THE ARCHER WITCH

EBP

HOUSE OF ROMANTASY

E. P. Bali's
House of Romantasy

This first edition published in 2023 by
Blue Moon Rising Publishing
www.ektaabali.com

ISBN ebook: 978-0-6455686-7-7
Paperback: 978-0-6456909-2-7
Hardcover: 978-0-6456909-3-4
Paperback (Pastel Edition): 978-0-6456909-4-1
Hardcover (Pastel Edition): 978-0-6456909-5-8

Illustrated Cover design by Carly Diep
Naked Hardcover by Etheric Designs
Map artwork by Najlakay
Chapter Background by Etheric Designs
Book Formatting by E.P. Bali with Vellum

The author acknowledges the Traditional Custodians of the land where this book was written. We acknowledge their connections to land, sea and community. We pay our respects to their Elders past and present and extend that respect to all Aboriginal and Torres Strait Islander Peoples today.

A NOTE ON THE CONTENT

I care about the mental health of my readers.
This book contains some themes you might want to know
about before you read.
They are listed at www.ektaabali.com/themes

E.P. BALI

THE ARCHER WITCH

THE ELLYTHIAN ISLES

THE GREAT
WESTERN OCEAN

LOTA CITY

LOTA ISLAND

TIGER ISLAND

LEVU VILLAGE

GULAB VILLAGE

JUNGLE
SCHOOL
TARAKA TOWN

THE LOTUS

SEA

BONEWEAVER ISLAND

Pronouncination Guide

Altara: Al Taa ruh
Atax: Ay tacks
Cheshni: Chesh nee
Daanav: Daah nuv
Ellythia: Ill ith ee uh
Geravie: Jer ah vi
Gulaab: Gul aahb
Harranpul: Har ann pull
Jessine: Jess eene
Kai: K eye
Keshmi: K air sh mee
Levu: Lair voo
Lobrathia: Lo brath ee uh
Malika: Maah lick uh
Odeelia: Oh dee lee uh
Pia: Pee uh
Rahana: Raa ha na
Reshmi: Resh mee
Rani: Raah ni
Raen: Ray en
Saraya: Sar eye uh
Trisane: Tris ayne
Ulanna: Ul ah nah
Vayashi: Vay ah shee
Yasani: Yuss ah nee
Zale: Zay-l (rhymes with gale)

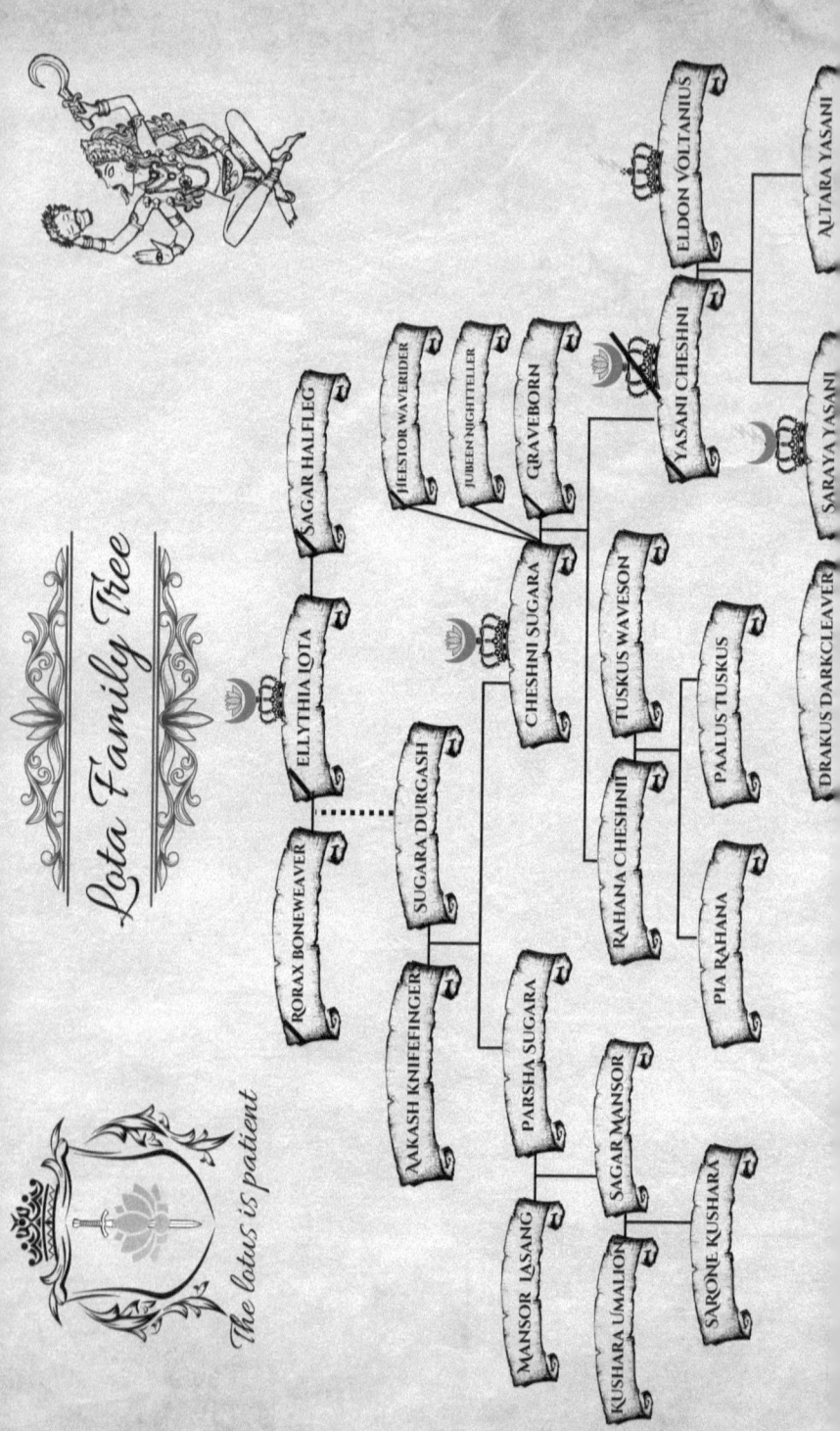

Lota Family Tree

The lotus is patient

RORAX BONEWEAVER — ELLYTHIA IOTA — SAGAR HALFLEG

HEESTOR WAVERIDER
JUBEEN NIGHTTELLER
GRAVEBORN

ELDON VOLTANIUS
YASANI CHESHINI
ALTARA YASANI
SARAYA YASANI
DRAKUS DARKCLEAVER

CHESHNI SUGARA

SUGARA DURGASH

AAKASH KNIFEFINGER
PARSHA SUGARA
SAGAR MANSOR
MANSOR IASANG
KUSHARA UMALION
SARONE KUSHARA

TUSKUS WAVESON
RAHANA CHESHNII
PAALUS TUSKUS
PIA RAHANA

Bonewearer Family Tree

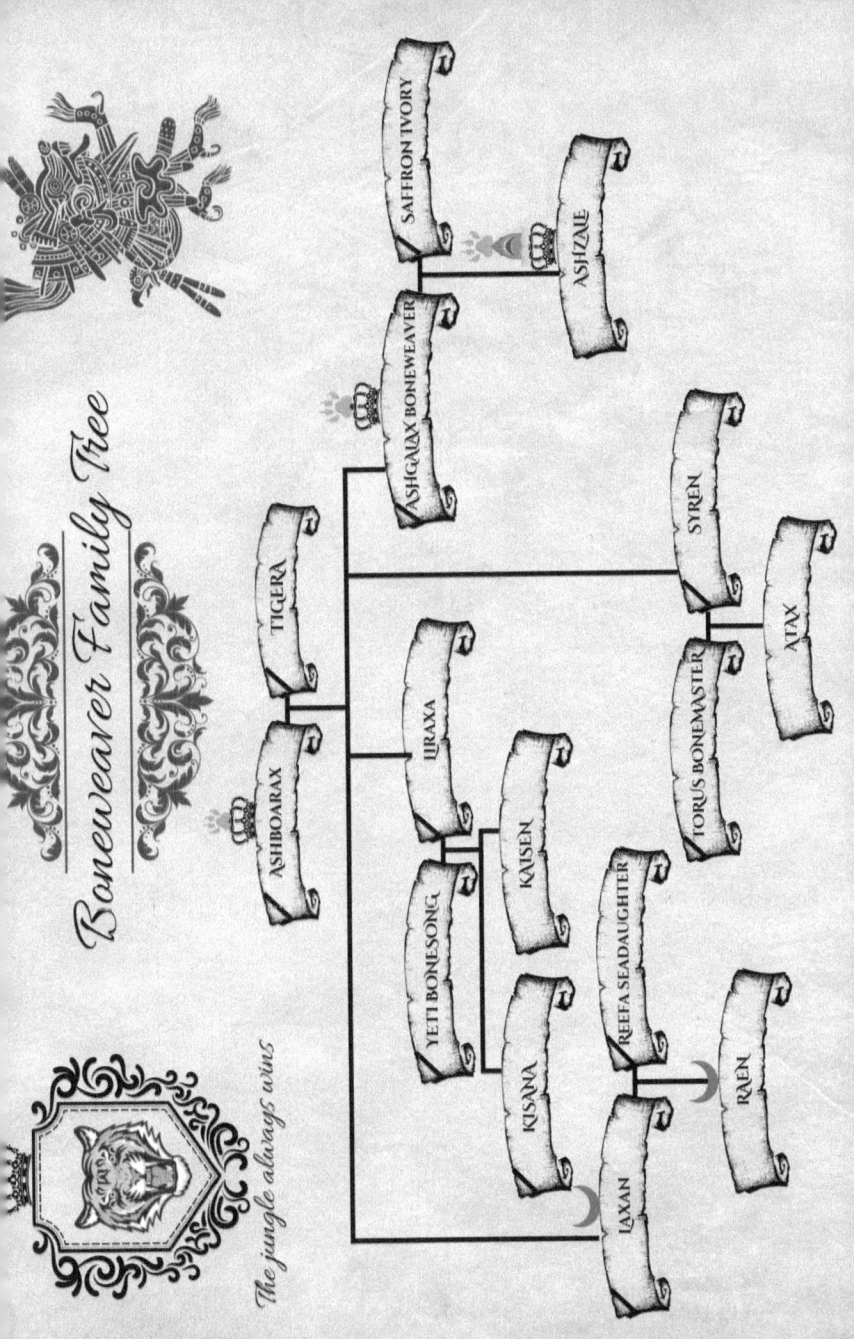

The jungle always wins

SAFFRON IVORY

ASHZALE

ASHGALAX BONEWEAVER

TIGERA

ASHBOARAX

URAXA

SYREN

ATAX

TORUS BONEMASTER

YETI BONESONG

KAISEN

REEFA SEADAUGHTER

KISANA

LAXAN

RAEN

For my sisters who've ever fallen into the abyss of ever-dark,
Sometimes if Light lets the Dark win it's only because she needed a
little more time to sharpen her sword.
And that's okay.
We fight again tomorrow.

PIA

The jungle was burning around me.

I stood in the midst of the dying battle, covered in demon ichor, my two swords in a tight grip as I caught my breath. With the ancient ruins of Castle Ivory looming over us, the last of the demons were finally being executed. We hadn't known the exact numbers of the demons that held Altara and the Old Ones captive, and once we'd launched our attack, I'd known we were in trouble. Luckily, Raen Boneweaver had released himself and the three Old Ones from their bone cages just in time, and together with the villagers of Leyu, we'd been successful in our rescue of my cousin, Altara...for the most part.

Next to me Malika stabbed a dying demon with a stolen sword, and the pixie we'd dubbed Trouble was flitting next to her ear, shouting his encouragement. Atax, in his black lion form, leapt through the air directly at a crawling demon. Malika stumbled back as Atax's jaws grabbed at the throat of the demon, shaking him as if he were a child's doll. Satisfied, the Old One dropped the demon to the ground and straightened, flashing into his naked human form, and scanned the dead bodies around us. There were two kinds, the blue-skinned Daanavs that came from under the Lotus Sea and the subterranean crimson-skinned demons.

"Put some clothes on, you brute," snapped Malika.

Atax smirked at her, ignoring my friend completely, before strolling to Raen—with his pants on—who was sending streams of water onto the fires burning the jungle around us. Malika gave me a look, and I shook my head at her.

We had bigger problems than naked Old Ones. Ahead of me Rani was pulling a sword out of a demon torso, the lean muscles of her arms glistening in the dawn sun. I signalled her to join me in heading to the famous bone cages that had long ago been used to imprison rabid beasts.

The three elderly ladies, Geravie and the priestess twins Keshmi and Reshmi, were frowning over the patch of singed grass Altara and Zale had disappeared through. Kai was on his hands and knees, sniffing the grass, his long white hair streaked with his own blood. Thankfully, all that was left of his near-fatal injuries were angry-red lacerations on his muscled torso. Leela, our second pixie, was frantically zipping about, her golden wings a blur as she panicked about Altara's disappearance.

I wasted no time. "Is the portal still open? Can we get through?"

Kai deftly leapt up to his bare feet, patting the hunched back of Geravie Harranpul, Altara's old nursemaid. "No, Your Highness," he said gravely. Even in the midst of a disaster, Kai's voice was mild, his sky-blue eyes a little unfocused. "All signs of it are gone. It must have been a transient entry point."

Malika swore from behind me and angrily kicked a

demon helmet like it was a ball. We all turned to watch it soar through the air and land onto the pile of demon bodies the villagers had assembled to burn. I turned back to Kai. "Can we get it back? Is there another way to get into the Eternal Forest?"

Kai screwed up his face as if he were thinking hard. "They are almost impossible to find, Princess, and they constantly shift. I've only ever known one person to find one and that was Zale."

I swore under my breath as Geravie wiped the sweat off her wrinkled forehead. "There's no helping it," she said. "They'll have to find their own way out."

The three elderly ladies had worked hard in the battle, and I think it had been the first time in a long time Geravie had even used magic at all.

"At least Altara and Zale are together," Rani said reasonably, her gangly form crouched down to rest. "She'll be safe. Did you not see her use her lightning magic? It was spectacular."

"Yes, but this is the Eternal Forest we're talking about," said Malika, angrily re-doing her braid. "How many people do you know have gone there and come back? And did you see, Altara had been cut open! Goddess knows what's going on in her head."

The elderly ladies exchanged grave looks. For Ellythians the Eternal Forest was a thing of legend and danger. It was hardly a place one came back from—such a thing only happened in the old stories. Geravie gave me a pained look, devastated as we all were by what we'd just seen of my cousin Altara and the awful dark state she'd been in after being strapped down to that table. Wreathed in dark smoke, I'd only been able to see Agnolthi's sign glowing on her fore-

3

head. It was something I would never forget. Altara had been chosen by the Goddess.

"Altara shot Zale with a special arrow," I said quietly to the group. "Did you see? Lisanthi's priestess from Levu was right about the conditions of Zale's cure. She shot him right in his black heart and…"

We'd all felt the shockwave of magic that had blasted around the entire area when Altara had shot Zale with an arrow made of darkness and lightning. It had made everyone stumble back, and half the demons had fallen to the ground, dead from the fell wave of magic.

"She had to have broken his curse with it!" Rani said excitedly. "That book in the temple was right about the prophesy; Altara was the key to Zale's conscience this whole time."

We descended into quiet after that, disturbed only by the sound of Atax and some village men striding through the demon corpses and periodically stabbing the living injured.

Reshmi, one of the twin priestesses of Agnolthi's temple, shuddered and made herself stand tall, assuming the leadership position. "Let us focus here for the moment. Heal the injured, and let's get everyone back to Levu to figure out a plan."

Raen, Atax and Kai seemed to enjoy helping and did a majority of the legwork, with Raen levitating our injured onto carts the demons had used to haul their prisoners. The three Old Ones didn't seem at all worried about their king having been shot and then summoned away from here through the portal.

When I asked Raen about it, he shrugged and said, "Zale can look after himself. He's been there before."

I raised my brows at the fact he'd revealed that Zale had

been there before but said nothing more on it, knowing that he was probably right that the Boneweaver King was more than capable. I'd never seen anyone fight the way the Old Ones had fought, and we were all once again reminded that these creatures had been born in a different time. They'd fought as if they lived for it. As if they *loved* it. Even so they had ended up as prisoners to the demons, so they were definitely not infallible either.

While everyone took a moment to rest and drink water before the long trip back to Malika's village, I wandered into the jungle to be alone with my thoughts.

After a minute of walking through the damp dark, I stilled as the air around me became charged with heavy, divine presence.

The shadow that had been following me for the past three years was an abrupt, hazy cloud at the corner of my eye. Whirling around, I saw Cholnayak, the Widow Goddess, standing as an old crone, frail and somehow strong at the same time. Her cloak was a deep silver, almost grey, and seemed to suck in all the light from around it. She hobbled up to me, fixing me with two, beady silver eyes. It was always uncomfortable being stared at by a Goddess—and Cholnayak more than any of the others. Her eyes held the heavy presence of a grave, her force like a suffocating corpse on top of my being.

"The sands of time run short, girl," she croaked in a voice that reminded me of the death rattle of dying lungs. "You have grown stupid and lazy."

I pursed my lips, but she continued her relentless verbal assault. "The stars die, the demons reap, the earth trembles with pain. And what. Are. You. Doing? Nothing. That's what." Her eyes were magical pokers digging under my skin, pulling apart everything that I was and laying it bare for her disapproval.

"What *can* I do?" I hissed at her, the backs of my eyes burning. "I am no one. I have no magic. There are others you should be harassing! What about my grandmother? Why are you not shouting in *her* ear?"

The shape of the matter around me changed in one abrupt moment. Cholnayak's hunched frame shot up, and she became seven feet tall, straight-backed and furious. The veins around her eyes turned black, her eyes now endless hollows of sheer nothingness, silver hair flying violently around her head. Colossal power lashed around my neck, pressing just enough to restrict my air.

"There are many dark things that walk in the shadows of this world, girl," she hissed. "But none of them are as dangerous as a Lota princess who has lost her power."

I choked under her hold, fear rising up my spine like an icy cobra.

"Find it, or you will destroy everyone around you, including yourself."

The absence of her presence hit me with all the force of one of Rani's shields, throwing me down onto the jungle floor, gasping for air as my body adjusted to the loss of her mighty divine presence.

Her visits were not always so violent, but she was clearly losing her patience with me. For what felt like the hundredth time, with mental fingers, I reached for my magic. As usual I came up against nothing, my awareness sweeping against my insides as if there were nothing there. As if I had never been born with magic at all.

Old shame grated against me, burning and biting at my heart. I sighed, getting to my feet, and brushed my hands on my trousers. However her delivery, Cholnayak was right. I had spent too long hiding away at Taraka school when my place was by my mother's side. At the side of the seat of Ellythia. Whatever my shame, there was a bigger battle going on here that needed to be addressed. It pained me to think of it, but everything was pointing me to one place.

When I got back to the clearing in front of Castle Ivory, I strode up to the group of Old Ones standing next to my friends, the old women and the pixies. They all looked up at me, and I took a deep breath.

"I need to go home and speak to my grandmother. She needs to know what has happened here."

Rani's eyes shone as she turned to look at me. "I will come with you."

Malika clenched her fists and nodded firmly. "So will I. It's about time our queen helped her people."

Leela landed on my shoulder, hugging my neck in sympathy.

I cast them a grim smile. "It will be messy. I will not be welcome there."

The two elderly priestesses and Geravie Harranpul shuffled around me. Geravie's face was ashen under her dark skin, the toll of the enormous magic she'd used now hitting her. Her voice was hoarse when she spoke: "Well, I can't let you girls go alone, now can I? It's about time I met with my old friend Cheshni again. We have a lot to discuss, the queen and I."

I glanced back at the row of cages made of bone, a place that had been traditionally used to house rabid Old Ones. A table had been put in the last one, the shackles on it lying open and empty. Just hours ago Altara had been strapped here, Raen had said, and a white Pentarog demon had been

7

cutting her open to the bone and feeding off her magic. She'd managed to free herself, heading straight for Zale.

"Star-soul mates," I mused. "I'd never thought I'd actually see it happen."

"What does that even mean?" asked Rani quietly.

Raen chuckled under his breath. "I should have known. They are creatures borne of the same star. Their souls are already one."

"They always did have a strange chemistry," Malika said. "Do you think that's why the Eternal Forest sucked them in together?"

My lips twitched without humour as Raen and Atax grimaced at one another in some silent conversation. I nodded at my friend. "Altara resisted it from the beginning. And whatever has come over her since her torture won't help at all."

"A mated Boneweaver male is a terrifying thing," Kai said thoughtfully. "Now that Zale knows Princess Altara is his mate, he'll stop at nothing to join them."

"Goddess," whispered Rani.

And as I cast my eyes across the piles of dead demons around us, I murmured, "Goddess help us all."

2

ALTARA

My body fell through time and space like it was made of wind, and I knew it was wishful thinking to believe that this was death.

The only thing I felt was irritation. I realised that I'd shot my husband in name, King Ashzale Boneweaver, right in his rotten black heart with an arrow made of my entire being—the solution to his curse as foretold by three old queens—and it did not kill *me* as I'd hoped.

Zale's wide, pain-filled eyes had been indication that it had worked to break his curse—he'd gone from a cold, murderous beast to tormented within seconds. I was certain he had his conscience back.

What had happened to me, to my body, before all of this was a foul shadow that was tucked away, far and deep, never to be thought about again. Never to be felt. Never to see the light of day. It meant that what remained of me now was the husk of a human girl.

Zale's fingers had reached for me just as I'd been torn from the island by a colossal force. Now I was only a shadow, lengthening and compressing as I hurtled downwards with nothing but cold air and darkness around me.

When I landed it felt as if I watched myself from afar, and it was nothing but a wraith of smoke and bone that thudded onto verdant grass—a girl made of sticky, midnight cobwebs that tasted like grief and sorrow. Inky tendrils of night floated from her body on a fell wind, curling around her in a sickly fashion so the naked, female form could barely be seen beneath. Only one thing breached that dark smoke: a glowing symbol on her forehead. A moon pierced by an arrow—the mark slapped onto her forehead by the angry hand of the Goddess Agnolthi.

When my body stood, I could feel soft grass beneath my bare feet, could see bright sunlight making the lush pine trees around shine a bright and impossible green.

A distant part of me might have appreciated the ethereal beauty of this place, but that self was locked away behind an obsidian and steel door and not available to me. Nor did I want it to be.

I felt no air on my naked skin. I felt no heat from the sun above me, nor any wonder at the fact that I knew this was the Eternal Forest, a place of myth and legend to the Ellythian people. A place under the island, accessible only through mysterious means. I barely understood how I'd come here and had no clue how to get out.

That *should* bother me. But it didn't. Instead I skulked forward and simply moved through the forest, noting with silent awareness that there was magic in the air. Something old but soft and fluttery like the wings of a butterfly reached out to me, observing my presence. I ignored it and moved on.

I do not know how long I wandered aimlessly through the forest, only that the sun set and two moons rose above me—

as if the night itself wanted to peer down and look at what went on here. The moons set, and still I walked as the sun rose above the canopy again. Some injury occurred in the soles of my feet, but it healed itself, and I did not stop to look at it.

Creatures ran at my approach. The trees seemed to hush as I passed them. Flickering lights in the distance dimmed well before I reached them.

The things in the forest did not want me to be here, and neither did I. I wanted to be gone. I wanted to be nothing. Power crackled within me, unused, slithering through me like sludge, dense and lazy.

My insides began making noises, and my throat became dry. Food and water were required, so I walked until I found food growing from dense bushes. Tiny pink berries that created their own light sat plump and juicy on thick stems. I instructed my body like a puppet, toggling the strings of my arms and fingers to pluck the berry and put it on my parched tongue.

"No!" someone shouted. I turned my head in irritation to see a small creature with glowing wings zooming toward me and halting metres away as if they did not wish to get too close. Through the film of dark smoke covering my body I could not see the creature properly, but I could make out that it was female—from the high-pitched voice and about the size of a human newborn baby. But she was no doubt a mature creature with full breasts and hips covered in a flimsy dress and long, golden hair. Her wings were yellow and shone like little rays of sun. This was familiar to me, but I did not care to search my memory to remember why.

She panted and spoke in a gentle, fearful voice, "Do you want to die, ancient one? You cannot eat that."

I took the berry out of my mouth and looked at it. Licking my lips, my voice emerged like the sound of autumn leaves being crushed underfoot: dry and brittle. "I do want to die."

There was a stutter in the glowing wings, and I got the impression of a feeling of sadness. "Why?"

But the answer to that question lay locked behind a door of silver cobwebs, brittle yet impenetrable.

"I do not know," I answered. Not only was my body foreign to me, but so was my voice.

"Then," the creature said, floating forward just a fraction. "You should not die. Eat these ones instead. The purple ones are safe, if a bit tart." She indicated a bush to her left where deep-purple berries sat small and without light. I walked to them and plucked three, eating them without question. They were sour, but I couldn't find it within me to care. It would settle the noise in my stomach, and that's all that mattered.

"Water," I stated.

The creature—the word *pixie* came to mind— bopped up and down as if she were nodding but with her whole body and said, "This way, ancient one."

I knew that was not my name, but it felt right to follow her, so I did. I was also vaguely aware of a warning in the back of my mind where I had been told about the Forests of Eternity being a dangerous place. That harm and death could happen to a person here.

It was just as well that neither pain nor death could really harm me because those were things I no longer cared about. So, I followed the pixie to a place where water bubbled and swished in a swift-flowing river.

Set on the bank was a whole community of pixies. It looked like a party with tables and chairs, food and wine overflowing. There was laughing, and someone played a flute in a tune I might have once called "merry."

There was a hush as I came upon the party, and the music stopped as the pixie guided me past them to the water.

I fell to my knees and with only my body's thirst in mind, cupped my hands and drank water whose crisp temperature I could not feel. I drank until my insides were full and got to my feet, staring at the flowing river. It glittered in the midday sun, and the sound it made was familiar. I'd heard this sound before when I was with another—when I was with Zale the first night we'd been alone together. When he'd told me my name, *Altara*, meant the Great Star in north. This memory did not stir within me the same emotion it did back then. My insides were dark and cold like the deepest part of this river.

The earth gave an almighty groan under my feet, and a colossal sound like mountains shifting resounded all around the riverbank.

The pixies began screaming, and I slowly turned to look upon them. Something darker than night shifted upriver, though there was no cloud in the sky. The pixies pointed at it and shouted. They darted for the trees, collecting their crying children, calling out in utter panic. Glasses and plates clattered to the ground and shattered in their wake. The darkness moved, spreading down either side of the bank towards us.

"Run!" my pixie screamed to me, her voice like awful bells. "We must run. The Fear is here!"

"I am not afraid," I murmured. "Not of this. Not of anything."

"You will die!" she screamed, pulling on her golden hair, the whites of her eyes visible all the way around her irises. "It will do worse than death to you!"

"Will it," I stated dully, and I did not move an inch.

13

The pixie looked at the trees her people disappeared through and then back at me. "Please, ancient one, whoever you are, you must run, or it will kill us both!"

My head snapped towards the pixie of its own accord, a frown forming across my brow as an old awareness crept through me. Now, we couldn't have *that*. I was, perhaps, condemned to death, but this small creature was innocent and had helped me though she need not have.

I summoned my bow, and when it appeared this time, it was in a puff of black smoke, and the wood was a strong and sleek obsidian night.

"You're insane!" the pixie screamed at me before fleeing into the trees.

Drolly, I turned back to look upon the oncoming darkness, knowing full well that this had to be one of the dangers someone had told me about. Rani. It had been my friend Rani, a girl of metal and heartbreak who'd told me about this forest.

I felt a sense of loss then, in amongst the tide of dark skulking within me. It was enough to pierce that heavy veil of shadow, and just for a moment, I felt a blow of pain in my chest like someone had taken a cleaver to my heart. I shoved that pain away and enveloped myself in the cold veil once again, turning to the task at hand.

Narrowing my eyes, I observed the dark cloud shifting toward me upon its own wind. It brought decay to the plants and trees as it tore past them. The trees sagged, the bushes yellowed and the flowers shrivelled before becoming overcome in black night. It moved forward, its magic a sick pall in the air, promising eternal torment and pain. The sky above me darkened into night, and I absently cocked my head to watch the change.

They'd carved my soul open when they carved open my

body. The worst had happened. There was nothing left to be afraid of. I was no more than a living corpse that stood, waiting, and nothing could hurt what was already dead. So, when the dark cloud enveloped me, I simply took what it dealt. It felt as if it were made of sand, tiny, sharp blades slicing my skin open, making me bleed, filling my throat and cutting away my air. I closed my eyes and held my breath, waiting for the malevolent magic in this thing to do its worst.

3

ALTARA

It tugged at me, trying to find a weakness, an edge it could manipulate, invade. It prodded me painfully, now slicing not at my skin but at my mind, pushing to pry it open.

It would not win.

An icy smile curved my lips as I felt the entity stutter around me as if it were surprised. It was old. As ancient as the land itself, perhaps, and had not yet met an enemy who did not fear it. Who did not have a weakness.

What are you? It seemed to ask in a loathsome, jealous anger.

"Hello," I whispered, my mouth filling with dark sand. "You are no longer the darkest thing here." Raising my black bow, I summoned an arrow, similarly black, and filled it with all my power. The arrow glowed with a fell, sluggish light, and I shot it into the Fear.

It pierced the midnight cloud with a shattering blow. An inhuman shriek of anger resounded all around me, invading my eardrums, and I smiled without joy again, feeling a tugging deep inside of me. I loosed another arrow into its dark depths.

Who are you? It shrieked, and I sensed agony. I relished that. That this time *I* was the one causing the pain. My veins rapidly filled with smoke and shadow that burned.

"I am nothing." I loosed another arrow. "I am no one." I loosed another. "What is dead cannot be hurt." With a final arrow the black sand around me vibrated as if it were having a seizure. In that moment I felt real death. A spirit leaving this world for the next, permanently. A thing that could not be undone. With a cry like a thousand mournful songs, the Fear fell around me, its spirit torn apart. Showered in midnight dust, I closed my eyes and simply felt the dying echoes of the screaming around me.

When I opened my eyes, the orange light of late afternoon glowed solemn and sombre. I stared dully at the sad, gritty remains around my feet, and knowing that I had destroyed it, I shrugged and went and sat in the crook of a low-hanging tree by the river. My wraith's body suddenly hung loose and weary, and as if my eyelids were being pulled down by the weight of all that dust, I fell asleep.

I WAS WOKEN BY A TENTATIVE TAPPING ON MY BARE FOOT. Frowning I blinked my eyes open and rubbed the sand and grit from them to try and form a clear picture of the mass of beings now surrounding me. Through my own curling shadows, I saw that it was dusk, a red tinged purple colouring the cloudless sky.

A crowd had gathered around me, but they were not crea-tures I'd ever seen in my world.

The person closest to me bowed. "My queen," she rasped.

I blinked at an old woman, so hunched she halved her own height. Her skin was white as a sheet, stringy black hair hanging limply down the sides of a narrow, pockmarked face. She wore a dirty black cloak, and her black eyes were wide and surprised on me. Distantly, I noted that she smelt foul, like old sweat and rotting meat. But neither this nor her appearance bothered me. What she called me *did*, however.

"I am not a queen." My throat was scratchy, and I swal-lowed down the dust that coated my airway.

She looked up at me, confused, clutching a twisted wooden staff to keep her from falling over. "But you killed the Fear, Your Greatness. You reign in its place now."

I looked behind her where other dark creatures stood, bowing low. Some were on their knees before me, and some were old hag like-women, hunched with age in old robes. There were also sharp-nosed, dirty goblins in rags, holding crude weapons. But the others were...beasts made of fur, fangs and dark coats. I saw the midnight pelts of wolves, obsidian-maned lions and even two massive snakes who stood as tall as a grown man, their hoods stretched out, a glimmering crimson jewel set on their foreheads.

All eyes were on me, predatory and intelligent with assessment. These were thinking and feeling beasts.

Something in the back of my mind registered this as important and mad and unlikely, but I was immediately distracted. Several bundles of golden light were being held in place by the goblins' wiry arms. I got to my feet and stared at the panicked face of *my* helper pixie and a group of her family being held captive. "Let them go," I ordered, pointing at them.

The hag at my side followed my finger, confused. "The pixies? But—"

Quicker than a flash of light, my bow was in my hands, an arrow knocked and ready to fly right into the head of goblin that held my pixie. When I spoke I barely recognised the dark promise in my voice. "I will not repeat myself."

The goblin let go of my pixie and held up his hands in surrender, then aggressively gestured to the other goblins, making a cutting motion with one dirty hand. "You heard the dark one!"

Immediately, the goblins let go of the pixies, and the group of tiny creatures dashed into the forest without looking back.

Two hags brought forth a bundle of black silk stretched out between them like an offering to me. I cast my eyes across the horde and saw all their eyes were not on my face as I'd expected but my body. Looking down at myself, I saw that although the shadows still surrounded me, it constantly shifted, and my bare skin was visible to all through the gaps.

I was not particularly bothered by this, but I remembered another time and place, where wearing clothes was considered right. So, since this clothing was being offered, I took it. It was a soft black silk, clean though smelling a bit off. I slid my arms through, and the hag before me presented me with a length of matching black silk and tied it around my waist to close it.

That sneaky door in my mind opened for a brief second, and I suddenly remembered that Rani's family were the premier silk makers of Isles, and I wondered where this silk was made. I slammed that door shut because she was not here, and I was not there with my friends.

Instead, I had these creatures.

"The litter is ready, Your Greatness," the hag said, gesturing. "We may go home now."

"Home?" I asked flatly.

"Your castle."

This is interesting, a back corner of my mind said eagerly. *Let's go see.* And because the front of my mind didn't care either way, I nodded and decided to allow them to lead me on. The beasts and goblins parted to reveal a chair made of twisted, dead and blackened tree branches sitting on a platform with long rods made for carrying. Six of the taller goblins stood by it. I skulked up to the litter, the beasts sniffing the air around me. The six goblins standing by the litter stared at me with shining eyes as if I were their Goddess and saviour. An abrupt thought launched into my mind, and I turned around.

"If anyone hurts the pixies," I declared loudly, "I will kill them."

Growls rose up within the ranks, followed by the goblins muttering. "Yes, Your Highness", "As you wish, Your Greatness." But one nasally voice said, "Why?" It belonged to a taller goblin brandishing a rusty axe slick with fresh blood.

Without even thinking a dagger flashed into my hand, and I hurled it. It lodged itself with a crunch in the centre of the goblin's forehead, and he crumpled to the ground. All around me the crowd of hags and goblins excitedly dropped to their knees, clutching their fists to their hearts as if I'd performed a miracle. The beasts lowered their heads, and I stared around at them with narrowed eyes.

These creatures worshipped violence. Shrugging at that

thought, I sat myself upon the black seat. The goblins hastened to work, raising the platform up by the rods and hoisting it onto their shoulders.

Some of the bigger lions and wolves surged to the front, followed by the hags. I was carried through the forest behind them, the other goblins forming a procession behind us. Some of the goblins and hags rode upon steeds—mostly boars with mighty tusks and in some cases, a goat. These steeds they treated as humans treated horses.

A tiny nagging thought of unease lurked at the edge of things, but I batted it away. This was interesting. This was good.

As the six tallest goblins carried my litter through the forest, the smaller ones occasionally ran up and held their dirty fingers high, bringing me offerings of small fruits, which I accepted, or the carcasses of dead animals, which I did not.

We headed west, directly toward the setting sun, and by some magic of the Forests of Eternity, the landscape rapidly changed.

We began in the pine trees, evergreen and tall, which then morphed into spotted mushrooms the size of trees, glowing, squat and patterned red and green that hurt my eyes. Critters made their homes in the trunks of these, looking out of carved out windows and doors, though they quickly hid as my procession passed them. Guttural screams sounded far in the night, and the squarks of animals being slaughtered by the predatory beasts up the front.

And the hags, they sang in husky voices, looking up at the twin moons, so I began calling them "witches" instead.

The forest became even darker and sparser, the lush trees giving way to spindly bushes, rotting, mouldy trees and blackened boughs, standing like skeletons in a cemetery. Rich, dark, soil gave way to sandy, dry dirt, and warm humidity gave way to a sharp, biting wind.

This suited my mood, and I observed everything with a dull sense of satisfaction.

Eventually, my eyes spied a black structure upon a hill. It was so dark it sucked in the moonlight into a massive gaping maw in the landscape. A beast made of black stone and mortar. The procession marched right up to it, and I could just make out a wide moat and drawbridge lying across greenish, sickly water.

The place was crumbling at the edges, but it was no less grand in its height and width for it. The entrance was a dramatic circular affair, bigger than any palace entrance I'd ever seen. It was wide enough to fit twelve horses entering side by side comfortably, and through it, I could make out a domed-high ceilinged hall.

This castle was a beast, and it swallowed me whole without hesitation. The procession carried me all the way inside after the horde of beasts who took up positions on wide stone benches formed into steps by the walls. It was clearly well made for this holding a court of beasts, and I wondered how long these creatures had worshipped at the feet of the dark entity I had slain.

At the end of the hall, raised on a dais up two steps, was a gigantic serpent's head carved from obsidian. Its mouth, open and fanged, was made into a magnificent throne perfect for a ten-foot-tall giant.

The two goblin guards standing before it fell prostate upon the black marble tile, and I ignored them as my litter was lowered.

The apparent leader of this group, the witch who'd first

awoken me, bowed, spreading her hands wide, her black cloak fluttering. "Dark one, we are home."

"So I see," I said flatly. "Lead the way—what is your name?"

"Magrin, Your Greatness." She bowed again and turned, making for the throne. I followed, my own silken robe flaring out behind me.

Magrin led me up the steps to the throne, but I stood there for a moment, scowling at the dark sculpture and at Magrin standing nervously beside it. Her eyes darted around as if she thought I was a hairsbreadth away from striking her. This place had been created for dark creatures, *by* dark creatures—bones were scattered in the corners as well as other debris, cobwebs hung from the high ceiling and a waft of something rotten occasionally drifted toward me. The beasts lining the hall were eerily quiet and still. Waiting.

Despite not liking the throne, I found myself nodding in approval. The cool quiet and dark was exactly where I wanted to be. Away from the world, inside a cocoon of my own silence, gestating against the grim dark that awaited me in the outside world.

So as the dark hall filled with the procession of excited goblins behind me, I strode up to the throne and sat upon it, propping my chin on a fist, my elbow on the hard plane of the armrest. With half-lidded eyes I watched the goblins, witches and beasts arranged themselves expectantly. I guessed that it was a little less than a hundred pairs of eyes trained upon me.

"What are they waiting for?" I muttered in annoyance to Magrin.

"We await your command, Your Highness," she said eagerly, rubbing her hands together.

"I wish for them to leave me."

Magrin stared at me, so I sighed and waved a hand at the group. "Go eat," I called in a bored, deep voice. "Rest. We have travelled far."

They all stared at me for a moment before Magrin snarled at them all, waving her staff at them. Then it was a flurry of activity as everyone left, the beasts first, followed by the witches and goblins.

The last all hastened to bow and quickly scattered through other doorways and entrances set in the sides of the hall.

Magrin turned her beady eyes to me, and I watched her blankly back. "Shall I bring your toys, Your Highness?"

I blinked in surprise, the dull dark around me twitching enough to peel away just a little. "What?"

Magrin spread her palms. "The ones the old king had here. They are by your rooms. We can go there now, if it pleases you."

I scowled, not wanting to move from my seat for some evil king's *toys*, whatever that meant.

Magrin wrung her hands, watching the last of the goblins leave. I frowned at her, realising that the old evil force that had called himself king of these parts of the forest had expected much of his minions. They thought I would be the same—have the same likes and interests as the evil being.

But my mind wanted nothing except to sit in its dark trance. I raised my hand, watching the smoky dark coil around my fingers and wrist, moving like incense around my skin, only thicker and darker.

In the stillness something *plucked* at the centre of me. Alarmed I looked down at my navel and spotted a golden thread not of this world, leading from my umbilicus out into the ether. A questioning movement plucked at it again.

THE ARCHER WITCH

I shot to my feet, sending Magrin flinching away. "Distract me, Magrin," I gritted out. "Show me these toys."

"At once, at once, Your Greatness!" Magrin stumbled over her own bare feet to lead me away from the hall, through a sloping passage and then underground, down a series of dark tunnels.

Deep in the bowels under the earth, where the air was hardly breathable, clearly made for non-human creatures, she led me to a sort of dungeon. Curiously, I followed Magrin towards one cell—no more than a tiny cavern segment closed off by rusty iron bars.

I stood before it, staring down at the two female occupants holding each other, huddled against one wall.

For the first time since before I'd come to the Forests of Eternity, my body went rigid with surprised alertness. Adrenaline scraped my veins as I registered the finely pointed ears, and even dirty in tattered rags, the supernatural beauty and lithe, athletic bodies borne of magic.

These were fae.

25

4

ZALE

The pain that exploded through my body was a beast I knew not how to slaughter. It wasn't made of teeth and claws; there was no flesh for me to inflict any damage upon.

It was this that made my fall through the portal into the Eternal Forest more torturous than anything I'd ever encountered before. Physical pain I could withstand. But this?

There were a thousand voices in my mind. A thousand screaming, laughing, sobbing voices, and I could not discern one from other. My day of reckoning had come, and now I would suffer for the dark things that I had done in the same way that every soul was supposed to from the time they were young. I had always been cold on the inside, like an icy tomb in winter, but now I was blazing.

I was thrown onto the forest floor with a smack that rattled my brain, and I leapt up, shaking my head to clear the buzzing in my mind. Almost as soon as I took a step forward, a wave of something disastrous flooded my core. My shoulders hunched around the sensation, and I grunted, recognising that another emotion was hurtling through me.

As two hundred years' worth of emotion tried to overcome my mind, I clutched my head, but the world slid sideways, and I fell back down to the ground.

I had spent my entire life as a ruthless beast, gutting my father's enemies, beheading any male who looked at my mother with the slightest predatory eye. When I had walked through my father's kingdom, any creature would cast their eyes down in fear, not knowing what violence Ashzale Boneweaver, the prince with no conscience, would do next.

And now here I was, thrown through a portal into the Eternal Forest, and I'd crumpled like a child against a tree while a pain I didn't think was possible attacked me. It was as if a thousand heavy blades were chopping my heart up into little pieces.

Memories, heinous, black and filled with blood, screamed through my veins, befuddling my thoughts.

Only a single, tiny part of me was holding on to a thread of sanity and seemed to know what was going on. I clung onto that thread, honing in on it as if it were my prey, and bit by bit, the pain flooding my chest faded just enough for me to regain control of my senses.

On the forest floor, leaf litter pressing into my face, I felt *everything* in retina-burning brightness. A hot sun beamed down on me, and I swore I felt each one of its rays on every cell of my skin. A bird squawked in the branches high above me, something rattled in the bushes to my left. A family of snakes writhed in their den ten metres away, a river flowed swiftly to my far left. My hearing and sight had always been good, but the sun had never felt *this* warm, the sound of water had never tickled my ear in *this* way and…that

27

sparkling thread at the centre of me felt like light and clouds and warmth. I placed a hand over my bare stomach as if I could touch that magic lying within me. It led somewhere. All at once I knew where.

Altara. My mate. Is that you?

There was no reply.

Something in my chest burst—my heart squeezed, *squeezed*, and I'm sure was about to stop working completely when something dark imploded under my ribs. I gasped, crawling onto my hands and knees, squeezing my eyes shut.

The island had ripped Altara away from me when I'd made to follow her through the portal. Rage furrowed my brow. My mate and I were made to be together; how could any entity think to remove her from me?

Altara, where are you? I desperately plucked on that string as my heart bled and split in two because I could feel that at the end of that golden thread was a darkness like solid midnight. Like the darkness at the edges of the death, it was grief and despair. Sorrow and heartache.

I didn't even realise that I was screaming until my throat burned like a blade had scraped it raw. Shutting my mouth, I shifted.

My spine elongated, my legs lengthened, fur erupted from my skin and my mouth burst into a muzzle. I'd always chosen my wolf form when the darkness that used to be at the centre of me became overwhelming.

I growled at myself, angry at this uncontrolled outburst, but I knew what it was. I was a Boneweaver male who'd seen his star-soul mate. Who'd felt that mate bond properly for the first time. It must have been masked while my heart lay in shadow, but now I had free reign to feel it.

That glittering thread that tied me to Altara felt like it was made of fine starlight. I knew the tale about my birth blessing ceremony. How the three queens had forged a key against the lock containing my cold heart.

Somehow Altara had found out about it and resigned herself to freeing me with her own life. She was going to give it all up for me. I couldn't have it. The look of cold apathy in her eyes would haunt me for the rest of my life. I never wanted to see that shroud her gaze *ever* again.

The shadow covering my heart had also covered my eyes, and my ability to see her clearly. I had stupidly assumed she'd been using magic to enchant me, that there had been something *wrong* with me, that she would be making me feel...

Like she was the centre of my universe. As if she were the sun that I orbited around. *Now* the mating bond struck me in the core with all the force of the earth shifting under me. It was a tether that nothing in the multiverse could destroy. My head spun with the force of it, and the sheer colossal longing that overcame me. I took a step forward toward where the thread was leading me. I was a force of primal desire now.

I was vaguely aware of something familiar crawling up my leg and shook myself out of the state I was in to reach down and chew the thing away—but I paused.

Wobbles was there, clawing up my leg, tiny shell fingers digging into my skin. Sighing I shook him off so I could look at him properly.

He'd been borne of Boneweaver Island itself, by the dark magic encasing my heart while I was strung up in my tomb. Once I'd left, Wobbles, as Altara had named him, and the other shadow monsters had come to serve me. But the magic had not been stable, and I suspected that had to do with Altara's presence interfering with my darkness. Now the shadow in me was gone; I'd expected all the monsters to dissolve back into the island. Except Wobbles, his head made of a conch shell turned upside down and the rest made of shell fragments pasted together with magic, had not fallen apart. He had an odd, golden sheen to him now but otherwise looked perfectly healthy.

He raised his spindly arms and flexed his shell fragment-fingers at me in a grabbing motion. Unexpectedly, a tiny seam opened in his conch-shell head and gaped like a mouth. In a tinny sort of twinkling voice, he said, "Wobbles help."

Well that was new. Wobbles pointed at my shoulder, and I remained still so he could scramble up to sit there, his long legs swinging like he was having a good time. One of his hands came down, and he patted me over my neck.

"Fear," he squeaked. "Pain."

I huffed in annoyance.

"Wobbles help," he repeated.

His voice was so tiny, but there was also had a little grit of determination laced in there. I grunted my thanks at him.

But Wobbles reminded me of the time he'd introduced himself to Altara. Of whom I'd been when I'd been around her.

I had done horrible things. Evil things. Things good males did not do. I had been a bad mate. I growled, low and long, and the creatures bustling in the forest around me went still and quiet.

They knew an apex predator was here, and he was ready for a hunt.

No force on this Goddess-given earth would keep me from my mate. Not even herself.

5

ALTARA

The two fae females stared at me with fearful, glittering eyes. The magic these creatures normally oozed appeared to have dulled with time, and it made for a mournful wail in my ears.

"Who are these people?" I asked sharply.

Magrin's wary eyes darted to me. "These are your wives, Your Majesty. Your playthings. The consorts. We have males if Your Highness would prefer." She gestured to the other cells down the row where bodies shifted and chains clinked.

Anger spiked through me, raw and concentrated. I clenched my fists into balls. "Release them all," I growled.

"That...that is not permitted."

The dagger was in my hand before I could think. I angled it towards Magrin's throat, pressing into her white skin. "Am I the monarch around here or not?"

"It is out of my control, Your Highness," she exclaimed, leaning away from me and my knife. "The magic! It is the magic binding them!"

I removed the dagger and straightened, assessing the

women, trying to sense what magic she was talking about. They both clutched each other as if they thought they were going to die.

"What magic?" I snapped at Magrin. "Explain it clearly. Leave nothing out."

Magrin pointed to the necks of the closest fae. I bent down, frowning at the small black chain around their throats.

"Black quartz, Your Greatness," Magrin said. "Unbreakable chains that forbid them from leaving your underground domain. Unbreakable magic the likes of…"

But I was no longer listening.

For the first time in my life, my magic was not eager to comply. It moved sluggishly, *reluctantly*.

I yanked on it angrily, and it recoiled from me.

Closing my eyes, I asked softly, "How long have you been here?"

There was no reply before a sharp movement from Magrin made the metal bars clang. I sensed a flinch but kept my eyes closed as a fragile reply came: "T-ten years, Your Greatness."

Anger shot through me, and I gave my magic a sharp poke. *Did you hear that?* I asked it. *Ten fucking years they've not seen sunlight or felt its warmth.* I was suddenly more awake and alert, my spine lengthening where I was squatting. The glittering power within me shuddered, then oozed out at my behest. It reached out for the black quartz pendant the first fae wore—so like Headmistress Jessine's blood magic pendant. My power surged around the quartz like a glittering hand, reaching, finding and drawing out the dark power that rested like a tightly coiled snake.

Promptly it sucked it back inside of me where I absorbed its malevolent power with a sharp intake of breath. My magic wrapped around it and consumed it like a meal, gobbling it up with relish. Glittering dust was all that remained of it. One of the fae gasped.

I opened my eyes and found the fae females staring at me with a mixture of horror and fear. Rising to my feet I gestured to Magrin, commanding in perhaps the harshest voice that had ever come out of me, "Open the cell."

Instructing my magic to reach out for the second fae's necklace, I urged it to do the same thing to this pendant and digested the dark power in exactly the same way I'd cured disease countless times by taking it into myself and making it my own.

I barely registered the interest at this new-found use for my power. I'd never needed my power in this way before, but this purpose felt as natural to me as healing disease. It made me wonder if what my magic had been doing this entire time was *healing* at all. Instead it seemed to neutralise anything evil it came across. Discomfort that was not physical wound through me, and I promptly shook myself.

Gesturing to the fae, I waved my hand to their now open cell door. "You may leave," I declared. "The magic on the pendants is gone."

The fae closest to me audibly swallowed and in a feeble voice said, "And the others--"

"Will follow you." I turned to Magrin. "They are not to be harmed on the way out. Let them go."

Magrin's mouth fell open. "But, Your Greatness! We cannot—"

I held my hand and took a threatening step towards her. "Let it be known that any creature that harms these fae will be killed *by me*. Understood?"

Magrin promptly shut her mouth and silently bowed. I turned on my heel and stalked to the next cell where three fae males sat bound in black chains around their ankles and wrists. Long, dirty hair framed dirtier faces. They looked up at me with confused, near-delirious eyes. They were also skinny, and I doubted they'd been fed well these last ten years.

"Magrin," I said sharply. The old witch flinched. "Ensure the freed prisoners have food and water for their travels back to…wherever they come from."

"Yes, Your Greatness."

"Who are you?" asked one of the fae males rather weakly.

"No one," I snapped at him. "I am freeing you. Shut up and do as you're told."

I'd never been a snappy, demanding or spoiled princess, but this shroud of dull dark over me had turned me into one. I had no choice but to be this way and hold that mental door shut—that force of the grief, guilt, self-loathing and shame. It waited at the edges of the shroud would kill me if I let it all in.

I knew that inherently. The only safe emotion was anger.

That would have all been fine except for the fact that my magic did not like this new state of mine. It had always been its own *thing*, a part of me and yet of its own mind. And while previously it had been a mere nuisance to try and restrain, *now* it was doing the opposite and ignoring commands completely.

If I wanted it to work, I needed to let emotion in. I relented just a little and thought about something safe.

I wondered where my sister Saraya was. We'd both been sucked into a whole new world, but she was the type of person that handled that sort of thing. Capable. Confident. I missed her so much that a harsh pang of sadness pricked at the corner of my eyes. We'd been *happy* together, even if a little battered. Even with our stepmother—

That door opened a slither and I slammed it back shut. No. *No.* I would not let myself spiral down that mad path.

But it was enough for my magic to shoot loose and seize the fae male's quartz-pendant, and this time, it shattered completely. The dark magic filtered back to me as the fae male gasped in surprise, staring at me in wide-eyed shock. I ignored him as deep within me, my magic gobbled up the magic of the necklace, consuming it until it was nothing.

I set about freeing the rest of them under Magrin's confused gaze. There were ten in total down in these cells, and they hobbled out of the tunnels as fast as they could.

Without thanks, but I didn't care.

After I was done, I became a little weary on my feet, and Magrin led me to a wide room where a sort of smelly nest of leaves, twigs and scraps of old cloth was set on the dirt floor.

Since there was nowhere else for me to go—and I likely smelled just as bad—I fell onto it and after sneezing a few times at the cloud of dust that rose up in my wake, I fell asleep.

I AWOKE SOME HOURS LATER, MY BODY ACHING ALL OVER—AND more than one twig poking into my skin. My mind was still in a haze, where everything had taken on a sort of dream-like quality. Nothing was quite real and neither was I. This was much better than the alternative.

Two goblin guards were standing awkwardly by the door,

and I realised that I'd awoken to the sound of their grunting voices.

"What is it?" I asked irritably.

"Visitors, Your Greatness," one snorted. "To pay their respects."

I stared at the ugly creatures looking up at me with reverence, their fists tight around short spears, tension lacing their bodies. They were scared of me. Rightfully so.

Right now I was capable of just about anything, and this news about visitors had my hackles rising.

Whatever I thought the Forests of Eternity was, I hadn't thought it would be so...*populated*. A forest was meant to have animals and a few sentient creatures, but this many roaming about? First the pixie party, then the collection in the castle and now more? It was uncalled for, honestly. But Geravie used to say following the flow of the river was the easiest or something like that. I'd have to take that advice now.

Geravie. I clenched my jaw as a pang of grief speared through my haze. My old nursemaid's face swam into my mind's eye.

She would be ashamed of me right now. She would say that I need a good thrashing, a slap across the face or behind. I could imagine her voice now, furious and fiercely telling me I needed to pull myself together or she'd make my bottom as red as the roses growing outside the Quartz palace.

I squeezed my eyes shut against that voice in my ear because the further down that path I went, the worse it was going to get.

Geravie hadn't known about the Butcher. Only that my stepmother had taken me away for punishment for the day. My body had healed with no sign of any damage. I'd returned different, my bones aching with remnants of that poison unless I distracted myself—much like how I was reacting now. Thirteen-year-old Altara had been strangely quiet for a few hours, but the hustle and bustle of the palace had made me put that mask back on. Had made me find comfort in Sam's arms. In his warm masculine mouth, his tongue, his fingers. Sex and sensual pleasure were immediate, distracting and satisfying in a way that nothing else was.

But the thought of Sam disgusted me now. I'd only been fantasising of one man—one beast—the entirety of my stay on Boneweaver Island. The smoke around my body stuttered and the long *creak* of a metal hinge started back up.

Stop. I needed to stop.

I cleared my throat and heaved myself to my feet as the goblins watched my every movement. My robe slipped open, baring a breast, and I leisurely covered myself. Looking down I could still see the smoke was still covering me, though its film was less dense. It seemed to come and go depending on the direction of my thoughts. I shoved every thought from my mind and pulled myself down into the heady comfort of darkness again. Smoke coiled slowly from my skin, dark as the night sky, and it surrounded me from head to toe.

"Visitors, you say?" I muttered. "Well, I suppose I'd better go see what they want."

They blubbered, agreeing with me, shuffling in their bare, hairy feet as they led me through the rabbit warren that was the underground portion of the castle and up a slope to the great hall.

Saraya would find this all so funny. I was a queen of this dirty ruined castle. Queen of the Goblins. I snorted, despite everything.

The entire "court" had gathered again. The huge black wolves, lions and this time, I noted gigantic black eagles also lining the steps along the walls, the witches in front of them and the goblins swarming like malevolent bees in the middle. Chattering excitedly, they'd left a path down the centre to make an aisle.

As soon as I entered through the side door, the horde quietened, only the sound of the heavy bestial breathing thrumming in the air like a primal, threatening song.

The old Altara might have put her nose in the air and pulled her shoulders back, stalking toward that mighty obsidian throne. But in this instance, I just didn't have it in me, and instead I ended up hunched and skulking along within my smoky shadows. I resumed my seat on the hard, cold, glossy stone, lifting one leg and tucking it up under me, bracing an elbow on the armest and resting my chin on that hand.

It was supposed to tell everyone what I thought of the world—or maybe what the world should think of me.

As soon as I was seated, two wolves loped over the draw-bridge and headed inside, leading a group of people—men.

That caught my attention. I observed them as they took the long walk across the hall. They had the lean muscular build of warriors and the swagger of cutthroats as they sneered at the goblins gathered on either side of them. I noted that they were wary of dark beasts standing further away, but they must not have thought much of the smaller creatures because one of them kicked at a goblin, then laughed as the creature tumbled backwards into his neighbours.

The group stopped a sensible distance from my throne, and when the wolves, having clearly finished their escorting job, darted away to join their pack, five pairs of hungry male eyes leered at me with great interest. They had the definite look of career thieves I'd seen in the poorer part of my homeland Quartz City. These were men who did bad things for both money and enjoyment. I got a whiff of alcohol, sweat and the tang of metal—they were armed to the teeth.

They gave me mocking bows, their arms spread wide. "Dark Witch, we have come to pay our obeisances," said the leader, long oily hair hanging limply by his ears. There was dirt and blood all over his face and jagged scars peeking above his yellowed shirt.

He ran his tongue over his yellow teeth as his eyes searched down my body in the same way a cockroach searched dirty ground. I was vaguely aware that through the smoke my robe showed more of my naked breasts than was proper, but I couldn't find it in me to pull the sides of it shut.

While I didn't mind the title, they all seemed to be giving me—*Dark Witch*—I knew at once that I didn't like these men. If I had fangs, they would be bared and snarling

My posture straightened of its own accord, my fingers twitching with the need and anticipation of summoning a weapon.

Pay our obeisances, he'd said. A big word that suited this castle.

"Have you now?" I had intended my voice to sound flirty, but it came out as flat as parchment.

"Yeah," drawled another in a nasally voice, flipping a dagger with old blood-streaked fingers. He pointed the dagger at me accusingly. "They said you let the carnal fae go."

Carnal fae struck something in my memory, but I couldn't think where I'd heard it before. Around the hall the beasts and goblins had gone still and silent, watching me carefully. They wanted to see what I would do, no doubt. They wanted to see what type of Dark Witch they were worshipping. Well, perhaps I would give them a bit of a show.

I kept up my bored appearance, even though my body now buzzed. "I do not like fae," I said. "They disgust me. And if you angle that dagger at me again, I will carve up your face like a pork roast."

The goblins sniggered in appreciation, the wolves on the right of the hall licked their long teeth but the men stilled. "See, there's the thing," the leader said, taking one very obviously threatening step forward. His hand rested on the pommel of his sword—a black, serrated, vicious thing. "I don't think you will. I don't think you can. You're just a little girl. Still fuckable, though." He gave a feral, hacking laugh, and the others followed in a cacophony of dirty male arrogance.

My lips stretched over my teeth in a sort of ugly grin. The man next to him stepped forward, sweeping a more respectful bow. He was cleaner than the others with short hair and a handsome shaven face that was currently looking upon me with heated interest. "I'm happy to serve, my queen. The name is Pox Sully, best sword this side of the Eternal Forest... if you'll be so kind as to *have* me."

I inclined my head, not caring either way—not caring that he clearly intended to be my bedmate. Pox came to stand next to my throne with his hands resting over his belt like my personal guardsman.

"Nah. I think you need a little lesson," the leader of the group continued. "Maybe with my cock." He grabbed his crotch and flexed his pelvis toward me.

The thought barely had time to reach my mind before my summoned dagger was flying through the air straight for his groping fist. With a thud it lodged itself through his hand and into his manhood, spearing him where he stood.

He screamed.

Pox titled his head back and laughed as the other men roared in outrage. But both me and the goblins were ready. The little creatures grabbed two of the men, jumping upon them with knives and long nails while I threw two daggers in quick succession—both of them missed, sailing through the air behind them.

I shot to my feet in shock, the smoke around me dissipating.

I'd missed my mark.

Summoning more daggers, I threw and threw, half of them missing, and by the time I got one man in the throat, the second was on top of me, stabbing me in the arm.

I let out a cry of pain and twisted away from him as he was dragged off me by Pox and stabbed to death, blood spraying all over the floor.

I sat back down with a huff, staring in horror at my own hands. They'd failed me for the first time since I was a child.

Lightning never missed its mark.

The realisation tore through me like an angry tornado, harsh and biting, the smoke around me appearing again and swirling fiercely. No matter what I had been through in my life, my magic was the one constant. The one thing I could rely upon. I chewed on the inside of my cheek as every dark thought I was suppressing rose to the surface, sucking me under like a riptide. I tumbled in those violent waters, my stomach churning, my breath coming in gasps. Cracks fissured in my skin, tearing me open.

I reached down and clutched the only thing that I had left —my mother's lotus anklet still on my foot despite everything. I felt the shape of the metal strong and sure, something I was no longer worthy of. How could I sit here and wear it as I defiled her memory with this pathetic person I'd become?

I looked around the hall, as if for the first time realising where I was. As the goblins began enthusiastically dragging the bodies of the fallen men away, every particle in my body went taut as I registered a familiar presence, and that golden thread inside of me hummed in response. My veil of smoke shot back around me, dark as night, solid as a storm cloud.

The witches shrunk back against the entrance of cavern, and the wolves let up a collective howl as a naked Zale Boneweaver strode through the entrance.

6

ALTARA

The King of the Old Ones stalked into the hall like the predator he was, and his presence hit me with all the force of a thunderclap. It always had.

In the time that I'd known him, with the shadow over his heart keeping him cold and distant, his entire personality had been made of ice and silver fire. He ranged from cold menace to open, violent rage. But any doubt in my mind that I had undone his curse was quashed from my mind because *now*, as he prowled into my castle as if it were his, he was all molten, volcanic heat that burned with unearthly power.

I was stricken on my throne as I felt the sheer force of him, the surge of his magic like a heat wave pulsing in the air between us, shimmering with restrained force. It brushed against my bare skin, sending tendrils of heat right to my throbbing core.

He prowled into the cavern taking up the entire space with his presence, his eyes consuming everything all at once but somehow still only fixed on a single point.

Me.

Pox, standing next to my dais, swore under his breath and shifted warily with his hand ready on his sword.

I couldn't breathe as Zale's ocean-blue eyes fixed me with the most primal, hungry gaze. I'd known he'd desired me before, but this look was pure, raw, untethered desire, and to be on the receiving end of it made me clutch my stomach in a pathetic attempt at self-preservation. His was a monster come here to devour me whole. To consume me. To possess me, body and soul.

He stalked up to my throne, entirely naked, a beast in the shape of a man, drawing me in with his own gravitational force.

I had never expected to face him again and I. Was. Not. Ready.

He cut an impossibly stunning figure. Tall and broad, a creature of muscle and sinew, his long black hair unbound and pushed off his shoulders to sweep his shoulder blades. My eyes were naturally drawn down the long length of his body, gleaming with the fine sweat of his travel, to his core where his sizeable manhood swung a little with each long stride. It was thick and long, as strong and proud as the beast himself.

Something inside of me was splitting open, and it was all I could do to clutch my stomach and hold onto the sides of myself with all my might. I would not let myself crumble before him.

As Zale came to a stop a few steps from my dais, his crackling force held me down, pinning me to my seat as heat and power hovered between us. As if one wrong move would send this entire place up in flames and us with it. I could not move. I could not breathe with him this close to me.

The beasts, goblins and witches had fallen silent, the ones

carrying the dead men pausing in their movements, simply staring open mouthed at him—a real, actual king by birthright and power. Not me, this fake queen sitting here, barely useful. Barely able to hit her mark.

Zale glanced down at the bodies of the murdered...and at all my daggers haphazardly lying on the black tiles. When his eyes looked back up at me, orbs of blue blazing light filled with deadly promise, the golden thread between us hummed and sparked with tension.

Every bone in my body ached. We stared at each other. Him, as if he could barely restrain the beast wanting to leap out from within him. Me, a barely human woman, a living corpse scrambling to keep her darkness around her like a shield.

When he spoke it was the guttural voice of the beast inside of him, and I watched his beastly irises expand. "I've come to claim you, Altara Yasani Voltanius."

It hit me in the soul as if the Goddess herself had reached down from the heavens and punched me with eternal force. I'd not heard my full name on his lips since our wedding— when I had walked down the aisle on the night of a full moon and under the priestesses of Agnolthi, sworn myself to both the marine demon Fangar Sharksbane and the Boneweaver King, Ashzale.

It seemed like a lifetime away, something that had happened to a different girl.

My thumb found his ring on the finger of my right hand, pearl set in obsidian—and I could not deny that it *had* happened after all. But now it was nothing more than a death wish for a dead woman. I pressed on it with my thumb, turning it around to face inward against my palm. Zale's eyes flicked down to my hand, and darkness seemed to gather around him like a storm.

"Want me to gut him, my queen?" Pox snarled, tugging on his sword hilt.

I raised a hand to silence him, but Zale didn't even bother to glance at the cutthroat.

"I cannot be your wife," I said.

A frown fluttered over his handsome features, but what surprised me the most was the flash of pain that painted his face with a broad stroke. His eyes were hot on my skin, and his voice was nothing more than restrained wildfire. "You made a vow. We are wed. We are husband and—"

"I cannot do it," I snapped.

"You have no choice." There was a king giving a command and it grated against my insides.

"Get out," I breathed, clawing my fingers into my stomach to try and control the emotions roiling like the sea. His eyes flicked down to my abdomen, and all I felt was heat. His heat. His desire for me.

"This is cowardice, Altara."

The words struck me like a slap. It was something Geravie would say. Something Malika would say. Something Saraya would say to me. I knew they would want to shake me out of this...stupor I was in, but they weren't here. Only I was. I was alone.

"I don't care what you think," I said flatly.

He cocked his head in a purely animalistic way. His eyes flicked down to the dead men still on the floor around him and the ten odd daggers lying uselessly and said, "Do you care what your magic thinks, Altara? Do you care that it's not working as well? That you're failing—"

46

I shot to my feet and pointed my finger at him like a weapon. "Get the fuck out."

He took a slow, deliberate step forward, uncrossing his arms and unhooking his dagger earring from his ear. In a flash it became his long, obsidian blade. The most lethal weapon I'd ever seen. His voice was fury and pain: "I will kill every single creature here if that's what it takes. I will drag you out of this hovel kicking and screaming *if that's what it takes*."

I wanted to take a meaningful step down from my dais, but that would mean getting closer to him and his lusty heat. I would succumb to it, I just knew. He was too powerful a force, drawing me in, making me wet just by the sound of his voice in my ears, making me *throb*. It was this that enraged me even more. "You think you could do that, do you?"

"Yes," he growled, his fingers tightening on his blade. "You are mine. You always have been."

I bared my teeth in defiance. "Well...I would kill you before you could try."

The corner of his mouth twisted up in pure male arrogance. "You'd never do that, my love. You want me too much."

"*You*—" My jaw dropped open as I trembled like a leaf, vibrating with anger. *My love*, he'd called me. *Mine*, he'd called me. He'd never called me those things before. Fuck. Fuck him. Fuck everything. Didn't he know I couldn't do it? Couldn't be a part of that, tainted and dead as I was.

He was smiling openly now, and I snapped, "I want to cut that smile off your face, Zale Boneweaver."

His wretched smile only widened, and he placed a large tattooed hand over his bare chest, and it was a coiled snake inked there, ready to attack. "I do love it when you threaten me, my precious wife." Then he looked around thoughtfully at the goblins, still silent and staring at us, and the beasts lining the walls. Probably in awe of Zale and his god-like body and power. "We could rule this castle together, if you like, though we'd have to make some changes."

My centre throbbed for him, and I knew I was wetter than the Lotus Sea as I lashed out. "This is *mine*," I snarled, pointing at the floor. "*My* castle. Not yours."

He shrugged, brushing a hand through his hair, and it only drew my attention to the powerful swell of his bicep. "If it is yours, then it is mine too. I'll give you whatever you want, my mate. Anything at all—whatever crumbling ruin of land you like."

"I don't need *you* to give *me* anything," I shot back. "I took this by myself."

"Maybe you can give something to me then." His eyes gleamed mischievously, and my stomach flopped on itself. "After all, you have yet to give me a wedding gift."

I gaped at him again, trying to find my words as his eyes stoked a blaze in my veins. "What do you want from me?" I lowered my voice in the way I used to, so long ago. "Want me to suck your cock for you?"

He never missed a beat, but the air practically fizzled between us. "I mean, I wouldn't say no, of course," he bowed in a kingly manner, spreading out both arms. "If it pleases you."

I had to gather the pieces of myself together before I answered. "The only thing that would please me right now is for you to leave me in peace."

He observed me, his eyes raking down my face to my body, leaving a trail of fire in its wake. I suppressed a shudder, knowing full well that my shadows had drawn back to reveal more of my body. I had not cared about how revealing this robe was before—that my breasts were heavy under it, and my nipples puckered against my rising desire—but I sure as hell cared about that *now*.

"You want me to leave?" he asked quietly.

I hated to admit it, but even rejected Zale still looked like a king. No woman should deny him—I knew that in my core. But it wasn't just him I was denying right now; it was everything he *meant*.

He was looking at me as if he could see through me and into my mind. He'd been there when the Butcher had opened me up like an animal on that table. His eyes went dark, as if he knew the black things that stirred within my mind. Pain flashed across his face again.

"I will go, my wife," Zale said quietly. "But allow our friend to say hello first."

Appearing from over his shoulder, likely to have been hanging onto his hair, Zale brought out Wobbles, the small monster made out of shell fragments of Boneweaver Island. I could not help the way my heart leapt when I saw his ridiculously long spindly arms and oversized head, and I could not help the way I automatically reached for him, stepping forward, my heart pounding in memory.

Zale smiled at me in a way that lit up his entire being, and it took my breath away because I'd never seen a look on his face like *that* before.

I stumbled a little in my step but recovered quickly, snatching Wobbles from him— careful not to touch his skin— before turning my back and siting back on my throne, setting Wobbles against my chest like a newborn baby and patting him on the back. He squirmed against me, then lifted his head, and in a tiny, crackling voice said. "Wobbles help!"

I looked back at Zale in surprise, and he was beaming at me as if I was the one who'd given him a gift.

"He talks now."

"So I see," I scowled back. "Leave us."

But Wobbles wriggled from my grip and clambered down my leg like a thief in the night. I watched him with dismay as he wobbled his way back to Zale, who picked him back up and settled him on his shoulder.

I had to keep the disappointment from my face as Wobbles turned to look at me, his intent clear. He belonged with Zale.

His master's face became serious and intent on me again. His voice was low and skittered across my skin like a feather. "When can I come back?"

It was soft. His voice was incredibly soft, and it was too strange and meant something I did not want to think about. "Never," I bit out.

"You heard her," Pox said, threateningly, levelling his sword at Zale.

A feral look took over Zale's face like he'd just remembered Pox was standing there. "You want to know what I think about that?" He shot forward, deflected Pox's blade and aggressively gutting the man where he stood. Pox's bowels slid out of his stomach with a wet gush onto the tiles. The man fell forward, landing face first into his own entrails. "That is what I think," he snarled, straightening.

Zale levelled me a look that scorched my retinas, that seared into my soul. Then the moment was gone, and he turned, stalking from the castle with his obsidian blade wet and dripping by his side.

I hadn't realised that I'd leapt to my feet until he was gone.

7
ZALE

I walked out of Altara's new abode practically vibrating with repressed emotion. I'd followed the thread of our soul-bond only to find her in this domain of perpetual night, guarded by malicious beasts and witches. I'd had to kill two lions before the moat to assert my dominance, which I'd hoped would serve to calm me a little before saving my mate because I knew what this place was. Who was supposed to own it.

Except I'd walked in there, not to save her from capture but to see her as a goddess of smoke and shadow, sitting on the obsidian throne, *ruling* the place. It was almost as if the Goddess Agnolthi sat on that serpent's throne in her darker, wilder form, all black emotion with only her arrow and moon mark blazing from her forehead. She'd oozed such raw, unhinged power that I could do nothing but move towards her, fixated, obsessed with that energy.

For that same wild power had spurred me on since I'd been born.

I knew of the thing that had owned this land before Altara

had come along. It was legend around here, a thing of terrible fear and torment, and no one, not even the carnal fae queen herself, would dare stray near its territory. That's how the most powerful beings in the Eternal Forest lived—separate, ruling their own lands and staying within their own borders. It had worked that way for thousands of years.

The fact that Altara was sitting on that throne, worshipped by these dark beings…it could only mean she'd killed it. My mate was *powerful,* and it made my heart swell in that weird way it was now doing when I thought about Altara. Wobbles had whispered in my ear, "Pride. Respect."

Huh. So that's what that meant.

Even heavy in that dark moving cocoon, she was the most stunning woman I'd ever seen, human or otherwise, and to look upon her was to know the real beauty of the world. My heart had almost seized on the spot, and every fibre of my primitive being wanted to leap upon her and claim her as mine. In that black robe that barely covered her perfect, luscious body? The beast in me had almost torn free before I'd shoved him back down.

She *was* mine, and everyone needed to know it.

As I'd stood before her throne, I'd been so enraptured, so struck by her power, my thoughts had all ceased to become anything except about her. The need to worship her with my own body. With my mouth, my tongue. The male beast in me had demanded to take her back, and I'd spoken out of turn. Of course, with the powerful being that she was, she would not simply obey me.

So I observed her closely.

In that moment it had struck me. An epiphany. A moment of bright, enlightened sight. Altara's power felt familiar and intoxicating to me because I'd been steeping inside that same power for the last two hundred years.

I'd been prepared for Altara's darkness long before she would fall into it herself. We truly had been made for each other.

So I'd baited her until she unfurled. She'd come out of that dark chrysalis of her grief, and she'd come back to life before my very eyes.

Warm satisfaction had laced through me as the fire stoked within her emerald gaze once again. I'd watched her for weeks as we'd travelled around Boneweaver Island together, and by the end, I knew every minute movement, every blink, her every breath like my own. At the time I had not understood my obsession of her, the star-soul bond being masked by my curse.

Altara at heart was a dancing flame that revelled in the movement of life itself. She was playful and joyful in her spirit.

She was not herself in the darkness. It was a part of her, surely, just as my own darkness was a part of me. The dark had been my domain since my birth, whatever my inherent qualities were, and I knew the deep dark that haunted the spirit like no one else. I knew what it would take to get her out of it.

I just needed to remind her of who she was. To accept the call of her own fiery nature. She was denying herself of it, punishing herself for the things that had happened to her and around her.

New sensations were clambering around in my own mind; it was like a whirlwind I was learning to navigate, and it was almost easier to stay in the centre of it and let it whirl around me as I watched. Emotions were uncomfortable things to be sure, and it felt like an internal assault.

It should have destroyed me, I mused, to suddenly be attacked by these feral feelings. But there was one thing that was centering me, keeping me focused with pinpoint accuracy—and that was my woman in that castle.

As I left, Wobbles patted my shoulder comfortingly. "Bad place," he muttered. "Bad for princess."

I grunted in agreement because I knew as powerful as my mate was, this was not her home. That goddess of smoke was not her natural state, and if she did not control that darkness, it would likely eat her whole.

I marked the various sentries the goblins and wolves had placed in the area around the castle. I'd had to kill a bunch of the goblins when they'd come at me at the border, and I was more than happy to kill them all if I had to. They were hardly innocent creatures—their favourite sport was hunting pixies and slaughtering them, tearing their wings off while their families watched. The last time I'd been here, I'd seen the worst of them, and in the last two hundred years, nothing had changed. But those huge beasts around her, lining the castle walls, were a different matter. Their size, savagery and darkness were as familiar to me as my own skin, and I'd marked their scents before I'd come in. They would know on sight and scent that I was a prime alpha beast, and a majority of them would submit to me without question.

I shivered at the implication as I headed east until the dead forest surrounded me, the blackened husks of trees looming like weapons.

"Flowers," Wobbles suddenly piped.

"What?" I asked faintly.

"Get flowers."

I pinched my nose as a memory came to me. Of my mother on her birthday and a bunch of pink hibiscuses that had been given to her by my father. The one time he'd graced her some semblance of kindness. Every other time he'd—some black emotion shot through me like a spear, and I stumbled, reaching an arm out to clutch onto the tree closest to me.

Perhaps I wasn't as immune to emotions as I'd thought. If any memory was going to be my undoing, it would be a memory of my father. The very source of my well of ever dark.

Wobbles said softly, "Grief. Sorrow. Rage." He poked me again. "Flowers." His tiny voice was nothing more than a squeak yet fiercely insistent.

Grief. That was a new one. I shook myself and focused on the soil beneath my bare feet, something I often had to do in calming myself down from battle-rage. It looked like it worked for this as well.

"Flowers," I repeated thoughtfully. Women, much like birds, liked flowers and other pretty, shiny things. I'd also seen Altara fingering her wedding ring. It made something warm me from the inside to see that she had not removed it. Perhaps Wobbles was right; Altara needed to know how I felt about her, that I could take care of her no matter how dark she went, and I knew exactly what type of flower would be best.

GOBLINS WEREN'T COMPLETE IDIOTS. THEY WERE SNEAKY AND cunning, getting into dark places before you even knew they were there. It just so happened that I had those same qualities, just a more aggressive version. The dark witches were dangerous; they knew the old magic of the wilds and would be more aware of what was happening to Altara than anyone else. As for the beasts...well *them* I could deal with as much familiarity as my own people.

I generally avoided shifting into small creatures as it was nuisance, but in this case I relented. I left my new flowers in the nook of a tree with Wobbles and snuck into the dark castle first as a hog—which Malika could *never* know about because she'd called me a pig once—so the goblin guards didn't suspect me because there were a few already milling about. Then I became a mouse and followed Altara's scent.

My scent would not change, even as a mouse, so the sleeping beasts outside and in the hall only blinked at me as I passed. There was a risk one of them would seek to challenge me, but apparently, they had enough sense not to. The two massive ruby-bejewelled king cobras watching me from beside the throne were definite candidates, and in fact, the other beasts seemed to defer to them. One was a male, the other female—mates, if I wasn't mistaken, and they watched me scuttle past with their round, sharp, serpentine eyes. If I ever thought they'd be a threat to Altara, they were as good as dead, but they seemed to be just as entranced by her as I was. Mice were natural prey of snakes, and I expected these serpents to understand just what I thought of them—that even in this form, I was not prey. Sure enough, just as I passed, both of them bowed their heads.

Satisfied, I scuttled on.

My tiny form was not for their benefit after all; it was for Altara. I did not want her to see me and chase me out like unwanted vermin.

I found my mate asleep, alone, in a gigantic bird's nest

and immediately assumed my human form to look at her better. I crouched over her, scowling at her bedding, knowing I could full well make her a better, more comfortable nest, big enough for both of us so that she could sleep on my chest, and I could pet her to sleep. Her face bore a little frown, her dark brows twitching a little in her sleep as the smoke around her made lazy patterns. The urge to take her into my arms and clean her off, wash her and bundle her safe into my care was overwhelming. I couldn't help it—I pulled out a stray twig through her tangles of hair. Her lips twitched, and I leaned down close to sniff at her.

She smelled so intensely of home that my cock twitched, wanting to do its job. I grimaced and pulled away, annoyed at myself for thinking of my own pleasure when I had to protect my mate. I summoned the flowers from outside and laid them gently at the side of her nest, so she'd find them as soon as she woke.

I left as swiftly as I'd arrived, hating myself for leaving her in that sorry excuse of a den. As I scurried out of the cavern system and back out of the castle, I spotted a group of goblins huddled around a campfire, gnawing on raw hog meat. I scowled in my mouse's face and hoped they were feeding my mate and was suddenly very sure that they weren't.

Well, now I knew what my next gift would be.

THE SECOND DAY, WOBBLES AND I TRAVELLED FAR TO FIND A tribe of pixies to trade with. Summoning worked a little differently in the Forests of Eternity. I couldn't simply construct anything the way I could on my own island. There was something about the intense magic here that corrupted that sort of work. I could move things from one place to another easily, but making a container was going to be impossible. I sent Wobbles into the village first, so as not to startle the creatures, and then went in after him, dragging the collection of rabbits I'd hunted. During my last time here, I'd learned that pixies in this land ate meat but found it hard to get any, being so small themselves.

They giggled and clapped at the fresh meat and gave me much in exchange. Happy with my supply, Wobbles and I left the pixie village and travelled back to Altara. That night I snuck back in and found her huddled under fresh twigs with a rusted can full of water next to her. Alarmed I quietly reduced the thing to powder, hoping she wouldn't become ill from its contents and replaced it with my new receptacle—a clean steel bottle and the collection of fruits and cooked fish the pixies had given me. When I looked back at Altara, she was stirring, rubbing her eyes. As she moved onto her back, the front of her gown pulled open, and I stilled, feeling my own eyes go as big as the earth itself. Her creamy brown breasts were exposed for me to see, beautiful in their size. Her dark nipples were peaked, and a feral heat whirled through me. She made a small noise in her throat and reached for her own breast, cupping it against the cold. Her perfect, bare-breasted form reminded me of a time she'd lain against me, naked and in my care.

I completely lost my mind.

My bare feet strode forward of their own accord. The beast inside of me had lost its patience. I dropped down to the nest by her feet and crawled up her body on all fours like a tiger, pressing my lips against her shins, her thighs. I got to her sex and inhaled her sweet, fiery scent and kissed her mound before moving all the way up and burying my face into her beautiful neck. Her warmth against me was my undoing. I needed her scent surrounding me; I needed her legs around my waist; I needed my cock thrusting deeply into her pussy, giving her pleasure as was my responsibility.

She squirmed in her sleep, and I raised my head to look down her perfect face. She really was the epitome of feminine beauty, and I watched in utter awe as her eyes opened a fraction, still heavy in that place between sleep and waking.

"Zale," she breathed, her sweet voice full of lust.

I groaned at that sound and lowered my face to her breast, licking across her nipple. She moaned in pleasure and my cock instantly became steel.

"Altara, my mate," I murmured against her skin, my voice guttural in the way it was when my beast took over. "I need to pleasure you."

"I was so cold," she murmured, a hint of a whine.

I grinned against her skin at her sweet voice and rubbed my heat against hers. "I'm here now."

Raising my head again I let my heavy body press against hers and brushed my lips against the hollow of her throat. "My mate," I whispered.

Her eyes flew open, emeralds alert and fully awake now. She made to scramble away from me, and I groaned in frustration and shot off her, turning and leaving her room at full pelt before I could do anything more. The tiger inside of me roared in protest, but I pushed him back down with all my might. I had acted like a foolish cub. She hadn't even been properly awake, hadn't been properly aware that this was not just a dream. I hated myself for letting my mating instinct take over like that. It wasn't safe for her. That's not what she would want.

I didn't even care to change forms as I left this time; the mouse was too slow compared to my human limbs. I ran my hands through my hair, groaning in anger, my cock standing at full mast for all to see. A pair of goblins came around the corner, and I was so angry with myself I brought out my obsidian sword. They stared up at my naked form and then down to my erect cock. I roared with rage and beheaded both in one sweep, pushing past their bodies before they could even fall to the floor and striding away from this fucking hell hole.

I *wanted* my mate so badly that I was out for ruthless murder, and the goblins and witches seemed to know this as they fled at the sight of me. The beasts in the hall merely watched on, probably aware of what a beast after his mate was like. Outside I killed two more goblins for daring to raise their swords against me and regretted it instantly. *Fuck. Fuck Fuck.* I needed her so much. But what choice did I have but to wait for her to want me back?

8

ALTARA

My heart pounded as I scrambled out of my nest. I took two involuntary steps forward after Zale, his retreating back simultaneously a knife to a gut and a cool wash of relief.

I looked down to see the new delivery. A large stack of fresh fruit, something wrapped up in banana leaf and a steel can. I bent down and opened it up. Fresh, clean water sloshed inside. Excitedly, I took three healthy gulps and relished the crisp, almost-sweet taste.

It tasted like heaven compared to the dirty water that had been churning inside my stomach for the last few days, and I was momentarily stunned at the forethought Zale had to bring this to me.

I stared at the now empty, dark entrance to the corridor Zale had disappeared through.

I'd spent most of yesterday sleeping, but when I'd woken once, I'd seen that he'd left a bunch of soft pink lotuses next to my bed. They smelled like my mother's garden back in Quartz.

I'd been angry that he'd just come and gone on a whim, thinking he could just leave me *flowers* like it was nothing. I knew it had been him, of course, because his earthen, masculine scent was all over the room—if not the remnants of his powerful presence.

A male like Zale couldn't just come and go without it being known. Or experienced.

After he'd left the throne room, I'd known that the bastard knew exactly what he was doing. Whatever strange and loathsome thoughts were hovering at the edges of me at the time, Zale's face had been clear and imprinted upon my retinas for the rest of my life.

He was always *with me* everywhere. When I slept on my nest of twigs, when Magrin brought me dirty bowls of water to drink, when I'd gone for a hunched walk around the warren of dark passages under the castle.

I haunted these passages, and Zale Boneweaver haunted me. The deep timbre of his voice followed me, the blistering intensity of his blue gaze and the heat that filled my stomach after that.

I'd never been looked at by a man that way and it terrified me.

Whatever had been between us back on Boneweaver Island—back when his heart had been in shadow and unfeeling—had now been elevated a thousand-fold now that he was free, and I had no idea what to do with that.

When I'd woken up to him on top of me, he'd been purely volcanic in his desire, and it had made me slick on sight. I thought I'd been having a pleasant dream when I'd felt his very real weight on top of me like he wanted to merge us together.

I wanted him inside me, and I wanted him as far away

from me as possible. How could I feel those two things with equal intensity?

Sitting back down on my nest, I swallowed the lump in my throat and reached down for the berries.

Somehow he'd known I was hungry. He'd known I was cold. He'd known lotuses would remind me of the Ellythian women in my life and give my heart warmth if not my body.

Something shifted in the darkness of the passage, and I knew who it was.

Everywhere I went Magrin was always lurking in the shadows nearby, watching me with curious eyes. There was some strange...power to her under all the wrinkles and alabaster skin. Like something lay slumbering within her she was trying and failing at pulling out.

I hoped I didn't have to kill her because she'd been helping me in the best way she knew how, and I was thankful for that.

But a little voice told me that Zale was taking better care of me. That I really only needed him, inside me, thrusting my darkness away with those eyes that looked upon me like he just *knew*.

I wanted to get up and follow him, chase after his retreating back and that bastardly beautiful tiger tattoo, but one thing was stopping me. That when I'd woken up and recoiled from him, the look on his face had been a mask of such terrible anguish that it had made me want to curl up in here and never see the outside world ever again. That I was not worthy of him and Wobbles. Or of anyone else. The others were probably frantically looking for us and I was holed up here like an ungrateful wretch.

I ate the berries Zale had brought me. I ate the meat Zale had brought me. I drank the water Zale had brought me, and with each bite and each sip, I remembered the feel of his trailing lips against my skin. I smelled awful—I knew it—and yet he'd still groaned over me like I was the most beautiful thing in existence. I wondered how his newfound emotions were treating him, though he looked well enough both times I'd seen him now.

He hadn't seemed consumed by dark emotions like I was. I supposed he was a veteran sailor of those seas. A seasoned warrior of those dark enemies.

The black smoke returned around me, dark and roiling, as Magrin shuffled into my room. I looked at her hunched presence—her beak of a nose, the harsh lines on the skin of her face. Her irises were dark pools of night, sunken into her skull, but today the black hood of her robe was pushed back slightly, and I could make out a black symbol freshly painted on her forehead. A crescent moon pierced by an arrow.

"Magrin," I said slowly. "Do you worship Agnolthi?"

Her fist tightened around her knobbly staff, and she eagerly bobbed her head. "The Witch-Goddess is our prime mother," she rasped. "Every full moon, the Nine dance. Tonight, we worship the darkness."

My interest sparked enough for a smoky tendril to ease off my face. "Can I watch?"

THE NIGHT SHOULD HAVE BEEN COLD, BUT I DID NOT FEEL IT AS Magrin and the other witches assembled upon the dusty grass behind the castle. The constellations spread out above us in the heavens, but by some strange plume of magic, the stars all shone red as blood. It heated my veins to see the witches coo and twitch at the sight of the night, their hunched bodies clutching their wooden staffs like weapons. There were nine of them, Magrin told me, and they bore the easy, often squabbling, sisterly familiarity of those who'd spent decades together.

Though the goblins stayed well away from us, some of the beasts joined along, and I could see that of those who did, the wolves, eagles and lions, were all females. The female king cobra slithered forward, and I observed her carefully. Drawing herself up to full height, she positioned herself to stand next to me, and this way, she was a full head taller than my five-foot-six frame. If this was a different time and place, if I were a different person, I would have run screaming. She was a powerful creature, her body the circumference of a tree trunk, and with her mighty hood drawn out, her forked tongue tasting the air, she was more monster than reptile.

We stood quietly side by side for a moment, the other beasts arranging themselves around us in resting positions as we watched the witches set a mighty cauldron on a fire in the middle of the grass.

"You are not what I expected." With great alarm I turned to stare at the serpent to see her mouth moving and forming Ellythian words in a soft feminine hiss of a voice. Her accent was sort of like Zale's and the other Old Ones, who spoke an older Ellythian dialect that was more formal in its cadence and grammar. It might not have been obvious, but as someone who'd been practising Ellythian to try and fit in, I noted it right away.

"You can speak?" I said dumbly.

She glanced at me, but there was a hint of pride in those predatory liquid eyes. "Most have lost the skill, but I remember."

I watched her mouth move in wonder. I'd never seen Zale, Atax, Raen or Kai do any such thing when they were in their shifter forms. Perhaps these beasts of the Eternal Forest where a different breed.

"Do you have a name?" I asked.

She tasted the air as she observed me, that crimson jewel on her forehead shimmering in the fire the witches had lit. After a moment she said, "In human tongue I am called Ulanna."

"Well met, Ulanna," I murmured. Manners had been instilled in me since infancy, and even in my current, sullen state, I couldn't get rid of them easily. The serpent stared at me for a moment before turning back to watch the witches.

She didn't say any more, and I wasn't in any mood for talking, even to this serpent, so I did the same.

Magrin built a fire unlike any I'd seen before. It was a light turquoise that reminded me of the water of a fae lagoon I'd once seen on Boneweaver Island. Rani had told me that such pools led directly to the ocean. I wondered if that had any link to this fire, that perhaps it was a sort of portal for magic too.

The nine witches circled around the cauldron, rhythmically thumping their staffs into the dirt at the same time. It shouldn't have, but by some magic, the ground trembled with each collective thud of the wood. A wind stirred through the air, smelling of earth, smoke and something sour. The witches abruptly halted, and as one, they brandished something that glinted. They held blades to the twin moons in the sky, as if asking their light to bless them then held their forearms over the cauldron and spilled their blood into it. A silver butterfly flit around my head before zipping away into the dark. I followed its path for a moment before shaking myself and looking back at the witches.

Magic thrummed through the air like a sentient thing, and the smoky coils around my body danced. As the darkness around me moved, I found myself moving too.

Not from my own volition, I found my feet moving me forward. I could barely feel the ground under my feet as I swept toward the witches, my gown slipping from my shoulders and falling to the ground. I wanted to feel this magic on my skin, I wanted to be bare to experience this.

The wolves behind me howled into the night, and when the witches saw me coming, drenched in that midnight darkness of my own soul, they crowed with glee, calling out in old, high-pitched trills and savage feminine cries. The sound spurred me on, an ancient call to my blood.

My very marrow responded, pulsing to the beat of my heart as the nine witches made space for me at the head of the cauldron. I summoned a dagger from my astral repository, and it appeared, black and dull. I slashed at my palm and feeling barely a tint of pain in the back of my mind, I stared at the welling dark droplet, letting it drip into the cauldron. The bubbling mixture spurted red and sparked with silver light.

The witches tipped their heads back and howled their own fell chorus, and then they were dancing.

Power from the magic they'd summoned must have given them a wild, feline strength, making their bodies go from aching to limber because they easily whirled around me and the cauldron, their robes flapping, their faces dappled in ecstasy. Red smoke poured from the cauldron, roiling into the sky in a cloud of anger and menace. The beasts behind me got to their feet and began a slow, circumnavigation around the dancing witches. Ulanna was in the lead, her powerful body slithering, her head swaying a little, caught up in the trance.

I watched them with heavy-lidded eyes, feeling the beat of the witches' pounding feet, their writhing bodies twisting, their arms slashing through the night. Images began to form in the red smoke lazily shifting above us, but I couldn't make out what they were.

High above it all, there was an image I could finally make out.

It was a golden bow, and I felt my own eyes widen as I beheld it. It had to be solid gold by the presence it bore, intricately inlaid with bestial patterns. I saw a mermaid, a woman with the body of a snake, a man with the head of lion. It was stunning and lethal and pulsed with old magic. Someone's hand plucked the string, and the twang it let out vibrated through my entire being. I could not blink; I could not breathe; my mouth was parted in a stupor of such awe that all thought left my body.

I didn't realise Ulanna had come up beside me until she spoke in a low hiss. "The Boneweaver Bow." Her voice gained a bite of anger. "Stolen by the Ellythian queens long ago, hidden away, never to be seen again."

My head cocked, considering this news, and I turned to look at her. By the time I looked back, the image had faded into red smoke once again. Disappointment spilled through me, sour and biting, and I looked back at the dancing witches.

"Agnolthi speaks!" Magrin shrieked, lifting her staff into the air. "Bring forth the tithe!"

The wolves parted and a smaller, male wolf came through, his head down, his tail between his legs.

"Are you willing?" cried Magrin, feverishly still caught up in the heat of the dance.

The wolf ducked his head in clear agreement.

"A sacrifice to Agnolthi," Ulanna muttered from next to me.

"For what?" I breathed.

Ulanna turned her entire serpent body and looked at me. But I could not look at her back as the nine witches raised their knives in the air and plunged them into the wolf.

I stared, my throat constricted by my own shock as the wolf crumpled to the ground, and Ulanna, never having taken her cobra's eyes off me, said, "For you."

Power like I've never known before slammed into me—foul, acrid, murderous. I screamed and screamed and screamed.

9

ALTARA

I woke up back in my nest, but this time I was surrounded by the beasts. Wolves slumbered on top of each other on my right, one with her head resting on the nest itself. The lionesses slept on my left, and the eagles were against the far wall, their wings around themselves, large eyes closed. Right at the bottom of my nest, Ulanna slumbered, coiled tightly, the ruby on her head twinkling sluggishly in her sleep.

It was the strangest thing to sit there and see the entire group of female predators sleeping peacefully together, their breaths synchronised, their wild and tangy scent perfuming the air. My body was strangely energised, my blood pounding heartily through my veins.

With a sick pang I remembered what happened last night. They'd sacrificed one of the male wolves. Slaughtered him *for me,* Ulanna had said. The urge to vomit struck me, and I clapped a hand over my mouth. The smoke around me stuck greedily to my skin, pulsing dangerously as I tried to calm myself, breathing the musty air of the cave through my nose.

Inside my body my magic hummed in my chest, my stomach, and I got the impression of a crimson tide cresting and falling. The power of that wolf was given to me, and my magic was trying to alchemise it like it usually did with foreign power. I felt tainted, *dirty*. I was wrong. This was entirely wrong. How could I have let them do this to me? I wanted to crawl out of the sleeve of my skin and burn it.

I scrambled to my feet and yanked on the silk robe someone has scrunched up and left on the side of the nest. My movements were jerky, and a rising anger, black as the coldest parts of the night, filled my entire being. I needed to go outside, needed to fill my lungs with fresh air to get rid of this heinous feeling.

Grabbing Zale's steel tankard from the nest, I made my way around the beasts. They remained quiet, but I sensed almost of all them prick their ears up and open their eyes at my movement. I strode out of the small cavern room and headed for the entry to the castle.

I got about halfway before Magrin came bustling down the corridor, jittery, sweaty, her robe askew.

She bowed low, clutching on her own throat as if she thought I was about to rip it out.

"What's wrong?" I snapped. I was jittery myself, this new, awful magic inside of me tumbled in my stomach like a body caught in crashing waves. I couldn't control it, and it was going to quickly drive me insane.

"Y-your Greatness, there is a small issue," she flinched, waiting for a slap that never came. "One of the hunting goblins took—uh—felt the need to—" She gestured to the throne room behind her.

I impatiently pushed past her and strode up the slope to the outside, that feeling corrupting my stomach suddenly become a maelstrom. I wanted to tear something apart with my teeth; I wanted to claw through these walls and lay it to waste. The air around me thickened with crackling energy, lightning sparked off my skin.

When I stepped into the throne hall, I stopped dead in my tracks.

The male beasts lying lazily around the hall stared with barely any interest at the two goblins who had a pixie on the tiles, with her hands and ankles bound, her golden light fading due to the rusty knife they'd stuck into her heart.

The image of her lying there, bound and cut open hit me like a mallet.

Not long ago, that had been *me* lying on a table, cut open but a cruel being, hopeless and powerless. I let out a feral shriek.

The goblins took one look at me and bolted. The male wolves began growling, and two of them launched after the goblins.

I had to heal her.

Rushing to the pixie, I reached into her chest with my magic, but the knife lodged in her heart had not been the first strike. Many wounds laced through her lungs and cardiac fibres. A savage pain like none other punctured my chest. She was so lacerated that I dared not take on this injury.

I could not save her. My face crumpled as I opened my eyes to look upon her fair face. How much did death insist on following me? How many times would I be helpless to do anything of value?

But I recognised her face right away. It was the same little pixie that had saved me from eating the poison berries.

Rage tore through me with all the power behind a thunderous storm, potent and crackling. Smoke shot around my body in a whirlwind.

When I rose to standing, lightning shot down my arms, encircling my limbs like deadly bracelets. Magrin and the other witches now stood by the cavern wall, pale and trembling. Ulanna slithered out from the underground passageway, her eyes wide.

"Those goblins are dead," I hissed at Magrin. "It looks like I'm going hunting."

The wolves let up a howl, and Magrin nodded frantically before rushing out of the hall.

I followed after her, my footsteps quick as my blood raged within me. These nasty creatures had no reason other than sport to kill those pixies—I could see it as plain as day.

But as I emerged out of the maw of the castle into the new night, I stopped dead. All the goblins loitering around outside and the two male wolves who'd lurched out stared up at the magnificent figure of Zale.

As if he were the God of Death himself from some of old tale, Zale stood before us, his naked body tattooed and shining, his long hair loose and tossing in the breeze. Against the light of the two moons in the night sky, I felt as if I'd stepped inside a legend. In his two large hands he held the severed heads of two goblins by their hair, blood still dripping from them. I had met Zale on a night just like this.

The full force of his bestial gaze hit me in the gut and sent me reeling, and I was left trembling from both the new magic and the pure need in me. So slowly, every inch of his body masculine grace, he lowered the heads to the ground. An offering.

Something ancient and primitive inside me snapped.

I had no control over myself as I flew toward Zale, still half crouched, his blue eyes brilliant pools of the ocean, reeling me in. His arms opened for me as I threw myself onto him and crushed my lips against his, hungry for his heat, his skin upon mine, for the sound of his lust in my ear. His hands found my thighs, and he pulled them up around his waist. Hot power scorched through me where his hands gripped my bare skin, the silk robe flaring out around me.

I bit his lower lip, and he growled in approval. Barely aware that he was walking us into the dark of the forest, the full force of my frenzied desire gripped me, my hands aggressively dragging across the huge muscles of his neck and his biceps, our bodies clashing in a desperate battle of lust.

His mouth hungrily devoured mine, demanding all of me —tongue and teeth and all. His hands possessively gripped me like he never wanted to let me go; he carried me easily into the deep shadows of the forest and sat us down, keeping me in his lap as he yanked open the black silk of my robe. He pulled away to look at my breasts, nipples peaked, my chest heaving.

His voice was a low growl, "Altara, I—"

"No talking," I panted, pulling off the robe completely, presenting my naked body to him. This was what I needed. I had too much energy, too much need and desire. I thought I'd explode if I didn't have him right now. In fact I *knew* I'd explode. The raging longing inside of me was beyond anything I'd ever felt, I needed him within me more than I'd ever wanted anything in my life. Our power buzzed around us, charging the air with crackling intensity.

His gaze was fire on my skin, and the sound that came from him was all animal as his hands came up to grip me around the waist, his mouth capturing one breast.

I gasped as his tongue swept across my nipple, sending rivulets of pleasure through my centre. The twinkling, golden thread between us hummed and sparked with strange light and moisture pooled between my legs. I dug my hands into his scalp, gripping him, clutching him with my thighs.

Zale swept his tongue over my other breast, and I tilted my head back, pulling him closer by his strong shoulders. I was being rough—perhaps too rough—and it was almost like we were fighting as Zale dug his fingers into my waist.

I angrily pushed his hair back and ran the flat of my tongue along his neck, savouring his salt and male musk—a scent that I'd somehow been craving for my entire life.

The hard length of Zale's cock was delicious and impossibly like wrought iron under me. I pushed him away, and he let me, while I sat back a little to look at him, breathing hard.

I had seen Zale naked before, the entirety of Boneweaver Island and my dark court had seen him naked. But fully erect, his cock hard and huge before me, *for* me, he was devastating to look at. A king of the jungle. An apex predator. And all fucking mine.

I looked up at him and saw that his eyes had blown out into their tiger form. A low rumble emerged from his throat, and I all but leapt back into his lap. The tiny tremble in his hands told me he was barely holding himself back, but I didn't care. I wanted him rabid for me; I wanted him feral and uncontrollable in his desire, just like mine was.

But it was lucky he had some control because I'd never had someone as big or as wide as him before. The force between us sparked with real light, and we both flinched before he grabbed me, pulling my body against him. My breasts flush against his chest, he fisted his cock, and I lifted myself as he pressed the crown of his manhood against my dripping entrance.

He groaned when he felt my slick heat, and I lowered myself onto him, impaling myself, relishing in the slow delicious way he was stretching me out. I gasped at the intensity of his girth, clutching onto his neck, digging my fingernails into him. It was painful. It burned like fire, but it was exactly what I needed.

His lips seized mine once again, his tongue lashing the inside of my mouth, possessing me completely as my pussy encompassed the full length of his cock. I tilted my head back and groaned against the insane feeling of fullness, a deep and profound sense of satisfaction spiralling its way through my spine. I simply breathed for a moment, my nose buried in his neck, my breasts heavy and heaving against his strength. I needed his scent all around me, filling me up to the brim, and with both of us sweating in the dark, that's exactly what I got.

"Altara." His voice was nothing more than an animalistic growl, and it sent a shudder through me. I placed my forehead against his, our breaths combining between us and flexed my hips, riding him slowly at first. The bond that connected us sung with joy, and Zale groaned with pleasure. His hand splayed out on my lower stomach, his thumb finding my soaked clit and circling as I rode him. His other arm curled around me possessively.

I rode him, claimed his body with mine, until my legs shook, and he took his cue, lying back down on the earth and pulling me with him. He lifted his hips, thrusting inside of me with long, torturous strokes. I trembled on top of him, pleasure and pain shooting through my entire form.

I moaned, long and loud, needing him to know how good this felt, how long I'd been thinking of having him inside me. But this made something in him snap, and he suddenly couldn't get enough, quickening his pace to thrust into me with a slap, the wet sounds of my pleasure almost obscene, but I *loved* that. On top of his big, hard body I felt safe and warm and whole, and something began unfurling within my centre. My clit ground against his pelvis, sending waves of rising pleasure soaring through me until I felt as if I was flying high on the night clouds above us. I moaned and shuddered over him, and he rumbled his approval, his chest heaving as he found the most perfect rhythm.

"Altara." The way his voice caught on my name made me raise my head and look at him, though he did not stop moving within me. "My mate. You are the most beautiful thing I have ever seen." My breasts were heavy, bouncing with each thrust as I stared at his face, the dangerous intensity of his eyes as they searched mine. "I'm going to fill your sweet pussy with my cum." He thrust into me hard, jolting me upwards.

It felt like an honest-to-Goddess dream, the way the moonlight framed his face, the way his eyes pinned me onto the spot, the way his cock was hot and relentless.

He moaned and grunted under me as if I were his undoing, but as I watched him, that heinous, dark magic inside of me pulsed sickly. Zale's eyes widened, though he did not stop his movement.

"Tara," he growled. "You need—" He licked his lips, frowning as if concentrating. Then he pulled me down to nip at my lip and broke off to whisper, "Give it to me."

I didn't know what he meant because at that moment everything was blasted from my mind as he changed his stroke, holding me fast against his core, driving up into me with a sudden relentless force that touched a place so deep that nobody before him had reached. I let out a strangled scream into the night, and all he did was ferociously repeat, "Give it to me."

I closed my eyes as the powerful sensation of my climax

building thundered toward me, a tsunami coming to toss me in its delicious waves. I bounced on top of him, my palms braced on the thick muscles of his tattooed chest.

I was an utter mess of shuddering, uncontrollable trembling as pleasure blasted through my spine, finally crashing into me. I screamed, bucking on top of him, grinding my clit as Zale gave a broken moan so deep in his chest: "Ah—fuck—Altara, my love—" He broke off and roared into the night. Gripping my waist with both hands, holding me like a steel vice, he came into me, his cock pulsing as I spasmed, crying out from the sensation of his hot cum filling me up. I felt as if I was floating, suddenly light, and I was distantly aware that it felt like I was pouring heat and energy into him, and it was so strange because I was not used to *giving* my power away—only accepting—and it took me a few seconds to realise that Zale was freeing me of that murderous, excess power given to me against my will.

Unable to hold myself up anymore, I collapsed onto him, and as he held me tightly, I felt each of his thick fingers pressing onto the skin of my waist. He breathed hard, his dick still moving gently in and out as if he wanted to prolong the pleasure just a little bit more.

Twin butterflies, glowing purple and blue, flit around us in their own dance. I watched the cadence of their wings flutter in a pattern as old as time. I felt so light I might have floated up into the treetops with them. I exhaled on Zale's chest as the thread that bound us together began to tremble and *move*.

A deep-seated satisfaction tore through me, almost blinding in the way that it was claiming me, inside and out. Some primal force inside me was rising up, up, *up*.

I sat bolt upright, cold fear consuming my heart, my head

suddenly clear, my senses completely aware of what we'd just done. What I was doing.

I had just fucked Zale like my life had depended on it. And Zale was now looking at me as if *his* life depended on it, as if…I were his and only his and nothing more than that. I had never given myself to someone this way before. I couldn't afford to do that. This was dangerous. This was much more than a simple fuck, we were—

Zale captured me with those tiger's eyes, bright blue with a brilliance I'd never seen in him. Before he could say anything, I launched myself off him, yanked up my robe from the ground and *sprinted* into the night—away from him and the intensity of his Goddess-forsaken blue gaze.

10
ALTARA

I could still feel the ghost of Zale's huge manhood inside of me as I ran. My pussy throbbed from the stretch of him, and something cold wheedled its way through my spine. I followed the pinpricks of light that was the goblin's campfires as I hurtled through the trees, slipping my robe on as I went.

No signs of pursuit followed me. No pair of thumping human feet or pounding of tiger's paws. He'd let me go.

The further away from him I ran the colder and more desperate I got. The thread between us flickered with its strange light, and I shoved the image of it away. Even though I couldn't sense him physically chasing me, I couldn't help but feel he was somehow still right behind me.

I slowed down to a walk as the castle came into view, massive and towering above me like some dark god in its own right. A shiver crawled up my spine as I stopped by the goblin's campfire. They and the beasts watched me silently as I turned around and observed the black forest perimeter for some sign of movement. The twin moons sat side by side in the inky night sky, and I suddenly got the impression of a pair of angry eyes glowering down upon me. Hastily, I turned and hurried back inside the castle, heading straight past the witches and beasts waiting within, and making for my nest.

I threw myself down on my bed of leaf litter and twigs, the heavy patter of the she-wolves entering my room and Ulanna's soft slither. As they plonked themselves down around my nest once again, I was suddenly very aware of the fact that Zale *was* still inside me, the substantial amount of cum he'd put in me dripping freely down my thigh. I didn't touch it, and my pussy burned in memory of his girth and relentless fucking. Perhaps if I ignored it, the whole thing might just go away entirely. It took me a long time to get to sleep, but I kept still and silent, afraid of the implications.

I did not have Saraya here to stop my body from ovulating and producing a pregnancy, and Zale had been so taken by his own lust that I wasn't sure if he'd been in his own right mind. *I* hadn't been in *my* right mind after all. Something else had taken over me completely.

SOMETIME LATER A COMMOTION OUTSIDE AWOKE ME, AND Magrin was at my door, pulling at her hair, panicking. "Your Greatness!"

"Say no more," I muttered. In a flash my bow was in my hand, and I lurched off my nest and bolted outside. I felt strangely light and energised and I didn't care to think about why.

As I ran through the tunnel, up the slope and through the

hall to the outside, the sounds of battle, namely goblins shrieking and the clash of steel on steel, reached my ears.

The thread inside of me twitched and spun, and I knew immediately who it was outside. Sure enough, when the dull twilight hit my eyes, I found Zale with a pile of goblins at his feet, the remaining living ones standing warily by the entrance to the cavern. The beasts simply sat there and watched with great interest. The other witches were no doubt still sleeping.

"Altara!" Zale roared when he saw me, his eyes wild, "I cannot stay away from—"

One of the more insane goblins ran forward, an axe raised, but Zale knocked him out cold without even looking.

"What are you doing?" I asked angrily. "You can't just come here and—"

"What I'm doing is wondering how many of these things I have to kill before I feel better about my mate running away from me!" His face was a mask of anger and torment, and his eyes scorched me, making me suddenly remember everything we'd done last night. How much I'd wantonly thrown myself at him.

I swallowed as guilt oozed through me; I'd not meant to let it get that far. I was not ready for what he'd wanted. "But what does that even mean?" I shot back, "'Mate.' I don't even—"

"It means," he said, taking one menacing step forward that made my heart skip a wild beat, "that we are one. Born of the same soul. There is no other sacred union. No other thing comparable in this life. That I am yours. And you are *mine*."

I closed my eyes against the intensity of his voice, of his words. The priestess of Lasanthi Temple back at Levu village had read as such from her book, in the story of Zale's birth.

His star-born mate.

But why was I feeling this awful, soul-crushing sensation? I should be happy, ecstatic that I'd found my soul's twin. Instead I felt the living smoke-skin around me darken further, protectively encompassing me from him, from the world.

"I think there's something wrong with me," I said quietly.

He blinked, then his eyes darkened as he pinned me with a glare. "There's never been anything wrong with you, Altara. I would know as someone who actually *did* have something wrong with him."

His shining eyes swallowed my breath. He was right, in a way.

"It hurts now—here"—I pointed to my chest—"All the time."

A flash of pain crossed his face before it disappeared. "Mine hurts too." He shook his head. "But you're pushing it away." He gestured to my coiling smoke veil with his broad hand as if to point out my current situation.

"I think it'll kill me if I don't."

He stepped forward in the way that predators do, silent, measured, sure. "I won't let it."

"It's something I have to deal with myself."

"You can heal any disease and injury on your own, Tara— you always have. But this is not a wound made of muscles and blood." Something in me twisted at that, but he continued, "It's a wound of shadow and cunning. It is a hunter, and you are its prey. It's a goblin creeping, about ready to attack when you aren't watching." He pointed to me. "You've got a goblin in your head, and it's shaped like the Butcher."

I flinched at the mention of his name out loud, and Zale's face became purely murderous, but the image his words conjured in my head was so ridiculous that I let out a hoarse laugh. Shocked at myself, I quietened. Perhaps the screws and bolts that held my mind together were crumbling apart.

"I watched you fill him with arrows," Zale said in a dangerous, low voice, his eyes flicking down to the black bow still in my hand. "That white demon. He's the one that hurt you, isn't he? And he'd done it before."

A blade of pain breached my calm, and I began to tremble at the memory of my body lying splayed on the Butcher's table, a child under the hand of a monster, cutting me open. But I *had* shot him, hadn't I? It hadn't been satisfying at the time because I'd worn this very cloak of dead apathy, but I found myself nodding as I thought back on it. I had shot at him relentlessly, perfectly, without any thought—pure instinct, pure hunter. I had shot at him, and he'd been so shocked he couldn't even fathom what was happening. My lips twitched at the memory of his astonished face.

"I will be there with you," Zale said, "when you finally kill him."

I looked up at him in surprise. The idea of killing the Butcher hadn't even been a wisp of a thought in my mind. He was nigh impossible to kill, fortified with my own magic as he was. Zale didn't understand that. There was a lot about me he didn't know.

"There's more good to do in the world, Altara. And...and I want to do it by your side."

I clenched my teeth against the onslaught of his words because they were a knife that cut deep.

"Good?" I rasped. I was shaking now as I stepped toward him. "Like the good I did when Fangar and the demons came for me? When they slaughtered Malika's people and destroyed their houses? Like *that* good?"

His blue eyes burned like they knew something I didn't.

The understanding I saw there tore me open anew. I couldn't look at him. I didn't *want* him to understand me and all the black and heavy parts that made up who I was. There were wounds in me that could not be healed. I was tainted. I could not be with him, *mate* or not, I couldn't be with anyone.

I turned away from him.

He opened his mouth to speak, but I held up my hand. "You need to go," I hissed. "Right now."

The emotion coming off him was roiling in hot waves toward me and my shoulders sagged from the weight of it. "I might have needed your cock, Zale," I hissed. "But I do not want *you* here."

He recoiled like I'd slapped him, and I hated myself for it, but I *had* to make him leave.

When he spoke, his voice was deadly quiet. "I will leave you even if I know that it's not what you need, Tara. I do it only because I want you to know that I respect you and your wishes. But I will tell you one thing before I leave: You *cannot* deny a star-bond. It is bigger than the both of us. They know it too." He pointed to the beasts poised behind me, listening intently.

Without a further word he was gone, and his absence was a cold, cold, shard of ice slicing through my heart.

But I could not be what he wanted. His mate, his queen. Though my body yearned for him, lusted after him; I was no candidate to be *his*. This was something I'd known from the beginning.

11

PIA

We arrived on the shores of Tiger Island one week after we agreed to leave for the capital. There had been clean-up and repair of Levu village to be done, stray demons to be hunted and arguing to be had.

I'd served my exile at the jungle school on Boneweaver Island for three years and leaving it as an adult woman to return, without the blessing of my grandmother, made an old, nasty feeling twist in my gut. I had been sixteen at the time of my leaving Lota City, friendless, magic-less and resigned to my fate as the shame of the ancient house of Lota.

In the long line of Ellythian princesses destined to ascend the Lotus throne, I was perhaps the worst failure, and neither my mother—the crown princess—or the queen—my grand-mother—were likely to forgive me any time soon. In fact, returning before my punishment's completion was a crime in of itself.

Now I was returning with friends in the form of two fierce young women, Malika and Rani, also exiled for their own sins, and who'd grown much in the time that I'd come to know them. We also had Geravie Harranpul, Altara's old nursemaid, a fierce and remarkable woman who made grown men pale in fear. We also had Keshmi Harranpul, one of the elderly priestess twins of Agnolthi's temple, who was knowledgeable in all types of lore and magic.

Perhaps the most notable addition to our entourage were two Old Ones. While Raen, their sorcerer priest and also the more civilised of them, stayed behind to guard Boneweaver Island with our two pixies, we had the other two with us. I was convinced that Atax and Kai were half feral, and it wasn't their preference for raw meat that made my mind up about it.

Atax walked next to us like a lion made human, fully ready to behead anyone given half a chance—I'd seen him do it a little too happily during our two battles together. Kai, our white-haired beauty on the other hand, walked around as if he were living in a fanciful dream, where the world and everything in it was his plaything. He was eager and bouncing like a puppy, but I'd seen him be lethal and precise like his leopard-self.

As the Old Ones had disappeared from Ellythia over a century and a half ago, the sudden appearance of two of the blue eyed, bestial warriors made the sailors on the boat we'd commissioned extremely nervous. And they'd already been wary of us since the huge surge of demons on Boneweaver Island. We assured the captain a majority of the demons were either dead or had run off with their leader—the white Pentarog Altara had tried to kill—but I couldn't entirely blame anyone for being nervous around the two menacing Old Ones, or Geravie and Malika stomping around the deck like angry feline creatures themselves.

We crossed the narrow strait between both islands and

then proceeded to make our way into the perilous jungles of Tiger Island—so named because of the large population of tigers in the southern aspect. Rani's silk farm was to the far north, and we would have to be careful about making our way through there.

On our first night we camped around a small fire, cooking sweet potato and cassava Kai had sniffed out and dug up— lucky for his good nose. Geravie, I could tell, was getting irritable, and I think it was because she was anxious about Altara being taken. Even though my cousin was a young woman now, nursemaids always felt a sense of responsibility over their charges no matter the age.

"You're telling me there's absolutely no way we can retrieve them?" Geravie asked for the second time. Her Ellythian was sort of rough after her twenty-year stint in Lobrathia, speaking their clipped common tongue, but no one would ever question her authority.

Keshmi, who was stirring the little cauldron of food sighed. "No way in," she murmured, "but..." She tugged on her silver braid in thought, looking up at the night sky. "I wonder if we could try scrying?"

I shook my head. "Her mental defences won't allow outsiders looking in on her, just like all the Lota princesses."

"Mmm," Atax agreed. "Hers were particularly strong. Do you remember when Zale tried to check her power that first night he did the testing?"

A sour feeling stirred within me as I exchanged a look with the girls.

"You mean," Malika said loudly, "when you stole us from our beds in the middle of the night like the insane animals you are?"

Kai rubbed the back of his neck his obsidian sword earring

swinging, clearly ashamed about the whole affair considering he'd plundered our kitchens and beaten a drum *as* we were being kidnapped. But Atax smirked at Malika.

"Ah, yes," he said, grinning as if it were a fond memory. "I remember the way you squirmed against that island monster. Completely helpless against it, in your nightgown—"

Malika threw a full-sized cantaloupe right at his head. Atax caught it in one large hand, and without taking his eyes of Malika, took a savage bite out of the fruit. Malika scoffed in disgust and crossed her arms, turning her beautiful face towards Keshmi as if he were dismissed from the conversation. But it only pushed her full breasts up and Atax's eyes darkened as he watched her.

Geravie huffed but a tiny smile twitched her lips. It was a strange way to flirt, granted, but very entertaining for the rest of us. I wondered when they'd get over their ruse of a battle and finally fuck each other senseless. But sex was a sore spot with Malika these days. It was sex, after all, in exchange for money to help her family that had gotten her exiled from her village in the first place. I personally thought she was the most faultless of us all. Pre-marital sex had never been taboo in Ellythia, but that man had not told her he was married.

Rani shifted on the log we sat on. "I wonder if it's worth trying anyway?" she asked tentatively. "The scrying? King Zale might see what we are trying to do and respond."

Geravie nodded eagerly, "Why not? What have we got to lose?"

AFTER DINNER WAS DONE AND WE'D WASHED OUT THE TINY cauldron, Kai filled it with water from the nearby stream.

We all sat eagerly around it while Keshmi began a scrying construction. It was a little complex because a clause for inter-dimensional visual needed to be added, and I had never actually seen someone use such advanced magic before. The elderly priestess was sweating within minutes, her shoulders hunched over her rapidly moving hands. With the power she was calling on to breach the gap between worlds, I was severely impressed, to say the least—and more than a little ashamed I couldn't help. Kai stared at Keshmi, his sky-blue eyes wide and unblinking. He bent down to whisper in Rani's ear, "I've never seen such an old human use that much magic. Is it safe?"

"Bite your tongue, young man!" Geravie growled at him, completely ignoring the fact that Kai had at least one hundred and fifty years on her. "Keshmi is a priestess of Agnolthi. This is her domain, not yours."

Kai's brows shot up, and he made a show of pressing his lips together and sitting back on his haunches. I suppressed the urge to laugh until a shimmering image appeared on the surface of the water in the cauldron. We all went still.

"Holy mother…" Malika whispered before she was shushed by Geravie.

Zale and Altara were standing opposite each other in some type of stand-off. Zale had a pile of dead creatures littered at his feet.

"What are those?" Malika said in disgust

"Goblins," Atax muttered. "Fucking filthy goblins. They'll sneak up on you and—"

Geravie shot him a wicked look for his interruption, and he shut his mouth immediately.

We all leaned forward, transfixed by the scene. Altara looked like a completely different person than the girl I knew just a few weeks ago. A fell magical smoke cloaked her body like a moving skin, making her look like a supernatural entity, a wraith goddess. Under the smoke I could just make out her body, thinner than before, and a flash of her angry face revealed emerald eyes a match to mine except hers were dull like old moss.

A shiver ran through me at the devastation I saw in her form. I knew torrential pain when I saw it. We couldn't hear what they were saying, but it was clear that both were upset.

It was also clear that Altara was sending Zale away when his shoulders hunched, and he turned around and walked away from her.

Altara stared at his retreating form for a moment, and my heart broke in two.

Kai leaned forward, his two tiny white braids dangling as he held a finger dripping with blood over the cauldron and shouted, "Brother! Atax and I are going to Lota Island to see the Ellythian Queen!"

Rani gasped and clutched my hand, watching Kai, who sat back, sucking on his finger.

I looked back into the cauldron and saw that there was no sign of his blood as the image of Altara, trembling now, retreated inside a huge black, crumbling castle. I let out a long breath, wondering if there was a chance for either of them to hear us.

Keshmi altered her construction, sweat dripping freely from her now, and I prepared to call her off. But the scrying water followed my cousin into the dark, through dank cave corridors where she lay down on a gigantic bird's nest and stared up at the ceiling—up at us with such dejection it made me feel sick because it was all too familiar.

"Altara what in Agnolthi's name are you doing?" Geravie said crossly, shaking her fist. "She's been cut up by an enemy, and she's lying there like a broken worm!"

Altara frowned before the image was cut off and Keshmi collapsed onto the grass. We all let out shouts of alarm, but Kai was already there, cushioning the tiny lady's head and with the gentlest hands, lowering her carefully to the ground.

Geravie and I immediately rushed over to her, but she was breathing and just fainted from exertion. We all sighed in relief.

"He cut her entire body open, Geravie," Rani said, her distress at seeing Altara making her voice catch. "I'm surprised she's not been made insane by it."

"I'm well aware, Rani," Geravie replied smoothly, running a cloth dipped in cauldron water over Keshmi's forehead. "But Altara has been trained for this since infancy."

"Trained in getting cut up?" Kai said, a large hand upon his heart.

Bless the creature.

But Geravie was nodding. "She's been training to take great wound and injury, awful as it sounds, since she was barely out of nappies. That's how her magic has worked this entire time. She's a veteran at it!"

Everyone around me cringed. I didn't. Because I knew the type of training Ellythian princesses went through. Kai and Atax seemed to notice my change in energy because they were both staring at me in that ever-observant animalistic way of theirs.

I cleared my throat and said quietly, "Geravie is right.

Aunt Yasani would have taught my cousins to deal with this exact type of thing, just as I was."

"That's cruel," Rani muttered.

"It is," Geravie said. "But the level of power Lota women carry is a heavy burden. With that privilege comes the acceptance of a lifetime of responsibility. She's ignoring all we've taught her." She heaved herself to her feet.

"What was that you did?" Rani asked Kai, her brown eyes wide.

Kai held up his finger, already healed, and nodded eagerly. "Magic always has a cost, and my blood is as good as any. I thought if I offered the island my blood it might let me talk to him, so he knows where to come when they get out."

"It's fair logic," I said, smiling fondly at the white-haired Old One. "I just wonder how long we'll have to wait to see if it worked."

12
ZALE

I strode away from my mate with my heart kicking against my ribs. Everything inside of me screamed to rush back to her and pull her warm body into my arms so we could be together as one for the rest of eternity.

Altara was pushing me away because she was scared; I could see it in her pain-filled, emerald eyes. The mate bond was an intensity of feeling she was not used to, and even for myself, it made me breathless with the force of my desire, my lust, the pure need to have her. I could already feel our bond growing since we'd made love and shared power. I didn't know how she'd obtained all that excess dark energy, but the fact that she was living with those nine crones was proof to me it was by nefarious means. The most I could do was relieve her of it as her Vayashi. I was more used to handling energy of murderous intent, and if I *did* actually murder someone, I'd rather that guilt be with me than with her.

Wobbles launched himself at me from where he was hiding in the bushes, and I didn't break my stride as he scrambled up my body to sit on my shoulder. I patted him unconsciously, thinking about my mate.

For Boneweavers a star-born bond was an uncommon thing. Our mates were usually chosen out of worthiness, males and females fighting one another to see who was a match. Star-soul mates happened every generation or so, that was why the three queens had thought of it as a cure for me to start with. It was a sacred thing, and anyone who wasn't a Boneweaver would be fearful of such power. In time she would come to be in awe of it, just as I was.

But right now, she needed distance from me to find her own mind about it. So I would give it to her because it was my responsibility to give her *everything* she wanted. But this would be in my own way. I couldn't actually give her real distance from me, for all the need I felt of the bond from my own side, but I *could* give her the illusion of distance.

A predator's best skill was in not being seen after all.

Her little nest was cold, and I hadn't been able to get out of my mind when she'd said she'd been cold that night I'd fallen on top of her, unable to control my own desire. The pixies had their own material I could barter for, so that's where I went once again.

My desire to protect and claim my mate almost had me missing the jolt of Kai's power I felt tunnelling through the air. In between obsessing over Altara, I had been wondering what trouble my brothers and the girls would get up to without me.

The Eternal Forest sent Kai's voice to me on an echoing wind. *"Brother! We are going to Lota Island to see the Ellythian Queen!"*

My chest filled with warmth as I heard the voice of my youngest cousin-brother.

95

E.P. BALI

"Happiness," Wobbles cooed softly. "Comfort."

"Is that what this is?" I asked him, patting my chest.

"Mhmm."

After a moment of processing this new emotion, I came back to reality. So they had plans to go to Lota City, which was at once insane and worrying. I wanted to return to the black castle and tell Altara because I suspected it was Pia who was wanting to return to her home city to get help. But this move was laden with risk for the second in line to the Ellythian throne, having been banished for maiming her betrothed and then losing her power completely.

The Lota family was notoriously harsh on their women. High levels of power meant high expectations. In my time Queen Sosha had been monarch and had subjected her daughters to great tests of endurance and pain.

It was this that brought my brothers and I some solace when our own training had almost killed us time and time again. "It's not just us," Raen used to say. "The Lota princesses have been diving into fires and defeating death since they were children too. We cannot be weak in the face of that."

This was why I'd immediately known Altara to be a good Vayashi for me when I'd sensed her power. I hadn't seen her Lota eyes at the time, but I'd recognised her power as equal to mine.

And then we'd had sex last night, and my mind had been blown into a million pieces. Not only by the mating lust but by the sight of the power I'd been privy to while I was inside her. Sex was the way mates power-shared, and next time, I'd give her a taste of *my* power.

Even now, in addition to the dark energy I'd relieved her of, I felt the buzz and crackle of her lightning inside of me. It was a new and distracting thing. Bright and heavy all at once. What a weapon. I could think of a hundred different ways to use this in battle.

This was also probably why I didn't notice the twenty carnal fae creeping up on me until five diamond blades were angled at my throat.

I stopped short kicking myself a million ways to the seven hells.

"Well, well, well," a deep, familiar voice drawled. "Ashzale Boneweaver has come back to grace us with his presence."

In an instant I was surrounded by the golden guard of the carnal fae.

Rassiel Brightblade's amber eyes were trained on me, stroking down my body, heavy with overt assessment. The scent of his lust drifted toward me, bold and strong.

I had been trying to avoid these particular dwellers of the Eternal Forest and failed miserably.

"This is not your territory, Brightblade," I said calmly, knowing too well he'd love it if I used his first name.

"Oh, I know," he drawled suggestively, scraping the tip of his blade down my throat, down my bare torso until he reached the waistband of my pants. "But really, you know we'll go practically anywhere for *you*."

I suppressed a sigh, counting how many of my amber-eyed assailants I knew from last time. "Two hundred years older and no less horny," I said, unimpressed.

Rassiel chuckled as one chuckles at a lover who's said something wonderful, completely oblivious to my rising irritation. He said with a purr, "Oh, I've missed you, Your Highness."

"I'm not coming with you," I snapped, my voice taking on its beastly growl. "I'm a mated male."

All twenty fae stilled, suddenly going on high alert, and I knew then it was the worst thing I could have said. Carnal fae loved nothing more than a challenge of the sex kind. They would pursue me relentlessly now, just to see how far they could get. Rassiel's pupils dilated all the way out as he took another step toward me, sniffing delicately.

"Oh, I do smell it now," he whispered. "You know she'll just love that."

The involuntary growl began deep in my chest, but it only served to delight them. They tittered about me as I said, "Still skulking around, is she?"

Rassiel smirked fondly, "Our fair queen will be so happy to see you returned to her. And when she knows a *game* is afoot—"

I saw red. "Touch her, and I will slaughter your entire court."

He had the sense to startle at that and chose his next words very carefully. "No touching, of course—never *touching*, Your Highness." He cocked his head. "But you know a debt is owed. You are obliged to come with us."

"I will pay my debt," I snarled so ferociously the other three fae angling blades at me immediately hopped back two steps. "But that is all."

"Yes yes yes," Rassiel drawled shrugging one shoulder as if we were talking about organising a dinner party. The carnal fae were familiar with dealing with aggressive males. If anything it was their *preferred* type of male to deal with. As annoying as it was, they all knew exactly what would get them killed and what would keep them safe from me. Now they were backing away with their hands in the air, their swords sheathed and making no sudden movements.

Rassiel gave a very slow gallant bow, sweeping his arms wide. "Your Majesty," he said in an exaggerated calm, gentle voice. "If you will allow us to escort you to our court."

It was this that saved his life, and he knew it.

I gave a short grunt, trying not to think about Altara left behind me, lest I kill all these assholes in one go, and shrugged my shoulder to tell a stunned Wobbles to leave me. He obliged, all but leaping to the grass from me, and I prowled past Rassiel, who couldn't help but look me longingly up and down.

13

ALTARA

After Zale left me, I returned to the hall with Magrin at my side, muttering what she thought were comforting words.

"Shall we organise a hunt, Your Darkness?"

I grunted in question.

"To kill the Boneweaver King. We will sever his head and hang it from our cavern as their kind do themselves. We will carve his body open and flay—"

I had her pinned against the wall by her thick throat before I even knew what I was doing. Breathing hard, I looked her in the eyes. She was trembling, but a part of that was excitement.

This was the type of thing they expected from me. The type of darkness that an evil witch would do. She was uncomfortable around me when I was moping or silent. But she understood *this* language and had learned to love it.

That door at the back of my mind swung open with a groan as I realised that this was the type of behaviour the Butcher himself relished. I looked outside, at the dark and silent night, not a cicada or bird daring to make a sound. He had taken me on a night just like this and together with his men, had cut me open like a sow. The entire time, it had been silent except for the sound of flesh being cut. My smoky curls solidified around me and I could barely see the old witch's face. I slammed that old door shut but it swung inwards and right back on its hinge. Irritated, I cocooned myself against the memories coming through that door. But it wouldn't be enough. I needed a distraction. And not of the sex kind.

Abruptly, I let Magrin go. She fell at my feet, blubbering apologies.

"I do not want him hunted, Magrin. I want a party."

She heaved herself back up. "A party?"

"I want noise and revelry. Beating drums and song-singing. *Loud* song-singing. And dancing too. Can you do that?"

The old witch nodded slowly, her face crumpled in concentration. "And..."—I swallowed—"there will be no *sacrifices* for me again. I wish to do target practice. Have some of the bigger goblins dress in leaves and bark, and I will practice shooting at them."

Her face brightened as if I'd given her a great gift.

MAGRIN WAS QUICK TO COMPLY, AND I WATCHED HER AND THE witches scamper around outside, weaving around the beasts, shouting orders and smacking goblins over the head. The goblins liked the idea of revelry, and they *did* have crude instruments of sorts. Drums with tanned animal skins beaten with bleached and in some cases fresh, bone of some forest dwelling creatures. In amongst it all, the serpent Ulanna and her mate watched me with great interest.

Magrin chose one of the smaller goblins to sing to me, and it was a truly awful off-pitch wheezing thing to hear but anything was better than the silence. Anything but the silence.

Agnolthi's sign was the full moon, and two of them hung high in the night sky above me. She'd come to me while I'd been tied down by the Butcher. Angry and eyes blazing with the type of volcanic fury I couldn't even comprehend. She'd spoken to me, and it had been enough to tear me from my stupor.

I jumped to my feet, and my bow sprang into my hand with a flash of dull light. It was a lethal-looking thing, all black and inlaid with gold. I looked at the pattern closely and saw that they were skulls patterned with butterfly's wings. I frowned down at it, but was quickly distracted by Magrin giving a shout, bustling around, pushing goblins into final position around the campfire. I crept forward, keeping my head low in the way of a predator. I imagined myself as one of the she-wolves of my court, prowling for the kill.

"Run," I ordered dully.

The goblins scrambled, and in the night, I only gleaned their movements from the campfire reflecting on their armour. They held dead ferns over their bodies by way of hiding, and I scowled as my smoky veil hindered my vision.

I aimed. I fired and most definitely missed the first.

Magrin was clapping next to me, as if she really was at an excellent party. My scowl deepened, and I loosed more arrows into the night.

A wailing shriek—a nick.

Metal plinked against metal, and I knew I'd missed yet again.

Swearing out loud, I stormed back to my dead log where the small goblin resumed his singing. I sat there for a while, brooding into the fire while the goblins played their ugly drums.

Wolves shifted, the eagles flapped their wings and the goblins gnawed at the bones of some animal they'd caught and cooked. In amongst it all, I sat with my thoughts, watching the fire as if it held some knowledge I did not have.

I should have known that in the darkest parts of the world, darker creatures were enticed by music.

It began slowly at first. A foul wind struck the camp, and the goblins raised their heads and looked up at the sky. One of the wolves gave a warning bark, and they all went still as deer. Ulanna and her mate swayed softly to music only they could hear.

All the hairs on the backs of my arms stood on end.

I was on my feet in an instant, heart pounding, my bow in hand. It was useless, I knew, but there was something approaching, and I *needed* to have a weapon in my hands.

The air around me changed, weighing upon me as if the weight of the entire planet was pressing down on my head. The drummers stopped and clapped their hands to their ears, letting out morbid screams that pierced the night like tiny, rusty spears. The wolves whined, long and low.

Time seemed to stop in the world around me, and my limbs became frozen as if encased in ice. The essence of terror shook the particles of my being, and I couldn't get enough air into my lungs to take a proper breath.

Something came towards me from the shadows, and the campfire blinked out as if snuffed by a giant's hand.

A presence solidified from the very darkness itself. By the light of the two moons, a hunched, old man came into view. His skin was yellow and waxen, and the bottom lids of his eyes sagged open. He smiled at me with a mouth filled with sharp, red teeth.

"Dark thoughts call dark creatures," he rasped, except his voice sounded like men screaming.

"Dear Goddess," I choked on my own saliva.

"There are no Goddesses here, girl of void and sorrow."

"Are you Death?" I managed to get out.

"You think Death is evil?" A spine-tingling chuckle. He wouldn't take those forsaken eyes off me, and by the seven hells, I *needed* them off me. I felt dirty. Rotten. Exposed.

"Dark thoughts call dark creatures, and death is only a reprieve."

I gulped and whispered, "So you said. What are you then?"

Silence stretched out between us like a living corpse, and I wanted to vomit. But I'm sure this was a creature few had actually met and came out bouncing. I didn't want to make a stupid, fatal mistake.

"I am not nightmare. I am not terror. I am the force that is worshipped by the truly depraved."

I was suddenly aware of the uneven beating of my heart, of the blood flowing through my veins, of how much my soul needed to get away from this creature. "What does that mean?"

"In your world I am called many things. Often apathy. Sometimes despair. Always hopelessness."

I stared at him in disbelief.

"You are not a dark creature by nature,"—he grinned at

me with those glistening crimson teeth—"but you want to be."

"A dark creature?" I repeated carefully, even as the smoke coiled loosely around my body, more transparent now. "I don't know about that."

"You are masquerading as one. You are wearing a shadow as a mask. Do you want power like mine? You could have it, you know. You could be what I am."

I recoiled from his foul, dark soul. "What? No! I don't want that."

"You are a lie, living in the body of a woman."

A hollow gaped within me, yawning wide, threatening to swallow me whole. I wanted to fill it; I wanted to scratch my skin and get rid of his eyes upon me. "I don't want it, I don't!"

"You want to know real darkness?"

I shook my head violently, but he kept stepping forward. Magrin was suddenly at his side, frozen still, her black eyes wide in terror, a mirror of my own.

"Kill her. And do it for fun. Do it because it brings you joy."

My gut clenches as if it's been punched. "No! That's not who I am." But I know I'd gained power through the death of another last night, and I'd done nothing to stop it either.

"Apathy is one pathway to the true dark. Shame is another. Be careful what you call for with your thoughts, child."

My thoughts. He was talking about the dark thoughts I'd been having about wanting to die. About wanting to kill those goblins. About wanting to crumple, here at the end of the world and become nothing.

"I have tread upon the stars of this universe since it was

new, and I have not met a creature like you in millennia. Come with me." His voice was the command of an evil general on a battlefield.

Something deep rooted inside of me rebelled. I whispered, "No."

"Come," he crooked, a finger and a pincer sunk into my chest, reeling me forward like a fish on a hook. It burned like my heart was being pulled out of my chest.

"No!" I cried, trying to grab at my chest and tear myself free of that dark power. "No!"

"You do not have the power to stop me," he smiled with those red teeth, his eyes wide and eager.

I squeezed my eyes shut and immediately, Zale's face was blinking up at me as we were intwined the other night. Butterflies had been flying around us, glowing purple and blue.

A power within me flared to life—hot, crackling. I pulled and pulled, drawing it up and up through my core out through my fingers. My forehead heated up and somewhere far, far away, I *felt* Agnolthi smile.

The dark master before me shifted, and when I opened my eyes, he was right in front of me, his terrifying face inches from mine. His pupils were pools of the living dead, and in them, I saw only pain.

But I had danced with pain my entire life. I had pulled it out of people. I had suffered through it. I had dealt it. Lying in the cocoon of my own darkness now felt unnecessary.

My magic lashed out, and my hand became an arrow made of starlight and the deep part of a storm. I crushed my white-hot hand into the dark god's chest. Bone shattered, flesh gave away and I felt his black heart beating a lonely and sorry beat.

The smile vanished off his yellowed forsaken face.

Leaning forward, I hissed, "I know you. I see you. And I rebuke you."

Tiny blood vessels burst in his eyes. I squeezed his heart, and in much the same way as I pulled from Fangar that one time, my magic pulled upon the heart of this dark god.

Magic surged into me, and its poisoned sludge was so vast I shivered under the strain of it. But my magic gobbled it up, neutralising it, and it became a fine gold mist that fed me.

For the first time in a while, I felt *strong*. It reminded me of a time when my mother whispered in my ear about my power and how I could use it. The smile that curved my lips was pure happiness as I thought about my mother and Saraya. I remembered Yasani Temple lying ancient in Taraka village and how the first time I'd seen it, I'd fallen to my knees at the thought of my mother. She left her homeland to have me. She left everything she knew for daughters she'd not yet met. She left her homeland so that one day I could return for Zale.

For the first time in a long time, I sounded like myself. Wildfire burned through my words. "My mother gave up her entire life to have me, and I have a duty not to let her down." I took a breath. "I have seen the worst life has to offer, and I know that I can bring light to those who do not have it. I know why I was born."

He was as still as the dark parts of the universe he hailed from, and under my hand clutching his heart, he inclined his head.

Then he was gone.

And all at once I knew what I was.

When I woke up, power thrummed inside of me, wild and ferocious. I realised that I was *still* pulling darkness towards and inside of me ,and my power was swallowing it whole, digesting and turning it into fine golden powder that felt like the dawn.

The sun beat down on my supine form, and I grimaced against the heat, rubbing my face and finding a layer of dust and grit over me.

Groaning, I rubbed my eyes open and with a jolt remembered what had happened last night. *Who* had happened last night. That dark god had sought me out.

I shivered as the terrible, cadaverous image of him wrested through my mind's eye, and I tried to concentrate on my surroundings instead.

There was death around me. I smelled its blood and muck in the breeze.

The entire front lawn of the castle was littered with bloodied bodies. All of the goblins had been massacred, and the dirt was awash with old blood.

I turned and vomited, though there was not much in my stomach to begin with. I wiped my mouth on the back of my hand and looked back at these small, dirty creatures that had worshipped me. I didn't think they ever cared for me so much, as they wanted a murderous leader to enable and encourage their lust for blood and death. Even so, I felt bad that I had been the cause of their demise.

A cough to my left drew my attention, and I knew that it was Magrin coming towards me in her dark cloak. My vision went blurry with tears.

"I am sorry," I breathed to Magrin. She looked down at me in what I was sure was confusion, and I could only shake my head at her. "I feel that this is all my fault."

"The dark master that came needed payment," Magrin said in a deep, melodic voice, *very* unlike her. "Such is the way of that being. And it is always taken in blood and death."

I looked up at her in alarm, before scrambling to my feet to get a better a look at the changed witch. Magrin was now a much younger woman, possibly only forty, her skin still white but now smooth, her black eyes now long lashed and glittering with amusement. Her body was no longer hunched, but *tall*—perhaps six foot—long limbed and straight backed. She still wore her black robe and hood, but a length of long black hair hung shiny and soft over her shoulder.

I gaped behind her as the other eight witches emerged from the castle, all tall and beautiful and looking at me with gleaming, serious eyes as if I was their saviour.

Magrin smiled, and her teeth were white and straight behind her red lips. "Look what you did for us." She swept an arm behind her.

I thought she had been indicating the witches, but instead, behind her, lay a mass of brown, naked bodies, adult men and women who looked like Ellythians, only taller and well-muscled, lying asleep on the grass.

"They will wake up soon," Magrin intoned, "and they will be very happy to be returned to their true forms, as we are." She and the witches bowed deeply before me.

Clutching my heart I looked left and right and realised that there were no beasts in sight. No animal bodies. I remembered the power last night, how I'd pulled magic from the dark god and made him leave. But even after that, I still felt my power pulling from around me, alchemising more dark power and making it my own.

"I made the beasts human?" I breathed in disbelief, wondering if I'd been wrong about my power.

"No," said a light female voice from behind me, "you dissolved the magic keeping us captive."

I whirled around to see a naked man and woman. Both were tall, brown-skinned with blue eyes but with black-slitted pupils like a serpent's. Both have a tattoo marking the backs of their hands. I knew who they were immediately. "Ulanna?" I breathed in disbelief. "What do you mean?"

"I never told you my surname," she said with amusement. "It's Boneweaver. We are Old Ones. Distantly related to your mate, our king. This is my star-born mate, Ulfas."

My mouth dropped open in a very non-princess like manner, but I didn't care. I couldn't help it; this was insane—Old Ones were living here.

Both serpents bowed low. "We owe you a debt, my queen," Ulfus said. He spoke slowly, his mouth forming the words carefully as if trying to remember how to use his human mouth. "When the dark lord took over this place, we had been bound in our animal forms for over a two hundred years with no way out."

"How is it that you are here?" I asked incredulously, looking about the stirring bodies of the Old Ones around me.

Ulanna took a deep breath. "After Prince Ashzale was imprisoned by the Reaper, the Old Ones eventually grew unhappy with the way his father reigned over Boneweaver Island. Slowly, we all left for other realms and continents. Our particular wave of immigrants were allowed into the Eternal Forest to find our fortunes here." Ulanna looked around the castle, pensive. "It was just our luck that we stumbled upon these lands."

There were groans and muttering behind us, and I turned to see the other Old Ones, sitting up and looking around at each other in utter disbelief. With some preternatural awareness, as one, they all turned to look at me.

My stomach was churning as the vile magic inside of me tumbled as if it was being washed in a basin, my own magic shovelling it around as if playing with it before its consumption. It made sense. So much sense, that I couldn't even find a way to dispute it in my mind. This was it. I had assumed my power was healing, just in a roundabout way. I understood now that healing was just one small part of a much larger power that I had. Excitement laced with something bitter poured through me. Zale's face flashed through my mind. I wanted to tell him about this, that his people were here and some of them were distant family. It would make him so happy to have his people back. A tiny part of me was surprised that I was concerned about Zale's happiness now, but I brushed it away with an impatient hand.

I cleared my throat and smiled at them all. "Well, does this mean we should have another party?"

Ulanna tilted her head back and gave a wild, rough cackle.

Magrin flashed her teeth at me, and she and the witches followed suit.

ULANNA AND MAGRIN FOUND ME SITTING AGAINST AN OLD, broken tree in the sunshine, thinking about Zale and what I'd said to him to make him leave and what the hell I should do about it.

Ulanna had fashioned herself some clothes out of brown material—a pair of loose trousers and a shirt—no doubt using Old One magic. I'd seen Zale and his brothers summon clothes out of their astral repository many times, and I assumed this was a magic they all shared. Magrin held a length of rich brown material with tiny flowery embellishments. I raised my brows at the workmanship.

"What is this, Magrin? It's beautiful."

She inclined her head deeply before she and Ulanna sat down opposite me. She passed me the material, and I took it gently from her. "The witches and I made this robe for your highness."

I still wore my silk robe, and in this position, it fell open, showing the inner curves of my breasts. It was not ideal now that there are so many males walking about. Before I might not have cared but now, I couldn't help but feel I wanted my skin to be only for Zale's eyes. It was not a feeling I was used to, and just for a moment I was inclined to rebel against it.

The fabric was incredibly soft under my hands, but also fiercely strong. It was imbued with magic that I could feel tingling under my fingers, and it shone in a certain light, as if cast with glittering drops of dew.

"The thread is imbued with the blood of all nine witches," Magrin said in her deep, melodic voice. When she spoke it was like every word was a chant, or a spell. "Wherever you go, we go in spirit, as is proper for the high priestess of Agnolthi."

I looked up at her in surprise. She knew that eventually I would need to leave. That this was not my home. But— "high priestess?" I frowned. "What do you mean by that?"

"The mark you bear on your brow is Goddess Given. It is a mark for the high priestess of our Order, though you are not ordained just yet."

The Order of Yasani. Agnolthi had not said anything when she'd given it to me—slapped it across my forehead actually. And at that time, she'd been furiously angry with me. It didn't make sense. I told Magrin so.

The witch only gave me the knife's edge of a smile, and I inherently knew that whoever Magrin had been in her hunched crone version, it was a version of herself that hadn't remembered quite how dangerous she was. This was a supernatural woman of great power. There was a lot that I could learn from her.

"Will you teach me, Magrin? What I need to know about the Order of Yasani? I have been given this mark, and yet I hardly know anything about it."

"Hardly know?" asked Ulanna. "The Old Ones have long worshipped Agnolthi, and even I can see you are more like our Goddess than anyone I've ever known. If you are not the human equivalent of Her than no one is. Your mate is a tiger, even. You bear her power, her magic. Her wild potency."

I exhaled a long breath remembering when my body was covered in smoke, and all I felt was the darkness. In truth I still felt it at the edges of my being, hovering there, ready and waiting for me to fall into it again. Except...I knew *that* darkness was borne of grief and sorrow and anger. That I was not those things in my heart. I looked at Ulanna, beautiful in her serpentine presence, a beast at heart, vicious and proud. And Magrin, who was dark and terrible, beautiful and cruel. Then there was me. I had been many things. Destructive, selfish, tormented. But I had also been wild and happy, protective and I'd never denied my body of its desires.

Magrin gave me a tiny, knowing smile. "The Boneweaver Bow is hidden in the world above, written upon in an ink only The high priestess of Agnolthi can read. You must find it."

I looked at her with interest before sighing. "That would mean I have to figure out a way to get out of here."

Ulanna nodded. "The island grants access as it wills. But I have a feeling it will not let you leave without your mate."

I nodded slowly. "This mate-bond is something I will have to understand better. I've never known anything like it. Honestly, it was the last thing I ever expected to come across. I assumed I would marry some fat lord and have my own dalliances whenever I pleased. But to have *one* man this... possessive over me? I don't know what to think of it."

Ulanna let out a low chuckle and showed me her right hand where there was a tattoo of an crimson jewel surrounded by black flowers. "This mating mark tells all that I am mate of Ulfas. A Boneweaver mate is a ferocious thing. I do not think any other woman would be able to handle a one like Ashzale Boneweaver." She looked at me ruefully. "You are a queen, born for him just as he is a king, born for you."

I was surprised that I didn't have the urge to squirm uncomfortably under her assessing gaze. Her words might have scared me once, but I was still unsure about how I felt about them now. These creatures seemed to want me as their leader and...I *would* take it as my responsibility to protect them, if I needed to. The dark cocoon of grief I'd been covered in had shown me a side of myself I'd never allowed through. A dangerous, dark part that was capable of violence, and now I knew I had that part. It...changed everything about how I saw myself.

I looked down at Magrin's gift and ran my fingers over the blood red embroidery. The images were of flowers but also beasts, wolves, tigers, eagles and even sharks. I couldn't help but smile as I admired the craftsmanship of it. I liked the silk robe, but now my protective dark smoke was gone, I could feel the cool weather once again.

Ulanna suddenly leapt to her feet, frowning into the distance at the forest floor. Magrin and I also got up in alarm.

A tiny white figure was awkwardly scrambling towards us, his movements jerky and frantic. I looked behind him, but Zale was nowhere to be seen.

Wobbles sprinted toward me as fast as he could. All at once, unbalanced by the weight of his oversized head, his spindly legs tripped and he tumbled onto the ground, somersaulting several times. But I was already running for him.

"Wobbles!" I cried falling to my knees to scoop him up.

The shell-creature grabbed my face with both hands. "Zale taken!" he cried. "Fae! Fae!"

My brows shot up. "Taken?"

Behind me Ulanna made a sound at the back of her throat. "Carnal fae," she spat. "Spiteful creatures, even if you saved four of them. They will have taken him for their pleasure."

I leapt to my feet, rounding on Ulanna as unexpected rage pummelled through me. Magrin tapped her chin. "They have an agreement, Your Highness. Well, *had*. Before the

Boneweaver King's imprisonment, he frequented the carnal fae realm."

I was simmering, trying to control my rising panic and anger that someone *dared* touch Zale... It wasn't right. "What type of agreement?" I bit out.

Magrin and Ulanna exchanged a look. Magrin said, "I do not know the particulars, Your Highness, but it was a Vayashi agreement."

In hearing this, anger whirled up in me like a fierce tornado. I'd never heard of a Vayashi until I came to Ellythia, but it was a person who could be a vessel for magic. Powerful creatures like Zale needed an avenue to funnel their excess power, and you could do that through sex—give a woman or man your power to help you calm down. Zale had told me that when he had too much magic, he became excessively violent and uncontrollable. The only problem was your vessel needed to be strong enough to hold your power. Otherwise you got what Pia accidentally did to her betrothed and ended up crippling him for life. So Zale finding a powerful fae to help him burn off his excess made sense...before he'd married *me.*

And I'd sent him away out of fear and uncertainty. After the Butcher, I'd felt dirty and unworthy. I didn't think I could be what he needed me to be. But he'd always known that I was made for him. He'd sought me out when I'd rejected him over and over again. He wanted me and no other. He'd never made me feel dirty. No, what was clear to me by the light of day was that Zale made me feel good and whole. Special and worthy. He'd given me those things when I couldn't give them to myself.

And now he needed my help. He'd been taken against his

will, and someone he'd been having sex with was likely wanting him back for the same thing.

We'd had sex, but it wasn't…it wasn't the way I wanted it to be, desperate and completely out of my mind.

I needed to find him and apologise for hurting him with what I'd said. The memory of the look on his face when I'd rejected him made the backs of my eyes burn. I didn't want to hurt him like that again.

Looking up to Ulanna and Magrin, I said. "I'm going to go get him."

Ulanna gave me a savage smile, and together, we stormed back to the castle. I wasn't so good at tracking, but if I could somehow use the golden thread linking us, I could find him.

Back at my nest, I took the remaining food Zale had given me and the canteen of water. Before I left I turned and look back at the pile of sticks and fabric.

"Goodbye, nest," I whispered. "You've served me while I was unwell. But I certainly won't miss you."

15
RANI

My heart sung a sad tune as I spied the familiar mountainous landscape of my northern homelands. We'd made it through the southern portion of Tiger Island without any difficulty. How many years had I spent running around here with Yulara at my side, climbing trees, playing with pots and pans in the shade of the big banyan tree? Little had I known that as young women I would fall in love with her soft eyes, the smooth lilt of her singing voice and the strength of her spear arm. Her hands were calloused but kind, her touch so gentle how could I not love her with all my heart? Our love had been so undeniable that our parents had all agreed and our betrothal had been set in stone when we were both fifteen. Our hearts had been full on our betrothal day, and we'd made love under the stars where we'd used to play as children.

Then I'd had the accident and my entire universe fell apart into nothing and all that had been left was the sound of screaming.

I had been a ruin then, and I was still a ruin now. Pia

watched me from the side of her eye, and I knew she was trying to gauge how close I was to breaking down. On my other side Kai hummed under his breath, some Old One tune that made my hair stand on its ends. His white hair gleamed under the bright sun in such great contrast to his brown skin, and I wondered whether he ever felt separate or apart from his brethren because of his appearance.

Maybe that was why I felt compelled to sit by him at the nighttime campfire. Why he felt the need to walk next to me while we travelled. Not in the same way Malika and Atax were compelled toward each other, but in the way I might be comforted by the solid and stable presence of a brother. No one would call Kai *stable*, exactly, but I found a solace by his side and the little part of me that I allowed to remember, missed my own twin brothers. They would be sixteen by now.

Kai turned to me when I glanced at him, cocking his head and smiling at me in a way that I did not deserve. I smiled back at him.

He was so pure that I was often struck into silence by him. His blue eyes sparkled with an off-kilter sort of innocence, but I knew that inside his bare muscled torso there was a killer. A beast that was capable of great brutality.

There was a dead rabbit in his hands, and he whispered over it.

"What did you say to it, Old One?" I asked when he'd finished. No matter how much time I spent travelling with him and Atax these past few weeks, I couldn't bear to call someone who was two hundred and something years old by their first name. It went against every Ellythian instinct and manners I had. And I did not think he would appreciate me calling him grandfather. I tried it with Atax the other night, and he just gaped at me. Now Malika called Atax "grandpa" just to piss him off.

Kai looked at me, and I saw at once that there was blood on his face. I got my handkerchief from my pants pocket and dabbed at his cheek. He closed his eyes and grinned in such a boyish way I couldn't help but smile back.

He spoke with his eyes still closed: "I said a prayer of thanks to the rabbit, and said I hope he goes back to Agnolthi's sweet bosom."

I put my hanky back in my pocket, and he opened his eyes, summoned a knife and began rigorously skinning the rabbit with a happy sort of grin.

How could there be such extremes in one person?

"Well I suppose that would be nice for the little creature," I said awkwardly.

"Which part?"

"The bosom part."

He chuckled. "Oh, it would."

"I met Agnolthi." The words tumbled out of me, and I immediately froze because I had not ever intended telling anyone about that time except perhaps my mother or Yulara. Pia, Malika Altara and I had been whisked from our beds to see the Goddess in the flesh, and she'd told us about how we needed to break Zale's curse. The moment had struck me like a mad blow to the heart because when she'd looked at me, I'd seen nothing but love in her amber eyes.

Ferocious yet kind eyes that reminded me of Altara's emerald ones. And when I had looked at Altara every time since then, I remembered the Goddess and how she'd looked at me like I wasn't a murderer. Like I was something more than what I'd done.

When I let it slip to Kai, I expected him to drop his knife.

To perhaps look at me in shock or horror or say something like, "Oh my Goddess, what do you mean?" Except he didn't do any of those things. His enthusiastic skinning of the rabbit continued as if we were talking about the weather.

"Oh, yes," he said, "her bosom was lovely the last time I saw her. That's why I said I hoped the rabbit would get to go there in death."

Now I was the one that was gaping at him. "What do you mean, Old One? You saw her too?"

He nodded, white braids bobbing. "Saw her plenty. Back in our time, the Goddesses all strolled around Boneweaver Island and the Ellythian Isles talking to us. Usually it was on holy days--they all have their day, don't they? Our high priestess, Zale's mother, told us that long ago, they walked about *all* the time, and then it got less and less as the centuries went on. Can you imagine, Rani? The Gods walking about here as if they were one of us?"

I silently listened to his rambling as I thought about such a thing. In truth I couldn't imagine it. The Gods were perfect beings, and this land was meant for us mortals, terribly imperfect. Sometimes I thought that the Old Ones were gods too, in that they were more than human, practically physically perfect and beautiful except that they happily killed things. I had not seen our Old Ones kill humans though—only demons so far.

"Have you killed a human?" I asked Kai. Yulara had told me that I had the tendency to be abrupt or say something unexpected, and I know it had happened when other people looked at me funny. Neither Yulara nor Kai had ever looked at me *funny*, although sometimes I caught Atax listening to what I was saying, even if he was not looking at me. At this question, though, Kai nodded vigorously. "Yes, Rani, I have. Lots, I suppose."

"What do you mean *lots*?" I asked carefully. "Like Ellythians?"

"Oh, yes. When we were cubs we trained to kill people. The king used to bring us little Ellythian children the same age as us to practise on."

I stilled, and I knew that across from the campfire Atax heard and also went still. This was shocking news. The most shocking, perhaps, that I had ever heard.

"I would plant flowers for them," Kai went on quietly as he fed the rabbit onto a metal spike for the spit. "After training, Raen would take me to say a prayer, and we would sow hibiscus or orchid seeds so they could grow. His father was Priest before him, you know, so he knew what to do. Then the king found out and punished us. After that I threw flowers into the sea."

"I'm sorry, Kai."

He paused and turned to look at me. The campfire was reflected in his blue eyes reminding me of a parrot of blue and gold I'd seen up north. He blinked once, then twice as if he was confused. His eyes darkened as they focused on my face. "I am sorry too, Rani."

And I knew he was not talking about himself.

THE NEXT DAY WE WERE DUE TO ENTER SALAARI, THE northernmost town I'd grown up in. The Umasri family was the wealthiest family of the island, and we lived on a large property only an hour from the sea where our silk farms were. Plenty of the townspeople worked at our farm so I was sure I would know them on sight as we passed though. As midday arrived and we begin to see some more foot traffic, I glanced behind me to where Atax had walked in his black lion form next to Malika. Both old ladies sat atop him with parasols they'd bartered for with two farmers we'd passed. Atax caught my eye and ducked his head. I nodded back. Malika stared at me.

Everyone was watching me now—seeing how I would react to being at home for the first time in three years. A silent tear fell down my cheek as we walked on.

I was fifteen when I'd left, and I was nineteen now, a woman grown. I was a lot taller, broader and more muscled, but I did not think my face had changed all that much. But I was wrong about one thing. I was not the wise person I thought I was. I was still incredibly naive.

The town looked exactly the same, and my first inkling that something was wrong came in the form of an elderly mother and son outside of the town smithy pointing at me and whispering. The young man, whom I didn't recognise, strapping with long black hair tied up, turned on his heel and sprinted down the street.

Malika swore under her breath and came up to me, looping her arm protectively through mine. On my other side, Atax, now in his human form, came to stand too. My heart swelled where it quivered under my ribs, knowing that this was not good. The elderly woman outside of the smithy turned away from us and ambled to the next shop.

Geravie and Keshmi, shuffled up to me. Geravie was grumbling under her breath. "We'll stay in town tonight," she said softly. "Are you going to see your family?"

"I'd like to," I said, my eyes still trained on the spot the young man had disappeared down. "And whether it is wise or not, we shall see."

"I do not advise it," Keshmi said. "Rani, you have not served your sentence as it was set by the chief."

Geravie made a disapproving noise, but it was Kai that said, "They should leave the past in the past."

I could only swallow the lump in my throat and continue forward. My heart wanted to cross this ground that I'd known so well, but my head was telling me that this was a very, very bad idea. They were my parents, my family. How could I just pass them by? I needed to try and see them, even if it was from afar.

But we did not even make it to the gate of my parents' property.

Having left Geravie and Keshmi at the town inn, the five of us headed up the sloping path leading towards the outskirts of town. Atax and Kai heard the horses first and bade us to move to the side of the path to let them pass.

I recognised them on sight, though I could hardly believe my eyes. My twin brothers Asham and Yetton leapt off their horses and stood side by side, their chests heaving, sweat gleaming off their faces. I stumbled past Kai, feeling for all the world like a snake was tied around my lungs, choking the breath out of me. They were grown—still growing but clearly healthy, strong and agile. Their hair was short and thick like my father's.

"Rani?" Asham gasped, his wide brown eyes looking me up and down. I let out a sob and reached for them, but Asham grabbed my hands in a tight, almost painful grip, looking up at me. He had our mother's eyes. "You cannot come here. They will kill you."

I gaped at him, and Malika and Pia were at my side in an instant. "Who?" Malika demanded.

The twins looked between us all, their eyes widening further at the sight of the Old Ones.

"Dear Goddess, it's true," Yetton said. "The Old Ones have truly returned."

"Listen, boy," Malika said sharply. "Answer me clearly— who is after Rani?"

The boys snapped to attention, looking back at my beautiful friend with assessing eyes. Malika was a stunning woman, but her face was almost always contorted into a fearsome scowl, and she had the power to back it up. And in that moment, though I loved her for it, her needing to direct her anger at my little brothers crushed something in me.

Asham cleared his throat. "Yulara's family. We were all at the house when one of the men from town sent word. We got here first, but they'll be coming."

"They are still angry with Rani?" Kai's voice was soft, but only an idiot would miss the threat behind it.

My brothers exchanged a look. Asham said, "They will come with men."

"Let them come," Malika hissed. "Rani has a right to see her family. It's been four years!"

"Four years can't bring Vasi back," Yetton murmured.

I clutched my stomach and stumbled away from them, trying to control my rising panic. I thought I had this under control, that somehow four years would be enough to heal this wound. But I hadn't realised that no amount of time would fix this. Would heal this. Nothing on this world could make what I did right. Nothing could bring back the dead. *Murderer.*

Strong hands gripped my shoulders and pulled me

forward. I landed on a hard muscled chest that smelled like the jungle and raw bestial power. Even with my eyes screwed shut, I knew it was Kai who had me. One of his braids tickled my cheek.

"Be still Rani," he murmured, and the rumble of his chest served to ground me. "All will be well."

I had not lost control of my magic since Altara had taken Malika's arrow wound back on Boneweaver Island and I had thought she was going to die. I felt my power now, broad and shiny bubbling within me, but I refused to lose control now. I clutched it inside of me so strongly I thought I might break it, but Kai's old forest scent grounded me.

My racing heart slowed, and I knew more heated words were being exchanged behind me. Kai patted my back as one patted a baby to sleep, and I hadn't been held like that since my mother hugged me before my exile. I want to see her, to smell her too. But this one thing I would not be allowed to have. Jagged old wounds in my soul bled open anew.

Galloping hooves sounded again, and I knew we'd tarried too long. The shouting was angry and I knew I must be on high alert if they had come to kill me.

It would be a deserved death. And my father taught me to face my actions on my feet. So I took a breath, placed a hand over Kai's strong chest and pushed myself off him.

Five horses reared to a stop on the road, and it was Pia and Malika who stepped forward. Atax and Kai assumed positions next to me though I could not look at either of them.

I recognised Yulara straight away, and I was ready for it. To see the love of my life again in her almost fae beauty, her long, black hair and willowy body. Like the Goddess Xalya herself, in her powerful form swinging off her stallion, eyes fierce as they searched the faces of us gathered here. She was always a strong girl, and in womanhood, her power was devastating. There was a new tattoo winding around her wrist in black ink but I was not ready to see what sat atop her breast.

A solid gold and quartz marriage necklace. A marriage necklace that was not mine.

For the second time in my life, my legs gave away, and I crumpled to the ground. The others on the horses, all Yulara's extended family, dismounted and strode forward.

Kai and Atax did not do me the disservice of helping me up. They knew I would not want that. Instead I gritted my teeth, wiped my eyes on my sleeve and rose from the ground. I looked at Yulara, standing next to her father, another man and a woman with a small pregnant belly—both proud, young and strong, and I knew at once what had happened.

I had been replaced.

Malika called out, "You are in the presence of the Princess Pia Rahana Lota, and I am Malika of Levu Village. We—"

Yulara's father slammed something to the ground. Malika and Pia parted so I could see it, though Malika's fists were clenched at being interrupted.

"You are not welcome here," Yulara's father spat. "How *dare* you try to return."

I looked down at what he had thrown, and my heart split in two all over again. It was our betrothal wreath, made of palm leaves, and red silken threads bound in a beautiful circle in the presence of the seven Goddesses of Lota City. But it had been cut with a blade and was no more than an ugly rope now.

I closed my eyes for a moment before Yulara's voice reached me like a poison poured a wound. "I am married now, Rani. Our betrothal can be no more. I am sorry."

127

Dear Goddess that voice had once been a beacon of love and hope for me. Now it was a bright blade gone dull. Silver tarnished with years of disuse.

I looked at her glimmering brown eyes, trained fiercely at me as if she was trying to communicate something. But I could not understand her. What bond we might have now laid on the ground before us. She never returned my letters although I wrote many in the first year. Perhaps I did not know this person at all.

"Return from whence you came, *demon* woman," her father spat. "You will not curse our lands with your black presence."

The men behind him unsheathed their blades, and I blinked at them in a sort of dazed disbelief.

"We will go," Malika gritted out. "But we will not forget this." She was looking at Yulara, whose gaze was darting between our party as if she were trying to read something.

"We will stay in town tonight," Pia said in a calm, deep, voice of command she rarely used. "We have elderly women with us. Tomorrow will be on our way, and you will leave us be."

The men stared at Pia, at her emerald Lota eyes, and though I could tell my old father-in-law did not want to, he gave a curt nod.

It was Yetton, my brother who said in a brave, loud voice, "You will not be disturbed. But if you are here after dawn, I cannot ensure your safety. This is reasonable."

They would kill me, I realised with dull shock. It was the fitting atonement for an adult. Back when I was still a teenager, my parents had fought the council to let me live in exile, though many had argued that I was no more than a rabid dog—unsafe for the community and best put down. I should have known they would still hold this in their hearts. But the knowledge that so many wished death upon me crashed upon my being with the force of a mallet.

They insisted on watching us leave, and the only thing I could concentrate on was putting one foot in front of the other. Malika lurched forward to grab my hand, and Pia came to hold my other, and with white-knuckled grips, we made our way down the road. I was so close to seeing my parents, but at least I got to see my brothers and both did not hate me. Had come to help me, in fact.

I knew that where Altara came from, in Lobrathia, such things, like sleeping with a man before wed lock, was considered amongst the worst crimes for a noble girl. For Old Ones their greatest shame came from cowardice or physical weakness. But for Ellythians mal-control of one's own magic was the worst sort of shame one could bring on their family, and I'd done that in the worst possible way.

I'd lost control and killed a boy with my power, and I deserved every harsh word and punishment that came my way. Though it crushed me into tiny pieces I might never be able to put back together, I would take what I deserved.

I could see the thoughts on Atax's face as clear as day as he glanced from me to Pia. If I, the daughter of a silk lord, was not welcome at home after what I'd done, how will the princess to the throne of Ellythia be welcomed home after what *she'd* done?

16

ALTARA

Since infancy I had been trained to be a warrior. To fight my enemies with a blade, bow or throwing daggers. But my real enemy had always been inside of me. A shadow that would always lurk at the corners of things. A shadow I would always have to fight. But it was in between that fighting that I might be able to live again.

I was still coming to terms with the fact that I cared for Zale, in a way that should be impossible, and I hated that Zale had been *taken*. And worse, something frightening was rearing its head at the mental image of some creature chaining him and locking him up like a common animal. Much in the same way the Butcher had chained me up. I knew Zale was a capable warrior, but faced by some fae queen that he likely knew from all that time ago, what would his reaction be? His...*feelings?*

The Old Ones were swarming around the entrance to the castle, the males pacing, clearly agitated by the news a Boneweaver had been captured against his will.

Ulfas was the first to approach me, his dark-blue eyes

blazing. Ulanna was close behind him. "We will fight, Your Highness," he said. "We will bring the king back."

His words and the sight of the males barely concealing their own violence ignited a further anger in me. I felt my own darkness rise up, that oily smoke coiling around me in a haze of barely contained anger. My forehead heated up, and I knew Agnolthi's sign was burning brightly.

Ulfas and Ulanna did not shirk way from me as I expected. Instead their eyes were bright with excitement and determination.

"*No,*" I said, my voice deep and low. My bow flashed into my hands, lethal in its gold and black form. "He is my mate. I will go after him myself."

Ulanna grunted her approval and nodded, understanding me completely. I strode past them, knowing that Ulfas was angrily prowling behind me. The Old Ones parted in a wave as I passed, growling in solidarity, their faces serious, their muscular bodies tense as if ready to spring at any moment. Looking at them all, I could tell which were wolves and which were the lions. Each group had a distinct sort of flavour scenting the air, but they all had a feral, hardly human sort of look. It would take them awhile to regain their human selves, I knew, and right then, they were wanting to fight. As I strode out of the castle, Magrin and the nine witches waited for me, standing in a row. Magrin was standing next to a large, beastly black mare, more monster than horse in her size and musculature. Her black coat was glossy in the sunlight, her mane thick and lustrous. She had no saddle or bridle, and when she turned to look at me, it was appraising with acute intelligence. I paused in front of them, and the mare tossed her mane and let out a snort.

"Neera is willing," Magrin said, baring her teeth. "She will only ride for the Witch-Queen."

I inclined my head in thanks, hiding a wry smile as I thought that after riding Zale, I could hardly be worried about riding any other sort of beast, however monstrous.

"I need to return to Ellythia," I said evenly to those gathered. "I know not where my path takes me once I find my husband."

Magrin and Ulanna nodded in agreement. "You are theirs as much as you are ours," Magrin said slowly. "The motherland is yours to rule, but there is the smell of war in the wind for the land above. We will always be here, and we owe you a debt of life. A debt of blood."

Goosebumps erupted all over my skin at her words as the witches fiercely looked upon me. I looked at them each in turn before swinging around to the Old Ones. The group of them were gathered there—seventy strong, I guessed, looking at the bright-blue eyes they all shared. I was reminded of Zale's brothers Atax, Raen and Kai as I looked upon the males, and the females were their exact feminine counterparts—tall, strong, lithe and fierce.

"I am glad to have met you," I said softly, knowing full well their supernatural ears could hear every breath of mine. "I'm glad that I came here."

They gave me growls and murmurs of assent, and in the back, a few of the wolves howled at the sky. The two king cobras stepped forward, and I nodded to them, suspecting what they wanted to say. For Old Ones leadership was based upon dominance and fighting ability, and those things could be easily intuited by their kind. It was why they'd known Zale for his station right away. It hadn't even need to be vocalised; the scent had said it all. I might not have the same ability to scent, but I could tell the two serpents were respected leaders. Ulanna stepped forward with a blood-red jewel in her hand, and I raised my brows at her, recognising the ruby jewel from her serpent form.

"Take my crown jewel, my queen," she said. "I will easily grow another, but it means that you will be able to call me if you require the help of your court."

I took the egg-sized ruby carefully, and its weight was satisfying and warm in my hand. It was like no other jewel I'd ever seen—a deep, blood red with facets that caught the light of the afternoon sun. Magrin showed me a series of hidden buttoned pockets in my new cloak, and I settled it inside one of them, safe and sound.

"Is it your desire to stay in the Eternal Forest?" I asked the Old Ones.

"The castle and these lands belong to the Nine," Ulanna said, respectfully nodding to the witches behind her. "We will return to Boneweaver Island when the Eternal Forest permits it, which I suspect will be soon, if the king has returned. I suspect it summoned you here to save us in the first place."

A feeling like sunlight expanded in my chest at her words. I had tried to make sense of the sentient magic that ruled this place, it clearly had its own mind and desires, and the fact that it had wanted me to find Zale's people made me feel accepted by this place. And wanted.

Thanking Ulanna she gave me a boost with her strong hands, and I mounted the mare easily. The black silk gown and witch's robe flared out behind me dramatically as I tested my balance. I hadn't ridden bare back for years, but somehow it seemed right.

"Neera is a *zekar*," Magrin said, looking up at me, her

brown eyes sparkling. "She will keep you safer than any horse."

The zekar mare snorted in agreement, and I grinned, delighted at the thought of this powerful creature working beneath me. I shook my head ruefully. If only my father could see me now: barefoot, bareback, ready to save my husband from some wild, pervert fae. I *think* he'd be proud of the bareback thing, at the very least.

I imagined that he would tilt his head back and laugh, his blue eyes twinkling with mirth. Right now Zale was the only family I had, and by Agnolthi's fair face, I would rescue him.

I also knew that I wasn't the best at hunting on the ground using tracks, but I did have that twinkling string linking Zale and I, that right now vibrated like it was agitated.

The Old Ones placed their fists over their hearts, and I inclined my head in return. Ulanna handed me Wobbles who leapt up to sit on my shoulder, his little body tense and nervous. Someone whacked my mare on her hindquarters, and I scrambled to grab her mane as she launched into a canter right into the forest.

The golden thread within me tingled and vibrated, and although I could not sense the beast at the end of it, I knew it was anger coming down towards me. I would have no mercy if they hurt him—I *would not*. Zale and I had both faced enough pain in our lifetimes and I would not stand to watch it happen again. They would all be dead. I didn't care if I'd saved a few of them to start with.

WOBBLES AND I FOLLOWED THE THREAD FOR A FULL DAY through the Skeleton Forest, and by the time the long rays of the afternoon sun were falling through the trees, Neera began to twitch as if she were sensing something was amiss.

We were being watched.

As Wobbles hastily scrambled off my shoulder to hide on Neera's back in front of me, I scowled into the shadows and summoned my bow in a flash of light. It returned to my hand from the ether, this time no longer a solid black but a gold and black swirling design all the way up the wood. I smiled without humour at its beautiful but lethal jungle patterns that I would have to appreciate properly later.

We slowed to a careful walk so I could discern any secret footsteps sounding through the undergrowth, but alas, the fae had no issue with being seen, because a commanding shout came up from the trees ahead.

"Halt!"

I sat straight with three arrows knocked and ready to shoot immediately.

"Who goes there?" I called.

Two tall fae stepped out of the bushes, armoured with glittering swords drawn. They wore garments almost too fancy for guards—silver doublets embroidered in a rainbow of colours and crisp golden pants. They were strikingly handsome in the supernatural way that all fae were with long arched points to their ears. The tallest one spoke, his amber eyes looking me up and down with a frown. "You are in carnal fae territory, *wench*. Turn around before we chain you."

I took great offence at his terminology and aimed at him with my bow. My voice emerged harsh, slicing through the air. "I am here for my husband, King Ashzale Boneweaver, you swine. Lower your weapons and take me to him before I shoot your eyes out."

Both fae glanced at each other, and six more fae emerged from the jungle, surrounding me completely in glittering silver, lethal alertness. Neera stomped her hoof threateningly.

"Did you say *husband*?" the fae guard in front of me said incredulously.

I snarled at him, "I am his wife, yes. I am Princess Altara Voltanius Boneweaver, and I bear his ring. We said our vows before his Boneweaver priest and two priestesses of Agnolthi. Where is he?"

The fae around me bristled and exchanged wary looks. "Dismount the zekar," the captain ordered.

"I will not be ordered by the likes of you," I snapped.

He made an effort to speak in a gentler voice. "You will do as we ask, Princess, or I cannot promise your safety."

"Touch me, and I will remove your head from your body." With a flash I returned my weapons to the ether and leapt off Neera, leaving Wobbles on her back. With adrenaline spiking through me, I landed in a crouch and straightened, adjusting my black silk robe, thrusting my chin in the air in a way that would have made my sister Saraya proud.

They were all incredibly tall, but I still managed to look down my nose at them as they gathered around and leered at me.

These fae were different from the ones that had come to take my sister for marriage. But where the fae of Black Court had held a sense of severe manners, these fae were sort of... wild. As if they'd been born of this very jungle itself and had crawled through it dirty and naked as children. They were not the domesticated, sitting-in-a-cold-palace type. These were the type of fae who danced around fires in pretty clothes and sung up to the moon at night, tankards of strong mead in hand. It was alluring to see, and I was drawn into this energy.

Carnal fae, a different breed of fae entirely.

Due to the afternoon heat, I'd long removed my witches cloak into my astral repository and remained in the black silk one. Because of it they were now staring at me like they were trying to see under the silk, and there was more than a little lust in their blazing eyes raking all over me, taking in my face and what they could see of my body.

"Take me to my husband," I ordered imperiously, "otherwise you will get to know how good my bow arm is."

Neera snorted in agreement, and I reached back to pat her on the neck as Wobbles scrambled into the grass.

The fae continued to stare at me, and I glared back at the captain, burning his eyes with my own. Anger was still swirling within me, a blazing storm lighting up my veins. I let a little bit of it show. Lightning danced around my bare hands, around the planes of my face, sparking off me just a little bit.

The fae warriors jumped back, and the captain twitched violently. I raised a brow and whispered a thank you into Neera's ear and kissed her on the nose. She blinked slowly, just once, before turning and trotting into the jungle.

I stalked forward. Hastily, the fae guards shifted to let me through, staring at me with wide, glazed eyes as if in a trance.

"Is it this way?" I asked breezily.

They jumped to action after that, forming two lines on either side of me as if they were *my* own personal guard, and by the time we reached the entrance to the carnal fae kingdom, I was smirking.

The forest opened up to a set of silver gates that dazzled like pure diamond in the light of the setting sun. I refrained from openly gasping as I beheld the kingdom in all its ancient glory. The entire place was enclosed by three rows of huge ancient trees, their trunks as wide as the span of my arms, their branches reaching so high up I had to crane my neck to see the canopy. The kingdom itself was woven of the forest, rows of lights glimmering from inside the lengths of the tall trunks with sturdy rope bridges linking them, illuminated with quartz-lamps of many colours. It was magnificent and wonderful, and I expected nothing less from the fae of the Forests of Eternity. I wondered how long they'd lived here and how they held their court in the middle of this wild place.

Two of the guards opened the gates, and I sauntered through, treading upon a paved golden path lined with a multitude of pretty hibiscus, frangipani and lotus. It was bright and colourful, and if I'd come here on good terms, I would have smiled in appreciation.

Alas, I was not here for a social call.

The captain rushed ahead of me as I turned down a winding path and headed over a small, rounded wooden bridge. A stream trickled beneath it, glittering with luminescent blue water.

"Your Highness, the Queen Odeelia has court—"

"Down here?" I asked, gesturing down the path where I could hear the buzz of low voices and the soft thrum of a lute.

The guard hesitated, but I didn't have time for that, so I just continued forward and let them hurry after me.

The path opened up into a theatre of sorts, which I thought was strange for a throne room, but it was filled with fae, sparkling in finely made gowns and suits of many colours. Though, I noticed, the clothes were gauzy with long slits and sheer panels that left nothing to the imagination of both the male and female bodies underneath.

Before a tall throne of gold and silver, coupled dancers in scraps of clothing leapt and twirled on a mosaic-tiled floor, writhing against each other in a seductive dance, splaying their limbs wide, moving their hips to the melody of the song.

A wicked grin crept upon my lips before I reminded myself why I was there.

"Your Highness," one of the guards hissed behind me, "You must know, the queen does not—"

I violently shoved him away because I'd just seen that sitting *next* to the occupied throne on a gilded seat all of his own was my husband.

Zale's ocean eyes were fixed on me, standing behind the dancers at the entrance to the open theatre. His figure struck me then. This was the man who'd held me in his arms after I'd been shot by demons. Who, despite having barely any conscience, had rubbed my back and whispered soft words into my ear. My heart hammered against my ribs as his eyes glimmered with emotion. He didn't hate me, I realised with cool relief. For my harsh words, or for anything, I didn't think he was even capable of hating me.

The captain of the guard rushed around the dancers and frantically whispered in the ear of the queen. Wobbles reappeared by my feet and followed the captain to amble back to his master.

I turned my attention to this Queen Odeelia, who was holding Zale captive, and I suddenly had no doubt in my mind that she *had* been intimate with him all those years ago.

Her skin was a hue of copper that made her look like she was lit from within. She had the finely pointed ears of the fae and their stunning, delicate, high-boned features. Her gown hung low off her fine shoulders, showing off the plump mounds of her generous bosom. Her hair was a glossy red so deep it was almost black and was curled down to her rosy nipples—which I could clearly see because her dress was a sheer golden gossamer that sparkled as if it were made of thousands of tiny jewels. She made for a stunning figure of supernatural beauty, and if I was not so irate, she would have taken my breath away.

There were five seats arranged on the left next to Zale on the dais, and there sat a fae warrior on each, both male and female, richly dressed and well-muscled, which they showed off in sheer shirts and gowns.

The fae queen raised a regal hand, and the musicians seated in the corner ceased their lutes, fiddles and pipes immediately. The dancers bowed their heads and hurried back into the crowd, walking backwards.

Without taking my eyes off the fae queen, I strode forward with unwavering purpose. Whispers broke out around me, though I cared not for what they said.

I halted a respectable distance from the throne and declared straight to her face, "I am here for my husband. King Ashzale Boneweaver."

The queen's amber eyes flashed in anger for a second before she raised her chin and smirked at me in a way that made me want to plunge my fist into her face and shatter bone.

Settling back into her throne, she said smugly, "You cannot have him. He is mine."

I had to push down my furore as I smirked back and said sweetly, "He is my husband."

Her reply was as quick as a whip. She'd been ready for this. "In name only, perhaps. You do not want him. You have not sealed the bond between you. A specimen like him deserves better, and I can give him that. I want him to join my mating group as king. You may take one of my other males if you wish. You are pretty enough to satisfy *someone*, surely."

I had to admit she was partly right in that I hadn't claimed Zale as I should have. But what does she know of what had gone on between us? Of what had happened on Boneweaver Island?

So I hid my anger, and my smile was razor sharp. "An interesting offer. I decline."

Her smile was dangerous, showing me teeth. "Oh, really?"

"Zale?" I looked at my husband, who had been watching the entire exchange quietly but with acute awareness. I could tell he was struggling with his emotions because he said through gritted teeth, "I am bound until I repay my debt."

Debt. Surprise spun through me. "And what is the nature of this repayment?" I asked.

Queen Odeelia's smirk didn't leave her face. "I want him to serve in my court for my pleasure for ten years."

Like fuck he would.

Something deep rooted in me snapped, and before I knew it, light exploded from my body. When it faded, ten bows knocked with black arrows were in the air, levitating and aimed at the queen and her harem. The court gasped.

Lightning skittered around my skin, and I levelled a gaze upon Odeelia, ready to cut her to pieces. "I think *not*, fae queen," I hissed. "I would sooner blow this place apart than see *my husband* serve *you*." I pointed a finger at Zale, and before I even knew what I was saying, it came out of me: "That beast is *mine*. I claim him."

I was breathing hard, completely unprepared for this, as I now realised. The queen cocked her head, all amusement gone, her face narrowed in predatory intent. "There's no need for that, Altara."

I scowled at her over familiarity. "I am descended from both the Volatinus Lightning Kings and Queen Ellythia herself," I snarled. "And you will address me as such."

Odeelia sighed dramatically, her breast heaving, likely on purpose to draw attention. "I met Ellythia, you know. All Lota women share that same"—she twirled her hand in the air as if searching for the word—"*deathly* seriousness. Wouldn't you agree, husband?"

The fae warrior closest to the dais nodded, though his face bore no amusement. "One really never forgets the eyes."

That surprised me. That meant these fae were more than two thousand years old.

"But an open weapon in my court is an insult I note," the queen continued. "You and I will battle for him."

A tiny needle of anxiety pricked at me. "I will not battle anyone for him. He is mine."

"Oh, you *will*." There was no humour in her eyes. "There is a debt of blood. Our laws are absolute. No one is above them. Not even a Lota princess."

I considered this news. Zale had a blood debt with this female. I wasn't happy about it, but there was surely a way out of it. They'd lived this way for thousands of years, and I completely understood creatures like this had their *rules*. I could have my way; I needed only to play by the rules to get it.

So I looked the fae queen dead in the eye and vanished my weapons back to my astral repository. I curtseyed as well as I could in my silk robe, though it showed a considerable length of my leg as I did. "I will play your game, fae queen, and at the end of it, I *will* leave here with Zale."

17

PIA

O ur ship docked in Lota Harbour just after midday, and as I scanned the dock, a sensation of foreboding funnelled through me, foul as rotting fish guts.

My throat closed up as the backs of my eyes burned as if my grandmother was already searing me with her furious gaze.

For the first time in three years, I was home, and I knew I would not be welcomed.

The sailors on this ship avoided our gazes once Geravie had laid into them about staring at *the princess*. I'd been meaning to keep my arrival private, but Geravie shook her head ruefully at me when I mentioned it.

"If you think you can hide anything from your grandmother, you're raving mad." She then choked on her own laughter.

I enjoyed Geravie's bluntness most days, but today she was wrong. It wasn't my grandmother that you couldn't hide anything from. It was her spymaster. My mother, the Crown Princess of Ellythia.

The mood of our group had steadily grown as dark as one of Malika's glares after our encounter with Rani's family back on Tiger Island. I glanced at my old friend, who had plastered a smile on her lips but couldn't hide the pallor of her skin. Or the sudden trance of profound grief that came over her once a day. Her night-terrors had come back, despite the long work we'd done years ago to make them go away. Kai had been a good friend to her in those moments, his easy countenance and child-like wonder never faltering. He'd slip his hand into hers and mutter something that sounded like a prayer, and Rani would sigh and nod as she calmed down.

Her pain made my heart ache, and that ache only grew as the gangplank landed with a resounding, threatening *boom*, and I saw who awaited us at the dock.

Atax came to stand by my side. "Is that—"

"Xalya's Guard—my mother's elite forces, yes," I murmured, cringing and looking down at the ten black-swathed female guards astride ferocious zekar mounts. The famed warrior assassins, their mouths and noses covered in black cloth, were chosen as toddlers to train under Xalya's high priestess—also known as Ellythia's commander general —were among our most feared warriors. Historically, they were sworn to the crown princess.

Atax looked down at me, his blue eyes searching. I imagined that trying to figure out political machinations two hundred years after you'd been around would be difficult. But he knew about the legendary Xalya's Guard as they'd been here well before Atax was born, and that meant he knew what I did—that my mother knew we were coming, and we were noted to be a substantial threat.

A part of that would be the fact we had two Old Ones

with us, but what drew black thoughts through me was that I knew she would've sent them even if I'd arrived alone.

Geravie demanded to descend first, and clutching my arm, we made our way down the gangplank, Keshmi clutching onto Rani close behind us, followed by Kai and then Malika and Atax bickering at the rear.

Farrah, the leader of Xalya's Guard, dismounted. I hadn't seen the wiry, hard-eyed woman since my leaving, but I knew her on sight. I had trained with her on multiple occasions, and once when I was thirteen, she'd fractured my forearm to teach me a lesson about arrogance. In return, months later, I'd broken her nose with the butt of my knife, and covered in blood, she'd laughed. It had been a lucky shot, but she'd respected me a little more after that. It was their job, after all, to break the princesses apart and forge us anew.

So my spine was a little straighter as I came up to her, specifically unarmed. "Commander," I said formally.

Drawn to full height, Farrah was six foot and easily towered over me and Geravie, intimidating as the goddess she served in her tight-fitting leggings and tunic. Her brown eyes were terrible above her black face covering as if she was able to see inside my skin to my blood vessels and organs and knew exactly how to kill me the quickest.

"Pia," Farrah said shortly, and it brought a chill up my spine at the edge of disdain in her voice and the lack of honorific. They had not stripped me of my title for my exile. Not yet, anyway.

Geravie had also grown up at the Ellythian Court and knew exactly what this meant. She gave me a dark look of command.

I cleared my throat. "This is Lady Geravie Harranpul."

Farrah inclined her head to the elderly lady. "I am aware."

She scanned the rest of our party, and I watched her mark each of us, stopping the longest on Atax and Kai, the last of whom was sniffing the air and looking around in wide-eyed interest.

"Is that a market?" he said loudly, completely oblivious to the threat and pointing at Lisanthi's sector where the first of the market stalls were set up. "Can we go and see?"

I suppressed a smile despite everything. The Old Ones never had markets. To my knowledge they had a sort of sharing economy and bartering system.

Farrah ignored him and assumed her commanding voice. "We will take you to Her Majesty. She is waiting for you." She indicated an open wagon behind the horses.

Geravie and I stiffened as we both recognised the worn, wooden farmer's transport cart. No royal carriage for us then. The message was clear.

Exchanging a dark look with Malika, I escorted Geravie to the cart, and we all piled in under the hostile eyes of Xalya's Guard. The only one of us *not* tense was Kai, who beamed at his surroundings as if he were a tourist on holiday. To be fair to the white-haired Old One, Lota City *was* a marvel of magic and human ingenuity. Six temples of the Goddess were placed like sparkling monuments in a hexagon around the palace, which stood front and centre of the city.

It had been made out of pure gold and quartz by the gold-smith Rorax Boneweaver, who had been Queen Ellythia's second husband. The Boneweaver King at the time had given the Old One to the new queen as a gift of good faith, and it was written that they'd had a long and happy marriage.

So happy that he'd built the entire thing himself, toiling over it for ten years before he'd considered it complete.

Kai knew this story of course, but he'd just never seen the

Lota palace. Old Ones were not permitted on this island, just as Ellythians had not been permitted on Boneweaver Island. It was risky, coming here, but both Atax and Kai had refused to let us come alone.

I wondered if that display of chivalry would be enough to quell my grandmother's rage or if it would be cause to enrage her further.

When we arrived at the palace I had to stop for a moment at the bottom of the gold steps to simply look up at its magnificence.

There were three bells atop the palace in a wide golden tower and they all rung in ascending pitch.

A mother of pearl bell for royal and noble births, which chimed like angels singing.

One gold bell for big life events like weddings and coronations which rung a clear soprano.

And one black bell for death, which rang as a deep booming gong.

Beneath the bell tower was a gilded façade, ten levels of windows and balconies with lotus and vine details that could take the breath away.

I had forgotten how beautiful my home was and how the burn of what I'd done still tried to tear apart my very spine.

It had not been murder, like in Rani's case, but maiming a warrior so he couldn't fight was the Ellythian equivalent. Caran had remained my betrothed, unlike Rani's lover, and my relationship with him...I couldn't even think about that right now.

We were escorted by Xalya's Guard straight to the greater throne room. This twisted something in my gut because I would have expected to meet and be chastised by my elders in the smaller parlour room. I had been a girl when I'd left and today, I returned as a woman, and it felt like I was being led to a public execution.

The buzz of voices coming from the throne room told me that we would have a large audience. I tried to give a warning glance to Malika and Rani, but Geravie's low grumble of disapproval was warning enough.

"Brought the entire court out, has she?" Geravie rasped, her throat dry from travel. "Fanfare for the returned princess, is it?"

She and I exchanged a look, and suddenly I was glad for Geravie and Keshmi's mature presence by my side. In the absence of Altara, Geravie had taken me under her wing. Fussing over me and the girls, shooting sharp words of wisdom like arrows—often straight in the gut. But in all honesty, her words always hit true, even though they burned in their delivery. Geravie had also known my grandmother as a girl; perhaps that would hold some sway in this confrontation to come.

The gilded double-doors were opened by the palace division of Xalya's soldiers, in Lota colours of pink and black. The air was thick with tension so dense I could taste it, and as I laid my eyes on the Ellythian Court for the first time in three years, I was truly stunned to see that my grandmother had called the *entire* court to arms.

Familiar but older faces stared down at us as we were escorted by Xalya's Guard down the golden carpet stamped with lotuses. Colourful gowns of silk and cotton in the latest fashion—of which I had no idea—were worn by the men and women. Sharp-working blades were strapped to almost every hip, even the children sitting against pant legs and poofy silken gowns. Old magic spun in the air—protections and wards against demons. This had been home for me—these smells, these colours, these sounds—and yet they scraped across my chest in a way that made my hackles rise.

At the carpet's end, my grandmother awaited me upon her high gilded throne.

The Queen of the Ellythian Isles was seventy-five, sitting hunched and narrow eyed. Her hair was silver, almost the same colour as Kai's, though dull in comparison, and she wore the same heavy-white embroidered gown she'd been wearing for the past twenty years.

The Ellythian colour of mourning was white, and she'd started wearing it the day Aunt Yasani had left for Lobrathia. She had even ordered for the death bell to be rung. It had been a grave insult at the leaving parade—as she'd intended —but the old Queen of Ellythia was well known for her obvious displays of disapproval.

Her face was lined like a map of grief, rage and calcula-tion, but it was her eyes that disarmed me the most. That had always disarmed me. She had a way of stripping a person bare with a single glance, seeming to pull out all your weak-nesses for her inspection and eventual disdain.

At that moment, there was nothing in those eyes except a cold green stare that sliced deeply, and I knew I would bleed for all to see.

My mother stood next to my grandmother's throne, her right-hand woman standing tall and proud with her favoured sword still at her hip. Some things had not changed. She looked barely any older—her brown face with its soft cheeks but sharp nose, her lips full but pursed. She was a beauty, my mother—had always been—and my father had once loved her. I knew he would be close by, watching me with Paalus, my younger brother, waiting to see who I was now and what would become of me.

My mother's expression was stone, but her eyes blazed with verdant fire. She raised her chin as she assessed me—her only daughter, her biggest disappointment.

When my grandmother spoke, her voice was like a rasp of gravel under a boot, filled with mockery. "And so Pia Lota returns, disgraced, unmarried, powerless and in the arms of two Boneweaver scum."

Atax stiffened, Kai looked at me in confusion and I commanded myself not to cry. *I am steel, I am bone and I have the blood of Ellythia in my veins. I will never cower.* So I raised my chin and stood with my arms behind my back in the manner of a good soldier. My grandmother only understood one language: strength. My mother, I would worry about later.

I swallowed and said in a confident voice, "Your Majesty, mother, may I present—"

My mother's voice was the clack of a nun chuck with each name she spoke. "Atax Bonemaster. Kaisen Bonesong. Malika Yashra and Rani Umasri." She looked down her nose at me. At my friends. "We are well *aware* of the enemies you've brought with you."

Geravie coughed behind me, and my mother inclined her head. "And the returned Geravie Haranpul and Priestess Keshmi Harranpul of Taraka village. Elders, you are welcome here. Your companions, however, are not."

Malika shifted uncomfortably behind me, knowing full well that if the Ellythian Spymaster knew about the Boneweavers, she sure as hell knew about her and Rani's exile and the circumstances around them. They would be just as disgraced as me in my mother's eyes. I wondered for the first time if I'd made a mistake in letting my friends come along. They would be exposed to court politics now, and while Rani, as a lord's daughter might be prepared, Malika had never been to Lota City before.

I remained as stoic as a quartz statue, however, as any show of emotion would only further condemn me.

"Put them in the dungeons," my grandmother barked, making Rani jump. "I want them out of my sight. Put the Boneweavers in tourmaline."

Atax moved, and I whirled around, but Malika was already in front of him. "They will kill you!" she hissed, pointing to the balcony on the upper level where a dozen archers were poised with tourmaline arrows knocked two to a bow.

Atax's handsome face was a mask of anger, and his voice boomed across the hall, "We came to parlay with you, Lota Queen. We are owed a common decency. Subterranean demons have come to Boneweaver Island."

My grandmother scoffed and waved a bejewelled, dismissive hand.

Commander Farrah took me herself, hands like iron clasped around my biceps, forcing me to follow her out. Malika sputtered in anger but did nothing to defend herself, and thankfully, neither did Kai or Rani. Geravie and Keshmi watched on with dark eyes, untouched by the guards. Around us the courtiers remained quiet.

As I was dragged away, I couldn't just let them have the last word. "Mother, if you know about everything, then you know about Altara Voltanius and King Ashzale Boneweaver. They will come—"

"If they are lost to the Forests of Eternity," she said coldly, "then they are likely lost forever. No one has returned from there in over a century."

"Bah!" my grandmother spat. "That girl is as useless as her traitor mother."

"No," I hissed at them both. "You didn't see her at the battle of Ivory Castle. You haven't seen what she can do!"

My mother looked down her nose at me, ever the superior princess. "Whatever you think she can do, it won't be enough."

The entire Ellythian Court watched in silent approval as I, the third in line to the Ellythian throne, was taken to the dungeons. Something primitive inside me threatened to break in two.

18
ZALE

Watching Altara face-off with Odeelia would go down in my life as the single most wonderful thing I had ever seen. At the sight of her, soldiers were marching in my stomach, some of them doing somersaults and I would never tire of that feeling.

My mate had arrived like a goddess of the wilderness in that seductive black silk robe, her dark hair long and untamed. Her robe was only held together by the length of silk tied about her waist, and though it didn't fit her properly, I doubted even Odeelia could have worn it better. The centre of her chest was bared to the world, and the curves of both breasts showed as the silk slid around her body like water. As she'd walked into Odeelia's court as if *she* were the queen, each one of her steps had revealed a delicious bronzed leg I could spend the rest of my life staring at.

I also had no doubt that there would be murder here tonight, done by my own hand if the fae males here continued to oogle her as they were now.

Mine, the beast within me roared, *so fucking mine*.

The low growl that rumbled through my chest was not something I was in control of.

"I will not," I grind out, "be responsible for my actions if any male here will not avert their lusty gaze immediately."

The fae males of the court startled where they stood, and their fear perfumed the air as they all looked from Altara to me. The arm rests of my fake throne crumpled to powder under my grip. I met Altara's emerald gaze, and my body relaxed a fraction.

Her eyes were not happy to see me like I would have hoped. No, instead they were blazing with the challenge Odeelia had given her. A scattering of lightning laced around her head in a fine arc. From the side of my eyes, the carnal fae queen shifted in surprise, glancing at me to gauge my response.

Altara had come for me. She had fought the battle in her mind and had reigned triumphant over it. Everything in my body was screaming at me to take her, to claim her, *mount her,* right here in front of all of them so they would hear how she'd scream my name. But something in my mate's eyes bade me to sit still. A new emotion filled my chest like a warm breeze.

I was thankful that Altara had brought Wobbles back to me when he whispered in my ear. "Trust. Respect."

I trusted Altara.

In the time that I'd known Altara, she'd tried to kill me, had killed multiple demons, had endured torture and had taken over the court of one of the most evil entities in this forest. Even without knowing those things, I would have taken one look into those fire-bright eyes and known that she had delved deep into darkness and come out winning. I trusted that she could do whatever she needed to do to win this.

But Odeelia would not give me up without bloodshed. I knew that as well I as knew Altara was my mate. An idea crept into my mind, as stealthy as a wolf and as cunning as a tiger. But for it to work, we would need to work together in a way we never had before.

So I forced myself to sit back in my seat, and never taking my eyes off my mate, gave a tiny pluck to the divine connection between us. Altara's face softened just a fraction, and I felt a tentative answering reply.

Suddenly I could breathe again, and I was not the only one caught in the seductive fire that was Altara. Odeelia, Tylus and the other members of Odeelia's harem were shifting. These fae had never met anyone like my mate before, and by Agnolthi, I would make sure they *met* her properly.

I had, never in my long life, let my lips curve into a joyful smile, but as I watched my mate thrum with power, I did just that.

Zale Boneweaver smiled at me, and I could've been swept away by the lightest breeze at the way it made my entire being feel weightless. He'd never been more handsome, fixated on me, in that moment, and a little, heady throb began between my thighs.

I might just forgive him for getting himself into this position. Maybe.

Zale's nostrils flared, and his smile dropped as quickly as it came, his entire body becoming tense. The carnal fae bristled with interest around me, and I was suddenly cognisant of these supernatural creatures and their ability to sense things that humans could not.

Shit.

"What a thing," the queen said slowly.

I tore my eyes off Zale and looked at her. The queen's eyes were a little glazed, her rose-petal lips parted, and her head cocked. If I didn't know any better, I'd think she'd had a whiff of strong blue ganja or some other drug.

It hit me then. There it was—her weakness.

I smirked at her and then at her collection of fae warriors, who were staring at me with similar, unfocused eyes. All creatures, even these thousands-of-year-old ones, had their weakness, and it just so happened that theirs might be a particular strength of mine.

Clearing my throat, I said in a low, seductive voice I might have used on a lover. "What is...so interesting, my queen?"

She seemed to snap herself out of it, and with a little shake of the head, her eyes became clear and bright once more.

"You must understand," she said, glancing at Zale. "I'm fascinated by two beings forged in the same star. I want to know what it means. The extent of the bond." Her eyes took on a mischievous gleam, and she made a beckoning gesture to someone in the crowd of courtiers hanging on to our every word. "Lassiter?" She gestured to me, and a feeling like a cunning snake slithered down my spine.

A handsome fae male broke off from the crowd and sauntered forward. I watched with raised brows as he approached Zale, reached out a long finger and caressed the side of Zale's arm with clear seductive intent.

Zale frowned. "Stop."

My fingers twitched, eager for a dagger, and I said, "You'll lose that hand if you touch him again."

I was about to summon a dagger when Zale moved so fast I barely had time to see it.

Lassiter was on the floor, screaming under Zale's obsidian blade. Guards rushed forward, but Queen Odeelia raised a stopping hand, her lips curved into a delighted smile. Blood spurted, and Zale returned to his seat as we all looked between the severed hand lying on the floor of the dais and back at Lassiter's now bleeding stump of a wrist.

Zale, back in his seat, was looking at me with a non-human gleam in his eye. "Altara Voltanius is the only being permitted to touch me." There was a vice around my throat at the heated look in those eyes. "And any male that touches her will die."

Odeelia waved a lazy hand and said in a bored voice. "Remove him."

As two of the guards hastened to carry the sobbing Lassiter away, the heat in Zale's eyes was enough to consume me.

"Except me," Odeelia's eyes were fixed viciously upon me. "Due to our blood debt, I am permitted to touch you, Ashzale."

My entire body became stone as I registered her words.

"You were not aware of Zale's blood debt," Odeelia said, the pleasure of this hidden knowledge dripping from her voice like wine. "Ten years of service in my court to *me*."

"I was not," I said as if it didn't bother me. But really, before arriving here, Zale and I were hardly in an open and honest relationship. We'd both been difficult to one another.

Odeelia's voice was cunningly casual. "Then you will not be aware that I found Zale standing over the bodies of several Ellythian teenagers when I first found him over two hundred years ago?"

I glanced at Zale, wondering if this *did* bother me. I'd known he was ruthless from the start because his curse had made him do awful things. His blue eyes glimmered with some repressed emotion I was sure he wasn't used to feeling. His expression shuttered, and I wanted to go to him and tell him that it was okay. That I knew he wouldn't have understood what he was doing.

But who was Zale now that the shadow over his heart was gone? Could he really be so different than the cold beast from before? He'd just taken off a man's hand for touching him.

I knew Zale had that side of him. I'd travelled with him around Boneweaver Island for long enough to know that. But from the way he'd come to help me in this forest with his little gifts of banana leaf wrapped food and clean water, and the way he handled Wobbles, with gentle hands cocking his head to listen to the shell-creature, I also knew there was great kindness in him too. Zale had done those things for me and Wobbles, not for *anyone* else, including Odeelia.

So I said nothing, looking at the fae queen with feigned bored eyes.

Zale shifted in his seat. "I was barely a man grown. Those humans were trespassers on Boneweaver Island. I had to kill them. That was our law."

"And how many children had you killed in your time?" Odeelia drawled.

My heart plunged into ice as I looked a Zale with sharp eyes, but he was shaking his head in dismay as Wobbles whispered in his ear. "Many." He inhaled deeply as he looked at me, and I could practically see the memories of his past flashing through his eyes, the pain on his face obvious for all to see. "But I was also a child at the time."

Horror spun through me, bile lurching up my throat, the backs of my eyes burning.

The queen was clearly having a good time with this because she smiled at me as she said, "Why did you kill those children, Ashzale?"

I hung on to his every word, and Zale never took his eyes off me, as if it were important for him that I see who he was. Where he came from. That was important to me too. He swallowed again and seemed to compose himself. "My father wanted us to train for war as early as possible, so he took human children from Tiger Island and had my brothers and I battle them. Some they spent months training so they would be at the same level as us. As we grew up, so did our fighting partners. Any demons we caught, we also trained with them."

My stomach churned at the thought of Zale's father being cruel enough to steal children for the purposes of gutting them. Zale had hinted that his father was awful, but I hadn't realised just how awful. To think Kai, Raen and Atax had been forced to do the same.

The courtiers around us muttered and whispered to one another.

"I'm sorry," I said to Zale, hating this queen for outing him in front of everyone like this. "It wasn't your fault."

He blinked at me as if he didn't understand what I was saying.

"Yes, it's all very sad, isn't it?" Odeelia said wistfully. "He was close to death when we found him on one of our trips out of the portal to get kava." She leaned in her chair as if to whisper conspiratorially to me. "It won't grow here." Settling back in her throne she said, "We took him, bathed him, dressed his injuries..." she trailed off with a wistful smile as if thinking about some lovely dream. I scowled at her, and the audience tittered like they too remembered the occasion. "Where was I? Oh, yes—he told me *everything* about his father and his mother. Such a lovely time we had, didn't we, Ashzale?" She turned to gaze upon him with a smile.

Zale had gone still.

I tried not to think about the fact that they'd fucked each other. Often. But I couldn't help the lightning that sparked off my body in response as my stomach roiled. I suppressed a gag.

"Jealous?" Odeelia said, her malicious eyes on me. "Isn't it lovely the sound he makes when he—"

"Enough, *fae queen*," Zale growled. "Or you will find yourself without a court to reign over."

The courtiers bristled with excitement, and I looked around at them incredulously. Perhaps living thousands of years made a person go insane.

"Such threats," Odeelia said a little breathlessly, a hand pressed to her chest. "Such violence. There, there. We must get ready." She clapped her hands. "We will begin our little game on the morrow. I will have my girls take care of you—"

"*No.*" Zale's voice was all guttural beast in its cadence. A few of the courtiers stumbled over themselves at the sound of it as my own heart pounded. *"My mate will not be taken away from me."*

"How positively murderous, Ashzale!" Odeelia chimed with delight. She clasped her fists under her chin and blinked at him with wide eyes. Zale only had eyes for me, though, and they were trained upon me with such feral need that my breath caught in my throat.

Without another word Zale was on his feet and eating up the distance between us, leaving Wobbles to tumble off his shoulder. I held my breath as Zale reached me, unable to take my eyes off the fire and darkness in his gaze. He grabbed me around the waist with one hand and cupped my cheek with the other. Our bodies pressed together as he lowered his forehead to mine.

"Tara." He said my name with such gentleness that all I could do was look up at him in a sort of shock.

I remembered the last time we'd been chest to chest, he'd

been inside me, stretching me out. I'd been so sore after being with him, but it had been an ache of the most wonderful kind. Heat rose up, spinning through my core. He smelled like the forest, male heat and lust—

Someone in the crowd sighed, and it reminded me we were being watched by an entire crowd of wretched old fae. Zale's eyebrows twitched in an irritated frown as if he, too, remembered this, and he released my cheek to pull me out of the theatre as quickly as he could.

Tucking me close to his side, we headed down the path away from the court, Wobbles scrambling to catch up with us on his spindly limbs. Zale's hand was clutching my side, every finger a burning brand on my waist.

I swallowed. "Zale, who the fuck does she—"

"Not yet, Tara." His voice was barely repressed anger.

He swept us past pretty gardens, sparkling streams and over quaint bridges until a little cottage like structure came into view. It had no roof and was no more than wooden beams strategically covered in vines and flowers. I scented jasmine and roses and heard the bubbling of a brook nearby as he yanked open a tiny wooden gate and pulled me inside.

I'd never seen a house like this before, where lush grass was soft underfoot and the roof was absent, open to night sky so that you could pretend your ceiling was studded with celestial jewels. Before us was a rounded space filled with blankets and pillows. Orange and yellow quartz lanterns illuminated the walls, and a bowl of fruit sat on a carved table next to the sleeping area as well as a silver pitcher of water and two cups.

I supposed carnal fae like to be prepared for bedroom activities, but I could hardly appreciate the aesthetic of the decor because Zale pulled me into his arms and kissed me like a man possessed. His lips were searing and desperate, his tongue dominating my mouth out of pure need. Lost in the feeling of his hot mouth on mine, I arched into him, and he pulled at the ribbon holding my silk gown in place. Completely naked and bared before him, he wasted no time, his palms hot on my hips.

"I need you," he rasped, searing eyes raking my skin. "I need you more than anything in this world. Tell me that you've come here for me, Tara. Tell me that you want to be mine."

I clutched at his shoulders, pressing myself against his golden tunic, inhaling his masculine scent. Conflicted emotions made for a storm in my mind. I wanted his body on a physical level, desired him like I'd never desired anyone. But there was still much to be spoken about, and I was completely unprepared for this level of sheer attraction between us. "I came here to get you Zale. I'm sorry for—"

"*Tara.*" His voice was strangled, his fingers digging into my waist as he buried his nose in my neck as he went still and tense, frozen in place, barely breathing.

"What's wrong?" I asked, distractedly running my hands down the broad muscle of his back.

"We can't—" he breathed, placing a kiss on my forehead. "We need to wait to have sex."

I stared at him agape. "What—"

He waved his hand, and a bubble of his dark power circled around us. "Listen to me, Tara. I think I know what we will need to do. But it means we need to store our lust."

20
ALTARA

Much to my chagrin, me, my burning sex and Zale spent the night apart. Needless to say I angrily tossed and turned all night in that bed.

Zale confirmed that my observations of the carnal fae queen had been correct and told me of a plan that he thought might work. I'd been so filled with vicious lust, that I'd told him to shove his plan up his ass. Without looking back at me, he left, fists clenched at his sides, his strides a predator's languid stalk. I'd stood there for a full minute frozen by the sight of him leaving me and the burning, spiralling need in my core.

I'd been fuming but could hardly feel rejected by him when I knew there was a blood debt in play. A debt that could not be broken by any means except to fulfil it to completion. And in Zale's case, it was ten *years' service*. It had all been in exchange for Odeelia's use as a Vayashi—a means to temper his power through sex—where matches for him were difficult to find. Once he'd found Odeelia, it had been an easy solution.

As the dawn sun filtered through the canopy, shining in my eyes, I summoned the witch's cloak Magrin had gifted me.

I ran my fingers along the blood-red thread. Along the inseam the nine names of the witches were embroidered, and I whispered those names as I felt each stitch, hoping Magrin had meant "wherever you go, we go" literally.

Magic like water thrown on burning coals sizzled under my fingers, and it was almost painful, but within seconds, the matter around me shifted.

Nine tall, black hooded figures surrounded me in their transparent astral form, keenly looking around my room.

"My queen," Magrin said in her deep voice, bowing low. "You require assistance?"

"I didn't think I'd need help so soon," I said wryly, "but the Queen Odeelia is intent on keeping Zale. She wants me to win him back in some game, but we don't know what to expect."

The witches murmured in discontent under the breaths. "She must be punished," one witch murmured.

"She must pay for this disrespect," hissed another.

"I agree," I said. "But you've been around here for a long time. Do you know what type of games this queen likes to play? I have a feeling it'll be nothing good for me."

"She will ensure you lose," Magrin said darkly. "Even if you match her, power for power, she will cheat and lie to ensure she keeps King Ashzale."

I swore under my breath, knowing this must be true. "So…you're saying I'll also have to cheat?"

The gleam in Magrin's transparent eyes told me she would love nothing more. I chewed on my lip as I thought about what that meant. I didn't really like Zale's idea. Even for me it had been heavy handed, and I wanted to see if I could win on my own merit. Magrin kindly made me new clothes for the coming tests. I'd been barefoot this whole time, and she insisted on making me boots and a skirt to match my witch's robe. The boots bore heavy magic in them, though they were light enough to wear, and Magrin, with a mysterious smile, said they would ensure I always remained steady on my feet.

An hour later two tittering female fae came to get me from my room. I gave them my most charming smile, but they continued to stare at me. I was about to ask them if there was something on my face when one of them said, "Do you not recognise us, Your Highness?"

I blinked at them dumbly for a moment before I got a flash of memory of these narrow faces inside a dank cavernous cell.

"Oh, from the Dark Castle!" I said with delight. "You two look far more healthy with some food in you."

They beamed at me, nodding. "We owe you a debt for saving us."

"It's alright," I said as we made our way down the wooden steps to the ground. "You never should have been held there like that. It was awful."

They exchanged a quiet look for a moment before the second one said, "Our kind deal in debts, Your Highness. We cannot forgo a service like that."

I waved a hand as they led me down the path. "You can consider your debt repaid—if you tell me what kind of game your queen is playing with me and my...husband today."

They exchanged a look again, and the first one said, "She wants to break the star-soul bond between you and King Ashzale."

I might have fallen over if I wasn't already being careful

with my feet. My stomach sunk into my nether regions. I didn't even know a thing could be done. Let alone attempted. The two fae stared at me in fear and worry as I contemplated this. Odeelia was thousands of years old. She would have knowledge others did not. The fact that she was even going to try meant she thought it might be able to be done.

Our souls were born in the same star. How could you destroy *that* bond?

"*Only death,*" Magrin's voice whispered in my ear. "*Only in death can that bond be broken. She intends to kill you.*"

My mind stiffened as I kept my body appearing relaxed. Of course, that solution made sense. I projected my mind through my witch's robe to Magrin and the nine, "*But would she go to such lengths?*"

My witches' silence was enough admission. A wisp of smoke coiled around my being as I descended into dark thoughts. I growled to them, "*Can she be killed?*"

I could feel Magrin shaking her head. "*She is an old entity, borne of this land and tied to it. She will die when this world ends.*"

A shiver ran through me, but I sucked my bottom lip into my teeth as I really thought about what immortality meant. "*No creature can survive a beheading, surely?*"

Magrin chuckled. "*This one can. The Eternal Forest would pull her parts together until she was whole again. But, Your Highness…there are other ways to harm a person without killing them.*"

The smoke around me thickened, and the two fae turned to give me startled looks when they sensed the change in me. I grinned at them, showing my teeth, and said to Magrin, "*Indeed, there are.*"

I stalked into Odeelia's theatre moments later, fae courtiers giggling, drums playing, a flute chiming. But as soon as I stepped onto the beginning of the mosaic tile, the music cut off as if the villain had entered the stage in a play. It should have been comical.

But it wasn't—because as my gaze narrowed down like a bird of prey on this pretty battlefield, I knew that I was ready to have blood on my hands today.

Zale sat on his own by Odeelia's side, ahead of her other warriors of the harem, on a gilded throne of equal height and majesty to the queen's. The message she was sending was clear.

Odeelia was stunning in a fine shimmering gown of red and gold silk. Sheer immortal perfection topped in a gold and diamond crown, her beauty second perhaps only to Agnolthi. Her amber eyes were fixed upon Zale as if he were her personal God and saviour. She *loved* him, I realised with a sort of brutish shock.

SHE'D DRESSED HIM LIKE SOMETHING SHE OWNED—A DOUBLET OF gold embroidered in black leaves with a matching black cape. He wore black pants and shining new black boots. His long hair was silken and loose, draped across one shoulder. A wrangled piece of gold lay at his feet as if he'd crumpled the metal with his bare hands. His expression was made from obsidian itself, dark, terrifying, violence tightly coiled into the skin of a predator made human.

Zale always looked like a king, in whatever state he was— naked or clothed. But like this?

He looked like an emperor.

Me on the other hand? I hadn't washed in days, my hair was a tumbled mess and I was sure I smelled a little. I wore only my witch's cloak, skirt and boots, and stitched in their own blood, I felt like I had my own court here with me.

Odeelia's voice rang out clear as the waters of a fae lagoon. "Today we are going to test the star-soul bond."

I pushed away the chill I felt at her words. It sounded almost heinous, this test she spoke of, especially as I knew she meant to sever it. If she meant to kill me, Zale would likely behead *her*, so she would no doubt use something clever to manipulate it into happening.

A phantom finger trailed down my neck, and I shivered, my centre throbbing with heat. I swallowed and looked at Zale. My husband was staring at me, his eyes ocean water made into fire. I looked at him in shock, and the golden thread between us vibrated softly as if he was trying to tell me something.

I crooked a brow at him, and the corner of his lip twitched as he blinked drolly at me as if to say *"Are we doing this my way?"*

Something flowed through the air of the theatre, subtle but heady, and like a drug, it seemed to move the fae. Quiet voices murmured in the crowd, someone sighed loudly and silk and chiffon rustled. I knew at once that the exchange between Zale and I was having an effect on them. I looked then at Odeelia, who was staring at me with a snake's venom in her eyes. I levelled a smirk at her and tossed my head.

"How do you plan on this testing, exactly?" I drawled.

Odeelia's red lips curved, her entire face cruel immortal arrogance. She raised one lazy hand, and with a burst of light, a delicate glittering string of silver wrapped around her hand, leaving the end to trail around Zale's large wrist. It was uncannily a replica of the glittering thread that reached from my navel to Zale. A replica of the star-soul bond.

Nope.

Struck by a force that was wild and primitive, all reason was tossed into the wind and I couldn't control my response.

I ignited, lightning tearing through me with a slap of anger, and a bow of pure dark light was in my hands. Before I knew it, an arrow of lightning was loosed toward Odeelia.

The fae queen held up a hand as if she'd been ready for it as her warriors leapt to their feet at the open attack.

My arrow exploded into light as it hit Odeelia's glimmering shield of magic, and a sound like booming thunder echoed all around us. The entire court flung their arms over their eyes.

But I didn't. Caught up in a storm of volcanic fury, I loosed arrow after arrow, each one sounding a terrible boom upon her shield, and with each one, I took a single step forward, advancing toward the fae queen in angry steps. My mind screamed that I would kill her—for insinuating she could replicate what was inside me. For thinking she could simply *take* Zale. For assuming her wit was stronger than my wrath.

Nothing was.

I'd known that as soon as I'd killed the malevolent spirit of the castle I'd taken over. I was capable of dark and terrible things, and I would relish the blood on my hands if it meant protecting those I cared about. Nine dark laughs filled my ears, and I knew my witches were with me as I viciously rained arrows upon Odeelia's shield, three at a time now.

How long would it hold? Even with her immortal power, I had arrows filled with Voltanius lightning. Then an idea struck me because I wasn't just a Voltanius—I was a Lota too, as Odeelia had reminded me last night. So I filled my arrows with *both*.

Void magic zipped down my fingers along with the lightning and into the three arrows I had knocked. The electric white lightning turned as dark as night. A thrill consumed me, and a smirk touched my lips as I loosened all three into Odeelia's shield, still holding strong.

This time there was no boom because the arrows lodged themselves into the shield and *pulled.*

Odeelia's own magic began to fill me, funnelled through those arrows, draining the power from the shield. From behind the shimmering surface of Odeelia's magic, I saw her amber eyes darken in recognition. But she could do nothing as I pulled her power into me, and my insides began to buzz with the wild, immortal power of the Eternal Forest itself. She had a heady, writhing power that felt like sex and lust, greed and gluttony, and my own magic gobbled it up and made it into my own.

Her shield came down with a soft hiss, and the light faded. My arrows clattered to the tiles, but I only had eyes for Odeelia, her face contorting into a mask of rage.

Her harem of warriors recovered first and launched themselves at me. I was already standing with my toes touching the dais, so they barely had three steps to have me surrounded, their glittering blades drawn and angled at my neck.

But Zale was on his feet at the same time, his own obsidian blade brought into reality with a whisper of air and angled at the fae male standing in front of me.

"One word, Your Highness!" called a fae warrior from behind me. "One word, and she is dead!"

The warrior in front of me, Tylus, I recalled, had his blade directly pressed against my windpipe. He was blond, handsome and as tall as Zale and suddenly his face went from an expression of anger to blinking rapidly with fear.

Zale had come to stand behind him. "If you touch her," he said in a voice of cold quiet, "nothing will save any of you."

The three blades I felt pressing on my back moved away, though there was no sound of weapons being sheathed.

"Stand down," said Odeelia through clenched teeth. "Tylus. All of you."

The fae warriors now sheathed their blades, a few of them grumbling under their breaths. I loosened a breath of my own as Tylus, in front of me, side-stepped to get away from Zale.

Except it was already too late for him. I barely had time to close my eyes before I realised what Zale—his face bearing only red murder—was about to do. He swung a heavy down-stroke and blood sprayed on my face. Screams sounded out, but I remained still as only a fell wind passed me and four more fae bodies thumped to the floor.

Odeelia shrieked.

I opened my eyes to see a massacre of fae around me, their blood spattered across the front of my witch's robe, though the droplets slid off as if the material was waterproof.

Zale stalked around me, his furious eyes trained on my own, his face and new golden clothes splattered with blood. He paused and raised his hand to stroke a thumb across my lower lip before he turned and stalked back up the dais toward the throne.

Odeelia sat trembling, white, her fists clutching her armrests, and it was only then I could see that the silver thread around her wrist had snapped.

"*You,*" she hissed, the whites of her eyes showing all the way around. "Owe me four warriors."

I looked behind me, raised my brows and pressed a hand to my chest as if to say, "*Who, me?*"

Next to her Zale examined his fingernails, the obsidian

blade back dangling on his ear. "I believe," he said mildly. "I told them not to touch her. And those four," he jerked his chin toward the four bodies lying around me. "Laid their blades on her. She owes you nothing. A warning was given and ignored. The punishment was dealt."

Odeelia's jaw clenched and unclenched, but even I could see the logic in this. Her eyes flicked down to Tylus, whose head now lay a metre from his body. "Tylus was my favourite," she hissed.

Zale's eyes flicked to mine and held them. His voice was as mild as a spring morning. "I thought I was your favourite."

Was it an ugly thing that my heart simultaneously warmed and pounded because Zale's eyes were telling me that *I* was his favourite?

"Enough," Odeelia spat. "I've had enough. I want her in chains. Caged. We will resume this tomorrow."

"Tonight," Zale corrected smoothly, always the king at court. "We will resume this tonight. And she will not be chained. The cage is acceptable."

I shot him a look to say it *wasn't* acceptable, but we both knew we were already toeing the line.

Odeelia stiffened in her chair and looked sideways at Zale, trying to figure him out. He looked like a king of her fae court and spoke like one just now, just as she'd wanted. To her eyes it might have looked like he was warming up to the idea of being hers because she gave a stiff nod to her guards.

Fae guards surrounded me, their bodies tense, their hands clutching their blades, clearly terrified to touch me.

As they stared at me in a silent command, an ugly sort of realisation swatted at me. I could not win this by brute force. Zale's initial lack of action should have indicated to me as much. So I levelled Zale with a gaze and reached down the gold thread connection to caress him. His nostrils flared, and he cocked his head ever so slightly in question.

An echo came to me, floated in on the forest wind as if it had been caught and carried just for me. An echo of Zale shouting to me when I was in a place of such darkness I could barely hear anything. *Altara! Meet in the place between light and dark. Do you hear me, Altara? Meet me there, and I will come."*

I inclined my head a fraction.

You were right. We'll use your plan, but we'll do this my way.

Because while we certainly weren't creatures completely wreathed in darkness, we definitely weren't made of sunlight either. No, ours was a wild and feral power, made of blood and thunder.

21

ZALE

After I left the throne room, I was in a state of rabid rage, but at least it was a familiar emotion, and Wobbles didn't need to blubber in my ear about it. Murdering a few fae today had done a little to help my mood. Being alone while my mate was locked in a cage—even if it was solid gold and as pretty as her—had me pacing about in my room, my tiger claws piercing through the skin of my knuckles.

I only stayed in my assigned bedroom for an hour before I calmed myself enough to leave. I leapt out of my treetop house and landed in a crouch on the golden paved path below. Following the glittering thread inside of me, I made my way to Altara's cage, assuming my black panther form as I did. I didn't want anyone to approach me as I watched over my mate, and though these carnal fae had always been fascinated by me in any form, they knew not to engage with me right now, when my pelt was as black as my mood.

I knew this place like the back of my hand, having frequented it on an almost weekly basis from the age of fifteen when Odeelia had first found me. It was a hassle to get in and out of the Eternal Forest, but with my constant need as a teenager and then adult, I became very adept at it. I don't think my father ever figured out where I went on Sundays, and even if he had, he likely would have approved. Odeelia was ancient and powerful, just the way he liked his political allies. My mother definitely knew. As High Witch of Agnolthi's order, she knew everything that went on around the island. She hated it, her eyes always sharp on me when I returned a little calmer, and she was always training the girls to grow their power in the hopes that one of them would make a suitable Vayashi for me. I burned through them in no time, however, and always ended up going back when Odeelia sent for me.

Stalking into the shadows around the series of huge golden bird cages Odeelia liked to punish her court in, I lay on my belly a little distance from Altara's cage.

She noticed me right away, as if she couldn't deny the heavy tension that lay between us. Her emerald eyes found mine in the afternoon light, and we simply stared at one another. Before I knew it, she sat up and let the hood of her new robe fall off her head.

I'd been jealous when I'd seen the robe initially, knowing that it had been my intention to get her new clothes when the fae had found me. But I'd scented old blood magic on it and realised it had come from Agnolthi's witches and that Altara had every right to wear it as their High Witch. But she wielded it like a weapon now. As I knew full well, she wore nothing much underneath it except a small skirt and those new magic boots.

Sunlight danced upon her face, highlighting the wild and beautiful planes of her nose and cheeks, casting her in bronze.

The robe slipped down her bare shoulder, and she let it, her emerald eyes gleaming with mischief. The beast part of me angered to see her caged, but another, more primal part of me was content to know she couldn't run away from me again. I was a possessive beast, and if Altara did not already know how much I hungered for her to be at my side, she soon would.

Except in this moment, I felt less like a Boneweaver predator and more like prey as she watched me with those eyes full of seductive revenge.

I knew at once that this was payback for refusing her last night and perhaps a test for what we needed to do tonight. But didn't she know that she was perfection incarnate, and any movement on her part was guaranteed to draw my full attention? Or indeed, the attention of any male creature? Her robe dropped further down, exposing one round heavy breast and then the other. Her dark nipples were peaked in the cool breeze of the afternoon, and as she tilted her head back and trailed her fingers lazily down first the column of her neck and down to swirl around her nipple, I felt like a rabbit caught in a snare, my entire being heated up like wildfire.

She allowed the robe to open further, exposing her stomach, and now her entire upper body was open for my eyes to feast on. I growled low in my throat, and she merely smirked with satisfaction, tracing her fingers up and down her skin in a way that made me desperate and writhing to have her.

Altara had me completely in her grasp, and I laid there wondering why I hadn't beheaded this entire court for her. Why I hadn't beheaded everyone in this entire fucking forest just to have her safe and protected in my arms. To whisper in her ear that I would never let anyone hurt her in the way the Butcher had, ever again. I could tear those bars apart and have her in moments, and I growled deep in my chest at the frustration, my long tail twitching irritably.

Eventually, Altara gave me one last smirk before she lay down in her cage to sleep, covering herself with that witch's robe once again. When I eventually gathered my wits about me, I realised this was her way of telling me that she agreed to my plan.

Lusty and desperate, I never took my eyes off my mate the entire day, and when the sun headed west and late afternoon arrived, the fae servants came to bring her food, and I slipped away, quiet as a cat and hard as steel.

Back in my room, I looked at Odeelia's chosen clothes with disdain. She wanted to dress me in her clothes, on her terms, a message to the world that she'd claimed me for herself. I'd done some minor magic yesterday and turned her all gold ensemble into gold and black, just to spite her.

Odeelia *hated* black in everything except my hair. But her preferences had never really mattered to me, even back in my youth, as I'd not cared about anything in those times except for finding a way to control my power. Accepting her preferences had been a means to an end.

Now a need in me had grown wild and true, and it was singular, obsessive and unchanging. That was the need for Altara. To be inside her skin, to fill my being with her scent and to call her mine so that the entire world knew what she meant to me.

So as I looked at my new clothes, I smirked as I manipulated the colour in the fabric and stitching, landing on a colour that reminded me of her. While the entire outfit I coloured all black, I made the embroidery a bright and unapologetic emerald.

I SAT BESIDE ODEELIA ON HER SHOW OF A THRONE, THE remaining members of her harem on my other side with a few new additions, all dressed in gold. The fae queen wrinkled her nose at my change of colours but said nothing as I barely cast her a glance. She knew full well that I was impossible to persuade, that the only thing keeping me sitting in this chair and in her court and not outside with Altara was a blood contract I'd stupidly made.

My father had thought about the consequences about taking my conscience away. I literally had not cared for anything, except my own self and my father's orders. I had been obedient to him and only him in all ways and the only time he hadn't controlled me was when I was out in the jungle by myself, and it was usually then I'd made question-able decisions.

All too aware of that star-soul bond between us, I knew Altara had approached the theatre. I knew the cadence of each step she took, could feel the current of her breath in the air.

Our first time making love had been rough and practically instinctual, and afterwards, I'd seen in her eyes that she'd regretted it. She'd only been drawn to me to get rid of that murderous power that had been given to her. The devastation I'd felt had been akin to her splitting my chest open with an axe. Didn't she know how mad she made me? How…alive I felt around her? How, if she gave herself to me fully, we would be unstoppable.

But I'd known where it was coming from. The Butcher had taken something crucial from her. She'd thought she was not deserving of love because of what had happened to her. I'd recognised it because I'd felt the exact same thing with what my father had done to me. If I were more man than beast, it might have broken me. But when it came to my mate, my beast reigned king and he was a single-minded monster that would maim and destroy to claim her.

Something had changed in Altara's eyes and she looked upon me with something more than fear or annoyance or irritation. She cared for me enough to come after me. She cared enough to threaten a thousands-of-years-old entity. And after trying it her way, she'd agreed to my plan, strange as it was. The fact that Altara finally *trusted* me, made me swell with joy.

The fae courtiers tittered and giggled about the room, but as Altara stepped into view, the earth ceased its orbit. I was vaguely aware that the entire court had gone silent, that every fae had sucked in a shocked, lusty breath.

A seductive smile played on Altara's deep-pink painted lips.

I could tell it was witch's magic in the air, though I knew not how she'd managed to get them to work their power here and now. For our plan to work, we needed the fae perfectly rabid with arousal and by all that was holy; if *this* didn't work, nothing would.

It was as if Luana, the Goddess of desire and seduction, had entered the mortal realm.

Altara's dress was made of pink gem-studded, silk ribbons, as if she were a woman made into a gift. The ribbons were tied at her shoulder blades so they came over her shoulders and over her nipples, pushing her breasts up and into the centre. Altara was not a small woman—no. She had a full figure with thick thighs that kissed when she walked and wide hips made for my hands. I knew she'd been trained in physical arts since infancy, so she had strong arms and legs, but she'd inherited heavy breasts and curved hips from her Lota side.

A Boneweaver male might feel the need to protect his mate from the jealous, lustful eyes of others, but there was always a sense of pride there and clothes had never been the way of the Old Ones. Our community had mostly existed without clothes, and even in the time before I'd been imprisoned, clothes were optional, something women usually liked to have for recreation or ritual, or to symbolise their beast form. Our priestesses wore the clothes of the temple to honour Agnolthi's robes, but otherwise, our bodies were worshipped for their power. My mother had sat me down when I was teenager on the cusp of manhood, when I'd started noticing the bodies of the girls around me. She'd sat me, Raen, Atax and Kai outside a birthing room and made us listen to the natural sounds of a woman giving birth, she'd made us watch our women fight in the pits and unashamedly taught us the inside and outside parts of a woman's anatomy.

But a woman's body had never entranced me in the way Altara's did now in this theatre.

Most of her skin was laid bare to the world, gleaming bronze in the quartz-light, with just a sheath of pink transparent fabric to cover her glorious behind. The ribbons crisscrossed over her belly button and converged to cover the area her pubic hair grew, cupping her sex then criss-crossing down the length of both legs.

She'd made her hair sleek, so it hung long and smooth down her back, and she sauntered in as if she were Luana gracing this forest with her presence and us, her favoured pilgrims.

181

I sensed the change in the air immediately. Odeelia's nostrils flared, her eyes trained on Altara as if she existed only for her, and a corner of my mouth lifted. Altara was gazing back at the queen, her eyes half-lidded and seductive.

I gave a possessive insistent tug to our star-soul bond, and Altara tensed and actually looked down at the plane of her bare stomach. She knew it was me, of course, and plucked it gently back. I reached out for her down that glittering thread and caressed her velvet-soft cheek. I narrowed my awareness onto her as she smiled, and I heard her heart race at my touch, though her eyes never left Odeelia's.

"Irritation," Wobbles mumbled into my ear. "Erm. Lust."

I jangled him on my shoulder because *that one* I fucking knew.

The fae court quietened around us, and I knew they scented my desire, but Altara wouldn't look at me, though I could tell she wanted to.

Altara was only dressed in ribbons, and she *wouldn't even look at me*. I was dying for her gaze to touch mine, to see how much I needed her.

"Anguish," Wobbles said carefully.

Fuck. A low growl escaped my desert dry throat. Every particle between us thrummed with desire, and I knew the fae were as entranced with her as I was. Lust made the air as thick as honey, and just as sweet.

With every hip-sashaying step she took, Altara's emerald eyes fixed on Odeelia's amber ones, the heat in me became a roaring furnace of need. I knew without looking that the fae queen's pupils were dilated, her breath coming in heavy bursts, practically panting as Altara approached.

I scented her then, my Altara, feminine and floral and all

the good things in the world converging in a single, beautiful smell.

She curtseyed in the most graceful way, and I was suddenly jealous, though I knew it was ludicrous, but she'd never curtseyed to *me*—though, I have also never bowed for her, have I? As I'm wondering why I haven't fallen to my knees yet, Altara gently took Odeelia's hand and fucking stroked her thumb across her skin, just once, and brushed her lips onto the back of her hand, never taking her eyes off Odeelia's.

I was sweating, and I'd never been so rock-hard under these fucking clothes, and it was a torture like I'd never known to have her so close and not be able pull to her into me. But I had to wait for the right time.

Already, the carnal fae had descended into a fervour, falling into each other's arms, drunk on the scent of the combined desire heating the air. I needed them rabid with lust. I needed them panting and feverish in order for my plan to work. I *had* to wait.

Odeelia was squirming in her seat, and I scented her desire too, though it disgusted me now. One of the males from her harem sauntered forward and sat on the floor against her leg, drawing his fingers below her gown and up her calf. Her shoulders were heaving, and she clutched onto the armrests of her gilded throne for dear life.

Altara's eye's flit toward mine, softening as they looked upon me, and I held my breath like I was under water because I'd waited so fucking long for her to look at me like that. I was also sure I knew what she saw in me. A man hardly able to contain himself, his eyes a furnace of Agnolthi's dark fires.

There was only one look she could interpret from that gaze: *I need you, Altara.*

She turned her back on us both and allowed Odeelia to get a good look at her ass as she sashayed back to the centre of the theatre, turned and obediently waited.

Odeelia snapped her fingers, and the group fervour was broken. The queen's gaze was sharp as a knife on Altara until she smoothed it away with centuries of practised, cunning grace.

She had to clear her throat, and I noticed her grip was tight in her lap, her cheeks pink.

I was agitated enough that I had to roll my shoulders before I set upon Altara through our bond.

22

ALTARA

I wish my sister could have seen this costume. We would have laughed for days over it. We used to play dress-up all the time, and I'd even gifted her a heinous outfit for her eighteenth birthday modelled off a girl she'd seen in a brothel. She'd never wear that dress, of course, being less adventurous than me, but it was just for fun. Today I got to live out my dream of publicly wearing something inappropriate and actually be seen by creatures who lived for that sort of thing—who would just appreciate my body more than just as an object for men's desires, but as art. As a study of the feminine figure in all its rich glory, *every* curve and divot.

As my eyes set upon Zale, his eyes burned into mine, and the heat of it sent my body into a sudden tremble. I couldn't take my eyes off his presence as he glowered at me, almost as if he was angry or hungry or agitated, and I bit my lip as I felt a caress down our glittering bond.

I realised then—it was not a violent rage that moved his body but violent *lust*.

The thought flared like lit tinder within me and sent my

breast heaving. A phantom finger trailed down the column of my neck, down the curve of one breast and then the other, coming dangerously close to my nipple.

I let myself gasp.

So did more than a few fae in the audience. I was wet within seconds, and Zale's ghost of a finger trailed down my stomach, down, down... This was exactly what I wanted of our first time, just with less of an audience.

Odeelia sensed something was happening between us as I completely destroyed her plans for whatever game she'd wanted to play. She must have felt the need to regain some control because she taunted, "Do you know the deep sound Zale makes just before he comes?"

Goddess, the fire that moved through me at her words. Without thinking I hissed, "I don't need to; I know his soul." I took a step forward. "Because it is the same as mine. We are two sides of the same coin, and that is something you could never understand."

Zale growled in assent, but I think he'd totally given into his desire now because he was staring at me, unblinking, and his phantom finger found my sex and moved down my slit. Tingles flooded my womb, my thighs, my lower stomach, and I closed my eyes at the sensation. When I opened them and looked at Zale, the sensation of his finger moving through me heightened as he slid a sweet finger around my clit. I let myself go and moaned in the back of my throat. For Zale's plan to work, this needed to be a show.

The fae of Odeelia's court stood with their eyes glazed over, their mouths hanging open, simply staring at me in a daze. Lust honeyed the air so heavily I felt it pressing upon my skin like a real, living thing.

Odeelia's eyes flashed at me, and she reached a finger out for Zale, stroking him down his forearm.

He physically snapped at her like a wolf and pushed her so violently she tumbled out of her throne and into the arms of the male sitting at her feet. The fae male roughly grabbed the back of her neck and crushed his mouth to hers, and she sighed into him, the straps of her gown falling off her narrow shoulders.

The carnal fae court took this as permission because there was a flurry of limbs, silks, moans and sighs. Fae fell to the floor on top of each other, and there was more than one cry as legs spread open, lips pressed and clothes were torn.

Not a single male warrior from Odeelia's harem paid attention to us as Zale stood from his throne, his aura dark as midnight and as static as an ocean storm. He stalked toward me with purpose in his eyes. It was at once threatening and arousing to see the Boneweaver King moving toward me like he wanted to devour me. But I'd never been a coward. I stepped forward with the intention of leaping onto him, but he was quicker, and with that predatory grace, he picked me up as if I weighed nothing and devoured my mouth with his.

It was a biting, wet, possessive, *claiming* kiss, and I met him tongue for tongue. I was crushed against his body as if he wanted to merge our bodies together by sheer force of his will, but it was a sweet, sweet burn. His hands were equally rough on my ass, squeezing both cheeks, and I raised my legs to wrap them around his waist. His erection was impossibly hard against my core, and I writhed against his thick length, grinding against him.

He growled, low and deep, and it vibrated through my ribcage, sending me into my own frenzy.

"Altara," he panted against my lips.

"I'm sorry," I replied breathlessly.

He squeezed my ass again, and I realised then that he was walking us out of Odeelia's court, leaving the sounds of the wanton sex behind us.

"Is it working?" I said, lifting my head to look at the courtiers.

Zale growled a bestial sound of disapproval, bringing my attention right back to him and his blazing-ocean eyes.

And then he was laying me down in a patch of golden sunset with soft grass under me. The lawn was scattered with flowers, and above us hung a row of hibiscus trees, perfuming the air.

On his knees he loomed over me, and I tugged at his black doublet. He swatted my hand away before pulling on the hem and whipping it over his head. His body was a study of male perfection, and he looked like some wild god, sprawled with obsidian ink. I barely had time to drink him in before he surged down to rest his forehead against mine. "Do not leave me again."

I placed my palms on the broad expanse of his tattooed chest. "I'm sorry, I—"

He peppered kisses along my jaw, down my neck and then on the other side as if I was a precious thing. He spoke in between his kisses. "Do not apologise to me—I will not have it." He pulled away again, holding my neck in one hot, broad palm and looked at me properly, his eyes dark and searching. "There are some things we must do on our own." He shook his head. "We will speak of it later—"

"Agreed." I traced a finger down his groin where his cock was huge and straining under his black pants. He tilted his head back and groaned. Suddenly, there was a knife in his hand, and he was ontop of me, his mouth trailing kisses over the ribbons covering my body, the knife following him as he sliced them open.

They were on me so tightly that with each slice of his knife, each ribbon snapped off with a pop and fell to the side. The sensation of scraping blade and soft lips against my skin was both confusing and enticing, my sex becoming slicker by the second.

By the time Zale's lips reach my core I was writhing with need. He kissed me right over my clit before slicing the ribbon off. I cried out as the flat of his tongue gave one long lick from ass to clit. He groaned, and I tore at his hair. Zale made a sound of pure animal lust as he consumed my sex, clutching my thighs with those calloused hands. My back bowed under the earth-shattering pleasure shooting through me, and I came instantly, masculine sounds of pleasure coming from Zale's throat as he sucked and licked. With a final kiss on my clit, he groaned. "Ah, fuck, Tara, my love."

"Don't *my love* me," I demanded under him. "Fuck me."

A feral gleam flashed across his eyes, and for a moment, I swore his irises dilated into his tiger's form. His voice was an octave deeper when he rasped, "You are so fucking mine, Tara."

I hardly ever blushed, but I did now, heat warming my cheeks and neck as Zale climbed on top of me, his eyes hungrily devouring my body, his skin hot against mine. He fisted his cock, and I was breathless at the sight of its kingly size until he pressed the crown into my entrance, easing me open. My back arched of its own accord as he reminded me of his sheer girth. He let out a sound of pleasure as he sheathed himself completely. I whimpered his name, and his face stuttered with some emotion that made me want to cry.

This had never happened to me before, but I couldn't take

my eyes off him as I panted to adjust to his thick width, enjoying the feeling of him filling me up completely, stretching me out with a wonderful burn. I didn't realise how whole I would feel when he was inside me, and of course, that first time, I'd been completely out of my mind. This time I wanted to be fully aware of everything we were doing to each other.

"Fuck, Tara," he whispered, "you tasted like heaven." I pulled him down to taste myself on him before he kissed his way down my cheek to my ear. "I want this for eternity," he breathed. "I want to be inside your tight little pussy every single day and make you fat with my babies."

I couldn't help the giggle that came from me, and then I gasped with realisation. "Zale, I don't want to get pregnant right now. We never—"

He raised his head to look at me. "I would never put you at risk like that," he whispered. "Boneweaver babies require a ritual. We are conceived through magic."

Relief washed over me. "Oh, thank the Goddess."

He kissed me on the lips. "As much as the urge is killing me, I would not impregnate you without asking you, my little cub."

I laughed at his term of endearment and then quietened as it hit me then. No other man had ever considered the risk of getting me pregnant before. Whatever my old companions Sam and Matt back in Lobrathia had thought about bedding the second-born princess, they'd never once been concerned about planting their seed, even when Sam had come inside me a few times. I'd simply made some excuse and asked Saraya to adjust my ovulation or most of the time, taken the contraceptive tea. I'd assumed men didn't know about these things, but how could they *not* know? They'd just been selfish with their own lust, I was sure of it.

"What's wrong?" Zale growled, and I realised he'd stilled while I'd been having these thoughts.

I came back to the present, my eyes finding him in the orange cast light of the sunset. "No one's ever been concerned about getting me pregnant before. I've always—"

"Altara," he murmured, gently thrusting out and then. "Do not speak of other men while we are making love." That feral look covered his face again, and I could clearly see that his pupils were stuck now in their enlarged, tiger's version. His voice emerged deeper as I saw the thoughts flash through his mind. "*I* am your mate, and you are *mine*." His pace quickened, and I slid my hands down the rippling muscles of his back, feeling him thrusting into me. "You have always been mine, Altara Voltanius."

I slid my hands down to his firm, round ass, digging in my fingernails, and it felt *right* when I said, "And you have always been mine, Ashzale Boneweaver."

As he pounded into me, he pressed his nose into my neck to take a deep inhale. I'd never felt so close to anyone, so close to this sensation of fullness and deep, soulful pleasure.

"Tara," he groaned. "Let me show you how a Boneweaver male fucks his mate."

And he did; he fucked me relentlessly, each grind of his hips hitting my clit just right, sparking fire and heat and rivulets of pressure. I cried out under him, and he tensed and groaned in his own pleasure as the wet sounds of our love-making consumed me.

Something deep within me rose up and up, filling me to the brim, exploding within me like stars shooting across the night sky. Zale's powerful masculine scent filled my nose, and within moments of deep thrusting, he became more beast than man. The sounds of his pleasure filled my body, and I lost myself with the sensation of the stars bursting and thunder booming. He raised his head to look at me, and I saw more than desire and lust in his eyes. It was a full and present knowing and seeing. He saw me—all my darkness, all my fear, all my weaknesses—and still loved me for it.

I came hard, screaming and sobbing his name, clutching onto him as a drowning woman clutched onto a life raft.

His hips stuttered, and he roared into the night so hard I swore the ground beneath us trembled. Tiny sparks of lightning flew from my body, and I knew it probably hurt him, but he showed no sign of it, only shuddering as I felt his cum spurting into me in warm, delicious bursts.

Power swam around us in waves, our combined lust and magic filling the space around us and threading through the air in a spell unlike any other. The fae in the theatre behind us cried out, but I could barely hear their sounds over the roaring in my ears, the sheer sight of Zale's heavy, strong body covering me, protecting me and filling me up.

The world seemed to vibrate, and Zale seemed to light up from the inside, his body working and sweating.

I moaned into his mouth, and he kissed me deeply, stroking my cheek with his thumb. When he looked back at me, a single tear fell from one of his eyes.

"I have waited so long for you, Altara," he whispered. "I promise to love you and protect you and honour you forever."

I closed my eyes and placed my hand over his where it rested on my cheek. When I opened them, his eyes were a soft caress. "I came for you to the island without even knowing it. Perhaps some part of me did know that my mate was here.

That another part of my soul was needing me. I will always be by your side, whatever happens in this life."

When he smiled at me, my entire reality narrowed down to his face, that pure, bestial, masculine beauty unlike anything I'd ever seen.

The cries of pleasure from the theatre were lusty screams now, and our magic filled the air in a dense cloud. Zale's smile became a smirk.

I arched my back as he slid the long length of himself out of me, and I missed him immediately.

Summoning my witch's cloak and boots, I covered myself, and Zale, naked, pulled me up to standing. I nodded at him, and together, hand in hand, we walked back into Odeelia's court. I felt like I was walking through water, heady magic caressing at my skin as we stepped back inside. We were met with the sight of a fifty-person fae orgy, a tumble of naked limbs, writhing, crying out and moaning.

The air smelled like sex and magic, and I shook my head ruefully at the sight, knowing that I'd likely never see something like this ever again.

Odeelia was naked and glistening with sweat as we came upon her and her half-clothed warriors lying over her. One was absently licking her calf, another the hollow of her throat as she cupped his head.

Zale and I loomed over her, our long shadows blocking out the light.

"I could destroy your court for your cruelty," I hissed.

"You could," she murmured, her amber eyes trying to focus on me and failing. "But you could not destroy a blood debt."

I regarded her seriously. "You're right." She stared at me. "Give me Zale for one month of Ellythian time and"—I bought out my forearm and summoned a dagger, pointing its tip against my skin—"and I swear on my blood that I will send my husband to you, and you can keep him forever. Do you accept this in place of the old terms of Zale's debt?"

She frowned and then gave me a lopsided grin. "Yes."

I cut my wrist open, and she opened her mouth. I let three drops fall before stepping back and allowing my magic to heal my wound.

Without another word we turned and left Odeelia's court by the front gate.

I looked up at Zale. "We actually fooled her."

He smirked. "Now all I have to do is hunt down your other husband."

23

MALIKA

Fuck this shit.

The entire Lotus Court could all get fucked as far as I was concerned.

Worse still Atax had sweet-talked his way into sharing a cell with me. And by sweet talked, I mean he grabbed me by my braid and refused to let go when Xalya's Guard came to take us. He must have been using some Old One magic because the Guard were wary and hesitant around him, and they were known for being ruthless and brutal to everyone. He allowed them to put the tourmaline shackles on him, and by allowed I mean, they wouldn't have been able to put them on him otherwise. He'd looked Commander Farrah in the eye and *dared* her to separate us, and by dared, I mean he'd said, "Try it, Priestess, and see me tear down your golden palace brick by brick." The positively black aura pulsing off him made the Commander of Xalya's Guard falter, and she let him have his way. They'd never met an Old One before, I supposed, and it set them off kilter.

I hadn't realised he'd liked me *that* much and still haven't forgiven him for it. Bastard. My scalp still stung. So I got to feel his groin against my ass for a bit, it didn't change a thing between us.

Sitting in the cell opposite him, I glared daggers into his face. He only smirked back, disgustingly happy with himself, no doubt.

Atax was the only person I knew who would smirk while imprisoned. He was completely deranged.

"What are you looking at, grandpa?" I snapped. "We need to figure out a way to get of here, you buffoon."

"You're so beautiful when you're angry Malika. I can't help but stare."

"Then you must be staring at her all the time!" Rani called from the cell next to us.

I rolled my eyes and then realised she couldn't see me. "I'm rolling my eyes, Rani! Everyone shut up and tell me how we're going to get out of this mess."

"We can't shut up and talk at the same time," Kai said mildly from the cell on our other side.

"Kai, I love you with all the depth of my being, but you need to concentrate here."

I stared at Atax right in his blue eyes, but he was already glowering at me. The hair on the back of my neck stood on end every time he looked at me like *that*. Like he was looking *into* me, threatening my very organs.

"Do you love *me* with the depth of your being, Malika?" He said my name like a warm caress down my neck, and my eyes flicked down to his large hands sitting in his lap. Large hands—perfect brown hands laced with large blue veins. "Absolutely *not*," I snapped. Crossing my arms. "Be serious, grandfather. I'm worried about Geravie and Keshmi. The *real* old ones."

Atax scoffed, ignoring the new name I'd given him courtesy of Rani's impeccable yet confused manners. "In case it slipped your attention, my little firebird, the Crown Princess said they were welcome. They'll be comfortable in fine rooms with roast chicken and waited on hand and foot, I'm sure." He leaned back onto the wall as if the matter was settled.

"The Crown Princess," I mused. "The *Spymaster*." I said it mockingly and might have regretted it to account for Pia's feelings, but I just couldn't care to hide my disdain. Because it was completely true: Pia's mother was a bitch. Her grandmother an even bigger one. I should feel bad calling the queen a bitch, but there was something incredibly dark about her, now that I've finally seen her in person. The stories had been bad enough—a stuffed old crone, glaring and bitter, her mouth as sharp as an Ellythian blade. She'd been kind once, apparently. But once Princess Yasani, Altara's mother, left everything changed.

It was Rani's soft voice that flew toward me on butterfly's wings. "Don't say it like that, Malika. That's Pia's mother."

Rani was far too kind and had to be protected at all costs from everyone, especially the shitheads in her town. There were people far more deserving of animosity, and they wasted their time hating her for something she couldn't even control at the time.

They should spend their time hating people like me—a girl who would actually stab someone, given the chance. I was happy to be that person, to be the bitch Pia and Rani couldn't let themselves be.

"She hasn't been Pia's mother for years," I quipped. "Never wrote back to her. Never checked on her or anything. She doesn't deserve our allegiance."

Everyone went silent then, and Pia's silence spoke loudest of them all because I knew a part of her agreed. Atax watched me, like he always did, that lion behind his eyes prowling through to fix me to my spot on my hard stone slab that even my comfy ass couldn't help with. His voice held an undercurrent of darkness and was so quiet that perhaps only Kai was the only other person to hear. "That's treason, firebird."

I shoved my chin in the air. "Pia is the only royal I owe my allegiance to."

A quiet chuckle from the other cell told me Rani agreed.

"I love you, Malika," Pia said quietly.

My heart swelled to the size of the sun. "I love you too." I paused for a beat and then said, "but you need to tell us what to do about this dungeon business."

"It's alright," she said, her voice thick. "They'll come for me. As much as she appeared to know, my mother will want more information. She's just keeping us here to show me and the Old Ones our place."

"Kai and I are used to being in dungeons," Atax murmured.

"Do you remember," Kai said loudly. "The King's torture chambers Atax? There was one that looked a little like this one except for the steel spikes covering the entire floor. One time he made all four of us stand in there in between the spikes for a week."

Atax looked away from me, shrugging. "Yeah, wasn't worse than the cobra venom he put in me that one time."

"He broke my fingers for trying to help you!" Kai said, almost jovially. "I thought we'd have to suck out the venom, but you recovered after a month of screaming. Had no voice left."

"Yeah, even drinking water hurt." Atax huffed in amusement.

Me, Rani and Pia quietly listened to this in horror. I scowled at Atax for talking so casually about the torture of he and his brothers.

"They used to break our arms," Pia said quietly. "To get us used to pain.'

I whirled around in shock and then realised I couldn't see her. "What the fuck do you mean?"

Pia shifted in her cell. "Seven times," she said. "Seven times to break a princess's arms to make her strong."

"Fuck, Pia." I cried, getting to my feet and pressing my face into the bars of the cell, though I couldn't see anything except the dark corridor. "I'm so sorry."

Atax sighed behind me. "Ah, and they called *us* brutal."

I turned to look at him, his black magic-stealing shackles clinking as he scratched an itch on his ear. It's then that I saw it—his obsidian blade earrings caught the dim light as they swung from both his ears. Obsidian blades that could cut through anything.

24
ALTARA

Zale and I walked through the dark of the night-time forest hand in hand for a little while in silence. Wobbles found Zale's shoulder again, having had wisely disappeared for our little interlude. My body felt electric, as if our combined powers and the buzzing inside of me were ready for action. My mind worked at lightning speed, thinking about what we'd just done and what it meant.

I was holding Zale's hand. I'd never held a man's hand before. Not in this way, a way that was comfortable, comforting. It was a foreign thought, but it felt…right. My mind zoned in on the touch of his large palm, his fingers curling around mine, steady and warm.

"It occurs to me," Zale said quietly, rubbing his chin, "that is the first time I've come up with a plan that didn't involve murdering someone."

I couldn't help my grin and didn't mention the fact that he *had* murdered four fae yesterday. I guess he didn't count them. "I've been wondering how you've been dealing with this new state of yours. I suppose this means it's growing on you."

"My mind is...busier than before," he admitted. He abruptly stopped and grabbed me around the waist, pulling me into the hard length of his body. I had to tilt my head to look at him as one of his palms found my cheek. The movement was so intimate that I blinked at the newness of it. Sex was intimacy, I knew, but this type of soft touch from him reached into a place deep within me I didn't know I had. I watched him inhale me, deeply, his eyes navy under the moonlight. His thumb caressed my cheek, and his lips twitched as if he, too, didn't know what to make of this new, softer thing we had between us.

"Perhaps you are a good influence on me, Tara."

I smirked. "I'm a good influence on everyone."

His eyes darkened. "Is it bad that I want you all to myself?"

His voice tugged on something in my lower belly. I wondered how I felt about that: *belonging* to someone else. But this was Zale, not merely *someone* else, and the thought of him with another woman made me want to gag. "I wanted to kill Odeelia for touching you," I said. "Wanted to rip her apart, hair by hair and—" He swallowed my next words with his mouth, and when we broke apart, breathless and suddenly very hot, he abruptly let me go.

"Stop distracting me," he admonished. "We must get some distance between this court and us." He cast me a wry look as I stood there with my arms crossed. His absence from my body was *not* welcome. "Do you trust me?"

"Not one bit, Boneweaver King." I strode ahead into the dark, not caring that I had no idea where I was going.

"Would you...ride me?" His voice was so tentative and yet laced with innuendo that I whirled around to stare at him. My ears popped as feathers burst forth from his skin, and suddenly he was not standing there before me in his human form. Wobbles was blasted off Zale's shoulder, but apparently being used to Zale's explosive shifting, landed next to me in a bent-knee crouch. Zale stood before us in his golden eagle form, huge and tall, with his mighty wings spread out on either side of him. He settled down, shaking himself as if getting used to this body and cocked a head at me, blue eagle's eyes flashing in the moonlight.

"Oh," I said slowly with a laugh. "You mean *ride* you." I jumped forward, keen to see this side of him, wondering if his feathers were as silken as they looked. I reached up to touch his beak and he leaned down and nuzzled my neck. A genuine giggle burst from me at the tickle, and I stroked his soft head, admiring the feel of the powerful muscles under all those feathers.

In that moment, my hand gliding over this powerful crea-ture, I couldn't believe he was supposed to be mine. Zale blinked at me and jerked his head toward his rear. Under-standing, I made my way around. Wobbles was already on Zale's back and scooched forward, clearly showing me where to sit.

"Where do I put my foot?" I asked, simultaneously putting my boot on the place his wing met his body. But Zale didn't seem to mind because his wing felt as hard as iron under me as I launched myself over his body as I would a horse. I wiggled into place, and he made a low sound at the back of his throat.

"Sorry, where do I—"

The asshole leapt into the air, beating his wings, and I surged forward to wrap my arms around his neck, squashing

Wobbles against my body to keep him from falling. The witch's boots helped to balance me as we ascended into the air—Goddess bless Magrin—the mighty beats of his wings rapidly propelling us skyward.

We cleared the tallest trees of the Eternal Forest within seconds, the wind rushing past me, my witch's robe flapping, and I hooted a laugh, trying to hold onto Zale while keeping the sides of my robe together. Zale noticed this and gave an amused cry. A bubble of clear dark surrounded us, and the wind around me disappeared, leaving me breathless but calm. I looked suspiciously down at Zale, wondering how he navigated the wind like this, but he wasn't bothered, still giving strong sweeps of his magnificent wings to gain height.

Eventually, Zale stopped his ascent, and we crested, his body coming parallel to the land. I allowed myself to ease off his neck little and looked out at where we were.

And what a sight it was.

Far below us the Eternal Forest stretched out for what did indeed look like forever—a black canopy of ever-dark stretching in all directions.

The night was clear with not a cloud in sight as we flew below the two crescent moons and many constellations of stars, none of which I recognised.

Zale reached out to me through our glittering thread, gently brushing my arm with a question. Raising my brows I allowed him into my mind…just a little.

His voice sounded in my head, much like Magrin's had, but with Zale's deep timbre, it made goosebumps erupt all over me. *"The stars are different here. All except one."*

He jerked his beak into the sky, and one star that I did recognise shone above them all. *"Altara."* The Great Star. *"We will follow her for a while before we land."*

"*How do we get out of here?*" I asked, frowning at the expanse all around us. "*We need to get back to the others, Geravie will be worried.*"

He told me then about how he was contacted by Kai, which likely meant they'd been scrying for us. His guess was that one of the priestesses of Agnolthi had done it, as it was in the repertoire of spells they taught their acolytes. My frown deepened as I worried what they might have seen while looking for us.

"*I don't think it was a good idea for Pia to go back,*" he said. "*She was a princess in exile, and for Ellythians, returning from punishment without its completion is asking for worse punishment.*"

Zale might have been gone for two hundred years, but he still knew the way the Ellythian Court worked better than I did. I was sure he was right, but on the other hand, Pia would know her mother and grandmother best, right?

I told Zale about what had happened at the Black Castle when the dark god came to me and how I'd woken up to find Ulanna Boneweaver and the rest of the Old Ones.

He said, "*I felt them when I first arrived at your castle, but it wasn't a priority when your life was in danger. I think they understood that*".

"*They were understanding enough when I told them I would likely not be back. Ulanna gave me her serpent's gem so we could stay in contact.*"

"Impressed," Wobbles squeaked. "Honoured."

"I am honoured too, Wobbles," I said, patting his conchshell head. "*She said they would make their way back to Boneweaver Island when the island allowed them to.*"

"*It won't be long now that I'm here,*" he said contentedly. "*Let them give Raen a little surprise*".

We lapsed into a pensive silence as I thought about this, absently stroking the smooth golden feathers of his neck.

Eventually, when Zale felt we were a safe distance away from the carnal fae court, he began his descent. I clutched onto him as he dived down, vaguely wondering if I could shoot an arrow whilst on his back. It'd take a bit of practise to get my balance right, but I was sure I could do it.

Zale chose a clearing to land in, and from this height, I could marvel at the glowing blue pools I could see dotted around this section of the forest. There were hundreds of them in different sizes and hues, clustered and steaming into the cool night air.

We landed, and without warning, Zale morphed back into his human form with an explosive *crack* of his bones.

I cried out and found myself clinging onto the broad expanse of his naked back, but Zale cackled like a madman and slipped his hands under my thighs to keep me in a piggyback. As Wobbles climbed up to his shoulder, I slapped his other shoulder in protest, but he only smirked and began walking us through a copse of trees, one of his thumbs stroking my thigh. I wasn't wearing any underwear, and with my core pressed to his smooth skin, I quietened immediately, hoping he wouldn't notice...or perhaps hopeful that he would.

We cleared the trees and were met with glowing blue and green lights mixed through rising steam. I gasped as he let me slide down his back, staring out at the twenty odd pools sitting unassuming and unoccupied.

I turned to look up at Zale when I got a whiff of myself. I wrinkled my nose. "I need to wash," I admitted. "It wasn't a great priority...before, and Magrin and the witches did the best they could to dress me from afar."

He kissed my temple and grunted in assent, taking my hand and leading me through the grass towards the biggest pool.

Something rustled in the trees on the other side of the clearing.

"If anyone is watching, I will have their head!" Zale cheerfully called out.

Giggles chimed, both male and female, before feet pattered away. Zale sighed, but I was in awe of the fact that here in this forest, there were so many creatures.

Dropping my robe immediately, Zale, to my surprise, stepped before me and crouched, unlacing my boots. I grinned at the vision of his kingly body at my feet, his fingers deft as they loosened the many laces before carefully pulling the boots off and setting them aside.

Naked and surprisingly content, I carefully climbed into the pool, feeling him close behind me. The water was warm, almost hot, and there were cakes of soap sitting in a woven basket off to the side.

I raised my brows at it as Zale waded in behind me. "The beings that tend to these pools are attentive," he said. "But discreet. They're strange little things, but they like grooming people."

I turned and quirked a brow. "Have you been...groomed?"

He cocked his head as if trying to figure out how he felt about it now. "Yes. But I did not have a mate then."

Something warmed my stomach as he said this, and delighted by the deep water tickling my nipples, I surged forward, heading for the soap. But Zale chased me and plucked the soap from my hand. He turned me around and placed his fingers under my chin and tilting my head back, kissed my lips, then my neck and began soaping me. Behind us Wobbles dipped his legs into the pool and kicked them to make tiny splashes.

Zale's hands were gentle on first my chest, then my breasts, the sliding sensation of the soap and his fingers at once comforting and arousing. His eyes were heavy with desire, but when I reached for him, he tutted at me. So I let him soap me up as he pleased, working his way down to my stomach until he got to the apex of my thighs and slid his fingers down my centre.

I fell toward him, a long moan brushing past my lips.

"We must concentrate, Tara," he admonished.

"What?" I said breathlessly as his fingers continued to slide through me, washing me with efficiency.

"I'm cleaning you—be quiet. I must do your hair too."

But I was squirming under him, trying not to giggle. "No, I—"

But he only growled at my protests, and to my great annoyance, left my sex to wet my head.

"That's not fair," I grumbled.

"There are leaves and dirt in your hair," he said, frowning in concentration and completely ignoring my wandering hands. "Can you float back?"

I could hardly argue with that, so I allowed my body to float on the water in front of him and placed a hand on his naked waist while he lathered up his hands. His strong fingers massaged my scalp so gently, and I was surprised at how good it felt to be treated like something delicate. He worked my hair more softly than any of my maids ever had, and I chuckled at the thought. Then I remembered he had long hair too—not as long as mine, but it was still the longest I'd seen on a male, although on *him* it looked at once beautiful and threatening. I stared at his frowning face as he worked. "Is sex different with your emotions back?" I asked.

He glanced at me with a smile. "The first time we had sex I was…shocked. Before it was just straight fucking to clear my energy. I didn't really think about it too much. I usually took them from behind so that their sounds didn't annoy me."

Unexpected jealousy flared within me, bright and bitter. "I'll kill any woman that looks at you," I said savagely, then frowned at myself for being that sort of woman. Was it a bad thing? Zale was my husband, after all. It felt natural to be that way.

His grin was wicked. "I know, Tara." His face softened in thought. "It's like nothing I've ever experienced. I…thought I was going to explode from the inside."

"Me too," I murmured. "I…I'm sorry about what happened to you when you were a child."

Zale put one arm on my stomach and another on my back to raise me to standing. "It's odd to look back on something you didn't have any emotion about at the time." He admitted. "Even with Wobbles helping me with my emotions, I still don't know what to feel. My father trained me to be a ruthless killer. To take what I want. And those things are habit for me, whatever my emotions are now."

"I still think you're a good person," I objected as he wrung water from my hair.

"I am not the *same* person." He sighed. "I did a lot of things I am not proud of and I cannot take those things back, but perhaps I can try and make up for them."

He was hardly less murderous, I thought wryly, remembering how easily he'd killed the fae that had touched me.

Zale pulled me into my arms and the warmth and smell of his skin was like a balm to my tired bones.

"Husband," I murmured, trying the word out in a way I never had before—in a way that wasn't mocking.

He ran his hand down my arm. "I like it when you call me that."

I traced the lion tattoo on his pectoral muscle. "Don't think you have it easy now, *husband*. These new emotions of yours might very well get us into more trouble than I do."

He laughed through his nose, watching my finger trace the beak of the eagle lower on his side. "Do not worry about me. As long as we are together, I won't go insane. Your presence calms me down." He kissed the top of my head, and from that spot, tingles rushed down through my entire being. It was such as loving gesture that it made me quieten. He liked taking care of me, I thought, and that feeling was foreign, coming from a man. His hands were possessive on me, but not in an overpowering way—more like the same way he might care for a favoured weapon. It made me feel powerful to have him hold me like that.

I didn't think being with a man, as his woman, could feel like that.

"How do we get out of the Forests of Eternity?" I blinked up at him, my lids growing heavy with a wave of tiredness as the day's events caught up with me.

He tucked a strand of hair behind my ear, his eyes warm on my face. "Let us rest for tonight, and tomorrow I will take us to some beings who used to help me."

He washed himself quickly and then scooped me up into his arms and easily climbed out of the pool. Using a clean brown towel, he set me down and dried me off as one would a child. I grinned and laughed at him, though somehow I didn't feel like a child under his care.

"We must help Pia" I said determinedly. "Whatever will

happen to her in Ellythia, she'll need our help to placate our grandmother."

Out of his own astral repository, Zale summoned a long white, clean shirt for me to wear and tugged it over my head. I had underestimated how good a bath would feel after so long living in my own filth in that dark castle. Fresh and clean with my eyes drooping, I barely noticed where he led me, but rather quickly, we were on something soft, and he tucked me against his side. With my back to his front and with Zale softly kissing a sweet line down my neck, I fell asleep.

2 5

ALTARA

I woke up on my stomach on top of something warm and firm. Under my ear a steady heartbeat thundered. Zale's broad hand swept down my back, leaving warm embers in its wake, and he continued down to palm my ass, squeezing gently.

"My mate," he said, his voice deep with sleep.

I blinked my eyes open to find the orange glow of dawn streaming through a canopy of trees. Tiny grey fuzzy creatures pottered in the grass around us, gently squeaking. They looked like floppy-eared rabbits but stood on their hind legs, and three of them were piling a woven basket full of strawberries.

"Go," Zale commanded, and they squeaked in alarm and scattered in haste, dropping the fruits as they went.

I let out a laugh of disbelief. "They're so cute!"

But Zale's hand was creeping under the shirt I was wearing, warming my bare ass cheeks, both hands now sliding upwards. I moaned in approval—the feel of his hands a sweet morning welcome on my hungry skin. I positioned my legs to land on either side of his, pressing my moistening centre on his groin where his cock was already iron. His hands pushed my shirt over my shoulder blades, and I obliged him, raising my arms so he could slip the shirt off completely. I realised that he was already naked, having never put clothes back on last night.

I looked down at him, his strong, tattooed, muscled body, his dark hair strewn across the soft blanket—a king under my command. I grinned at him, but his eyes were serious as he slid his hand behind my neck and pulled me toward his nose, inhaling deeply.

"Mine," he rasped. "All mine."

Something in my lower stomach swooped at the sound of him possessively claiming me in *that* animalistic voice, and I found that I didn't mind it at all. His cock strained under me, huge and thick, and I barely had time to say anything back before he lifted my hips up high, the crown of his cock springing up to kiss my entrance. I moaned at the feel of him and placed my hands on the plain of his chest. There was a fiery heat in his eyes, and I was breathless just to look upon him. He squeezed my hips and lowered me inch by glorious inch onto his huge manhood. I whimpered, breathing through that delicious burn as he stretched me open. He groaned. "Ah, fuck, Tara. You feel so fucking good around my cock."

I stared at him, panting, as I allowed myself to take him completely, claiming him in my own way. "Oh, Goddess!" I gasped, the sensation overwhelming me, and I rocked my hips a little to test the movement out.

Zale hissed, the veins in his throat and arms showing the restraint this was taking him. I leaned forward to run my fingers over his jugular, and he bounced me on his cock, making my breasts jiggle. I laughed breathlessly at the command he had over my body because every other man had followed *my* directions, and I had never let them assume control of me like this. But Zale under me, moving me in the way he wished, was a new and supreme kind of pleasure. That this beast would sate his desire, moaning and writhing from me was a thrill. That I could make him lose control of himself was an alluring sort of power.

I moved myself on his cock, rocking and sliding my hips, enjoying the rivulets of pleasure spiralling through my pussy and up my spine.

"You're so wet," he bit out as I rode him, picking up my speed until he lost it completely and grabbed me around my waist and flung me to the grass while we were still connected and began fucking me against the ground. I yelped in surprise, then groaned, tendrils of punishing pleasure rising and coiling like smoke inside of me. I grabbed his face with both hands and kissed him, our tongues dancing together, wet and warm. He broke off to lick one of my nipples, his tongue sweeping over my skin as his cock pummelled into me over and over again until I was consumed by the feeling of him and that thrum of our magical bond. I saw stars in my vision, and everything burst into magical flame around us. I cried out as ecstasy burst from me, digging my fingernails into his skin. Zale roared my name, pumping his cum into me in glorious warm bursts. I wanted all of him, I realised— wanted all of his sweat, his skin, his cum in me, around and over me. Panting, his heavy body came to rest on top of me, and we simply breathed each other's scent. I'd never felt more sated in my life, never thought this level of pleasure was even possible. As Zale's chest moved against mine, his fingers curling around my waist as we just breathed, a tender feeling unwound inside my core. The thread that bound us shone like sunlight, and I realised that I didn't simply want to be his. I *needed* to be his, and I needed him to be mine.

A s we dressed a question came to mind: "You called me Altara Voltanius, back at the court. Not Boneweaver."

"Why would you need to change your name?" He frowned. "Ellythian males take their wives' names, but Old Ones keep their names as they are. You are mine, and I am yours. Anyone with a nose can scent that. For Old Ones it is a language greater than any voice can speak out loud."

"But humans cannot scent. They do not speak that sort of language."

"Of what concern is it to me what humans think?" Zale cocked his head. "And Ellythian humans all have magic, so they can feel these things anyway."

It was a good point, but I wondered if my grandmother would see it that way. How she would react to one of her grandchildren being married and mated to a Boneweaver king?

I glanced at Zale, his powerful, tall form, his muscles flexing as he pulled a black shirt over his head. He seemed infallible, like no power on earth could stop him. But Magrin's words in my ear echoed, *"There are many ways to harm a person without killing them."*

Something in me clenched, dark and cold around my heart. The thought of something hurting Zale made me want to hurl and kill someone at the same time. A whisper of dark smoke fluttered around my vision, and Zale reached for me, pulling me into his arms.

"Breathe, my little star. Send the dark thoughts away."

I looked up at him in shock. "How is it that you're dealing with this better than I am?"

His gaze darkened. "I am used to thinking dark thoughts, Altara. It's all I knew for two hundred and twenty-six years."

I let his eyes hold me while I breathed and felt his breath moving in and out of that powerful chest. He was alive and well and whole, and so was I; there was no need to worry about something that had not passed. He tucked a strand of hair behind my ear and smiled as if he found something endearing. "Turn around."

I obliged him, if only to see what he was up to, only to find him combing the now dry strands of my hair with some type of comb. "I can do that," I protested.

"You can do anything, Tara," he murmured as he started to braid my hair. "But I am your mate. It is my job to take care of all your needs, no matter how small."

That warmed the last of the coldness in me, and I chuckled. "That means I have to take care of you too."

He grumbled, "Only if you want to." Surprisingly deft with braiding, he tied my hair off with a length of twine, and I turned around.

"On your knees, sir."

He gave me an amused smile as if he didn't quite understand what I was trying to do, and I scoffed at him, tugging the bone comb from his fingers as I started on his hair. His glossy locks landed down to his shoulder blades, and I'd seen him wearing it in a ponytail often enough, so I combed it and tied it low with the cord Wobbles handed me.

"So pretty," I said, satisfied.

He leaped to his feet and grabbed me, crushing his lips to

mine in a punishing kiss, nipping my lower lip before pulling away. "Let's go home."

We hiked on foot this time, staying in the shade of the trees for half the day before a strange grey mist enveloped the forest.

"It's not dangerous," Zale assured me as I inhaled the mist. It tasted strangely sweet on my tongue. The bubbling of a river sounded from nearby, and eventually, we came to a great lake, its water a robust pink bordered by purple trees. There was definitely something strange in the soil and air here to bring about such colours.

An old rotten boat rested on the shore with mouldy paddles. "I must repair this so we can use it," said Zale, hauling the dinghy higher upon the shore and looking at it with experienced eyes.

"You know how to repair boats?" I asked, frowning at the decrepit thing. "It looks ancient."

"I don't think anyone's used it since I did last. Ah—here, see?" He pointed to a spot on its hull, and I squinted at it. Roughly engraved were the letters *AB*. Ashzale Boneweaver.

It was such an unexpected thing for him to have done that I let out a laugh. He narrowed his gaze on me. "What?"

"Nothing," I said, summoning a dagger and carving my own *AV* next to it.

Zale fixed the thing with planks of purple wood from a tree he felled himself and hammered it together with the butt of his obsidian blade. I admit that I stared a little too long while he swung a summoned axe against the thick trunk of the tree over and over again, the muscles of his shoulders and back making his tattoos move seductively.

He worked fast, but by the time I woke up from a nap and he was finished, it was late into the night.

The purple trees glowed in the dark, illuminating the entire lake like we were in some ethereal dream. I plonked myself inside the repaired boat, and Zale pushed it out into the water. He deftly leapt in, taking up his new paddles to row us to the other side of the lake which I realised was actually an inlet—a termination point to a small river.

"We must be quiet," Zale murmured. "Or they will not come."

"Who?" I whispered, looking around wide eyed into the purple light. The trees were reflected into the water of the river, making us surrounded by dappled purple on every side.

Zale smiled faintly as if remembering something pleasant. "You'll see."

Since I loved a good secret, I sat on my hands and eagerly watched the trees passing us by.

I'd never been a romantic. Sam had brought me flowers once, and I'd chastised him for it, and of course, I'd never actually courted anyone—none of the lord's sons in Lobrathia had been suitable at all. I'd relegated men to a space in my mind that was only really for two things: fighting and sex.

But this? Rowing down a calm river with the stars above us and the luminescent trees around us, with Zale doing all the physical work, his large muscles coiling and tensing was... Well, I couldn't imagine anything more romantic than this. My stomach warmed like glowing coals. The only thing missing was wine. I looked at Zale, who was scanning the trees ahead of us with acute intensity, not paying any attention to me at all. I purposefully shifted in my seat, and he smiled without looking at me.

"Tara." His voice was a gentle caress tinged with meaning. It made me squeeze my thighs together.

"Zale," I countered, albeit a little breathlessly.

His smile widened into a grin, and I simply stared at him and his perfect face. "Why are you staring? Are you trying to decide how best to assassinate me?"

I grinned wickedly. "Can you die from having sex?"

His smile dropped and his face became serious. "I think so."

I quietened, wondering what he was thinking. "I want you to know," I began carefully. "That I do not judge you for what you did in the past. It means nothing to me."

"It should." His features darkened completely now, a grey cloud covering his body.

I crossed my arms. "You've done good since then. Taking me on romantic boat rides, for example."

His lips twitched. "Is that what this is? I thought I was trying to save your sorry behind."

"My behind is not sorry at all. And if you continue talking like that, you won't be seeing it ever again."

Zale stopped rowing, his shoulders tense, his eyes upon me like hot pokers. "No one is taking you away from me again." His voice was so dangerously quiet I stilled under it. My cheeks heated at the possessiveness in that voice. I would not take that lying down.

"I seem to remember that it was me who saved *your* sorry ass from Odeelia's court."

Zale began rowing again. "I'll give you that one. But that tactic won't work at Cheshni's Court."

Mention of my grandmother's name soured my mood

immediately, and I swore under my breath. "Goddess Almighty, I dare say it won't."

"They're going to see your priestess mark and not know what to think."

That stopped me in my tracks completely. I hadn't seen myself in a mirror for a while, but I could feel Agnolthi's mark was on me. What it meant, however, everyone except me seemed to know. The memory of Agnolthi's volcanic eyes made me twitch with fear and excitement all at once.

Zale tensed in his seat and stopped rowing again, letting us coast gently forward. "There they are," he breathed. "Don't turn around, just wait until you see them on the bank."

I obliged, trying to keep my weight balanced so we didn't keel over into the water.

In the next lot of trees that passed us by, huge white-feathered birds roosted on the long branches.

"Not birds," I whispered. "Owls."

They were as big as Zale was in his eagle form, and almost as intimidating. Pure-white feathers but deep, knowing, amber eyes looked upon us.

Zale inclined his head, and the two owls on my left bowed back. Surprise spun through me light and fluttery. "They're beautiful," I murmured.

Zale's eyes watched something behind me. "Try and be still, Tara. The boat might—"

I keeled sideways as the boat rocked violently, but just before I hit the water, the boat righted itself, and a firm wing pushed me back into my seat. Two huge owls sat on the rim of our boat, one on either side and I had to cane my neck to look at them properly.

"The jungle always wins," boomed a low voice coming from the white owl on my left.

"The wind carries all secrets," Zale replied seriously.

"Ashzale," said the owl. "We meet again, and the winds tell me you are a king now."

"A pleasure as always, Lightwing," Zale said, looking steady as ever. "My mate called you beautiful."

Both owls turned to look at me, and I blushed as their amber eyes took me in. Talking to animals was no longer a strange thing for me since I'd spoken to Ulanna, and well, even before that, my mate was a beast too, wasn't he?

"You are kind," Lightwing said. "Be welcome in our domain." He turned back to Zale. "I take it you are looking to leave?"

"We are," Zale said, smiling at him.

Lightwing exchanged a look with the second owl. This one was tawny, I thought, but his colour was made grey when mixed with the purple glow of the trees.

"We are pleased to see you well. But there is word from the east, King Ashzale," this owl stated. "Dark words. Dark deeds as sent by the king of Black Court himself." He plucked something out from under his wing and flopped it into Zale's hand. It was a piece of parchment. Zale opened it, revealing a black wax seal and a message written in black ink.

Profound dread wound its way through me as Zale's entire body became coiled and tense as if he were preparing for an attack. Black Court was in the Dark Fae Realm, and whatever it was, had to do with the fae on the Continent.

"What's wrong?" I asked reluctantly.

Zale's throat bobbed up and down. "He is back," Zale said. "Tara, the Reaper is back."

Just as I'd predicted, my mother called for me three days later. She was nothing if not poetic, and the three-day rule had stood for as long as the Lota family had reigned over this island. As Commander Farrah and the soldiers of Xalya's Guard escorted me out of my cell, I gave Rani a consoling smile. My poor, sweet friend would worry herself sick over this, on top of everything else she was mentally dealing with. We'd spoken at length about what to expect when the time came for me to be taken, and since we'd had nothing to do down here, my mother expected us, correctly, to fret. Atax and I had kept everyone mostly calm, though Malika would not be quelled by anyone except me. A few sharp words, and she'd quietened her plans to escape using Atax and Kai's obsidian blades.

It was all well and good to get out of this gaol—but what then? Our purpose here was to speak to my mother and grandmother. That was paramount. We needed a plan to fix the rising demon problem on Boneweaver Island, and a way to get Zale and Altara out of the Forests of Eternity.

Both things would be difficult.

I was sore and exhausted, hungry and sweaty, as I dragged my booted feet over the golden marble tile of the familiar corridors. However sorry a state I was in, I had faced worse during my childhood education. My brother Paalus and I, along with the other royal children, had faced a gruelling training as part of our curriculum. It involved pain and starvation and training for torture.

Demons could not be underestimated, and our grasp on security had been tenuous these last twenty years that we'd lost the Temari Blade. Worse, Umali had not declared a high priestess for her Order in years, so we did not even have a temple leader to help find it.

The gilded halls of the Lotus palace were almost comforting in their familiarity, as I was directed to my mother's offices. I've been questioned by her before but only in mock training situations. It was almost funny that the techniques she'd used to teach me to defend against, she would now be using against me.

Physical torture was bad enough, but magical torture would be a slap to the soul. At one time I would have been able to defend myself. Now I hardly had the means to. The only thing I did have was the strongest mental fortress my mother had ever seen. After the incident no one had been able to breach it. The official palace healer had said that it was a response to what had happened, and it might very well be what saved me now.

Farrah and her Guard strode me through the open doors to the suite of the Crown Princess—a place that might have once been mine.

Now? I risked being disowned completely. We all knew it, though I'd dare not speak it out loud these past years. A Lota princess without magic did not exist. Therefore, *I* could not exist as Princess.

My mother waited for me, her slender back facing us as she looked out the wide windows that overlooked the city. Her lean frame was even leaner compared to three years ago, making the smooth muscles of her biceps stand out where I could clearly see them under the capped sleeves of her close-fitting gown. Her hair was in an elaborate braid worn in a mature style down her back, the gown a crisp emerald green to match her eyes. Our eyes.

They seated me in a wooden chair, uncomfortable but sturdy under me. I recognised its varnished strength because I was sure I'd sat in this very same chair before. Ellythians never threw away their furniture.

"Mother," I said politely, bowing in my seat, my shackles clanking. They were plain steel shackles, and it was an insult to be wearing them, but…a warranted insult.

My mother slowly turned around from the window, and behind me, I felt Xalya's Guard taking up quiet positions by the door. Someone clicked it shut, and the sound was a knell that set off the tension in the room. It was thick between each of us, beginning with my mother's disapproving eyes and ending with my tight ones.

The backs of my eyes burned, but I would *not* show her weakness. When she spoke, her words were fingernails gouging at my soul.

"You disgust me," she hissed. "Have you not brought shame to us *enough*?" Her posture was ramrod straight, the sheathed blade at her side, shiny and—I knew—sharpened compulsively daily. The Lotus Blade. The hilt was an emerald set in gold, passed down from heir to heir for a thousand years. It was an honour to carry the blade of Ellythia's daughter, Matrika Lota, and one that would likely not pass to me.

It was odd that despair did not find me upon realising this. Instead a sort of fresh relief swept through me in the way of a cool ocean wind.

"I come out of necessity," I said calmly. "Not because I am disobedient."

"You bring two Old Ones to our doorstep. Two old enemies." She stalked toward me, lethal grace in a mature frame. Everyone knew that Rahana Lota was a master swordswoman. She could cut me to pieces in three swipes, and I'd seen her do it before. She taught me and Paalus sword craft, before handing us over to Xalya's priestesses, after all. I closed my eyes briefly because suddenly those graceful strides reminded me of a time when we'd practiced together. When, hopeful for my future, she had made an effort to be kind and loving. Hoping that I could be an honourable queen one day, forged and made by her to be the best. Aunt Yasani leaving had been a near-fatal wound for my mother that I did not think she'd ever recovered from. She had never wanted the throne in the first place, but the fact that my grandmother refused to give it to her was a blow of a thousand bloody whips to her pride, nonetheless. It had made her hard over the years. And bitterness had made way for brutality. But she'd never taken that out on her children until I'd made an error in judgement of colossal proportions. I could have salvaged the family name and put Aunt Yasani's deflection behind us, left for the history books. Instead I'd made it worse. Showing everyone how defective the Lota line had become.

One mad queen.

One abdicated queen.

One crown princess who didn't want the throne

One princess who had no magic.

We were well and truly a defective family. Ellythia would be ashamed to see her noble line ruined in this way.

I found that my hope suddenly lay with my cousin Altara. A girl with enormous power. Perhaps Ellythia could win back our name yet. If only Aunt Yasani had never left, and I would have been content to be a princess without a burden on my head.

"There are only four Old Ones in existence in Ellythia," I said in response to her question. "They come because they want to help. They are not enemies."

I knew she did not believe me by the set of her lips and the ferocious cross of her arms. She couldn't be a good spymaster when it came to me. She should have given the interrogation to someone else less biased. I didn't think she hated me, but she didn't trust me, which was worse.

"How naive you are. Three years older and still daydreaming fanciful stories in that lazy brain of yours."

I bit the inside of my cheek to stomach this barb. It's an old one, and I haven't heard it in years. It's strange hearing old retorts, and old insults thrown at me because I'm not the same person that left here, but my mother could only see me in one way: As the disappointing princess, she might have to disown. Exile had been a pretty solution. Keep me away, and the world might have forgotten about me and my uselessness.

She slapped down a letter on the table. "Tell me you are not a part of this."

It was marked with the black wax seal bearing a dragon. I raised my brows as I recognised it. Pulling it toward me, my shackles clanked loudly.

The Green Reaper has awakened. Prepare.
—*King Daxian Darkleaver of Black Court*

SHOCK WAS AN ICY BUCKET OF WATER OVER MY HEAD. THE Continent housed the Fae Realm, both light and dark, and Black Court was where the crypt of the Reaper lay, where he'd been sleeping for the last fifty years after a battle in a distant realm that almost killed him.

"The Reaper?" I breathed. "The Reaper is alive?"

She eyed me, raising her chin when she realised I was not aware of this.

"Not only alive, he is back, and my spies tell me that he has taken over the subterranean demon court under Lobrathia. He aims to take back up his campaign to rule over the Continent."

But he would come for us first. A chill like I'd never known locked me in a cage of ice. "Dear Goddess."

We didn't have the Temari Blade to protect us. We didn't have the Boneweaver Bow. We had nothing except our might and magic.

And then my mother asked a question that grabbed me by the throat, "Have you been fucking demons in the time you've been away?"

I stared at her. "I have not fucked *anyone*, Your Highness." How could I, after what I'd done?

She levelled me with a gaze made to peel off my skin and carve my bones into tiny pieces. To be on the receiving end of one of her lethal glares was a nightmare made reality.

I mastered my fear under that gaze. I promised myself that I would not cower under her fury. That I would not show weakness. So I gathered my wits together and said, "What are you going to do?"

She continued to stare at me.

Of course, she wouldn't tell me. Handing Boneweaver Island back to the demons had been fine *before*. But now the Reaper was back? We'd let him have one third of the Isles without a fight.

It had been a mistake on my grandmother's part, and arrogance had been its cause. My mother knew that, but would she try and repair the damage or in her pride, make it worse?

"Raen is still there," I urged. "Raen Boneweaver. He is the Boneweaver King's sorcerer and will protect their island."

"How quickly you've forgotten," she scoffed. "They taught you nothing at that school."

My mind raced as she gave me a moment to try and figure out what she meant. Of course, I failed because she made a disapproving sound and said drolly, "Ashzale's father was sworn to the Reaper. His son was to be the Reaper's greatest weapon."

It was my turn to stare.

We'd been so focused on the demons that we'd forgotten the truth of Zale's story. The priestess at Lisanthi's temple had shown us the written record of Zale's birth. That his curse of heart-shadow had been placed by the Reaper. When he'd grown too powerful, Zale's father had demanded the Reaper kill him and his brothers. But the Reaper refused and instead, put them to sleep in their tombs until the time came to collect them and use them for his war.

I suppressed the urge to swear out loud because I could see how this would look from my mother's perspective.

"Altara broke the curse," I quickly said. My mother's eyes

showed their first hint of uncertainty. She would have sought the truth of Zale's story as soon as she had word of his reappearance. "Altara is his star-born mate. The key the three queens made. She broke the curse around his heart, and now he would have his conscience back. The Old Ones fought *with* us, against the demons. They killed them all. They will not align with the Reaper."

My mother narrowed her eyes. "You think you know the minds of the Old Ones? Two-hundred-year-old preternatural beings who kill for pleasure? They are savage beasts full of the Reaper's magic. Whatever they have told you—whatever you think you know about them, you have been blind. They have you fooled."

I shook my head. "You do not know them—"

My mother slapped me with the force of her magic. My head violently flipped to the left and it smarted as if she'd spat on me. I had been hit by her many times in the training arena, but she'd never struck me in anger. It left me in a reeling panic. I clenched my teeth to stop the backs of my eyes burning, but I couldn't help the tear that slid out as I felt a dark web of realisation settled over me. This woman was no longer my mother. She no longer thought of me as her daughter.

Rahana Lota lowered her head to hiss in my ear. "Do not tell me what I do not know."

And then I remembered. She hated being accused of not knowing something. She prided herself on being all knowing. It was arrogant, but it had been borne of the betrayal at the hands of her sister. She could never have known that Yasani was going to leave her, and since that day, she'd made it her personal business to obsessively know everything about everyone so that no one would betray her ever again.

I swallowed down the emotion finger-crawling up my throat and said instead, "I know them, mother. They will not deflect to the Reaper."

"Take her," my mother said with such disgust I felt like waste on the bottom of her shoe. "Get her out of my sight and throw her into the Pit."

Panic enveloped me like a cobra's tail wrapped around my throat. "Please, no," I choked, staring at her in abject horror. In her face all I saw was obsidian night, shadowed in grief and disgust.

Xalya's Guards grabbed me by my arms and hauled me backward. The chair tipped back with me, and I had to lift my feet up to avoid dragging the chair as they roughly pulled me toward the door. That snake of fear around my throat tightened as I realised she would not let me see my family. "Let me see Paalus!" I screamed. "Let me see Father!"

But as my mother watched me being dragged out like some Daanav spy, I saw the severe set to her eyes and mouth, and it sent me spiralling into a mad panic. She considered me a traitor to the court. She would never let me see my father or my little brother. Instead she would leave me to waste away in the abyss of sensory deprivation that was the Pit. The punishment we gave to our worst criminals.

27
ALTARA

It was not often that I was rendered speechless, but as I sat in a boat with two giant owls and Zale, I stared at the three of them.

"The Reaper is back," I repeated lamely in an attempt to fill the tense silence. Something truly terrifying flashed across Zale's handsome face before it vanished. I was left looking at dark-blue eyes like the deep sea simmering in the moments before a storm.

The Reaper was a story. A creature I had relegated to the back of my mind as a thing of myth that had lived two hundred years ago.

Yet I had felt its power. I had known it and felt it in the magic that had held Zale's heart. The dark shadow that had taken so much from him. He was very real and very malevolent.

"I assumed he'd be dead by now?" I said in what I hoped wasn't a stupid voice. "It was all so long ago..." My eyes dipped down to Zale's chest where I'd shot him in the heart with my arrow of void.

"He lives," the golden owl said. "It took him this long to wake from the injuries from an old battle in another realm, but he walks the Dark Fae Realm as we speak."

I sat bolt upright. "The dark fae realm?" I looked from Zale to the owl. "My sister is there! She was betrothed to the Crown Prince of Black Court."

Zale's gaze on me was eagle sharp. This was the first he'd heard of it, of course. I hadn't told anyone in Ellythia about it; there hadn't been time—or reason to.

"Your sister?" The white owl, Lightfeather, said slowly. He exchanged a significant look with the golden owl in a way that had me wanting to shake them both.

"What do you know?" I asked sharply, gripping the sides of the boat.

"There has been disruption in Lobrathia," Lightfeather said solemnly. "Demons have orchestrated an attack. They hold the Quartz throne now."

"*Demons?*" I shrieked. "Goddess! And my father? My sister? What do you know of them?" I was trembling now, my heart pummelling against my ribs in panic. This could not be happening. We'd both left my father to ruin; it was completely our fault.

"Tara," Zale's voice was a spear into the shroud of my rising panic. "Let us listen to what they have to tell us."

I swallowed, looking at him, trying to focus. He gave me a single nod that told me he knew the enormity of this and understood. That single movement gave me more heart than anything that had happened between us so far.

"The Princess Saraya had been taken by the subterranean demons until recently. She and her mate have made it back to the fae realm."

Relief poured through me, warm and true. My sister was

capable—I knew that. But her mate... She and the prince of Black Court had been down there together?

"This letter came from the King of Black Court," Zale said. "He was the first to know, Tara."

I nodded at Zale. The dark fae king had been a remarkable figure when I'd seen him at Saraya's betrothal. He had to have this under control, hadn't he?

But I could not miss the way Lightfeather shifted on the side of the boat, his huge claws scraping the wood.

Zale rowed us toward the riverbank where more owls— white, tawny, golden and in some cases, black—watched us with sharp, intelligent eyes. Some muttered to each other in soft voices.

One of them caught my eye. A tawny with proud eyes, who stood away from the others, straight backed and strong except for the torn wing he tucked tightly to his side as if to protect it. As we got off the boat, I wandered toward him, scanning the injury. I could tell that this owl did not wish to be approached, but I felt compelled by my own power to move toward him.

Zale said nothing as I peered through the purple lumines-cence of the trees, but I felt him close behind me as I tenta-tively inclined my head to the tawny owl.

"Greetings," I called softly.

After a moment he bowed his head and narrowed his eyes upon me. I knew at once that I would have to approach this with care.

"It would do me great honour to restore the integrity of your wing, noble sir. I have such a power."

The owl visibly stiffened, and I would have heard a pin drop within that forest with the way the other owls watched with bated breath. He said nothing.

I felt Zale's heat at my back, and I looked up at him to see if he had any ideas.

"Wing-brother's injury was caused by goblins," he murmured.

Ah, so the very goblins I'd ruled over, and this owl knew that. No wonder he didn't want anything to do with me.

"I can only ask for forgiveness by rectifying the harm caused," I said solemnly. "I am sorry, wing-brother."

The owl spread both wings, one full, one stunted, and clumsily lowered himself to ground level. "I would be grateful," he said in a deep croak. "To be touched by the magic of Agnolthi's priestess."

Ah, so the mark on my forehead had value after all.

I smiled at him and let my power loose. It zipped forward eagerly, enveloping wing-brother's wing and funnelling the injury back at me. My arm stung with sharp pain, but I held my ground and gritted my teeth as my bones cracked and split in two, deep in my bicep.

Squeezing my eyes shut, I teetered backward, but Zale was there to catch me, his hard chest warm at my back, both his arms coming around my waist.

My own magic flooded my arm, sealing the crack and fusing the bones back together, simultaneously growing the bones in the owl's wing and regenerating tendons, ligaments and feathers. I was sweating and panting at the exertion, but I pushed through.

Zale lowered his head, and brushing his lips against my ear, he whispered, "My beautiful, strong mate."

"Awe," Wobbles squeaked from Zale's shoulder.

I flushed as Zale's taut warmth and smell became a pleasant distraction from the burn of healing. Before I knew it, I was done, and when I opened my eyes, wing-brother was standing before me, staring at a brand new wing, stretched outwards, strong and healthy.

The owls hooted around us, in joy or surprise I couldn't tell which.

"You are of the old blood," wing-brother said a little breathlessly, his beak clipping on the vowels. "Princess, I cannot thank you enough."

"Your health is thanks enough," I said, rubbing my eyes.

Wing-brother stepped forward eagerly, his golden eyes shining bright as he flexed both his wings out to show me. "My name used be Half-Wing," he said solemnly.

"What name do you choose now?" Zale asked, then to me, he said, "Outsiders are not permitted to know their names unless they are told so. Everyone else must address them as *wing-brother*."

The owl bobbed his head and thought for a moment. "Whole-feather."

I grinned. "A fantastic name to be sure!"

He bobbed his head again. "If you wish to relay a message to your sister, I will carry a verbal missive for you. Such was our service to the queens of Ellythia in the Old Times." He glanced about us to the owls watching from their perches in the branches. Lightfoot was right next to us. "Perhaps we should take up the mantle once again."

"You would do that?" I asked as Zale kissed the side of my neck, not caring that I was wet with sweat.

The tawny owl bowed.

"No one else could be entrusted with a message crossing the Lotus Sea," Zale said seriously. "Now the Reaper is back, messages could be interrupted. We must be careful with communication now."

That sounded ominous. To me, lords spoke like this

during times of war. I swallowed the lump in my throat and turned to look at him. "You really think he's back to...what, exactly?"

Zale's gaze was trained into the distance, and it was the first time that he spoke to me without looking me in the eyes. "He will try to do what he always wished. My guess is that he will resume his campaign to take over the Continent." A dark feeling crawled its way through my middle, leaving me feeling unbalanced. "Send your message, my love," Zale said in such a soft voice that I stared at him. But his eyes were still searching the forest behind Whole-Feather, though his gaze was unfocused as if his thoughts were elsewhere. "And then we will go and warn your grandmother that war is coming."

Whole-Feather bowed, and I spoke my message to my sister. I kept it short, hoping that she would relay a message back to me as soon as possible, and told a white lie about me still being "happy and safe at the Ellythian School." I saw no need to worry her about all that had gone on, especially given the turbulence in her own life. Captured by demons! I needed to know exactly what had happened to her and her betrothed.

Once I was done, Lightfoot flew down to the forest floor opposite us. "Shall we?"

Zale nodded and shifted into his golden eagle form, shaking his head and stretching his wings out as if he enjoyed the sensation.

With slightly more confidence this time, I stepped up onto his back behind Wobbles and held his neck tightly.

We were off within minutes, the purple trees shifting and stuttering around us as the wings of the entire parliament of owls, and Zale created a gale force wind with their ascent into the sky.

I sent my awareness down the bond—this time toward

Zale, down that glittering thread between us. There was a tension in him now, something dark and foreboding that made his gaze intent and his muscles taut.

"Zale?" I asked nervously.

"Yes, my little star?"

I didn't know why I was so relieved when I heard his voice in my head. I smiled faintly as above us thousands of stars sprawled in a canvas of jewels in the night. The owls around us were silent except for the flapping of their wings.

"The Reaper put the darkness around your heart," I stated the obvious like an idiot, but I needed it to be said out loud by him. The Reaper was made out to be some type of dark god in the old story. Powerful and cruel. It would take no less to do what he'd done to a baby.

"He did."

"Will he know…that it's gone now, do you think?"

"He will".

A chill shuddered through my bones, and I dared not ask any more, but Zale said, *"I will not let him hurt you, my mate."*

Because I was the one that had undone it. I could not help but think that I had taken a lot of things inside my body with my power, but somehow, the Reaper's magic felt a whole lot more dangerous than anything I'd ever taken before or since.

Of everything I'd taken, they all became a part of me, a little bit. Did that then mean the Reaper's magic was a part of me too?

I shivered at that thought. *"This Reaper person,"* I asked slowly. *"In the stories they called him a 'dark god,' but what is he exactly?"*

"Gods don't interfere with mortal affairs on that level," came the reply.

"Bitter," Wobbles squeaked. "Resentful."

I chewed my lip as Zale continued, *"And they certainly don't try and take over the entirety of the planet and make their own dark realm."*

"Is that what he tried to do?"

"Try-ing. That's been his aim from the beginning. He was fae once. But he corrupted himself so completely by killing his mate that he turned into the darkest sort of creature possible."

"He killed his mate?" I breathed out loud. Unable to hide the disgust and revulsion in my voice. The thought of mates killing each other made me feel sick to the core.

"He did. The worst part of it was that he is extremely powerful. He does not have a match. In a one-to-one battle he is undefeatable. Luckily, it takes more than one powerful creature to take over the world, so his aim was to assemble an army. That is why my father trained my brothers and I so much. In the big battle to come, he wanted us to be the ultimate weapons. To help the Reaper take over the Continent and Ellythia so that we would be lords in the new world. He trained us according to the Reaper's instructions. Broke us over and over again as children until we became creatures of battle and blood and not much more."

My stomach turned. Everything bad the happened in Zale's life was because of the Reaper. He was created to be a weapon, to be used on the whims of a dark creature. *To be used.* I shivered again.

"His earlier attempt at taking over didn't work; he barely took over the Solar Fae Realm. When we woke up initially, I would have thought the Reaper had come to call us for the next attempt...but the power that woke us, your power, felt different. I knew it wasn't him. I was just content to be out of his mind-prison and try and take over Boneweaver Island and then Ellythia again."

A rueful smile twitched at my lips at what I remembered of Zale wanting to march to the capital with his army of demons to take over. Then the smile slid off my face as I realised the Reaper wanted him to do this very thing.

"*Zale*", I asked slowly. "*Do you still want to take over Ellythia?*"

I could hear him laugh down the thread.

"Nostalgia. Incredulous," Wobbles piped. I almost smacked Zale on the feathered head.

"*I had to check!*" I said angrily. "*I'm not entirely sure what's going on in your mind.*"

Zale quieted, all sense of humour gone. "*When I found you in your dark castle sitting covered in smoke and shadow, I knew then that I found all I needed. I knew then that I was made for you.*"

I went quiet and still at the emotion I felt coming down the thread, and I waited for Wobbles to say something, but he was also quiet where he sat leaning against my belly.

Zale continued, "*And now I know that I have my people back as well, I couldn't be happier, Tara.*"

"Content," Wobbles whispered. "Satisfied."

Swallowing the lump in my throat, I said. "*The Reaper won't like that, Zale.*"

"*I know*".

We lapsed into silence again until Zale indicated something in the distance. As we approached, I realised it was two glowing butterflies, dancing and swirling. It was way too high in the sky for butterfly flight, but here they were. From the forest below us, a swarm of the insects rose up and around the owls and Zale, fluttering in a pattern of light and colour. I was enchanted and dizzy all at once.

"*It's the Eternal Forest,*" Zale explained. "*The butterflies always carry the will of Forest. As I suspected, we've achieved what it intended and now we have its approval to leave.*"

The owls gave hoots of warning.

"Hold on, wife," Zale said sharply.

A light split the night sky, blinding my retinas. Zale let out a deep call into the night, and it skittered over my skin like droplets of water. All I could do was clutch onto him, keeping my body low and pressed against Wobbles and his back, my face pressed into the feathers of Zale's neck.

Warmth spilled through me and instinctively I knew it was the sun. I opened my eyes and blinked against a blue morning sky.

The air was salty, the wind sharp on my face. Under us was the sea, and before us was a green coastline.

"Welcome to Lota Island", Zale said.

My heart leapt as next to us Whole-Feather gave a low hoot and veered off into the west toward the Continent where he would hopefully find Saraya and come back to me with a reply of some sort. Something to tell me that she was alive and well. Something to tell me that our homeland was not full of demons like the owls seemed to think.

The idea of demons overrunning the palace, the city, killing and maiming was simply horrifying. That was my childhood home, the place our parents had raised us with love before their demise. I hoped my father was okay and that my stepmother didn't have anything to do with this. But suspicion crawled through me like tiny sharp bugs because I knew that my stepmother had a connection to demons. That she knew the Butcher. I'd never considered the wider implications of that connection until now. Hopefully Saraya could shed some light on it.

I was quickly distracted by the sight of my mother's homeland, *her* childhood home, coming into view as we rapidly made our way toward it.

The harbour spread out below us, filled with large ships,

some probably even from Quartz, carrying quartz and blue ganja, wheat and maize. Behind it Lotus City was sprawled out, golden, magical, glimmering and proud. The city in the shape of a hexagon, and the biggest temples I'd ever seen were set at the points of it.

That was when we saw the first tourmaline arrow headed right towards us.

ALTARA

"**H**old on," Zale said calmly into my mind, veering to the left to avoid the arrow.

"Wee!" Wobbles called out as we sharply turned to avoid another arrow.

"What do we do?" I asked, trying to get a good look at who the hell was shooting us without asking any questions. The Ellythians of the capital were clearly the kill-first-and-ask-questions-later kind of people. "They're mad!"

"They're not mad," Zale said darkly. *"They know who I am."*

The dark shadow in my gut grew a little bigger. They thought Zale was their enemy—Boneweavers were not permitted on Lota Island unless given permission, and Zale's father had worshipped the Reaper as his personal God.

"I'm going to request a parlay. Hopefully they remember what it means. Don't let go."

I was about to ask what that involved when Zale suddenly flashed back into human form. I screamed at the top of my lungs as we free-fell, me and Wobbles piggy-backing on Zale's naked back. He threw something at the ground and flashed back into his eagle form. I scrambled to adjust my position as his wings snapped out to catch the wind. Wobbles seemed to have no trouble digging his fingers into Zale's neck.

"Motherfucker!" I screamed at him, slapping his shoulder in rage.

"I gave you warning, little star."

"Fuck you, Zale!"

I swore I heard him laughing in my head, and I smacked him again. We'd lost height, and Zale wheeled toward the city, making directly for the golden palace. Below us there were shouts of alarm, but arrows no longer zoomed through the air. A huge white flag with the sigil of a tiger's head whisked toward the palace, easily visible against the blue sky. I wondered if it would be enough for them to trust us.

The thought of seeing my girls again filled me with hope, but their presence here, especially Pia's, was also cause for concern. I hoped that they'd made it alive and well.

Zale continued his descent, unusually slow by his insane standards, in a circular motion, giving the golden palace enough time to see that we were no threat. It was not lost on me that my mother ruled then abdicated this very throne twenty years ago, and here I was, her daughter, returning with a Boneweaver husband, an enemy of the kingdom.

Lota City was bigger than Quartz, and from this height, I could see everything. The architecture and the layout were stunning, intricate and the work of over two thousand years. I wanted to study it all, to soak it up over weeks, walk the streets my mother walked—see what she'd seen.

"Have you been here before?" I asked Zale.

"I was not permitted," he said, wryly. *"My father would never reveal his greatest weapon. They knew of me, though."*

Of course, they did. The story of the black-hearted Boneweaver Prince was legend.

Below us, in the square before the golden palace, multiple companies of warriors, male and female both, were gathered as if ready for a big attack. They were dressed in the different colours of their station—black, purple, and white. They were armed with spears, swords and even two rows of archers in formation, their arrows strung and ready to fire. At the head of the palace entrance stepped out a narrow figure dressed in a green gown and a glittering sword at her hip. She shaded her eyes against the sun, watching us as more people gathered behind her. Neither Pia nor our friends were anywhere to be seen. A chill shuddered through me as I felt the tension strumming the air like a knife held to the throat. Perhaps we hadn't planned for this thoroughly enough.

As Zale prepared to land, my skin prickled, and my heart pounded against my sternum. Eyes, so many eyes, were on me and Zale that it made me glow and want to hide at the same time.

Magic tickled my skin, and I realised with alarm that I hadn't accounted for magical protections. I sent a plucking of alarm down our binding thread, and Zale sent me a reassuring stroke back. Clearly, they had some; I just had to be thankful that Zale knew what he was doing. No doubt they'd had a similar sort of magic in his kingdom back in his day.

We landed in the centre of the warriors lining the courtyard, and I could more clearly see the distinctions between the warrior factions. I wanted to know what they meant, wanted to know *everything* about my mother's people and how they'd been living while I'd been in Lobrathia. Despite the weapons angled at us, excitement flooded me as I lightly dismounted from Zale's back, and it evaporated in a poof when I sensed a dark ribbon of malice shooting through the air right toward me. I fortified my mental walls just as it hit me, a presence that tested my magical guards like a dagger against stone. I narrowed my eyes at the crowd of people standing at the top of the golden stairs at the palace entrance, wondering who was rudely trying to gauge me this early in the piece. They had no manners at all, honestly. Zale shifted back into his human form, Wobbles clambering to sit on his naked shoulder.

"Pants," I commanded.

I sensed a chuckle down the thread, and he obliged me with dark pants, boots and a black shirt. Together we strode toward the crowd of nobles gathered before the palace doors. I scanned their faces and fine gowns, noting that even the most finely dressed women were armed. It warmed something within me to see women holding pretty weapons that they no doubt knew how to use. My mother had trained us with weapons in the way of her people, even despite Lobrathian courtiers turning their noses up at little girls holding swords. At the same time, I knew they would use those same weapons upon us if we were deemed to be a threat. My heart clenched once again when I still couldn't see Pia among the faces here to meet us.

In another life she might have run out of her palace pink cheeked and pulled me inside with a grin, demanding that I meet my long-lost family members. But in this life, that was not to be.

At the head of the nobles stood the green-gowned woman, holding Zale's first white flag scrunched in her fist as if it were a rag.

Though her fists were clenched, her emerald eyes stared at

me wide, her mouth slack as if she'd seen a ghost, a hand coming to her chest.

I knew she saw Yasani. I looked too much like my mother. And I knew immediately who she was because she also looked like my mother, only taller, narrower, *harder*.

Aunt Rahana

And then the moment was gone because her eyes flicked to my forehead and her face became wrought iron under my gaze. An ashen hand gripped the hilt of her sword as if she wanted to behead us both. There was a fury in her eyes I'd never seen on my mother's face, and it broke something in me because in Ellythia, your mother's sister was a second mother to you.

It set my teeth on edge, and a little of the darkness in me reared its ugly head. A wisp of shadow coiled around my body. It was a lazy, oozing coil, snaking around my limbs, but I felt everyone around us tense as they noticed it.

My aunt stiffened, her eyes widening before they narrowed into slits. I was suddenly sure it was she who had tested my mental defences.

I gave her my best curtsey, sweeping my witches cloak wide. "Aunt Rahana."

Her voice was as sharp as the honed edge of a blade. "You will address me as 'Your Highness.' I am no aunt of yours. You do not have a claim to this family."

Alright then. She wanted to play. This was my only aunt. I only had one uncle on my father's side, and I wanted to make the most of it because her expression was offending me, and the memory I had of my mother. The smoke around me grew denser.

"I am Yasani Lota's daughter. I have her eyes. I have Lota

power. I am descended of Ellythia, and you cannot change that, whatever my mother's transgression against you."

Her eyes flashed dangerously. "You walk on dangerous ground, girl."

"I am a princess born and raised, Aunt Rahana."

"You were not raised here."

I lifted my chin proudly. "No, my mother raised me and my sister and taught us all she knew."

Aunt Rahana's eyes shifted then to Zale, clearly done with me. "Your *kind* are not permitted on this island. You know the law, *Ashzale Boneweaver*." She said his name like a curse, and I wanted to gut her for it.

I was surprised when Zale bowed to my aunt, and so was everyone else because both the women and men behind my aunt muttered and stared wide eyed at my husband. Zale's voice came out deep and smooth, a king come to visit his neighbouring kingdom. "Your Highness, you must forgive my transgression. I come to parlay."

Rahana's fingers gripped Zale's flag with white knuckles. "The queen will decide what you've come to do. Until then you will allow us to shackle you."

Zale exhaled as if this was annoying him. On his shoulder I heard Wobbles mutter in his ear. "Annoyance. Impatience."

I had to hide my smirk because Zale already knew *those* emotions. It was the positive ones he had trouble with, and I didn't think we'd find much of that here.

"I think not," Zale said smoothly, showing no sign of dark emotion. "It is not protocol."

"Neither is arriving without permission," Rahana shot back.

"The Reaper is returned. There is no need for permission in times of war."

Everyone went quiet at that, and the tension rose considerably, a vibrating shiver in the air.

"*King* Ashzale is my husband," I announced, holding my hand up, the pearl and obsidian wedding ring for all to see. "And he will be treated as such. You cannot shackle a king."

Rahana quirked a cruel brow at me. "And you expect to be treated as a queen?"

I tossed my head just a little bit. "I have not had a coronation yet, so no. But I am a princess, *and* priestess of Agnolthi's Temple. I will be treated as such, yes."

There was muttering behind me now. Nothing else spoke louder than the mark on my forehead, clearly Goddess-given. A fluttering of cloth behind us made me turn to see a group of women and men dressed in lilac robes rushing up to me, and as one, descended onto one knee. I sensed Zale smirking next to me.

"Pride," Wobbles squeaked breathlessly. "Honour."

I stared out at the group of perhaps twenty young people. A woman at the head of group touched her fingers to her forehead and then to her heart. "We pledge our allegiance to the high priestess, Altara Yasani Lota. The lamp is lit, the cauldron burns. Blood speaks."

High priestess? I thought in a daze. Magrin had said the same thing.

And then I felt it. My witch's robe thrummed against my skin, full-body goosebumps erupted on my flesh as all around us the particles in the air stilled.

Zale stepped away from me, and I stared at him, but the look in his eyes was blazing, meaningful. My heart stopped as he bent down on one knee and looked at me like I was the only woman in the universe.

A force like a rupturing volcano blared from behind me,

and the heat wave swept around the entire courtyard, forcing everyone to their knees, except me. Every cell in my body lit up as time slowed down. Slowly, not breathing, I turned.

Agnolthi stood halfway up the steps to the golden palace, and the entire world darkened around her. She shone through it, colossal, divine power emanating off her perfect, wild form like the crash of a tidal wave, the tremble of an earthquake, the chant of a song older than time. She was as I remembered her from the temple in Taraka, and yet my memory could never do her justice.

She was astride her golden lion, who stood as a beastly, savage king, his eyes everywhere all at once. Her golden-brown skin glittered with its own light, covered by a sheer black gown that showed the lush body underneath. Her face was painted with black symbols across her forehead, down her slender nose and across high cheekbones. Her lips were painted a glittering red, and her dark hair, as long as mine down to her hips, was silken but wild and unbound.

When she looked at me with emerald eyes, I felt my womb quiver under the weight of Her.

She slipped off her lion, and I saw in one of her inked hands she held a bone-hilted knife. I blinked, my chest a ball of fire and ice, my magic roaring in my ears, pushing and straining. Agnolthi lifted a single finger as she sauntered down the stairs, and my power stilled like a serpent in a trance. She smiled at me, and my heart near gave away as I fell to my knees.

Agnolthi grabbed me by the throat, but her fingers were gentle, and when she spoke it was with the old melody of the beasts and birds. Her mouth did not move but everyone in that clearing heard clearly: *"The thread weaves a silent story, blood never lies, my Altara."*

All I could do was gulp up at her, my entire world becoming only her firm fingers on my skin, her amber eyes on mine.

"You are dark, and you are light." Thunder boomed above us. *"You are pain and you are joy"*. Lightning flashed, illuminating the courtyard. *"You are illness, and you are healing."*

Agnolthi held up her knife, the blade glittering as if made entirely of diamond. My veins became fire, my heart a tempest storm. I could not breathe, but I knew in my bones what was going to happen. Dark and light surrounded me, pain and joy filled me to the brim. Behind it all I felt Zale's heavy presence behind me, warm and sure.

Agnolthi pressed the tip of her blade to her own finger and anointed my forehead.

"Will you listen to the song of the wild, untethered void?" she asked.

Somehow, I found my voice as my body ignited. "I will."

"Will you speak for quiet stars that burn old stories in the night sky?"

"I will."

"Will you dance in ancient forests under the light of all full moons?"

"I will."

"Do you accept the pledge of the dark and light from this day until the day of your death?"

"I do."

"Altara Yasani Lota Voltanius, you are High Priestess of Agnolthi's Temple, Order of Yasani. Do not disappoint me."

Her final words were like a beast's jaws, swallowing me whole.

Agnolthi departed as abruptly as she'd entered, and it left the entire Lotus Court reeling from the absence of her magnificent force.

The Goddess always had her own timing, but it was strange seeing her here on Lotus Island instead of back on my own island...and without my mother here to lay some sort of sacrifice in her honour.

Instead I had Altara, who had stood like a Goddess herself, the only being I would fall on my knees for. Agnolthi's force had pressed upon me, wild and savage, and I hadn't been able to help the shift into my tiger form. I padded behind Altara to stand by her while she took her high priestess oath, foreign feelings stamping across my chest. Foreign and yet right. Wobbles had whispered in my ear, "Respect. Honour. Trust."

My eyes had found Agnolthi's steed, standing upon the steps to the palace, and his amber eyes had looked back at me, flashing with something menacing that made my cells ignite. *Worship her, as I worship Agnolthi*, his voice sounded in my head. I'd given him a single nod, and he'd blinked his gaze lazily away from me, as if were nothing more than a common land creature. The challenge had excited me for a single mad moment—as if I'd challenge Agnolthi's divine lion, a God in his own right. He was her stabilising force, made to attend to her every whim. To show the world that she was master of the most ferocious beasts.

Just like how Altara was master over the beast inside of me.

And now, as my mate stood on feet steadied in her witch's boots, my heart swelled and sung like a bird, high pitched and keening. I yearned to be inside of her, to claim her as mine in front of everyone, but I quelled the ancient urge within me and decided we had to show them without outright mating. As Altara turned to face the acolytes of her order, I, still in my tiger's form, stalked to her side, rubbed my face along her thigh and stood next to her, baring my canines in an obvious and open threat.

Some of the acolytes were in the process of pulling themselves off the floor as a majority of them had tumbled down when Agnolthi arrived. Others were leaning on each other, visibly pale. The eldest of the group had their hands over their chests and were looking up at Altara in awe as her mark glowed a deep pink that hurt the eyes.

"Thank you," Altara said quietly. "I will come to the Temple after I have met with the queen."

All they could do was nod, and they remained on their knees as Altara turned toward me and placed one glorious hand on my head.

I rubbed myself against her, growling in approval, marking her further. She gave a small huff of amusement at my eagerness, then turned back toward the palace entrance where the Ellythian nobles and her wretched aunt were gathering their wits in the wake of what they'd just seen. Agnolthi had given them her divine back, had not even faced them when she appointed Altara high priestess.

Nothing could have made me more smug.

She'd done it in front of the entire Ellythian Court and military factions. This was, perhaps, the only thing that would grant us safe entry to the palace. We had the approval of a Goddess, whose authority could not be matched. They had no choice but to let us see Queen Cheshni.

I bared my teeth at Rahana Lota, wondering where her husband was so I could assess him. But no one stepped forward to be with her as we stood there.

Rahana, slightly ashen to my keen eyes, had one hand on her sword and bared her teeth at me. I decided then that she likely kept her husband locked away in a closet—we would have to ask Pia when we saw her. It disturbed me that I could not scent my brothers or the other Lota princess in the wind.

If they were not here, then they were being kept away.

My hackles rose, and I hissed through my mouth. Only Altara's hand on my side kept me from leaping through the palace and finding their scent. If they were keeping them captive, I would tear this place down and fuck my ancestor Rorax Boneweaver for building it.

Suddenly, I felt the urgent need to let everyone know that if they hurt a single cell on Altara's body I would destroy them all. I let my magic flare out in an angry wave before realising that the thought of Altara being hurt was not wise for me to focus on.

I began to pace behind Altara, unable to keep still.

"Possessive," Wobbles whispered in my ear from where he held onto my neck. "Enraged."

The courtiers shifted uneasily as Altara took a deep breath to steel herself. "Allow me to see my grandmother, please, sister of my mother."

Rahana clenched her jaw and unclenched it, clearly wanting to deny my mate again. But the nobles behind her muttered and exchanged frowns. If there was one thing Ellythians held sacred above all, it was the seven Goddesses. To deny a high priestess was to deny their divine calling. Never in all seven hells would they let themselves do it.

Rahana had no choice, and she knew it. She gave us a single seething nod of assent before she whirled on her heel and strode back through the palace doors, the nobles hastily giving her way before she could shoulder them aside.

Ladies in waiting hurriedly came down the steps to rush toward Altara, but they saw me and hesitated.

Curtseying deeply from a distance, one said, "If it pleases Your Highness, High Priestess, please follow us."

I felt Altara's soothing touch down the thread of celestial magic that bound us. *"Be calm, Zale,"* she said. *"All is well."*

"All is not well," I muttered, though her touch calmed me instantly. *"Where are my brothers? Where are your sisters?"*

Her uncertainty came down the thread, and she glanced firey emerald eyes at me before she ascended the stairs to the palace that her mother had abandoned so long ago.

We were led to a small drawing room to await the queen. I did a lap around the perimeter and sensed no threat, no weapons and no magical means of attack. The Lota palace was opulent, gilded in light and quartz and oil paintings of old battles. But it was also teeming with ancient magic, and within it, I felt the power of the Boneweavers funnelling through its veins and arteries like a living pulse. Rorax Boneweaver had put his entire self into the architecture, and it showed. I knew that Atax and Kai would have felt the same, and perhaps felt a little more at home here because of it.

Still I could not scent them, and it made me rumble, deep with unhappiness.

"Come here," Altara said in a voice like silk that wrapped around my heart. I glanced at her, and there was a soft light in her eyes that warmed me to my black, rotten core.

I padded up to where she sat in a gilded and red velvet chair fit for a queen. She held out her hands, and I surged into them immediately, a purr tumbling through my chest. I nuzzled into her lap and filled my lungs with her scent. Strong but soft arms came around me, and she rested her cheek against the top of my head. I felt complete and whole in Altara's arms. Everything felt right in her lap.

Her scent had changed very slightly, and I knew it had to do with the magic that now bound her to the Order of Yasani as their leader. Her power was always her own, but I could now feel through our bond that she would be given the hidden secrets of her Order.

My mother always had knowing eyes that saw beyond what others saw, and I wondered whether Altara would develop the same.

"You will not be in your human form to meet your grand-mother-in-law?" she asked, the hint of a smile in her voice.

"I cannot. My control hangs on by a hair."

"Do you sense some threat?"

Yes and no.

"There is something dark here, my mate."

Altara inhaled my scent, and it brought me an extraordinary amount of joy to feel her doing that.

"Ecstasy," Wobbles murmured.

I growled in annoyance, and the creature gave a little pat to my shoulder.

"I feel it too," Altara murmured. "Something is crawling under my skin, but I cannot put my finger on what it is. Could it be Aunt Rahana?"

The woman was a vessel of bitterness and anger, and I was surprised she hadn't burned herself to cinders already. To think that this was Ellythia's crown princess made me...

"Disturbed," Wobbles whispered.

Fuck. I *was* disturbed by it. That level of darkness destroyed everything around it, and did not make for a stable throne. If we were to fight against the Daanavs and the Reaper, this leadership was not ideal.

Altara stiffened as a knock came at the door before it opened. I already recognised it as the lady-in-waiting and allowed her to enter.

"The queen will see you now," the teenage girl breathed, glancing worriedly between me then my mate.

"Thank you," Altara said, ever graceful.

I had noticed it before in the Carnal Fae Court, but it didn't strike me until now how much of a graceful princess Altara was. She wore only her witch's boots and cloak, and yet she walked down the corridor and into the assigned parlour room as if she wore a ball gown made of diamonds.

The room was full of people I could only assume were Altara's extended family. Green eyes, bronzed skin, curved yet athletic bodies. An ancient line as old as Ellythia: the great and noble house of Lota.

We were not graced with the throne room. Instead we were presented to the queen sitting in a royal chair, her family milling about the room.

This was to be a private affair then.

Altara strode toward her grandmother and made me jittery to see her dressed in a white Ellythian gown of mourning.

We stood before Queen Cheshni sitting scowling and sharp eyed before us. I knew something was wrong immediately. There was a fell gleam in her eyes. Emeralds that should have burned bright were instead dull as old metal and biting like venom. They passed over Altara, looking her up and down, before raking over me. I sent a warning down our thread, but Altara showed no sign of receiving it because her heart was pounding, and she was not blinking.

This woman had given birth to her mother, and I was sure she saw some familiarity there.

Altara did not curtsey; she merely stood still, staring as if all the wind had been blown out of her. I wondered if she was in shock.

"So, Yasani's spawn comes to Ellythia," Cheshni said in a voice like the creak of a rusty door swinging open. "Parading as Agnolthi's high priestess."

Altara recovered from whatever reverie she was in because she then curtseyed as if she were happy to be here. I did not move an inch.

"I am honoured to meet you, grandmother." My mate's voice was deep, melodic and firm.

"Bah!" Cheshni pointed a crooked finger at her granddaughter. "You aren't one of mine. Not anymore."

"You are wrong," Altara said mildly. "I see my face in yours. I was in your womb at one time."

Cheshni's lip curled in distaste. "I should execute you for even mentioning it."

My growl filled the room like a thunderstorm, and I was

about to take a step forward when Altara ran a firm hand over my head, and I leaned into her warmth.

"Brought your little pet with you, eh?" Cheshni sniped. "The little prince cat who was put to sleep for all those years."

Only Altara's hand continuously stroking my head, her gentle reassurance down the bond, stopped me from launching myself at the old woman. Altara might have removed the shadow around my heart, but that beating muscle was still black as far as I was concerned.

"Ashzale Boneweaver is my star-soul mate and my husband under Ellythian Law," Altara said calmly. "And you will not speak of him in that way."

Cheshni scoffed. "This is my kingdom, girl, and every man, woman, child and mage is loyal to *me*. They would take you and cut you up into pieces with just one word from *me*."

My rage rose, and I vibrated with the need to destroy our enemies. Altara rested her hand on my head in warning.

"You could try, but I promise you, it would not end well." Altara glanced around the room at her supposed family members who were now, to my great pleasure, shifting uncomfortably, hanging on to every word.

"You are not frightened of me." Cheshni's voice was filled with dark humour and some old part of me remembered my father.

"I cannot be afraid of anything when I have met with despair himself."

"Then you are stupid," she spat. "Despair is for the weak."

"You do not know what I have suffered at the hands of demons," Altara hissed.

"We have all suffered at the hands of demons," a lord said. A teenage boy was by his side, and I knew at once from his scent, that this was Pia's father and brother. Not in a closet then. I hissed at him because he knew nothing.

"Ha!" cackled the queen.

I felt Altara's rage pummel down the thread, heady and potent like volcano erupting, and it caused my mate to explode with darkness veined with light. Altara was triggered by the insult, and I protectively moved in front of her, shielding her from this queen with my body. I sat on her feet while all around me magic shattered every single one of the windows in the room.

Turning to look at her, I saw her body was covered in a veil of black smoke like a second skin, but through that, made out of pure, blistering light, were cuts, abrasions and bruises in her organs, bones, muscles and skin.

It took me a moment to realise that they were every illness and injury ever taken by my mate in her healing of others. On her skin were a thousand deep lacerations, and on her bones, vicious serrated cuts. I now saw every wound the Butcher had given her.

I saw it, and my vision became a red mist of rage. I let out a roar.

The walls of the room and the shattered glass on the floor vibrated under its force, and the Lotas cowered against the walls.

Despite it all Altara stood tall.

I felt something down the bond then, some awareness Altara had. Some inkling of understanding. With a crack of lightning, her bow was in her hand, glimmering deep blue and white with the crackling, wild power of a storm.

She loosed a black arrow of void straight at her grandmother.

Everyone gasped, and someone screamed, but the arrow

sailed right inside the elderly woman, disappearing completely into her chest.

Something malevolent screamed. It was a howl of rage, pain and madness. I leapt onto Altara, pinning her to the ground as from the queen erupted an avalanche of the most malevolent magic I have ever known.

It was frighteningly familiar.

30

MALIKA

I had never been the panicking sort of woman—more the
throwing-a-dagger-at-the-wall-to-let-out-my-frustration
type of woman. So when Pia did not return from being taken
up to the palace, I fell into a blind rage.

"Where is she?" I screamed through the cell bars for the
fifth time, my cheeks pressed hard against the cold metal.
"Where the fuck is Pia!? Bring her back, you spineless
fuckers!"

No one replied, and my voice only echoed down the
empty stone corridors. "Fuck!" I shouted, smacking the steel.
A burn spread through my wrist, but I relished the pain.

I turned to see Atax watching me from where he sat cross-
legged on his stone block, a bemused expression over his
achingly handsome—I *mean*, arrogant face. "I don't think
Xalya's senior priestesses will appreciate you calling them
'fuckers.' I believe they are celibate."

"Fuck you, grandpa."

"Don't talk to your elders that way."

I was more than ready to reach around his throat and

throttle the life out of him when my eye caught his obsidian earrings, swaying as he moved his head. An idea struck me like a fist, and I was angry enough and mad enough to see it through.

Kai's innocent voice floated toward us from the cell next door. "Maybe her mother is housing her in a nicer accommodation? She is a princess, after all."

"Doubt it," Rani said darkly in the other cell. "Pia said that was unlikely, given the initial reaction."

"People change their minds," Kai said, a sweet note of hope in his voice.

Atax watched me with a feline gaze, then arched an eyebrow when I remained standing by the bars, staring at him. I stepped toward him slowly, letting my hip settle with each step—a saunter if I knew one. His eyes darkened as he honed in on my swaying body, his own muscular form going predator-still. If I looked closely, I swore I could see that lion prowling beneath his skin, proud but sharp. Lethal but graceful.

My heart pounded in a frenzied beat because what I was about to do with this lion turned man was dangerous and dumb, but I was at my wits end. We'd been in this cell for days, and no one would help me get out of this place saying my ideas were idiotic. Rani never called them that, of course, but the meaning behind her flowery words was the same, and it grated against my skin.

It was now or never. He'd only give me one shot, I was sure.

"Atax," I said, trying to keep my voice normal, knowing he'd suspect my seduction straight away if it was obvious. "I think I'm going mad." I stood before him, breathing a little hard, and I saw him note the movement of my chest. I had average-sized breasts, but I'd use them to my full advantage now.

"Malika." Atax's lips purring across my name were gentle, and it suddenly pulled me off guard. He normally had a mocking bite whenever he said my name. And then he ruined it. "You were *always* mad."

My plans fell to the wind and on a whim. I lunged at him, my fist aiming for his jaw. He caught my fist in one hand, pulling me into his lap and moaned in mock arousal. "Oh, Malika, please stop." But his hands were so fucking strong I couldn't shake my fist out of his.

I shrieked in anger, "Let me go!"

He let my fist go, and straddling him, I swung again. He caught my fist a second time. I jabbed at him with my left, and he caught that one too.

He was now holding both my fists on either side of his head, and I felt so open and without a defence, sitting chest to chest with him this way. His lips were close to mine now, but his earrings were also close to both my hands. On sudden inspiration, or more likely, desperation, I leaned down and crushed his lips with mine. He opened his mouth without hesitation, and I sunk into him, allowing myself this one thing even if I'd promised that I never, under any circumstances, would. But this didn't count; it wasn't real, because I had an agenda. *It didn't count.*

"Is that what you want, firebird?" he murmured against my mouth, his voice hitting me straight in my lower stomach.

Rani gagged next door, and Kai sniggered, but I only had sapphire eyes in my vision.

"Yes," I panted. He allowed me to twist my hands out of his grip. I clutched the sides of his face, his scruff rough under my fingers as I opened my mouth against his, groaning when his tongue swept across mine. He wanted to dominate me, fight me, but I'd never let him win. I bit down on his lip, and he growled in surprise, but just as his hand came around my waist, I deftly unhooked his obsidian earring from his left ear and leapt out of his lap.

I was back on my side of the cell as he stared at me stunned, then at the lethal jewellery I had dangling from my fingers. He touched the now empty lobe of his left ear, and his disbelief turned into something else as he narrowed his eyes. My heart skipped a beat at his dark look of menace. But I'd never let him know he unsettled me, so I smirked.

"I've always wanted one of these," I said lightly, hooking it into the second hole on my right ear. The hook of the earring was still warm, and a miniscule part of me heated up at the fact that I had a piece of him on my body now. "Does it look nice?" I purred.

Slowly, so slowly, it made me burn like living fire, Atax got to his feet. Every move of his was calculated, lethal, masculine efficiency—a real, terrifying warrior even Xalya's Guard were afraid of. When he looked at me, his eyes reeled me in, those sapphires becoming chips of blue stone.

His voice was an octave lower than usual. "Give it back."

Ignoring my shot of fear, I quickly unhooked the sword from my ear and held it tightly in my hand. How did it work? Whenever the Old Ones took the tiny blades off their ears, the metal elongated to its normal size naturally, but when I'd taken it off, it didn't do that. There must be a way to activate it.

Atax lunged for me, and I danced out of his grip to the back end of the cell. His nostrils flared, and I knew that in this tiny space, I didn't have much of a chance at escaping him. Atax glanced down at my cleavage when they'd jiggled as I'd pounced backwards. Smirking, I dropped the tiny sword into my brazier. Atax's eyes followed its path to my breasts, his pupils dilated as he stared at the plump mounds. I squeezed my thighs together to try and ignore the heat now furiously pulsing there.

"You think that'll stop me?" he asked quietly.

I bit on my bottom lip, wondering if he would, in fact, put his hand down there and knowing that I would, in fact, like that too much.

Admitting this angered me, and I snapped at him: "I'll cut off your hands if you do."

Atax licked his lips. "Might be worth it, firebird." He stepped to the left, a beast stalking prey, but his tourmaline shackles restricted his hand movements.

"Just let me try it," I said a little breathless as I felt the tiny blade stabbing my sternum. "Tell me how to make it big." This was my only shot, after all. After this there was no way he'd fall for it again.

"No."

"Come on!" I urged. "Don't be a brute; let me try. I think I could saw those bars open quickly."

"No."

It disgusted me to do it, but I put on an over-sweet, high-pitched voice. "Please, Atax?"

His smile was wide, his sapphires now as bright as the sea on a summer's day. "Say it one more time. Beg for it, firebird."

I glared at him, but at that moment, I would have done anything to get out of this cage. I dropped my voice and looked up at him from under my eyelashes, all doe-eyed. "Please, lord lion?"

His eyes turned heavy, his lids dropping a little. His voice so soft that it brushed the apex of my thighs. "One more time."

I took a step closer and cleared my throat a little, my heart trying to leap out of my chest, and I was annoyed that he could probably hear it and scent my arousal. "Please—"

I didn't get to finish because he lunged for me so quickly that I didn't even understand where I was in space or time until I was on my back with Atax's face down my shirt and his hard, massive erection against my thigh.

With great, clit-throbbing alarm, I felt his tongue slide down my cleavage and right back up in two wet strokes. Totally out of my mind, I let out a wanton moan, and when he came back up, his earring was dangling on the end of his tongue, and his mouth was wide in a savage grin.

The sight of him over me with his pink tongue hanging out sent my mind seizing. I knew I was gaping. I knew I was wet. I knew my pussy throbbed like a wound that could only be soothed by him. *Bastard.*

I was just about to tell grandpa to get off me, but I didn't get to, because right at that moment, the entire palace groaned as if it had been struck. The very land shook viciously on its foundation.

"Earthquake!" Rani cried.

Atax looped his shackles over my head and shoulders, pulling me close to him. I punched at his shoulders because if it was just an earthquake, I didn't need protection. His body rubbed against mine, and suddenly my brain shut off, and all I knew was his long hard length against my thigh.

Magic surged around us, dark and terrible, and Atax looked down on me, brows raised in alarm, holding the sword earring between his lips now.

"It's not an earthquake!" Kai shouted.

Dust fell from the ceiling, the stone brick around us trembled, and with an all-mighty shudder, I watched the roof of the cell crack in a spiderweb pattern. Atax looked up at the long fissures and his head whipped back down to me just as a slab of the ceiling broke off and hurtled toward him, lying on top of me, magic-less in tourmaline shackles.

I flung up my arms around us and screamed.

31

ALTARA

The most vile power I had ever known slammed into me—old, cruel and sharp as poison. I choked on it as my magic whirled in a maelstrom, chasing it around the cavities of my body until my power scrambled to gobble it up, piece by disgusting piece. The rotten magic hit me in a continuous wave, and I didn't realise I'd fallen on my ass until Zale's tiger body was upon me, covering me as if he could defend me with his muscles. I shook under him until the screams coming from my grandmother faded into nothing. My ears rang, and a giant wet, hot tongue scraped across my face.

"Ew, Zale, stop," I gasped.

It should have been terrifying to see a tiger's face staring down upon me, his gaze wild, heated and murderous. But it wasn't. With a growl Zale pounced off me, and I heaved my suddenly heavy body to my feet, that foul-tasting magic bearing down on my insides. I staggered forwards to see the members of the Lota family plastered against the walls of the parlour room, their faces disturbed, ashen and shocked, while

Aunt Rahana shook my grandmother by the shoulders. Suddenly, I realised the gravity of what this looked like. I'd *shot* the Queen of Ellythia. It looked like I'd come here to murder her.

"She's breathing," Rahana snapped when a guard stumbled forward to assist. Then, whirling around with her face twisted into a mask of rage, she cried. "Seize them!"

"Wait!" I cried. Then I gagged, about to vomit my insides out as the foreign magic churned in me. "She had rotting magic in her! Didn't you know?" When no one moved, I said quickly, "That's a part of what my magic does—it takes foreign magic and converts it. I take it into my own body." I struggled to explain it as I'd only just come to terms with it myself.

It was an elderly lady sitting in the corner who croaked in surprise, "She speaks of void magic."

I stared at the woman, trying to figure out what relation she had to me. She was almost as old as my grandmother, silver-haired and green-eyed in a fine gown of pink brocade.

"Please," Rahana said drolly. "Aunt Parsha, void magic hasn't been seen since Matrika and her daughters walked the earth."

Aunt Parsha? She was likely to be Cheshni's sister then, a princess. And Matrika was Ellythia's daughter, who reigned queen after her thousands of years ago, but I had no idea about the history of that magic.

"That was *dark* magic," Princess Parsha rasped. "I saw it with my own eyes. What was Cheshni doing with it inside of her? How long has it been in there?"

"Enough, Aunt!" Rahana said angrily. "Tuskus, get the healers. The queen has been attacked and needs attending to.

We can discuss the crime later. Guards, take them to the dungeons at once."

"This is Agnolthi's high priestess," Parsha said angrily. "We will need a Priestess Moot."

"Fine," Rahana snapped. "Send the summons."

Parsha turned her old emerald eyes toward me. "And my sister's granddaughter will not stay in the dungeons. I do not care what Yasani did. This girl is an Ellythian, through and through, and a senior member of the palace now."

I knew it already, but it was still a shock to hear it said like that, in this room from an elder of the court.

Rahana ignored the elderly lady, but everyone else in the room seemed to listen to her.

"Thank you...Grandmother," I said softly.

Parsha smiled in approval and snapped her fingers. A set of palace guards with the lotus crest on their breasts stepped forward.

"Guest rooms for the High Priestess and the Boneweaver King. Under guard." She heaved herself to her feet.

"My friends," I said hurriedly, glancing at the queen who was grumbling and shifting now. Relief washed over me as I saw she wasn't mortally injured from my arrow. "Where is Princess Pia and my husband's brothers?"

Zale shifted into his human form and thankfully, quickly summoned pants on himself, but not before Grandmother Parsha got a good look and flushed pink.

"Indeed, where are my brothers?" Zale asked in a dark voice.

The others in the room shifted awkwardly as I eyed Zale. He had clearly calmed down enough to trust his human form, but there was still a terrible aura of violence around him. He took my still trembling hand in his large, calloused one. I got the feeling he did it to steady himself.

"You and your Old Ones have come here as a question, King Ashzale," Parsha said, fixing him firmly with an emerald eye. "We do not know your intentions, husband to the high priestess of Agnolthi or not. I'm sure you understand that given your history with allying with the Reaper, and the fact that he has returned to the Continent, we must be careful to protect our people. Your brothers will remain under our guard."

So they knew about the Reaper being back. To my surprise Zale nodded. "My father turned on me; I understand betrayal. Do as you deem to be fair." He shot a dark look at Aunt Rahana, still bent over the queen as two attendants in purple robes ran in to attend to her.

Interesting that the temple of Agnolthi took on the healing role for the city, and now *they* were under my jurisdiction.

Parsha made a sound of approval, and still jittery with unease, we exited the room with the palace guards on our tail. I did not miss the fact that she had not told me where Pia was.

But I didn't get to push the question, because out in the palace proper, it was chaos. Dust coated the golden tiles, guards were sprinting through the corridors and to my utter surprise, deep cracks high on the palace walls were healing themselves in sheaths of golden light.

I swore under my breath, guessing that this had to do with the surge of magic I'd let out of my grandmother. Zale's hand squeezed around my own before shooting to the guards, "Are the Old Ones and three girls being kept in the dungeons?"

They gave each other a startled look before hesitantly nodding.

Zale's voice dropped low. "And are your dungeons underground?"

The two men nodded again. "There's been some disruption to the foundations there, part of the ceiling caved in."

Terror speared through me, and I froze immediately. "Our friends!" I exclaimed, smoke coiling around my form. "Take us there right now."

Their hesitation made anger twine around my panic, and it showed in the dense smoke now covering my skin, my lightning shooting around me in threatening waves. Zale stroked a thumb over the back of my hand, and it helped me focus my thoughts.

"If you value your lives, you will take us there," Zale commanded in a way that no one in their sane mind would deny. "We will go to our confinement *afterwards*."

They glanced at me with worry before turning back down the corridor and leading us to a set of golden stairs that led under the palace. Quartz lamps flooded the area with light, unlike our Lobrathian dungeons which were kept dim on purpose. There were shouts coming from deep within the bowels of the dungeons, and I lurched forward and pushed past the guards to sprint down. I felt Zale directly behind me as I came upon a collapsed section of the dungeon, our path now blocked by sandstone.

Zale nudged me behind him as he flung his arm out, and abruptly, the stones separated down the middle, forming columns either side of the passage. Raising my brows I caught Zale's eye, and he winked before frowning up ahead.

Atax strolled around a corner with an ashen but conscious Malika in his arms. "Let go of me, you brute!" she slapped him on the chest, but it was weak and barely a pat on his expanse of muscle.

"Malika!" I cried, running toward her as my heart unfurled with joy to see them alive.

My friend's brown eyes widened in shock. "Oh my God, Altara!" She reached for me with both arms, tears streaming down her face. "You're back!"

"I should have known it was you two," Atax said wryly as Malika and I hugged, though he wouldn't let her down.

Rani and Kai came up from behind them, Kai giving a mad shout and jumping right into Zale's arms and wrapping his legs around him like a child. Zale laughed as Kai kissed him on both of his cheeks before jumping out of his arms and grinning at me, his sky-blue eyes bright with joy.

Goddess, it was good to see their faces.

Rani sobbed before putting her wiry arms around me and picking me up, burying her nose in my hair and crying her eyes out. "Tara!" she wailed and began blubbering words I could barely understand.

"This whole situation is a bit of a mess," Malika said angrily, but the effect was blunted by the fact Atax was cradling her like a newborn

"Tell me about it," I said, kissing Rani on the forehead as she released me. "But let's get out of here."

There were guards everywhere now as we exited the dungeon, and we came across Prince Tuskus on his way in. He nodded at us. "I'll head in to make the repairs now," he said.

"I can help!" Kai piped, rubbing his hands together. Covered in dust, his silver hair coming out of its braids, he looked a little crazier than usual, and it was hard to believe there was a trained killer underneath all that.

Tuskus eyed him uncertainly before Atax made a noise of great annoyance. "Malika held a whole section of the ceiling off us until Rani placed metal supportive beams all around," he said, a bite of anger in his voice and something else as he glanced at Malika and Rani. "We need to fix it before anyone else gets hurt. I'll come with you."

Tuskus and the guards stared at the Old Ones for a moment before my uncle shook his head. "The castle is self-healing thanks to Rorax Boneweaver. We've got it from here." He indicated two sets of guards. "Take them to adjoining guest rooms."

Malika sighed in loud relief while Rani took my hand and refused to let go. She was trembling from head to toe with adrenaline, her eyes darting around, her shoulders twitching. In an odd move, Wobbles leapt from Zale's shoulder and landed on Rani's shirt, clawing his way up to sit on her shoulder. She gave him a pat as he leaned against her neck.

"Looks like you saved them," I said proudly to my friend as the guards led us to the upper levels of the palace.

I watched her carefully and noted that Rani did not smile as I expected, but sort of grimaced like she was in pain. I squeezed her hand.

"She did," Kai said loudly. "It was a marvellous feat of metal magic."

"Let me down!" Malika protested. "I can walk."

"I know," Atax said dismissively.

Zale cast me a smirk, and I felt a twang on our thread. "Ah, I missed you all."

Kai stared at Zale adoringly and Malika cast me a disturbed look before making googly eyes at Zale. "Are you normal now, Boneweaver King?"

"Normal," I snorted. "As normal as an Old One can be, I suppose—and by that I mean he's still fairly murderous."

"You can't talk," Zale smirked at me. "After what you pulled back there."

"That was you, Tara?" Kai gaped at me.

I was wary of the six guards listening around us when I replied with a stiff nod.

We were deposited into a suite with four adjoining rooms, which Rani told us had been made for visiting nobility. Malika, having grown up in a Boneweaver Island village, gaped at the gilded chairs, fine oil paintings, high scrollwork ceilings and decorative lotus wallpaper. Zale and I took one room, Atax and Kai the second and Malika and Rani the third.

"Dare I ask where Pia is?" I asked as we sat in the suite. "Or Geravie and Keshmi?"

"The grandmothers are fine, but they took Pia," Rani whispered. "She said that her mother would want to interrogate her, but it's been two days, and she's not returned."

Atax, who was still holding onto Malika like his life depended on it, had no choice but to let her go as she swatted him across the face. Grumbling Malika leapt to the floor, landing lightly on her feet before swearing loudly, "Those fuckers better not have hurt her!" She then nodded to the mark on my forehead. "You can find out where she is, though, right? They'll listen to you now you're priestess of Agnolthi?"

"High Priestess," Zale corrected.

Rani gasped.

"I've made a tiny error of judgement," I said sheepishly. "I attacked the queen; there'll likely be a trial."

Rani made a choked sound while Malika jumped up and down. "Someone had to do it!"

"Firebird," Atax admonished. "You're not supposed to

attack the queen, you know. That's grounds for execution. High priestess or not."

"It wasn't an attack, as such," Zale corrected quickly, raising an eyebrow at me at Atax's new nickname for Malika. "We—" He looked at me in question, and a dark thought seemed to flicker under those blue eyes. "I sensed the Reaper's magic around her, Tara. Is that why you went to pull it out?"

I swallowed and sat down on a purple velvet chair, suddenly finding my bones weary. That magic was still inside me, getting digested. Thinking back to when I had laid eyes on my grandmother and sensed a strange ever-dark in her. It had been foreign, an invasion, a terrible, dark thing, and my magic had yearned to consume it. "I didn't even know what I'd done at first," I admitted. "The bow and arrow were in my hands, and the arrow loosed before I knew what I'd done. I think my magic just knew there was something terrible and awful that needed to come out of my grandmother. It was weighing her down like an evil robe." I turned to look at Zale. "I hope she's okay. What if it kills her to have it removed?"

Zale shook his head. "I heard her breathing, and her heart still beat strongly. But—" he looked meaningfully at Atax and Kai. "I've sent word to Raen through the wing-brothers, but... the Reaper has returned to the Continent and it was definitely his magic all over the queen."

Kai frowned, and Atax paled. "Zale," Atax said stiffly. "He will know we are awake. He will come for us."

"I know," Zale said as Rani audibly gulped and took a seat next to me. "We need to ally with Ellythia. But they still see us as the enemy. We need to deal with this trial first."

"What is a Priestess Moot?" I asked. "I've never heard of it."

"It's rare, but when one of the royals or priestesses do something wrong," Rani said quietly, "they call a Priestess Moot. The high priestesses of each temple are summoned to the Round Table, and together they decide what the punishment will be."

"Punishment?" Malika asked angrily. "Tara has done nothing wrong! Saved the queen from the Reaper's magic, that's the way I see it!"

"Maybe so," said Rani. "But that will be up to them..." She scratched her head in deep thought. "In fact, I think they'll likely decide Pia's fate at the same time. It was at a Priestess Moot, after all, that they decided to exile her in the first place."

Power thrummed through me, strong and pure. But alongside the feverish magic churning in my body, a dark feeling settled in my stomach. Agnolthi had made me high priestess, and my very first act in that position had been to shoot the queen. I wondered how that would be received by my peers, extremely powerful women blessed by the other six Goddesses themselves.

32

ALTARA

We were summoned that evening.

After we'd separated to our individual rooms that afternoon, we washed up, ate the given food and basically fretted about Pia and our position here. Geravie and Keshmi arrived, sweeping me and a surprised Zale into their arms with kisses on our cheeks. Geravie wiped more than a few tears, and I forced her to sit down with a glass of strong wine before we started talking.

Rani and Malika told us what had happened during their travels to Lota City, and in turn, Zale and I gave a brief version of what had happened to us in the Eternal Forest.

"So Fangar can take Zale's place at the fae queen's court?" Atax said with a grin.

"If we can find him," I said carefully. "But basically, yes. I specified that I'd return my *husband* to her within a month. Odeelia didn't know that I'd been married to two men."

"Brilliant!" Malika had said viciously, "at least that bastard Daanav will come into some use."

She had every right to hate my Daanav husband Fangar

Sharksbane as much as I did, as he'd led the demonic charge into Levu village, killing many of her people. The repairs were still ongoing with Raen's help. I also wasn't going to mention that it had been Zale's fault I'd had to marry the both of them. I suppose this was his way of making up for it.

Rani was quieter than her usual self, and I noticed Malika cast her a worried look more than once. I barely had time to converse with her about it when a smart knock sounded at our door, and us girls all violently flinched, adrenaline pumping, hands on weapons.

The Old Ones didn't show any surprise, no doubt having heard the footsteps approaching. Kai leapt to answer the door.

"Good evening!" he said excitedly. "Are you here for high priestess Altara?" He stepped aside to reveal two black-swathed Xalya's Guards, whom Malika had told me all about with great venom. "Celibacy?" she'd scoffed at the time. "What a joke."

I was surprised when they both, one male and one female, bowed to me. Their voices muffled behind their face coverings when they said. "We summon you to the Priestess Moot, High Priestess. The other leaders are gathering at the Table."

"Very well," I said. "Let's go."

But they stood aside to reveal two teenaged, purple-robed acolytes of Agnolthi. "We must dress you in the formal robes," said a girl with long curly black hair and a shy smile. "If you will allow us."

I glanced at Zale in surprise, but he was smiling. "My mother wore those robes," he said quietly. "It will be another kind of joy to see them again."

Wobbles piped from his shoulder, "Nostalgia. Grief."

I breathed through the sudden tightness in my chest. "Come on in then. We don't want to keep them waiting."

Leading the way to the bedroom Zale and I shared, I heard Atax teasing Zale about Wobbles just as the girls shut the door behind them.

"Does he tell you when your cock is hard too?"

I rolled my eyes as both girls blushed.

"Apologies," I said, taking off my witch's robe. "The Old Ones have a…different way of life than the Ellythians."

"Oh, I find it very exciting!" the curly-haired girl said. "Beasts of legend have returned! It's like all the stories were true. They even bring their own magic—there's so much to learn from them!"

"Indeed." I smiled at her. "Even for me I have much to learn about my own temple. You two will have to teach me what I need to know."

The girls exchanged excited looks at the prospect, and my heart warmed to them immediately. I anticipated problems with my new appointment. Agnolthi might have approved me as being the leader of her Order of Yasani, but the leaders of the temple might not enjoy the hierarchy being moved around. I might be a second-born princess, but I'd been privy to nuances with power plays from the cradle.

The girls, curly-haired Hassa and giggling, red-cheeked Issel, were deft in dressing me in the robes of the high priestess of Agnolthi. It was a gown of purple silk embroidered with black beasts and symbols of fish and flower petals. The imagery brought a smirk to my face as I remembered the "flower" at the centre of Agnolthi's temple on Boneweaver Island. The girls had to sew the bodice to sit tightly around my bust, and there were cut outs on the sides that showed the curve of my waist. The gown then slinked down to the floor hugging my hips. It was completed by a wide, purple silk hood and attached cape that flowed behind me like deep-purple water.

It was a stunning gown, and when I walked out into the corridor, Zale waited alone, the others having gone ahead. It was the first time in my life I'd ever seen him go ashen. His blue eyes glistened as he held his hands out to me. I took them, and he kissed both my hands one at a time.

"If they want my execution, husband, I want you to take another wife," I said, half-jokingly.

The way Zale's eyes darkened into pools of midnight death told me that he did not, in fact, take it as a joke. "If they plan to execute you, wife," he growled, "I will tear this place and everyone in it to shreds. My ancestor built it; it is within my right to turn it to ash."

A shiver crawled down my spine at the serious, violent threat that I knew he would follow through on. I made a mental note never to joke about my death ever again. A tiny whimper behind me suddenly made me realise that my two acolytes had heard our conversation. I turned around to try and reassure them Zale wasn't going to kill them or anyone any time soon, but neither of them appeared fearful. Instead Hassa and Issel were staring up at Zale all bug-eyed and drooling. Issel's cheeks were bright red, her eyes as round as coins.

"Your Majesty," Hassa bowed, practically glowing with excitement. "I think it would be rather perfect if you arrived on a lion like Agnolthi herself! Everyone would go *positively* mad!"

"Oh, Goddess yes!" Issel squealed. "I beg of you, *please*, High Priestess! The last high priestess was nigh twenty years ago; it'll bring everyone so much joy!"

Despite the impending threat of my day of judgement I couldn't help but grin. "I knew I liked you two for a reason." Turning to Zale I arched a brow and caught him staring at me with a sort of dazed look on his face as Wobbles whispered in his ear. "Is it alright if I mount you, Your Highness?"

Zale shook his head a little, then realised what I'd said and smirked at me. He pulled off his shirt in one sweep and vanished it into the ether. "The day I have a problem with you mounting me, wife, is the day you need to cut my head off."

Wobbles leapt off his shoulder just in time as Zale flashed into his lion form. Behind me both girls couldn't help but cover their excited shrieks. As Wobbles and I climbed on top of him, the two girls quickly walked to the front, leading the way like bridesmaids.

I heard the buzz of many voices as we approached the great hall. The girls warned me that a crowd of all the courtiers and nobles of the Lotus Court had gathered to await the verdict for both myself and Pia. It was from there that I would enter the room of the High Priestesses' Round Table.

My nerves set my veins on fire as the yellow glow of the quartz-lights of the hall came into view. Hassa looked back at Zale to make sure we were following—or it could have been a look of warning because when I saw the great hall, it was *crowded* with finely dressed Ellythians with no space for us to get through.

Zale let out a rumbling, low growl, and the people closest to us jumped in fright and hastily leapt out of the way as Zale never broke his stride and prowled through, no doubt glaring at anyone who looked our way.

The Ellythian nobles gaped at us as we padded through the crowd, and though I did my best to hide my smirk, I failed, and it shone through, meeting each person eye for eye. If I was going to be given a punishment tonight, I would take it with my head held high—damn them all because I'd done nothing *that* wrong.

When we got to the set of gilded doors, I spied Rani and Malika waiting with Geravie, Atax and Kai.

"Fuck yes!" Malika mouthed at me.

I gave her an indulgent smile.

Milling about closest to the door were the youngest acolytes of all the temples dressed in their colours. Purple-robed boys and girls of my own temple waited for me with wide eyes. A few older purple-robed members looked me over, no doubt assessing me for my competence to be their leader. I didn't really know the answer to that myself, but at the very least, I hope I'd do my mother proud tonight.

Zale stopped right at the doors and upon some bestial urge, raised his head and gave a loud roar. The sound rattled my bones as I felt it rumble through his back and up the centre of my body, but I suppressed the urge to show any sign of the thrill it gave me. A primal part of me throbbed at the sound of my mate announcing my entrance and his protection of me. Several nobles covered their ears, and I briefly saw a commotion over someone who had fainted.

I slid off him with an imperious look at them all before turning and nodding at those of Agnolthi's temple and striding through the gilded doors. To my surprise my own acolytes followed me in, and as I entered the big room, they streamed through to join the crowd of acolytes that were lining the walls, making the room crammed full of silent people.

They all made way for a magnificent ornate round table that sat proud and ancient. Eight seats were set around it, five of which were occupied. At the far end, opposite to the door sat a throne, no doubt meant for the queen, so it sat empty. Five high priestesses stood upon my entry, and I stared out at my peers with careful interest.

The one closest to me, in black fighting leathers, no doubt Xalya's high priestess, nodded at me and indicated a chair between hers and one at which an elderly lady in white stood before—no doubt Cholnayak's high priestess. I nodded back, shoving my nerves down and strode to stand in front of that wooden chair. Keshmi stood with the group of purple-robed priestesses and acolytes and smiled encouragingly at me. I nodded to her, grateful that I knew someone in this room.

"We welcome Agnolthi to the Table," announced the elderly lady beside me. Hassa had warned me that at this Table, the high priestess represented their Goddesses and so were referred to accordingly.

"Be welcome," they all murmured.

Five pairs of eyes latched onto mine, and I couldn't help but *feel* the sheer feminine power coursing around the room, heady and potent. Like a storm of many colours, pulsing and testing the air. It felt like life, death, pain, power and joy were concentrated in this very room.

I raised my chin and swallowed the lump in my throat. "It is an honour to be here."

They nodded, and as we all sat down, I couldn't help but glance at the empty seat next to Xalya's high priestess. I counted the faces here.

In Cherimani's seat sat a young lady my own age dressed in pink and gold, her face bright with a smile, her arms adorned with golden bracelets.

In Luana's seat sat a voluptuous woman in her early thirties. Her dress drew my eye because she wore a golden

embroidered red bustier which left her stomach bare. A delicate golden chain was strung around her waist and she wore
an Ellythian dancer's saree, specially wrapped in many folds
like loose pants around her legs. She was picture of seductive
beauty, and I couldn't help but grin at her. She cocked her
head and grinned back.

I eyed Lisanthi, the Mother's seat, upon which sat a
woman in her late forties who wore a modest red dress that
covered her arms in full sleeves.

Cholnayak's seat wore a white saree, which covered her
head in the traditional dress of a widow, while Xalya's high
priestess was in her fifties, her fighting blacks worn from
years of use.

"The Goddesses whisper that Umali's seat has been
recently been chosen," Xalya's high priestess and general of
Ellythian forces announced. "But she has not presented to the
Lotus Court yet."

"I see," I said, wondering who it could be that she hadn't
arrived here yet. It was then that I noticed that we had an
audience above us too. A balcony was lined with senior
members of the court, including Aunt Rahana and Grandmother Parsha. Zale, Malika, Rani, and Geravie were also up
there, their nervous faces watching intently.

Everyone except Pia was here to witness my trial.

"Well," Cholnayak said, "let us begin. High Priestess of
the Order of Yasani, representative and voice of Agnolthi, you
are called to trial today for the"—she cleared her throat and
said in an incredulous voice—"attempted murder of Queen
Cheshni Lota. High priestess of Xalya, what is your assessment of the queen's health?"

"The queen is well," said the woman next to me. "I do not
see any physical mark, any injury or evidence of attack."

"Lisanthi?" Cholnayak asked.

The high priestess in red shrugged. "No injury, either. She is unconscious but well. In fact her essence is better than when I saw her last. As if some dark force has indeed left her."

Cholnayak grunted irritably. "That, too, was my assessment." Interestingly, she shot a dark look up at the balcony towards Aunt Rahana. "I have been saying this for a while now, though, to deaf ears. The Lotus Seat has been compromised. We are all in danger. Agnolthi has saved us."

I sat there in a state of shock for a moment, staring at Cholnayak. There was muttering in the balcony above and also whispers from those around us. Cholnayak's representative fixed me with a steady black eye, her white hair gleaming under the yellow quartz light. "What was your assessment, Agnolthi?"

I swallowed again as all eyes, including those I felt of the women and men of my temple, turned to stare at me. To judge me. "Upon meeting the queen for the first time, I sensed a dark magic in her. My magic responded quickly, and I acted in the fastest way I could—by shooting her with an arrow made of my own magic so that I could pull it out of her. My...magic digested it, as one digests food. I have done this before. It..." I looked up at Zale, who nodded at me encouragingly. "It felt exactly the same as when I relieved King Ashzale from his curse." I paused and looked around at them. "I believe this was the Reaper's magic." The room fell into a hush. "What I don't understand is," I said maybe boldly, maybe stupidly, "is how no one else detected it."

Cherimani's priestess let out a laugh. "Indeed, how *did* we miss it?" She cast a dark look at the seat of the queen.

"Agnolthi," Luana said to me, her voice husky and low. It

skittered across my skin, soft and kindly. "You are new to the Table; there will be much for you to learn, but traditionally, it has been Agnolthi's role to detect dark psychic forces entering the kingdom. We all have our roles to play."

"We *did* detect it," Ellythia's general said, turning to look me in the eye. "But we were forbidden to act."

Forbidden to act? I glanced up at Aunt Rahana, whose teeth were grinding where she sat in her seat next to Parsha. The Queen of Ellythia's word was law above all else. I turned back to the general.

"Are we prepared?" I asked her seriously. "For war?"

She nodded. "I have been prepared for the last twenty years, when your mother took the Temari Blade and left us open to Daanav attack."

The crowd murmured, and I tried not to take it as an insult, but there was a bite to my voice as I said, "She cannot apologise for her sins as she is dead. But I will contact my father to see if he knows anything about it."

The general stiffened at that. "We do not ask for help from the Lobrathians. We never have, and we never will."

"If it is there, we must retrieve it," I said, trying to reason with her. Didn't she see that this was the most logical solution?

The other high priestesses shifted uncomfortably.

"Well, I think it's a good idea," Cherimani said, the golden bangles on her wrists jingling. "It is ours, if they have it; we should get it back from them."

"The demons have Quartz; they can't possibly have it," the general said darkly.

It was my turn to stiffen. Right. My home had already fallen. Things were more dire than we'd thought. I fell silent in my seat, reluctant to speak here, in the place where I was a newcomer and not at all well versed with the way of things.

"One thing remains clear," Lisanthi said, "the Reaper is coming. Our temples are ready to face it. The only remaining one is Agnolthi's temple and Umali's across the sea. How will you prepare, High Priestess?"

They all turned to look at me.

I had no idea how to answer that question.

"I have yet to even meet the people of my own Order," I admitted. "I will meet with them and put a plan together."

The thread between Zale and I quivered as he reached out to reassure me. Zale knew about war; he would help me too. The other seats nodded as if this was reasonable.

"Then," Cholnayak said, "we can close this case in the name of the seven."

I whipped around to stare at her. "Do I not get a punishment?"

Cherimani and Luana laughed outright.

"You saved the queen," Xalya said begrudgingly. "You did your duty. There can be no punishment."

Cholnayak banged her wooden staff against the floor three times.

33
PIA

I had no idea how long I stayed in the infinite darkness of the Pit. The minutes merged into hours as I stood there—just breathing, just thinking. Eventually, as was always the way, the thoughts began twisting into something ugly. I'd been in here three times before, though never for this long, but the trick was to make up a story and live it out as if it were a play in your head.

In this one I imagined Aunt Yasani had never left, and I'd never been considered the eventual heir to the throne of Ellythia. I would have been allowed to align myself to one or two Goddesses, pursue a career of my choice and choose a husband out of the ranks of the nobility. I'd probably learn sailing craft and travel all around the Continent and into the Great Western Ocean and have strange and wonderful adventures with interesting people. I'd just gotten to choosing my imagined crew of talents, Malika and Rani being two of them, when the unmistakable sound of the Pit door opening hit my ears with an unearthly, ghostly wail. The metal gears grounded, the magic in them forcing the movement with colossal force until a slither of light hit my eyes.

Cold wind whooshed past me, and rough hands gripped my limp biceps, metal shackles clamped around my hands and ankles. I squeezed my eyes shut against the onslaught of sensations. Their fingers were like knives against my skin, the light like pokers stinging my eyes. I released a sigh as Commander Farrah's voice grated in my ears.

"You're going to the Priestess Moot," she muttered.

I registered that with dull acceptance until she said, "Your cousin has just come out."

"W-what?" I said, my voice like sandpaper.

She snorted, and I knew it was because I sounded like a weak, stammering child. Clearing my throat I remembered who I was. Altara was here. *Here!* But come out of where? "What do you mean, Commander?"

When she didn't answer me, I swam through the murky waters of my mind, trying to find purchase on my scrambling thoughts. Light hit my retinas painfully, and I squinted through it as the pain grounded me. I gasped for air like a woman coming to the surface after a long dive, the sights and sounds of the palace crashing into me like ripping ocean waves.

I was stripped and shoved into a bath, roughly scrubbed of the crystals of urine coating my legs—there was no bathroom in the Pit either. Broth was shoved down my throat, though it did nothing much to ease the dizziness and little for my dry throat. I was wrangled into a dressing room, dried and roughly clothed, then grabbed around the biceps by Xalya's Guards and hauled out of the room and through the palace.

My head swam, my legs ached and yet my heart warmed at the thought of Altara returning.

Goddess help us.

One of them heard me because quite suddenly, she appeared with a violent crack of lightning that only I could hear. The metallic smell of blood swam through the air. It wasn't Cholnayak. It wasn't Xalya, and it *definitely* wasn't Luana.

As the Guards pulled me down a long corridor, at its end, wreathed in licking-black flames, stood the Goddess of rage, Umali.

Terror struck me, sharp and bold, and Xalya's Guards ended up dragging me along as my legs gave way completely.

She'd never shown herself to me before, and none of the paintings in the palace had ever done her terrible countenance justice. Her naked skin was midnight blue, wild dark hair sweeping down to her hips, whipping in its own fell, electric wind, covering her heavy breasts. Around her neck she wore a garland of bleached demon skulls. In one hand she held a sword, in the other the severed head of a demon, its black blood dripping on the golden tiles of the palace floor. Her black eyes hit me with the force of a maelstrom, deep and wide and soul crushing. I could not breathe; I could not blink; my blood raged in my veins.

"Umali," I wheezed, pleading, praying.

Her black-red lips curved into a dark smile, the tips of white fangs showing. Blood trickled from her mouth down to her chin.

I immediately knew what this meant.

Something was coming. Something terrible and huge and so chaotic it would cause mass casualty.

When she spoke it was the roar of a tsunami that met me, but I could not reach up to my ears to cover them.

"The Order of Temari lives again, Grey Princess. Across the sea High Priestess Saraya Yasani Voltanius bears my mark, fights in my name, kills at my behest. Listen to the song of the dark, for it is coming for you."

She disappeared as if she'd never been there, and I was left wheezing and reeling. Xalya's Guards dragged me straight through the doorway and down another corridor.

"Umali," I wheezed again. Dear Goddess, what had she said. Saraya? High Priestess of the Order of Temari? My *cousin* Saraya, Altara's sister?

"She's gone mad," one of them exclaimed. "It was only two days."

Unexpectedly, I was slammed against the wall, leaving me choking on my own saliva. My head pounded, my throat, dry as bone.

"Girl? Did you say 'Umali'? Did you see her?" Farrah gruffed at me, but I caught the sense of urgency.

With great difficulty I focused on the two guards before me. Farrah's eyes searched mine with haste, and I tried to speak, but it came out as a wheeze.

"Water!" Farrah snapped.

A canteen was passed and pressed to my lips. Cold water coursed down my throat. I spluttered, then gulped it down gratefully.

"I saw her," I confirmed, my shoulders heaving.

They both recoiled for me as if I'd said something heinous.

"Goddess," the second guard said, pressing a hand to her own forehead. "She hasn't been seen since—"

"War," Farrah spat at her. "The last bloody war." She was angry, her shoulders tense, but her eyes were fixed on me with eagle-like focus. "War is here. It's on our doorstep, isn't it, girl?"

I stared at them both. We all knew what Umali meant. She meant bloodshed. She meant chaotic change—violent change. I gave them a stiff nod and said nothing more.

Quietly, and with less aggression, we passed through the palace until we got to the great hall. The place buzzed with urgent noise, and my heart sunk at the thought of crossing through a sea of Ellythian nobility in the state I was in. I doubted I looked good at all.

So I did what I could with two sets of shackles on and made my back straight and raised my chin, walking with the swagger of an experienced swordswoman, albeit a little jerky. The Priestess Moot would decide my fate tonight, and I'd been naive not to have seen this coming. I thought my mother would just sit me in the Pit forever until I died. Her face after she'd told Xalya's Guard to take me there would never leave me. It was colder than anything I'd ever seen.

"What did they give Altara? And for what crime?" I asked just as we reached the yellow light of the hall.

Farrah glanced down at me. "For shooting the queen with a magical arrow. She's the high priestess of Agnolthi," she muttered. "She was cleared of charges. The queen is free of whatever black magic was on her."

Shock winded through me so fiercely that it removed all panic from my entrance to the hall. I didn't even care that everyone was staring at me as I took in that my grandmother had black magic on her. But more than that...Altara was High Priestess of the Order of Yasani, and Saraya was High Priestess of the Order of Temari. My cousins. Pride was a golden tide that flushed every dark thought away from my being, and I couldn't help but smile. The backs of my eyes burned because it made sense. Yasani's daughters couldn't be queens of Ellythia, but they'd made their own way back here. They'd done for the family what I could not: They would make our ancestors proud and bring glory to the Lota House once again.

And hopefully mask my complete non-performance in that area.

We were at the doors before I knew it, and when I stepped into the room of the Round Table, I was fucking *beaming* like a mad woman.

My eyes found Altara, flanked by Keshmi and the other purple-robed acolytes sitting at the seat of Agnolthi and her emerald eyes, a twin to mine, glittered with emotion. I was lifted by the wings of this vision. That my mother had thought she would never make it out of the Eternal Forest, and. Here. She. Was. Powerful and a high priestess, no less. That was a slap to my mother's face I was sure, and I was devastated that I missed it by being stuck in the Pit. It didn't matter; she was here, and that meant Zale was here too. I checked the balcony and found him standing by Malika, Rani, Kai and Atax. I nodded at my friends before glancing back at Zale, my brother-in-law. He was hard to miss, of course, and his blue eyes were on me, a slight crease between his brows. There was worry there, I noted with surprise, and by the Goddess was that different from the last time I'd seen him— cold and nonchalant about everything.

I pulled myself back to the Round Table and tried to focus my flighty thoughts.

The last time I'd appeared before the Priestess Moot, Agolthi's seat had been empty. The circle was now complete. Ellythia was whole once again, and it brought me an insane level of joy to see that. I grinned at Altara with all my teeth, and Goddess bless my cousin, because she was the most beautiful thing I had seen in a long time when she grinned back at me.

I think I really *am* crazy.

"Princess Pia Rahana Lota." Otha Dhumvar, Cholnayak's high priestess, stared me down with her dark, intelligent eyes. She looked exactly the same as she did three years ago at this very Table and not a bit less sharp.

I hid a grimace and bowed as I remembered what Cholnayak had said to me back on Boneweaver Island. Something in Otha's gaze told me she knew about *that* too. I wondered what the Goddesses shared with the high priestesses. They sure liked to bother *me* a lot.

"Three years ago," Othar continued, "for maiming your betrothed, and the inability to control your magic, you were exiled for ten years to Taraka School."

"Handed over to Danaavs, rather," Altara said mildly. "I thought it a rather odd punishment to send our girls to the enemy."

Everyone in the room stiffened, and I wanted to kiss her.

"You'll have to forgive my ignorance," Altara continued, "but under what wisdom was this punishment given? *To anyone*?"

"The crime was a heinous one," the high priestess of Xalya said. "The queen determined the punishment needed to be just as heinous."

"So it was not a punishment approved by the Round Table?" Altara's raised brows circled the room.

"The Ellythian's Queen's word is law, Agnolthi's servant," Lisanthi's high priestess said matter-of-factly. "And as the queen is priestess prime for all seven goddesses of our fair kingdom, she also rules the Round Table."

I could tell that Altara was fighting back a smirk. "And if the priestess prime is not here?"

Luana's servant, a girl I did not know, sat back in her chair and chimed with a smile that would melt any man's pants off, "Then the high priestesses must be unanimous in our decision."

The relief around the room was palpable, even as I felt my mother's glare down upon me. All six high priestesses turned their attention back to me, and I knew what would come next.

"Princess Pia," Cherimani's representative leaned forward, eager and rosey-cheeked. "Has your magic returned?"

I swallowed my shame like a medicinal potion. "No, High Priestess, it has not."

Silks ruffled, someone above us coughed, and my throat burned. In this room they could do anything to me. They could decide my execution. They could strip me of all titles. They could even make me infertile, if they wished. This Table had done that for bad crimes. They'd also done worse.

Ellythia's general tapped her finger on the wood of the table. "The sentence was not served. You returned without permission."

Before anyone could say anything else, Altara piped in a low voice, "Why *did* you return, Princess?"

My cousin had given me a chance to speak, and speak I would. "To warn of the threat to Ellythia. To tell the queen that the subterranean demons launched an attack on Levu village on Boneweaver Island."

Everyone went still as if struck by a spell. The general's finger paused its tapping on the table as she turned to me, her face ashen. "How many?"

"An entire company. With a Pentarog assassin. They were working with the Daanavs."

Someone gasped. Cherimani's pretty mouth dropped open. The entire table looked up at my mother, who now stood still on the balcony. She'd not told them, I realised with surprise. She'd not told anyone about what she knew about the attack. Was it arrogance? Or stupidity that she'd let the demons do as they wished on Boneweaver Island? Because everyone knew what this meant. Marine demons and subterranean demons had only banded together in the time of the Reaper's last campaign. War was here again.

Cholnayak's priestess turned to the general, and her voice was sharp as a blade. "Bhairavi, you know what to do."

"Immediately." The general waved her hand in the air, and a map of all three of the islands that made up the Ellythian Isles was revealed, glowing dots for the location of each one of the forces, most of them concentrated on Lota Island with a small contingent on Tiger Island. We all watched as she moved her hand in a complex pattern only she knew, sending white beams of light to two of the dots marked black and purple.

"I will not allow it." My mother's voice struck the air like a hammer.

"You are overruled, Crown Princess," Xalya's voice snapped, and with a flourish, she sent out two magical signals. Before dawn two companies, one of Xalya's and the other of Agnolthi's war mages, would be on ships to Tiger Island to man the southern border.

My heart broke and was healed in the space of a single moment. I dared not glance at my mother's face because I knew what fury would be etched there. In the absence of the queen, the Round Table ruled Ellythia; that was old hierarchy established two thousand years ago. For the first time since my grandmother had taken the throne fifty years ago, the Lota family had been overruled by the Round Table. It was a slap to my mother's face to be treated as second best, once again. Whispers broke out in the balcony, and I knew word would get out to the entire nobility within the hour.

I did glance at Altara then, but she was already looking at me, the success written all over her face. With one arrow of her magic, she'd single handedly saved us.

We had hope yet.

"Done," Bhairavi, Ellythia's general said, her face a little flushed. "I will triple the watch and prepare for invasion." She turned to Altara. "Whatever plans you have for your temple need to be accelerated. We need Agnolthi's battle mages ready to act."

Altara nodded. Everyone turned back to me.

"The message has been received, Princess," Bhairavi said, her dark eyes searching my face as if I had more secrets to reveal. "The issue remains that you still disobeyed orders. This could have been a written missive to us."

I wasn't going to tell them that I had written to my mother multiple times over the last three years without reply. I'd stopped sending them when the pigeons returned the letters, unopened.

"The other issue," Cholnayak said, "is that we have a Lota princess without magic."

My stomach turned at that. *A Lota Princess without magic does not exist.* They were thinking about stripping me of my title. Something golden but heinous unfurled within me at the thought. I listened with bated breath.

"Imprisonment works just as well as exile," Lisanthi said

thoughtfully. "She could serve the rest of her five years in the dungeons."

My stomach clenched at that, but what was five years in the face of a full life with promised freedom?

Cholnayak's voice sounded like footsteps over a grave. "I propose she take the white robe."

My heart stopped in my chest. She wanted me to join her White Widows. To serve Cholnayak in monkhood meant a vow to never take a man and never bear children; it was the ultimate renunciation of material life. My job would be to cook and clean, to care for the dying and deceased. Considering what I did to one man, it made sense to deny me of another ever again.

The entire room went quiet. They knew it was a harsh punishment, but it was fitting, poetic even. From somewhere far away, in the back of my mind, I heard a deep, rasping cackle.

Bhairavi, taking pity on me, perhaps, sighed. "She could also take the black robe. Swear to serve in Xalya's army for the war to come. Without magic she can serve in the foot soldier's division, without rank or title."

Lisanthi's priestess nodded. "Nothing else would be fitting. A life lived in service is perhaps the only way to regain any honour after the crime."

I could only stare at them. I'd known it was coming, but to either take the black robe or the white? It was not death, at least, and both were humiliating in their eyes. But to me? It smelled like freedom, and I was a woman who yearned for a sip from that golden chalice.

"I think we should let her decide," Cherimani said, her high-pitched voice kind. "Choosing her own path is a punishment on its own."

In amongst the six sets of sharp eyes, I found Altara, who met me with a strong gaze that said, "I am with you."

I wetted my lips to try and hide my budding excitement—they would know for sure I was mad if I showed I was happy about this. I would no longer bear the Lota name. I would no longer be a princess. In the way that bastards do, I would bear the name of my patron Goddess. I would be free to choose my own way. Choosing to leave Boneweaver Island had been my first choice for myself, and now I made a second. "The black. I choose to be an acolyte of Xalya."

Ellythia's general gave me a curt nod. "Very well. You will return to the barracks with me tonight." She looked around the Table. "Anything else?"

I cleared my throat and said before I lost my nerve, "Umali appeared to me."

"Umali appeared to you?" my mother hissed from her seat high above. "You're lying."

To my knowledge no Goddess had yet appeared before my mother, so I understood why she assumed I wasn't telling the truth.

"Yes," I said confidently, glancing up at her. "She informed me that the Order of Temari lives again, and that Princess Saraya Voltanius is Umali's high priestess."

A wave of gasps sounded from the balcony around us, and the priestesses shifted in their seats. I felt Altara's shock and nodded to her reassuringly.

"Lightning does not yield," Luana mused, citing the Voltanius house motto and twirling a golden braceleted hand in the air. "Yasani's two daughters as high priestesses. It smells of fate."

Otha Dhumvar grunted in agreement. "Saraya Voltanius

will not come here if the rumours are true, and she is wed to a half-fae, half-God."

Half-God? This was news to me, and I could tell it was also news to Altara when she glanced at me, her eyes wide. She nodded slowly. "Subterranean demons have taken over Quartz. I am waiting to hear back from her. I am hoping wing-brother will return soon."

Everyone turned to stare at her. "Wing-brother?" Cherimani laughed, clapping her hands. "Truly?"

Altara gave her a smile. "Courtesy of my husband. They are friends of his we met in the Eternal Forest."

More than one person made an impressed sound. Bhairavi simply stared at her.

I could have laughed, and as the high priestesses exchanged a few more words between themselves, I knew Altara deserved to sit at the Round Table.

"Very well," Othar said, turning to me with a sigh. I could swear she looked a little disappointed that she wasn't getting me as an acolyte. "Princess Pia Rahana Lota. Henceforth, you are stripped of your name, your titles and any ties to land and family. You are put into the care of the Holy Mother of War. You will take her name and be known as Pia Xalya."

As Othar pounded her staff three times, it was like a tiny, golden gate inside me clicked open.

Looking up at the balcony, I saw the tense shoulders of my mother's back as she stormed off. Malika and Rani were both holding hands and looking down upon me, crying. I might have freedom from my title, but I paid a high price. For every day of these past three years, Rani, Malika and I slept, ate, trained and bathed together. We'd also laughed, sobbed and screamed in each other's arms. Now we'd do none of those things together, ever again.

34

ALTARA

I watched my cousin leave with Ellythia's General with my gut churning. She'd been stripped of her title and status and was condemned to serve in Xalya's army for the rest of her days, and yet...she'd grinned at me. Like she was *happy* about it. Unease squirmed its way through me, and I was suddenly not sure that Pia was entirely *alright*. I supposed people dealt with grief in different ways, but still.

The worst part of it was that the entire thing was my fault. If I'd never defied my stepmother and run away from home to come to Ellythia, she would never have sent the Butcher and the subterranean demons to hunt me down. Because of the demons, Pia had taken it upon herself to come here with Rani and Malika to ask her grandmother for help, thus illegally ending her own exile. Now she was paying the price for me. I glanced up at Malika and Rani, now sobbing into each other's arms, but was quickly distracted by the other high priestesses getting up to leave for the night.

Cholnayak's priestess tapped me on the shoulder. "You must learn to merge your magic." She nodded at Zale still standing on the balcony, watching us, his tattooed forearms braced on the railing. "If we have Old Ones on our side, we can consider ourselves lucky. Merge your powers, and you will help us in the war to come."

A small cough sounded at my side, and we both turned to see Cherimani's priestess standing there, but her smile had disappeared.

"There is still a darkness in him, high priestess," she said seriously. "When the Reaper comes, it is because he is coming for the Boneweaver King too. Is his allegiance *truly* with us?"

Her honesty caught me off guard, but I saw the others listening in closely. I knew that what I said next was important.

"His loyalty is to me," I said evenly. "We are star-born mates. Once I broke his curse, wherever I go, he goes."

"So the old legend is true," Luana's priestess said breathlessly. "I see the connection between you two as clear as the sunlight. It is a blessed union." She beamed at me, then up at Zale.

"I see it too," Lisanthi's priestess said, though her voice was whisper quiet as if she were disturbed by something. "But..."—she exchanged a look with Cholnayak's priestess— "I also see the bond between him and the Reaper."

A knot twisted inside of me at that, and I stared at her. "But I broke the curse," I said softly. "The darkness around his heart is gone."

"You might have removed the magic of the curse," Lisanthi's priestess said, "but you cannot remove the bond the Reaper created when he made the curse when Zale was a newborn. Their magic is tied."

I glanced up to find the balcony empty. The girls and the Old Ones, including Zale, had left. "How do we destroy such a bond?" I asked, looking around at the four remaining high priestesses.

"You are the high priestess of Agnolthi," Luana's priestess cooed, cocking her head to study me. "If you cannot find a way then no one can."

"Altara," Cholnayak's priestess said roughly. "That means he is a risk to us all."

BACK IN OUR SUITE, WE ALL SAT AROUND THE HEARTH FIRE, WITH Geravie and Keshmi joining us. Pia's absence was like a thorn in my side, and I couldn't help but see her smiling in my mind's eye. We sat quietly nursing goblets of wine, each of us with our own thoughts, except Kai, whose charcoal pencil scratched softly on a piece of parchment. He was adept at sketching and declared that he wanted to draw Lota City to show Raen when they got back to Boneweaver Island. No one had the heart to tell him we didn't know when we'd be going back.

The knowledge that Zale and the Reaper shared a bond just like the one I had with Zale sloshed around in my gut like sewer sludge, and I wanted to hurl at the thought of a glittering black thread linking the two of them. I glanced at Zale who sat with Wobbles muttering in his ear, and I wondered how much of the high priestess' conversation he'd heard and whether he knew about the bond. I didn't want to think of him as a risk to the Ellythians, but if the magic I'd felt coming from my grandmother was any indication, I knew the Reaper was powerful. I hoped my grandmother was alright. They told me I could see her tomorrow, in my new role.

Casting my eye about the room, I saw Malika and Atax quietly arguing about something in the corner. She touched the dangling obsidian sword earring on his left ear and Atax said, "Firebird, if I ever give it to you, you'll know I've gone truly insane and should be put down." Malika crossed her arms and scoffed.

Atax, for his part as Zale's commander, would follow Zale until the end of his days, I knew that in my heart. And Kai, sitting opposite Rani by the hearth, with his silver braids brushing the parchment, would also follow his brothers until the end. My heart cried out for Rani, who shook her head as Keshmi offered her tea. As the two older ladies ate a late supper by the dining table, I strode over to Rani and sat next to her, putting my arms around her shoulders and leaning my chin on her lean shoulder. She stilled under my hold, and I pulled back to look at her.

"I wish I could have seen it," she whispered without taking her eyes off the orange flickering flames. "Agnolthi in front of the palace, making you high priestess."

Nodding, I remembered the first time I'd ever seen Agnolthi, the three girls and I had been summoned to the temple in Taraka Town. It was a special moment among many that I'd shared with them.

"Me too, Rani. And I heard what happened in your home-town. I'm sorry I wasn't there to blast them back to their houses."

Rani glanced at me with a grimace, and I realised then that something small, but critical had changed in her like the shutter on a quartz-lamp being closed. The girl I'd travelled with around Boneweaver Island had hope in her heart and worn kindness on her sleeve. *This* girl carried the weight of the world on her shoulders, and her eyes bore a grey despair that scared me.

Because I'd seen it in myself.

"Oh, Rani," I whispered.

"I'm fine." She suddenly straightened and gave me a brave smile that didn't reach her eyes. "I'm glad you're back. I'm glad we're all back together."

We didn't talk about Pia. Instead Malika came to sit next to us, and I told them about the Eternal Forest and the strange grey bunnies that liked to groom people, the steaming pools of blue light and the white owls that talked in serious voices. They drank in my every word as if it would save us from what was coming.

I glanced up at Zale periodically and watched him stare into the dying fire, the shadows cast across his face. When his eyes flicked to mine, he smiled, rubbing a thumb across his jaw. The celestial thread between us twanged slightly.

"My mate, he said into my head. *I worry about what is going on behind those eyes of yours."*

I did not want to hide anything from him.

"The high priestess of Cherimani said you and the Reaper share a bond, kind of like the one we share."

His mental voice was harsh when he said, *"It will never be like ours."*

So he knew about it. Or felt it. But the possessiveness in his voice reassured me.

"But what does it mean?" I pressed. *"If you are tied to him in some way—"*

"We will need to find a solution, my little star," he said simply. *I will have Raen look into it."*

I immediately felt better that he'd thought about this and had a plan. We had a plan, and that was good.

"*I will see if anyone in my temple knows —*"

He gave a small shake of his head. "*It is best if as few people know about this as possible, Tara. The Ellythians already expect us to turn on them. I don't want to startle them further.*"

I sighed, knowing that was true if the side-eye looks from the courtiers gave any indication. I understood it—I really did. If I didn't know my little band of Old Ones personally, and I'd heard the legends about the way Zale's father had trained his son and nephews to be the best, most ruthless, possible killers, I'd be looking at them with a wary eye too.

After we bade everyone goodnight, and I gave Atax a look of warning to stay out of Malika's room, my mate and I turned in for the night.

Wobbles scrambled off me as he seemed to know when I needed him gone. Lucky for him, otherwise he'd be rubble by now. The Priestess Moot had been one event I'd remember for the rest of my life. To see Altara sitting in Agnolthi's seat, in the height of her power, surrounded by other powerful women, unravelled something warm in me.

I was, however, extremely surprised that I'd been allowed in. My family had been considered Lota enemies since the time my father sold his soul to the Reaper. In the two hundred years that we'd all been gone, the Lota family had not forgotten. It was a legend told to young children, a story that had lingered in the back of the mind: The Emperor of Demons would one day return, and when he did, the Boneweavers were supposed to ally with him.

It was also not lost on me that I now had a court of my own people out there. We had beasts we could work with, warriors who would fight at my side if need be. And in the war that was coming, we would need everyone on our side, but my mate, most of all.

Altara was, apart from myself, the most powerful weapon we had. And now that I'd heard her sister was high priestess of Umali, mated to some half-god creature, it gave me some heart. It also gave me some ideas. The Reaper was headed right toward me. And against power that no one could match, the only thing we could be was careful and clever. The gears of my mind had been steadily turning since we'd left the Eternal Forest. I knew what was coming and the seed of a plan was growing in my mind

"So how do we merge our magic?" Altara asked me, sitting in front of her mirror, brushing out her beautiful long hair. "The high priestess of Cholnayak said we should try that."

I stared at her for a moment and I wondered if she'd read my mind. I smiled and realised that nothing in this world could make me feel like Altara did, and the warmth in my chest at the vision of her was a balm to my worn soul. It was a foreign feeling, and one that I was more than ready to get used to.

"Sex, Altara." I knew I was gloating, but I was so fucking excited by the concept of being inside her again. "Sex is how we do it."

Her own smile was laced with eager promise, and it went right to my cock. "Well then. Now we know they're not going to kill us, I suppose we can do that."

"Even if they were going to kill us," I said darkly, "I'd still find a way."

She laughed, low and seductive, and it drew me in like a fish on a hook. She sauntered toward me and placed a small hand on my chest, her wedding ring glittering, tutting with mock disapproval. "Oh, Zale. You have no idea who you're dealing with. You are not the first man I've had."

I knew exactly who I was dealing with. I viciously grabbed her round the deep curve of her beautiful waist and pulled her toward me, getting in her face. "I want the names of every man you've fucked, Altara, because I'm going to fly all the way to Lobrathia and rip their throats out with my teeth and present you their cocks in a velvet lined box."

Her eyes went round at the edges because she knew I was serious. "Whoa! Sam is a nice boy. You'll leave him alone."

"Sam?" I growled, imagining a brawny palace guard spying on Altara while she practiced her archery or rode her horse...*or as she changed her clothes.*

Something sharp and hot stabbed me in the throat, making me bleed, and I abruptly let her go to gape. My hand went to my neck and came away sticky with crimson. "Tara?" I said, shocked.

My mate's lightning skittered over her bronzed skin as she pointed a finger at me. "You were squeezing too hard—*and* threatening my friend, Zale. There's a lot more where that came from!" She lifted her hand as sparks flew from her five fingers in a threatening wave.

My cock twitched as I stared at her raw power, then something dark and oozing filled me as I realised I'd hurt my mate.

"Horror," Wobbles squeaked from the floor. "Regret."

Altara nodded in approval. "The only acceptable response."

I stared at her in shock, clutching my chest as pain wracked through my body. "I'm sorry, my mate. It won't happen again."

Her face softened. "It's alright, I think you were getting jealous at the thought of me having sex with someone else."

I looked down at Wobbles aghast, and he confirmed with a sombre nod. So that was where the sudden anger had come from. The thought of hurting Altara was a physical pain I could never recover from. I would rather die a slow death by a thousand cuts than allow that.

"Hey." Altara's fingers were on my face, warm and comforting, her sweet and spicy scent filling my nose, making me groan. "Help me take this off. It'll distract you."

I prowled after her as she went to her dressing room, pulling at the laces to her high priestess gown. The style was a little different compared to the one my mother wore, thank the Goddess, because I didn't really want to be thinking about my mother right now.

Staring at Altara's naked shoulder, she cleared her throat, and I shook myself before undoing the ties of her cape and helping her unravel the rest of the silk.

She twirled around and stood naked before me, and it was with a sort of daze that I stared at the heavenly glow of her skin, shimmering bronze in the soft-orange quartz light. She was so fucking beautiful that it could make a man weep. It hit me then. I *had* her. I actually had my mate all to myself. She was safe and whole before me, and all I could think about was how I could make her happy. The beast in me roared with joyous approval, and I didn't even need Wobbles to tell me that's what that warm, ravenous sensation was.

Before I could do anything, Altara dropped to her knees, unlacing my pants with a feverish look in her eye. I could only stare at the picture of her kneeling there when abruptly, she released my cock and it sprang free, already hard.

I couldn't count the number of women who'd taken me

into their mouths, but to see Altara's perfect pink lips kissing the fat crown of my cock sent a wave of tingling magic through my entire body. Her hands were so small as she held me and when she licked me from base to tip, I tilted my head back and moaned like an animal.

"Tara," I whispered, holding her jaw on either side and rubbing my thumbs over her cheeks, soft as a peach. She blinked up at me, the long dark fans of her lashes like a butterfly's wings as they fluttered over her jewel eyes. The way she was looking at me made me feel like I was the only man in the world for her. Like she *wanted* to be mine. That she desired me as much as I did her. It healed something in me that I hadn't even known was broken.

She put her lips around me then and sucked on my head. My balls tightened in response, and I stroked her hair, like a river of silken midnight. Taking me further in, she hummed at my taste, and her wet, soft mouth sent my body into a rigid stupor. She sucked me hard, up and down my length, licking and moaning as I stroked her jaw. Her naked breasts sat plump, and I lost myself at the sight of them, wanting to lick and bite at her sweet nipples. I knew that her skin tasted like heaven; I knew that her pussy *felt* like heaven, and the knowledge that she wanted to be with me so intimately that we could power-share drove me rabid with heat. I was groaning and clutching her head as she sucked me off, her cheeks hollowing out, my hips bucking as the tiger in me hissed at the sight of my mate. When her left hand went down to her pussy and she played with herself, I almost lost it, my body coiling and twisting until I was so wound up that I was ready to burst. My cock hit the back of her throat, and I was consumed by the feeling, grunting, my abs tightening, my mind struggling to contain my thoughts. But I couldn't come in her mouth. If she wanted to power-merge, we needed to come at the same time.

Without thinking I pulled myself out of her mouth and reached down to grab her around the waist. I hoisted her over my shoulder, slapping her on her naked, round ass. She squealed in outrage, punching my back in a way that tickled me. I headed straight for the bed and threw her down.

"Wait, you gnarled beast!" she panted, bouncing on the bed in a way that had me staring, round-eyed with lust.

My voice, though rough and dark, still managed to sound offended, though I was really not. "I'm not gnarled."

She burst out laughing, and the sound was music that filled me up like a whirlwind golden storm. A growl tore through me, and I climbed on to the bed and pulled her on top of me. I needed her to control me a little, else I might come too soon.

"If you want to power-share with me, my wife, I must fuck you senseless."

But the vision of her naked, plump, curves sitting on top of me was almost enough to make me finish. I groaned, savagely squeezing the base of my cock. Altara laughed at my turmoil, low and deep.

"You think this is funny?" I panted, dragging my gaze up her perfect form.

"It's so funny to watch King Ashzale trying not to come too soon."

My eyes snapped back at her. "I always make you come first."

"Mmm," she nodded, tapping a long finger to her chin as she ground her wet pussy against the base of my cock. I tilted my head back, savouring the sensation. "We've fucked all of three times, Zale."

I've fucking had enough of her teasing me so I grabbed her hips and did what I knew would make her stop. I lifted her and pushed the crown of my cock into her sweet, sweet entrance.

She let out a breathy moan, and I sat up, her fingers coming around my neck. I loved the feel of her hands on me so much that I couldn't wait any longer and shoved her down, impaling her onto me. She gave a little shriek, and I watched her face, going still and observant for any sign of pain. She was so tight around me, her pussy clutching onto me as if it never wanted to let me go. But she was also wet, *so* wet with her sweet honey I knew I'd need to taste her after this.

"Too much?" I asked, trying to slow my breathing.

She shook her head, unable to speak, so I licked up the side of her neck, giving into the bestial need to mark her with my scent and taste her all over at the same time. The star-bond must've taken me over because suddenly I was ravenous for her skin, and I licked her up the other side of her neck and then up her sternum, grunting like a madman at her taste.

She giggled, and I rumbled in my chest because how I was feeling was not funny at all, and I punished her with an upward jerk of my hips. Her breasts jiggled perfectly, and I shoved her mouth onto mine, swallowing her moan.

I'd need her to come a few times in quick succession, so I lapped at both her nipples in turn, bouncing her on my cock and moving her hips back and forth until she was breathless and moaning, digging her nails into my shoulders for more. I lay down, bringing her with me so her clit ground against my stomach as I relentlessly pounded my length into her, whispering praises into her ear. She cried out my name and bucked, grinding her hips, and I told her yet again how much I wanted her. "Sweet star, you feel like heaven right now." She groaned in response. "I'm going to fuck you like this every day until the end of time. Lick your sweet pussy and fill it up until you're overflowing with my seed."

Her magic rose up, seeking me out with tendrils of light, shimmering around the room and smashing against my chest. She shattered in my arms, shuddering and gasping, and I didn't stop, fucking her through her orgasm. Her pussy tightened around me, those inner walls squeezing my shaft, and I couldn't help but fall in love with her even more. The beast in me locked my arms around her, refusing to let her go. But I was sane enough to remember the plan.

"My mate, direct your magic into me," I breathed into her ear.

When I felt a trickle of her lightning around us, I flipped us over and turned her around like a doll, and she let me do as I pleased, which brought out a new side of me. Pulling her hips up and back as if I was doing the breeding ritual, I eased into her wet sensitive pussy. She cried out, grinding her ass against me, and I leaned down and licked up her precious spine. She moaned my name, and I lost it, grabbing her hips and fucking into her so hard she moved up the bed on each thrust.

She grabbed onto the headboard. "Zale!"

"I know," I gritted out, my voice an octave lower, and I felt my pupils dilate. "I can't help it." I could see every strand of her hair now, every sweet centimetre of her skin, and it only made me want her more. "I'm going to fuck you until you can't walk." Sucking on my first two fingers, I reached around, circling her swollen clit, rubbing my fingers in her delicious wet slick. I brought my fingers into my mouth again and sucked on my fingers, relishing her divine taste, and rubbed the remainder of her scent on my lips so I could smell her better as I fucked her. Her taste spurred me on, my hips rutting into her of their own accord, until her front was plastered against the headboard, and I had to yank her back toward me, holding her by her breasts as I devoured her mouth. I swallow her cries, still fucking her as I swept my hands down her perfect breasts and the smooth line of her stomach, back to her clit again. She lay her head back onto my shoulder, and I suckled on her neck hard enough to bruise.

"I have so much cum for you, my mate," I groaned against her skin. "So much fucking cum for this tight little, princess pussy."

She came with a scream, and I slammed into her, shuddering as her noise made me come. "Tara!" I roared, and I let my power out, alongside my cum, thrusting while shoving it into her, filling her up. Her magic pulled on mine, drawing it into herself through her core, and in sheer, undulating ecstasy, I rumbled like a tiger, the beast in me roaring with happiness as I allowed my mate to take from me what she needed. Altara let out a little growl of her own, and I grinned savagely, pulsing into her pussy as I felt her golden power trickling up to me through my core. It kissed my cock, my balls, before filling me up from the inside out. Sparks let off around us, bright white and electric, and my body felt charged like the sea before a storm.

"Dear Goddess!" Altara moaned, wiggling her hips. "You're still hard."

"Only for you," I panted as her electricity and void filled my head and made me feel like I was swimming in deep water. "Always for you." After barely a second of thought, I rumbled in her ear, "One more time, my wife."

WE LAY SWEATY AND SATED ON THE BED AFTER A TOTAL OF SEVEN rounds of blistering sex. My mind was in a daze, my body feeling light and heavy at the same time as I held Altara close to me, licking a bead of sweat off her shoulder. Our combined magic pooled within us, strands of light and dark twining around each other until you couldn't tell which was which and whose was whose. All of a sudden my skin felt like it was on fire.

I knew it was coming, but when it finally happened, I didn't realise the colossal, world-ending joy it would feel like.

Pain burst from my hand and the tiger inside of me purred as Altara leapt onto her knees, yelping. I looked at my hand now covered in glittering celestial light, a message sent by the star that made us. It was stunning and beautiful, and by the Wild Mother was it painful, but it settled down. When the light faded, Altara gaped at the back of her right hand. I stared at my left.

Inked in glittering celestial magnificence was a butterfly, it's wings dark obsidian flecked with light.

On my mate's hand was a black tiger, its snarling face bearing bright-blue eyes. I lay back and blinked up at her as my entire being became so full and calm it was like I've never known peace before. I didn't know that love could feel like this, but it was like walking through the gates of eternity. Altara blinked back at me, her face twisted in deep emotion I could now feel in my own chest.

I took her hand and kissed her palm. "I love you with every part of my rotten, black being. I waited for you for so long, but I would have waited two hundred years more if it meant I could have you. We were made for each other, Altara."

She audibly swallowed and leaned down to press a gentle kiss on my lips that burned like the sweetest type of brand. Her lips brushed against mine, and I breathed in her breath as she whispered, "And now the Gods agree."

W hen I woke up the next morning, my head pounded like a giant was squeezing it. I groaned, twisting around to find Zale's arms tight around my waist and—

"Oh Goddess," I breathed, realising that he was *still* inside of me. We'd made love yet again, after our mating marks appeared.

A deep chuckle sounded behind me as Zale's fingers splayed before my face, that dark butterfly inked there. But he wasn't showing me his mark—lightning zapped between each of his fingers in a dangerous, concentrated wave.

"It's a nice trick," he said, a little too smugly for my liking.

I gave him a sharp elbow to the gut, and he just chuckled all the more as he pulled out of me. I couldn't believe we'd slept like that all night, but I supposed it was part of the ritual to power share. Leaping up to my knees and supressing a wince at the burn between my legs, I glared at him. "How'd you get the hang of that so quickly?" I demanded, then looked at my own hands. "What powers will I have?"

He smirked at me and made the lightning dance up his

wrists and arms. "Oh, the trouble we are going to get up to together, Tara. Don't worry, I'll teach you."

I slapped my knees impatiently, but it only made my head pound further. I squeezed my eyes shut, and Zale's male scent consumed me as his huge hands pressed gently on either side of my face.

"It'll go away," he said softly. "You just need to drink water."

"I've never needed to drink water to fix anything," I mumbled as he grabbed the pitcher next to our bed and poured me some. "I have healing, remember?"

"Your body is just integrating my magic." His eyes watched me like a hawk as I drained the goblet. "The first time is supposed to be the worst."

"Do you have a headache?"

"Yes."

Well, that made me feel a little better.

We bathed and got ready to meet the new day. It would be my first time assuming the duties of a high priestess, though because Agnolthi had only ever chosen a temple leader from the ranks of the Boneweaver women, the role here was different from the other leaders. I would be expected to help orchestrate the battle mages and make plans for the Reaper's arrival, but every other system was already established.

After that we would head down to tour with the other temples. It was just my luck that because of the Boneweaver's long history of worshipping Agnolthi, Zale would be allowed to come with me into Agnolthi's sector.

The entirety of Lota City was divided into temple sections, with each housing the various businesses associated with that Goddess and the temple at its head like a palace. Cherimani's district held the education sector, all the schools and universities.

Luana's district was the pleasure section, where the pleasure priestesses, entertainers and artists worked. The market was primarily in Lisanthi's district, including all the food and cloth trading. The army was housed in Xalya's section, including training grounds as well as the weapons makers, blacksmiths and fletchers. Cholnayak's district bore the cremation grounds and healing, though they specialised in the care of the elderly.

Agnolthi's district lay between Cholnayak's and Xalya's, and was the centre for healing, apothecaries and the specialised schools for magic.

Umali had no district in Lota City, as she was an unstable and chaotic energy and therefore deemed unsafe to keep close to the main populous. Out of respect for her, the ancients built her temple across the sea in Lobrathia, where it could watch over the Lotus Sea between the Continent and Ellythia. A seventh, honorary platform had been made for her, upon the place called Ellythia's hill by the palace, where the Blade of Temari had been speared into the soil for two thousand years' worth of protection until my mother took it and left these shores for Quartz.

According to the high priestesses, the sword was Saraya's responsibility now. I could not help but wonder at this fact— that my mother had taken it and Umali had chosen Saraya to be her earthly representative. Girls were chosen before birth for the role, and it had the feel of fate about it.

But I said nothing as we left our room and met the Old Ones, Rani and Malika in the middle of our suite.

Atax and Kai went absolutely berserk as we entered, hooting with laughter as they stampeded toward us, pointing at our hands.

"I fucking knew it!" Atax shouted, grabbing Zale in a bear

hug. Kai ran straight for me, grabbing my hands, kissing my fingers and crushing me in his arms.

"You're my sister now," he said thickly. "One of us through and through." When he pulled back, he rubbed at his eyes, and I kissed him on the forehead before he pounced on Zale.

Atax wrapped his arms around me and lifted me off the floor, kissing me on my crown. "My queen!" he shouted before Malika came and admonished him for not being gentle with me.

He let me go, and I sheepishly showed Malika and Rani my new mark. Both girls stared at it with widened eyes.

"So it came because you..." Malika wiggled her eyebrows at me, and I shot Zale a look.

"I put a shield around the room after our first round, wife," he said through our thread. *"As much as I wanted everyone to hear you scream, the others needed sleep."*

My shoulders deflated with relief as Malika poked me playfully in the ribs before inspecting Zale's marking.

Rani's eyes brimmed with tears as she held my hand, though I noted that her eyes were already red when we'd come into the room. "I'm so happy for you, Tara," she whispered softly. "This is a bond like no other, isn't it?"

"Mating marks are supposed to be uncommon but not rare," I said. "Zale said he's only seen a handful. But hopefully the power-sharing will help us in what's to come."

She nodded with a sort of detached interest and immediately my heart twinged for her. Hers was not a wound I could take for her, though it made me distressed to admit it. I held her hand, and she reluctantly looked me in the eye.

"We'll get through this, Rani," I said softly, "together."

"I know. But please, you have much to do today, I would feel like a right dungfly if I distracted you."

"You're not a dungfly," I said indignantly. "You're one of my most treasured friends, and I would run into a burning house if it meant I could help you."

She looked at me sharply then and shook her head vigorously. "Do not speak that way, Tara. I must make my own way out of my...problems."

I, more than anyone, understood that.

WE LEFT OUR SUITE TO MEET GERAVIE AND KESHMI, BOTH OF whom exclaimed when they saw our mating marks and gave me significant looks. I smiled sheepishly at them, knowing we'd have much to talk about later. With them was Pia's father, the grim looking Tuskus Lota, and my cousin, the twelve-year-old Paalus.

He was a wiry boy with strong arms and a straight back from being trained by his mother. A thick shock of black hair was tied to the nape of his neck, and his emerald green eyes looked upon me with great concentration as he kissed my knuckles. It wasn't until Zale offered the boy his arm to shake that his mask of stoicism broke, and fear flashed across his eyes.

"Your Highness," Paalus said softly, grasping Zale's forearm in the way warriors did.

"We are family now, Paalus," Zale said easily, "You should call me Zale, as my brothers do."

My belly warmed at that, and Tuskus gave us both a strained smile. He'd effectively lost his daughter last night.

On top of that, it mustn't be easy to be married to a stormy woman like Rahana, and the strain of recent events was clear in his shoulders and brown eyes.

Pia's position weighed on me too, and I would be lying if I said I wasn't going to be paying attention to every law and rule around here to see if there was a loophole to get Pia out of her fate. Who was next in line to the throne after Aunt Rahana now?

Grandmother Parsha, I realised with mild shock. No wonder everyone had listened to the elderly lady's direction so readily yesterday.

"We've come to take Zale and the Old Ones to tour the city," my uncle said. "Your acolytes will take you to the queen along with Lady Harranpul."

This was a change of plans I wasn't expecting. I wanted Zale by my side to help me figure out battle plans, but at least I had Geravie and Keshmi. My acolytes from last night, Hassa and Issel, along with *ten* other acolytes of all ages, excitedly awaited me in a corner and I tightly clutched my witches robe around myself.

A strum of warmth down our thread made me look up at Zale. *"Just reach out to me if you need anything, High Priestess."* With a kiss of my hand, he let my uncle and cousin lead him and the others away. I couldn't help but feel a soul-deep tightness in my chest at his retreating back, but I shook that dark feeling away, admonishing myself for being stupid.

Malika winked at me, though it was half-hearted with her eyes a little puffy from crying about Pia last night. "I'll make sure they don't get into any trouble."

I gave her a small smile as my acolytes surged forward like a flock of excited birds. "We will take you on your rounds to see the palace's most unwell," Hassa piped. "Traditionally, when Agnolthi's priestess visits the city, that is what she does."

"And today that means the queen," I sighed. *"Magrin?"* I called silently. I'd put my witch's cloak back on this morning. *"Are you with me?"*

"Always", came the deep reply, followed by a delighted, *"High Priestess."*

Two of the senior acolyte's eyes almost bulged out of their sockets, and I realised they likely felt the magic of my cloak active in the ether. Their eyes swept down the material in a sort of shock, and I decided then, that if I was going to rule my temple properly, I needed to throw my weight around a bit.

"I was given this fair robe by the Nine Witches in the Forests of Eternity."

The entire group gasped.

"It's true!"

"That's were she said she met the wing-brothers!"

"Oh, Goddess!"

"How are you still alive?"

"No one's ever returned!"

I let a smile on my lips as I nodded. "I'll tell you all about it."

When we reached the queen's suite, my acolytes went from buzzing with excitement to quiet and tense. Glancing at them I knew that they were likely scared of the queen. Chol-nayak's Widows stood guard, two middle-aged women in white fighting clothes and cowls bowed to me, and one of them went inside to check with the maids if the queen had been readied for the morning.

But it wasn't a maid who stormed out moments later but Aunt Rahana. She stood at the door in emerald Ellythian fighting robes with her arms crossed, her eyes dragging down my body with blatant disapproval. With that magnificent sword strapped to her side she looked as if she were ready for battle at any second.

"Haven't you done enough?" she snapped.

A dark ribbon of her power prodded at my mind, and savagely, I clamped down upon it. Rahana flinched as if she'd been struck, then glared at me. The urge to step forward and threaten her was overwhelming, but with the eyes of the ten acolytes on me, I took a deep breath. I had to lead by example now, and as much as Zale and I loved a good battle, violence was not going to be the best way in the Lotus Palace.

Perhaps it was Zale's magic, or some added power being high priestess, but I seemed to assume more power over the void-shadows within me. I was easily able to allow a tendril of threatening shadow coiled around my head as I looked my aunt in her eyes. I had no real hate for her, but I *did* have a healthy suspicion. What was her game? "The Reaper's magic was upon the queen, Crown Princess. You would do well to let me see that it has all been removed."

"Every time you are in that room, I will be there," Rahana hissed, tilting her chin upward. "You will not visit her without me."

"Very well," I said lightly. "There is much we can *all* learn, isn't there girls and boys?" I glanced at my acolyte's ashen faces and then back at my aunt who narrowed her eyes upon me before whirling around and storming back inside.

Hassa tugged on my sleeve with wide eyes, and as I walked past Cholnayak's guards, I tried something I wouldn't normally do—I tapped on the door to her mind.

She straightened, hurrying after me before I felt her

mind's presence alongside mine. *"What is it?"* I asked curiously.

"High Priestess," Hassa said tentatively as we crossed a sitting room. *"Behind her back, they call the Crown Princess 'The Stingray'."*

"Why's that?"

"Because once her barb gets you, you don't come out alive. If she marks you as not in her favour, you are never seen again."

Dear Goddess. In Lobrathia, they'd called my mother the "Lotus of Ellythia." How did her sister turn out to be the complete opposite?

"And you think she's marked me?" I mused.

"She marked you the moment you arrived on the back of the Boneweaver King."

I refrained from shaking my head as we followed Rahana's aggressive prowl into a darkened room, sombrely lit with yellow quartz-light. It smelled of incense...and the sweet, sour smell of death. A cold trickle of unease snuck down my spine like a demon's caress as I walked into my grandmother's bedroom. Within it two maids were tucking the covers around her as she mumbled croaky words.

The maids bobbed curtseys at me before scurrying away as Rahana assumed a position on the other side of the bed, her arms crossed as she watched me, her eyes like needles on my skin. I ignored her as I looked upon my grandmother, wondering what illness I could eliminate from her elderly body.

Keshmi and Geravie stood by my side, dropping deep curtseys toward the queen. She wore a loose white nightgown with patterned tiny pink lotuses that didn't suit her famed Umali-like demeanour at all. Her long silver hair was unbound, but neatly brushed, splayed over her white pillow.

Her brown face was deeply lined, and I wondered what a lifetime of memories those crevices held. What she'd seen and what type of queen she'd been when she was young. Beneath the hollows of her cheeks, I could imagine the ghost of a timeless beauty who'd once ruled just and fairly.

After a few murmured words with Keshmi, I allowed my eager magic to reach out into my grandmother. No active trace of the Reaper's vile magic lay lurking within her body, but deep scars remained, dull, dark and jagged.

There were only a few times in my life where my magic swooped around a person's body and simply…lurked. As if it wanted to help but couldn't. As if it wanted to take all the pain and suffering away but could not. Something primal in my heart cleaved in two. My eyes burned like hot coals.

I could not stop the tears that fell, and from the side of my eye, I saw Rahana's arms uncross themselves and fall limply by her sides. I did not look at her.

My grandmother was dying, and my tears had just confirmed it for the entire room.

Geravie patted my back and took my grandmother's hand in her own. "Old friend," she whispered. "We once sat in the Lotus theatre and laughed at Luana's magicians. Such joy there was in your spirit. What happened to you?"

I screwed my eyes shut against the image of Geravie crying, but a croak like a battered door opening made them snap back open. *"He is coming!"* she cried.

We all stared as Queen Cheshni's bony chest heaved with strain as she raised her head and stared at Geravie, grasping her friend's hand with her shaking one. "Tell them; he is coming!" she urged, eyes wild.

"Who, Mother?" Rahana's voice was flat but commanding.

Cheshni's head swung over to look at her daughter. "The Reaper!"

"We know, Grandmother," I said quietly, placing a hand on her forearm. "We know he has awoken."

My grandmother looked at me, her green eyes glistening and maybe only half-lucid as she scanned my face in a sort of shock.

"You are one of mine?" she wheezed.

My eyes blurred, and I knew this version of my grandmother won't have long with us. "Yes." I whispered. "I am Altara."

"Ah." Her smile was wide as she closed her eyes, thinking of some memory. "I remember the day the missive came. *Saraya and Altara.*" She said our names like a prayer, and a soul-deep pain wracked through my body as I wished Saraya was here. Something more than the Reaper's magic had consumed our grandmother's mind completely over the years. Bitterness and rage had combined to change her on a bone deep level. But only when Cholnayak, when death, came knocking did we leave the boundaries of the bonds we'd once placed so readily upon ourselves.

I could not tell my own parents, and something in me wanted to make my grandmother proud. I had to tell her. "I... I am High Priestess of Agnolthi. Saraya is High Priestess of Umali."

She opened her eyes and gasped as if surprised, then smiled again. "My granddaughters. Yasani's daughters." She hesitated then, a frown gracing her face. "You...you must tell her that I am sorry."

I swallowed. "I'm afraid you will have to tell her yourself...in the next life."

Her eyes widened. "She is dead?"

Not moving a muscle, I blinked slowly, once.

Cheshni gave a heart shattering wail that came from a place only mothers possessed. "No! I did this! I did it! I could not stop her!"

A gust of air flying past us told me that Rahana was storming out. Still I thought, *still*, the impact of my mother's leaving was felt by her family here. I closed my eyes and saw her funeral pyre from five years ago, an ocean of black mourning clothes, the flames stoking high into the sky. They'd given her an Ellythian burial in Quartz, though cremation was not commonplace. In the darkened room with the sounds and smells of death here, it felt like it was happening all over again.

Geravie slipped her hand into mine and squeezed, just as she'd done that very day with Saraya's hand on my other side. But as my grandmother wailed, my left hand remained empty. Saraya was fighting battles with demons of her own.

"I'm sorry!" my grandmother shrieked, clawing at her face, writhing in her bed. "My Yasani, come back! Please come back to me!"

As the door slammed behind Rahana, something glittering caught my eye—a thread of light, dull but still shining with an ethereal quality, stretching out between mother and daughter. It was not unlike the star-soul bond I shared with Zale, but it was feathery and aged, and I instinctually knew that it was a bond of life between them. The bond a mother had with her child. As I stared at it, the thread leaving my grandmother's naval, my consciousness fell *into* it and voices, sights and smells overcame me, whirling and collapsing, rushing past me, some on soft wings, some on dark leathery wings. *Memories*, I thought, these are all of the memories between Cheshni and Rahana.

W ith my heart pounding, I noted that one of them zoomed straight for me. I allowed it to head straight into my chest, and it dissolved into my skin. I was sucked into a room cast with the warm glow of yellow quartz-light.

But the room could not have been colder for the tense band that lay between the people in the room, quivering as if it might snap any second.

I found my mother immediately, sitting in one of the gilded chairs of the very parlour room they had received me in yesterday. I wanted to fall to my knees. To crawl into her lap and ask her for forgiveness, for help, for comfort. But I was so struck by her presence, even in a memory, that my body froze. Yasani was stunning in her prime, her skin plump, her body strong, her hands calloused. There was a jewelled crown on her thick black curls and a brilliant light in her emerald eyes. She was Queen of Ellythia in this memory.

Rahana sat next to my mother, her young eyes wide and adoring as she looked up at her older sister. My grandmother sat on a couch opposite them, twenty years younger, streaks of grey in her midnight hair, her body held straight, her eyes alert but kind. Other members of the Lota family were around them—Parsha for one,—a few older men that must be their husbands and a younger man and woman holding a little girl, who must be Parsha's children and grandchild. Brilliant-green eyes dotted the room like jewels, and Yasani had them all captivated.

My mother took a deep breath, her hands clasped in her lap. Her gown was a brilliant gold, and she wore elbow-length white gloves and a sash. She looked every bit the sombre queen about to give bad news.

"Mother Jacaranda's prophecy for my reign was not one I expected," she began slowly.

I closed my eyes upon hearing her voice, a little higher than I remembered it, but the smooth, decadent cadence filled me with a deep, primal longing. I blinked away my tears and remembered that the Mother Jacaranda tree was found deep in the Fae Realms and every new monarch went to see her after their coronation. The tree gave them some prophesy about their reign, usually a warning or piece of wisdom about what was to come for them. My mother must have just come back from her visit there. Pia had once told me such a story, but to see it happening in real time gave me full body chills.

"She said that I have a choice to make," Yasani continued. "That either I reign long and well here or..."—she paused and seemed to steel herself—"or live a much shorter life and go to Lobrathia where I will give birth to two girls who will be the most powerful women the world has seen since Ellythia and Matrika themselves. And without them the world will fall to some great evil."

Rahana gasped, her hand flying to her mouth as she looked between her sister and her mother with terrified eyes.

An old man who must have been my grandfather, came to stand by Yasani and put a light hand on her shoulder.

My eyes were drawn to Cheshni however, who had begun to vibrate like a branch about to snap. She stared at Yasani, unblinking, and it hurt all the more knowing what was to come.

Yasani looked her mother evenly in the eye and said, "I have sent my offer of marriage to the Voltanius King, and his missive has returned." She took out a folded piece of paper from her gown pocket. "He has accepted."

Rahana stood up, trembling, her mouth a thin, straight line, but Yasani would not take her eyes off her mother. "I will announce my abdication, and I will leave for Lobrathia in three days."

Magic whirled around Cheshni, biting, chaotic. Dangerous.

"You would choose imaginary children over us?" Rahana cried, her voice shrill with panic. "Over me? Over your family?"

Cheshni's voice was deep and quiet, lethal rage held back on a tether. "If you go, Yasani, you will forfeit your family, your people. You will never be allowed to return."

Yasani raised her chin. "I know, Mother. For the greater good, it is a sacrifice I am willing to make."

Rahana began sobbing and threw herself at Yasani's legs. "Sani, please don't leave. Please don't leave me."

Sani. My heart broke in two. It had the cadence of a childhood nickname and Rahana used it in a desperate plea.

"I have to, Raha," my mother murmured.

Rahana raised her head from her sister's knee to look up at her and the pain overfilling her eyes was a devastation I'd never seen in a person. With a sob Rahana scrambled to her feet and fled from the room, her young body wracking with sobs.

The memory dissolved, and I was left, trembling where I stood as the present world came back into focus around me.

My grandmother was still crying out for my mother.

When I made no move to do anything, Keshmi breezed forward and whispered a spell over my grandmother, stroking light fingers across her forehead. Slowly, Cheshni quietened, and her cries became mumbles, her chest settling down into soft breathing.

My hand around Geravie's had become a vice but my old nursemaid did not show any sign of caring. Instead she tucked in the corners of my grandmother's blanket and steered me out of the room.

OUT IN THE FOREVER-SUMMER SUN OF LOTA CITY, I WAS ABLE TO relax a little and calm myself in the wake of what I'd seen. This newfound power of mine—to see the bonds between people, plucked at my vision from all corners. Shimmering strands of different colours and light connecting family members, friends and in some cases strangers. I shook my head and willed my mind to turn it off, though I had to consult Magrin to get instruction on getting it to go away. She gave me breathing techniques to calm me down, and they were similar enough to my archery breathing that they did the trick. And whenever I wanted, I could make them come back with the flex of my mind. Zale had never mentioned a power like this, so it made me sure it was Agnolthi-given.

My acolytes seated us in an open, horseless, self-driving carriage with a huge purple shade across the top so that it allowed us a good view of the city and gave us a cool breeze at the same time. While my purple-robed acolytes walked beside us, not minding the slow stroll, I relayed to Geravie and Keshmi what I'd seen.

It wasn't news for either of them though, as at the time, word of what the Jacaranda tree had said spread within the palace, and Geravie had written to her twin cousins on Boneweaver Island about the great adventure she would go on to raise her promised children.

"So you knew this whole time?" I asked Geravie aghast. "Why didn't you tell us?"

"It's not something you tell children," she said smugly, sitting back in her seat and sipping chilled coconut water from an iced canteen. "Can you imagine how much more of a problem you would have been for me then?" She put on a higher-pitched voice to emulate mine. "Geravie, I'm the chosen one. You can't make me eat eggplant! Geravie, let me show more cleavage! Geravie—"

I swatted at her playfully while Keshmi gaped at us both. I sobered instantly. "I can't imagine what Pia would have gone through, growing up and hearing that about her cousins, and now losing everything completely…"

Geravie sighed. "And Rahana turned into *that*, so I can't say I blame her for well…frankly, last night, she looked relieved to be leaving it all behind her."

I chewed my lip, thinking the same thing. Her face had smoothed over, her shoulders visibly lowering, though I'd never noticed how tense they'd always been. And that wild grin she'd borne…

"She will do well in Xalya's forces," Keshmi said softly, peering out at the golden city under the morning sun. "She was always an excellent swordswoman."

I murmured my agreement as Agnolthi's temple came into

view on the outer edge of the city toward the southeast quadrant. In this area were the apothecaries, herb growers, quartz-instrument makers and the magical schools. At the head of them all lay a structure made of silver and purple quartz, a monolith in the shape of Agnolthi and her lion mount.

She towered above us, tall and supreme, the Mistress of Mystery, Queen of the Stars, Wisdom of the Wild. As we rode up to the silver temple gates, marked with "Order of Yasani," what looked like the entire working population of Agnolthi's sector, over two hundred purple-robed men and women came out to see me. I smiled and waved at them as best I could, all the while a knot the size of the temple was growing in my stomach.

The acolytes waved us through to the temple entrance, and when we got out of the carriage, Keshmi fell prostrate immediately. She was so overwhelmed by the detailing in the structure of the sculpture that made up the temple, that they couldn't get a straight word out from her. Geravie kindly took her by the elbow and led her up the quartz stairs.

I emerged from the carriage to a round of bowing and cheering that skittered through my bones, leaving a deep warm glow. Grinning up at the senior priestesses standing on either side of the grand entrance doors, I made my way up, wishing that Pia, Malika and Rani had been here with me to see it. But alas, they were no doubt touristing the city with the Old Ones, dealing with their own emotions. Hopefully they got to visit with Pia.

The senior priestesses, three ladies aged between thirty and fifty, all kissed my hand, their eyes going wide at my new mating mark before they urged me inside. Their serious faces reminded me why we were here.

We needed to plan for war.

Inside the temple seven statues of Agnolthi, in her different forms were stationed around the centre with a huge, empty, cast-iron cauldron sitting in the middle.

What followed next was a series of meetings with the various leaders of each division of the temple—Teaching Witches, Healing Witches and Battle Mages. All three were already preparing their ranks for war, and I was shown their well laid plans in detail.

As a princess I'd studied old wars and battle techniques with my tutors, so I was versed in the necessary preparations. What I wasn't well versed in was the magical side of battle, as in Lobrathia, there were no people with magic, and my mother had taught us only about covert methods of magical defence.

The battle mages trained with Xalya's army, as there was plenty of crossover in powers, but they kept their ranks separate when it came to battle. I was reminded of Malika, who would have been besotted with the training regimens for Agnolthi's elite unit of war mages. They could set and create explosions from afar, launch arrows from two hundred feet away and set up gigantic shields of protection.

Since we had no Blade of Temari, to protect the islands from the demons, the throne was relying upon Agnolthi's Order to produce the city's shields.

Luckily for me, with Agnolthi's High Priestess sitting on the Boneweaver throne as queen, all these things operated independently of me. I was only needed if there were intra-temple punishments to be dealt and on the battlefield itself, to direct the movements of the wider groups.

We were finishing up a long afternoon of meetings when Joshi, the youngest senior priestess responsible for healing, sighed wistfully. "It would be an honour to one day see the original temple on Boneweaver Island. It has been a dream of mine since I was little. Perhaps now it might come true."

I smiled at her. "Of course, I would love that if the priestesses would allow."

Keshmi grasped the woman's hand and smiled. "We will be looking at retiring soon, and a new keeper of the temple will be needed to help the high priestess when she rules as the Boneweaver Queen."

Joshi beamed up at us as a mild shock ran through me. *"When she rules as Boneweaver Queen."*

The Old Ones from the Eternal Forest were waiting for us. Zale and I had a kingdom to rebuild. But there was one colossal thing standing between that and now.

I wasn't allowed to think on it too much, because Hassa sprinted into the meeting room, her round face flushed. "High Priestess, there is a disturbance at Cholnayak's temple, you are being called—"

"Why is Agnolthi's high priestess being called for white-robe business?" Geravie asked gruffly. "We have enough to do here."

"It's...the high priestesses' companions, Lady Harranpul," Hassa stuttered. "I believe one is called Rani and the other—"

A feeling of oily doom wrapped around my heart.

"Say no more," I said quickly. "Priestesses, we will resume when I come back tonight for the evening rituals. Will that suffice?"

They bowed their thanks to me, and I swept out after the acolyte with Geravie and Keshmi on my heels. Cholnayak's temple was right next to Agnolthi's so our carriage made quick work of eating up the distance.

We heard the cries before I saw who it was. My heart fell into my stomach, a dark feeling consuming my bones.

"No," Geravie said in disbelief. "No no no!"

Before Cholnayak's ivory temple, the White Widows stood guard, two holding down Malika on her knees as a new member was initiated into their order.

In the centre of a bleached-white courtyard, on a wooden stool surrounded by fifty white robed women and men, sat Rani, her back straight, her head bowed. Donned in a white robe and caul, her head was being shaved by the High Priestess of Cholnayak herself.

Malika's sobs echoed around us, but no one paid her any attention. They were used to family being upset about initiations into the white temple.

Geravie and Keshmi rushed out of the carriage to stand at the edge of the group seated on the courtyard ground. I rose from my seat, feeling as if I was floating in a nightmare made of dark water, under a night with no moon. One of my acolytes helped me out of the carriage, but I barely noticed her, my eyes only on Rani's now bald head as she muttered her vows.

"Altara!" Malika desperately sobbed, sounding like she was a universe away. "Make her stop—please, make her stop!"

I stared and stared at my old friend's athletic frame, hunched under the weight of grief and self-punishment.

The high priestess put down her razor and marked Rani with a fingerprint of black powder. Now it would be the only colour she wore because Cholnayak ruled over the new moon. In a voice that carried across the entire courtyard, the high priestess announced, "You are forgiven, Rani Umasri."

My own breath caught as tears streamed from Rani's eyes, tightly shut against the bright sunset.

It was only when the high priestess stepped aside that

Rani finally took a deep breath and looked up to meet my choked gaze. I saw her audibly swallow, but there was a grim determination in her brown eyes, her mouth set into a firm line. She'd made her decision.

I gave her a single slow nod of understanding.

Relief washed over her features, and she clenched her teeth before nodding back. She left the platform, heading into the temple under the instruction of senior priestesses. Malika wailed as Geravie, and Keshmi ran toward her, and the three of them hugged tightly. I met the high priestesses' eye then and pressed a hand to my heart in thanks.

For taking my friend in.

For forgiving her when she could not forgive herself.

For giving her a path when she could not see another way.

Rani had sworn to a life of renunciation of the material world, including her friends. She would tend to corpses, as was the job of the younger initiates, and train to fight with their White Widows. She would like that, I knew. Maybe then she would find peace in her heart.

Malika, Geravie and Keshmi plodded toward me, and silently, we sat in the carriage and made our way back to the temple.

"I want to see Pia," Malika mumbled thickly. "She won't know. She needs to know."

The three of us were quiet as we exchanged looks. Geravie took Malika's hand and wound her fingers through hers, and in the gentlest voice I'd ever heard her use, she said, "We can't sweetling. She's undergoing initiation at the moment."

Like Rani, though it went unsaid.

It wasn't for a few minutes that I realised who was missing. A shadow pierced my heart.

"Where is Zale?" I asked, sharply. "And Atax and Kai?"

Malika frowned in between dabbing her eyes. "What? I don't know they were just here." She looked around, frowning as if she'd see them on the passing street.

"Maybe they're back at the suite," Geravie said gently. "Maybe they thought to meet us back there."

It was dark by the time we reached the palace and the terrible, oily feeling of doom that had begun at Cholnayak's temple only grew denser, choking me until my heart pounded against my ribs, threatening to shatter every single bone in my body. To shatter my mind.

But I dared not speak my thoughts out loud.

Instead I coiled into myself, cold midnight shadow winding around my body, twitching with silent, violent promise. Malika frowned at me through puffy eyes, trying to search my face for the source of my sudden tension. But all at once she seemed to read something on me, and her tears stopped. Her shoulders stiffened, her hands balling into tight fists.

But we would not speak the morbid words that hung between us. Not yet. Not until we saw for ourselves and knew for sure.

I skulked back to our suite with Malika hovering behind me like death's own shadow. With every step I walked towards the room we shared with the Old Ones, my heart twisted an inch further, the shadows coiling around me a little more.

When it came time for me to open the suite doors, my hands hovered upon the golden handle allowing the cold of the metal to seep into my skin. It did not warm beneath my touch. I would not allow it because I knew in my very marrow of my spirit what I would find within. I pushed it open.

It was empty. Cold. No scent or sign of our Old Ones.

As Malika stormed around the suite, flinging open all the doors, I clutched my stomach with a trembling hand marked with that blue-eyed tiger and reached out down the thread that bound me to Zale, plucking it in a cold question. But the thread led into the dusk, giving me nothing back.

As I looked down at the blue eyed tiger on the back of my hand, my heart began to fracture.

"He will come for us," Atax had growled last night.

"He is tied to the Reaper," Cherimani's high priestess had warned.

"You come here as a question," Princess Parsha had said.

Geravie and Keshmi were behind me, their movements tense. "They might still be on their way back?" Keshmi said, trying to sound hopeful and failing.

Malika thundered out of her room, and when I saw her, my entire body began to shake violently. Her skin was ashen, her eyes tight and red in fury. In her hand was a lone, obsidian sword earring. It was a single, damning symbol.

"I'm going to kill him," she hissed, clutching it in her fist so tightly that blood welled and dripped down her wrist in a dark red ribbon. Her voice was laced with the crimson flames of rage. "Tell me, sister. Tell me they have not left. *Tell me* they have not deflected to the Reaper."

Outside our window there was a scream.

38
ZALE

A tax, Kai and I were waiting outside Agnolthi's temple with Tuskus and Paalus Lota when a fell wind ruffled my hair with dirty, malicious fingers.

Bull ants crawled across my neck and immediately my two bothers and I went on alert.

"What was that?" little Paalus said in fright.

"Stay close to your father," I commanded. "You need to get back to the palace."

"What is it?" Tuskus whirled around to look at our surroundings, and though nothing seemed outwardly amiss, I knew better. Purple-robed priestesses and acolytes plodded about under the afternoon sun, attending to their day's tasks as normal. An old woman swept the temple's steps, four girls played magical jump rope in the corner, the rope looping around of its own accord.

"Go," I said, a little too sharply to my uncle-in-law. He gave me an unappreciative look before climbing back into the carriage with his son.

But today was not the day for apologies. And anyway, I

didn't really know how to apologise to anyone who wasn't Altara.

Atax gave the horse-less chariot a slap on the side, and they were off back to the castle. I wouldn't be able to forgive myself if something happened to Altara's boy cousin. Enough had happened to her sisters-in-arms as it was—Malika and Rani had decided to go into Cholnayak's temple for a visit, and I'd let them, sensing they were safer away from me and my brothers right now. As usual, I was right.

I stiffened when another dark breeze prickled my cheek like tiny blades. Kai twitched, and we all stiffened as the echo of Raen's voice was carried on the wings of the wind, his voice distant and dull. *"Boneweaver Island has fallen. He is here. We are coming."*

Atax swore in three different ways as I tried to figure out the best way to get out of this. But just as I reached down the thread connecting me to Altara to warn her, my mind was seized by the dark hand of a giant.

Atax, Kai and I froze before the purple quartz gates of the Order of Yasani as a memory from two hundred years ago came hurtling into me with all the force of a charging shark. We'd been waiting for this, but next to me all I felt from my brothers was a feeling of absolute horror.

On my shoulder, Wobbles screamed and crumpled into dust.

Frozen in place I could do nothing with neither my physical body nor my magic as I sensed the darkness breeze past the Ellythian shields.

It had been the same two hundred years ago when he'd come to lock us up. My mind raged at the thought of leaving Altara, at the thought of being taken away from her.

I still remembered the way my mother's eyes had

widened in terror as she'd reached her hands out as if to help me, but now, there was no one around to notice that the Reaper was here, and I couldn't even turn my head to look at Agnolthi's temple where I knew Altara was sitting. Where she wouldn't even know that—

A giant force ripped us from reality and hurled us into the ether.

All three of us screamed into the void.

It was unlike the force that had pulled Altara and I into the Forests of Eternity. That force had been filled with celestial power, savage, but noble.

The Reaper's power held the shadow of murder, the stink of betrayal and the cadence of treachery. I tried not to let myself be filled with terror and rage and I shoved those emotions away and tried to think of a way out of this. But as we were slammed down with the force of a crashing wave onto sharp coral, the breath knocked out of me, three of my ribs shattered and Kai's scream broke my heart in two.

Altara's face in my mind healed those two pieces together but couldn't fix my broken bones. Smoking darkness surrounded us, and breathing hard, I lurched to my feet as my brothers did the same, injured grunts echoing in my ears.

Before us stood Raen, his handsome face ashen, features made of stone, though he was not physically injured. Next to him stood a figure just as tall as him but cloaked in a heavy black robe.

The smell of burning flesh stunk up the air, and I suppressed a gag as my entire world fell apart around me.

It was not a face one could ever forget. The Reaper, in his true form barely had a face. His skin was a mangled pink and white, as if it had been burned long ago and the tips of his fae ears were slashed. In place of a nose or mouth he had three pairs of eyes, set beneath each other, and each one was blood red all the way through. Just looking at him made you want to claw your own eyes out to get rid of the image.

Two hundred years later, he still had that nauseating effect on me.

"Ashzale Boneweaver," he spoke into my mind, the skin of his white, thin lips curving into a malicious smile. *"Two hundred years have gone and now I call upon you and your brothers, my faithful servants."*

"My father was your faithful servant," I spat, stepping forward. "Not I. I was never given a choice."

"Nor will you be given one now."

My eyes flicked to Raen, and I suddenly realised what was wrong. His eyes. His blue eyes that had once twinkled like the deep ocean were now cold. Dull. My eyes had looked like that once. I've never known the sharp sting of panic until now. Before I could do anything, the Reaper's magic gripped my mind with lethal, concentrated force and flooded into me like a revolting tidal wave.

I was freezing, slowly, and from the inside out. My very arteries chilled to a temperature so low I was surprised they didn't turn solid and kill me then and there.

The ice reached my finger tips and my eyes swivelled to Atax and Kai, similarly frozen, their eyes wild as they searched mine. I watched as Atax's eyes went cold, followed by Kai's.

Not Kai. Not his light, his joy. But I watched it right there as his baby blues turned frigid with malice.

Just as my mind was about to break into two, the panic left me.

Because inside the recesses of my mind was my mate's face. A mischievous, devious smile graced pillowy lips that I wanted to press against my own. But she drew away from me, pressing her index finger to her lips as if telling me to keep a great secret. She walked backwards, glittering eyes never leaving mine. A trap door appeared beneath her, and she descended down a ladder into a shadowy corner of me and pulled the door shut.

I jerked back into the present, and at that point everything left me in one forceful sweep. Everything except for cold obedience.

That glittering thread that bound me to my mate didn't glitter anymore, and I studied it with a veteran's calculation.

Raen came to stand beside me, and I nodded at him. Raen nodded back, scanning my body for injury and then, noticing my broken ribs, flicked his fingers and they healed. "Boneweaver Island is the Reaper's," he said in a slow, measured voice. "We will move to secure Tiger Island when given the command."

"But first," the Reaper said, twanging the black bond that tied me to him. *"A test."*

No one stopped us we entered the queen's chambers on four padded feet each. A tiger, a leopard, a black lion and a panther in the Lotus Palace. How my father would have choked on his own laughter to hear of it. When I said no one stopped us, I meant that we left the bodies of six of Chol-nayak's guard and two maids littered on the golden floor. They were already dressed in white for their funerals. How fitting. Atax had paid a quick visit to another room before returning here, a manic gleam in his eye.

"Better be quick," Atax said, changing back into his human form and rolling his shoulders, looking at Queen Cheshni's wheezing body with disgust. I noticed that he'd lost one of his precious obsidian blades but I said nothing of it.

"Why?" Raen, the tattoos on his face lifting with a smirk. "If anyone else came, we would just kill them."

"A blood bath!" Kai shifted into human form and clapped twice, the dark grin on his face showing me a mouthful of bloodied teeth. "Take your time, brother. *Please.*"

So all joy had *not* gone then. Kai, in his essence was a playful but bloodthirsty beast. Now with his conscience gone, there was nothing to stop his joy for a good kill.

Now in my human form, I strolled up the Ellythian Queen lying with her eyes closed on the bed. Looking down upon her, I stared at her elderly face, shaking my head at how weak humans were. She had magic in her, but it was dying, nothing more than dregs left at the bottom of a wine glass. Her eyes opened a fraction and between the lids are her irises. They were green, like banana leaves.

They are also the eyes of my mate, though hers were green like gems from the deepest parts of the earth. A memory came to me. Of her gasping as our mating marks burst into reality. I growled at the image, looking down at my left hand where a butterfly lay marked in celestial ink.

Raen came to stand by my side.

"Just do it," he muttered, irritated. "Or do you want me to?"

Raen had served to temper my lack of morals once. All those years ago, my darkness had spread to him, but it had not consumed him like it had me. With a hand on my arm or two arms around my body when I was really angry, he'd get

347

me to contain my bloodlust. Now we had *no one* to tame any of us. Now, we were free to do what we'd been trained from infancy to do.

Behind me, Kai was shredding the red velvet curtains with his claws, laughing to himself as they fell in heavy ribbons. Because of what my father had done to him , more than the rest of us, his lack of conscience now allowed him to take action on every one of the whims he'd had before. There was no thought behind his impulses; he just did what he wanted. He was going to be chaos incarnate, and I grinned at the thought.

Something tugged on the thread inside of me, and I frowned down at my naval, because if *she* was calling me, my instinct told me that I needed to go to her. I just had to do one thing first.

I casually summoned my obsidian blade and made a deft stab into the queen's heart. She was all skin and bone, so the cut was straight and clean.

Her eyes flew open as she gasped. "Death!"

"Yes." I stated. Pulling on the black tether inside of me, I called, "It's done."

An inky black claw gripped me and my four brothers, and we were pulled into the void once again.

39

ALTARA

Wreathed in a volatile midnight shadow I stormed to the balcony doors, flung them open and lurched outside, Malika hot on my tail.

Outside my heart missed a beat at the vision of a huge bird in the night sky. Just for a moment I let myself think it was Zale. That we had been wrong, and here he was, golden and glistening and mine and…good.

But it wasn't Zale, it was Whole-Feather, the huge tawny messenger owl I'd sent to Saraya. He circled the city, and the Ellythians below gasped and pointed, some cheered and clapped as the wing-brothers had not been seen in centuries in Lotus City. I cast my magic out to Whole-Feather, letting him know where I was, and immediately, he turned around and wheeled right for the balcony.

"Dear Goddess!" Keshmi cried. "I never thought I'd see the day!"

"Step back!" cried Geravie in warning. "These balconies were made for them to perch on."

Indeed they had been because Whole-Feather made an

easy, quick descent, and we all shielded our faces as the strong downwind created by his broad wings battered at us. Finally, he came to settle, his claws scraping against the balcony ledge.

"Ah," Whole-Feather said. "The winds tell me there is a new High Priestess of Agnolthi! It brings me joy to sit at the Lotus Palace once again, though I am afraid I bring bad tidings."

I stared at him dully as Malika muttered behind me. "Can't be any worse than what we've got on going here."

Pushing everything aside, all the terror, pain, grief and betrayal...just for a moment, I inclined my head to Whole-Feather.

"Greetings, Wing-Brother. You are always welcome. What news?" Dark tendrils obscured my vision as my shadows roiled threateningly around my body.

Whole-Feather seemed to register this and made quick work of his message. "The Princess Saraya is now wed to Drakus Silverhand or Darkcleaver, King Wyxian's true first-born son."

I frowned as surprise gives me momentary clarity. "Drakus? He was the commander that came to betrothal, wasn't he? *He's* now married to Saraya?"

"He is her mate, yes. There is more."

Her mate.

Geravie made a noise of great surprise.

Whole-Feather continued on to relay Saraya's message in her words. If I closed my eyes, it was as if she were standing right there, talking to me directly. Her story included the events of her capture by the demons and subsequent marriage to Drake, my now brother-in-law, and their eventual escape from the Demon Court. They were now in Black

Court, headed toward the Darkcleaver palace to prepare for the Reaper's arrival there. It ended with. "I intend to take back Lobrathia as queen."

My heart gave a weak flutter of joy at that. Of course, she would. My big sister always pulled through. She was the most reliable person I knew. Me on the other hand...I clutched at my heart, imagining Saraya as Queen of Quartz, killing demons with *her* husband. My fists clenched, and I bit out, "You said there was bad news?"

Whole-Feather bowed deeply. "My condolences, Your Highness, High Priestess. Your father was taken to the demon court by your stepmother. It was there he lost his life."

Everything in my world turned dark. My body ceased to be anything except shadow.

"It was there he lost his life."

The words echoed in my mind like an Ellythian funeral chant, slamming into my chest causing a great fissure between my ribs.

"It was there he lost his life."

Behind me Geravie said something, but I was not able to hear her through the sound of my own heart breaking.

My father. My poor, unwell father was no more. I should never have left Lobrathia.

I inclined my head to Whole-Feather before stiffly turning and striding inside. The others were exchanging words with him, but I couldn't find my ears to hear them.

My insides were going to explode, my heart was bleeding from a wound that would never be able to heal. I'd left my father there to die. Saraya had probably *seen* father die.

I opened my mouth and screamed out every last bit of air in my lungs.

The windows shattered. Geravie cried out but Malika and Keshmi held her back from coming to me.

I fell to my knees, swathed in wild grief. Lightning sparked from my fingers, violent and dangerous, but I could not care less as my world collapsed around me.

A tiny pluck on the thread within me froze me on the spot. I held my breath as Zale's awareness came again.

"Where are you?" I hissed down the thread. *"Where the fuck are you, Ashzale Boneweaver?"*

There came no reply, but I could feel him there at the end of it, covered in a shadow that was dangerously familiar.

"My father is dead," I said down the thread. *" My mother is dead. My grandmother is dying, where the fuck are you?"*

High above us, one of the palace bells began to toll, a deep, solemn gong.

Geravie smothered a loud sob. I turned on my knees to look at them all. Malika was squatting, her head between her legs as she pulled at her hair.

"The queen is dead!" Geravie cried. "That's the death gong. It means Cheshni is dead!"

I punched the floor with all my might. With a crackle of violent lightning, it left a crater in the floor. Rising to my feet, I stormed out of the room, a girl made into a wraith. A skeleton made of darkness and death.

That urgent pluck on the thread came again, and I roared down the bond. *"I'm coming for you. I'm coming for him!"* I let my power surge down the bond, violent and fierce, and found Zale's location. Geravie, Keshmi and Malika hurried behind me and as I stormed through the chaos of the palace, sparking lightning and shadow, panicking servants fled at the sight of me, guards' mouths dropped open, courtiers froze and stared.

I ignored them all, heading straight through the palace entrance hall and out the giant golden doors.

It was dark outside, the palace grounds frantic with activity, but not because the queen was dead.

"Breech!" someone shouted. "Breech!"

A white robed figure hurtled to us at a full sprint, bald and lithe. Behind her was a shorter figure swathed in black fighting robes. Two figures we all knew well.

"Where is Kai?" Rani shouted, waving a parchment above her head "Where is Zale?"

"The city's defences are down!" Pia cried, her face flushed. "The Reaper is here!"

We strode to meet our friends, frantic eyed and panting as they beheld the chaos around us. Pia's eyes were on the palace bells high above the ramparts of the golden building.

I paused my step as Malika reached out to them. Pia and Rani took one look at me standing still as a predator, swathed in midnight grief, and kept their distance.

"Kai left me this in my room at the temple," Rani panted. "It's me and Yulara. It feels like a goodbye. It's not, is it? What does it mean?"

On the parchment was a charcoal sketch, a true likeness of Rani and another woman of similar height and athletic build. They were holding hands and laughing, Ellythian wedding necklaces sparkling with light.

Geravie and Keshmi caught up to us by then, sweat coating their faces. But every cell in my being stiffened, and I made no move to go anywhere, because I felt that Zale was *here*.

One of Xalya's Guards let out a shout, and we all turned to see Ellythia's Hill, where, against the night sky and a full moon, the silhouettes of five figures stood like the harbingers of doom.

Rani cried out. Geravie and Keshmi smothered their cries. And it was all because the last figure was a huge being in a heavy black cloak with nothing but poisonous-green flames for a head.

Nausea rolled in my stomach as those flames licked up into the sky, potent and vile. Between one breath and the next, they were gone.

Instinctively, every soldier in the courtyard whirled around to search for them. Someone shot up a purple shield dome around the palace, but with the sound of glass shattering, it was gone in the blink of an eye.

I smelled him first. The smell of flesh burning and rotting. Keshmi vomited onto the grass, and she was not the only one.

They appeared before us, and every soul in the square became frozen against their will.

Kai, Atax, Raen and Zale stood like warriors of old in a solid, threatening line, obsidian weapons drawn as if they intended to use them.

Next to Zale stood the Reaper.

The creature of nightmares, the threat against our world. The being that intended to use the Old Ones for his campaign to spread his darkness across the Continent.

He was as tall as Zale in a heavy black cloak with the hood hanging across his back as sickly green flames pulsed from his neck. I dared not wonder what lay beneath those flames. I felt his power around us, an oozing, nauseating thing, as if all the dark things in the world had converged into a single creature, his aura clear for all to see.

That power did not speak of death. It spoke of nightmares. It sung of curses uttered in foul ancient tongues. It crooned of vultures waiting for men to become carrion. The hairs on the back of my neck stood on end.

I would be lying if I said I did not find *something* familiar about that power.

"My father turned on me. I understand the betrayal." Zale had once said those words in front of me, and I'd thought he meant it.

Rage filled me, and I was the first to move as a black, dangerous bow appeared in my hand, and with a pluck of the string, an arrow of void flew toward the Reaper. Rani cried out but Zale simply stepped forward and plucked it out of the air with one hand before it found its mark. The movement was familiar because he'd done this very thing not all that long ago. The night we'd met, in an old forest far away from here.

How my heart had been filled and ripped to shreds in the space between then and now.

Enraged, I was loading another arrow when Pia's voice pierced my fervour with her own arrow made of sharp words. "No, Tara, look!"

I stared at the group then. Properly.

My fingers trembled, but the ashes of my heart froze at the look in Zale's eyes.

Cold. Dead. Quiet.

Like long dead parts of the ocean where nothing stirred. Where nothing *could* stir because no light lived there. My spine tingled in warning as my eyes flicked to my brothers-in-law. I hadn't seen Raen's pretty, tattooed face in a long time, but a Boneweaver's eyes had never been *that* icy. Atax's mischievous glint had turned black and Kai...

Kai's sky-blue eyes glinted with insane bloodthirst. It

chilled me to the bone to see his boyish charm just snuffed out.

"No," I whispered, even as dark tendrils of grief solidified around me. Zale had once had a shadow-cloaked heart, but this time, his entire being was shrouded in shadow. Now his brothers shared that fate.

And then Zale spoke, a savage twist to the knife already lodged in my gut. "My mate. My allegiance must be to the Reaper." His voice was just as dead as his eyes.

I saw it then. Allowed myself to see it. An obsidian thread of cold shadow led from all four brothers to the Reaper. As if he held them on a leash made for monsters. Our own bond was still there, the celestial light shining between us. Sense illuminated my mind then. Perhaps I could appeal to our bond.

I whispered, knowing full well he could hear me despite the distance. "You would leave me?"

Zale's fingers tightened on his vicious serrated blade. "We made a mistake."

My anger snapped out like a whip because we'd *never* fucking made a mistake. "He killed my father!"

Three arrows were loaded now, aimed at the Reaper, who remained quiet and still except for his flickering flames.

"My love, do not," Zale said.

How could that term of endearment sound like dull blades in my ears now? I loosed the arrows.

Zale moved. And when he was still again, three arrows were clutched in his bare hands. "Come with me, my mate."

I'd never felt our bond more strongly in that moment, or perhaps it was our combined energy influencing me, but I actually took a step forward.

No one behind me said anything, clearly terrified out of

their wits and frozen by the Reaper's magic because even Xalya's Guard were not moving a muscle. How a creature could be *that* powerful befuddled me.

The only thing that remained moving was the death gong from the palace bell tower.

Clang.

A thought made of love and light inside my heart was terrifying me.

I had come upon this earth for Ashzale Boneweaver. And he'd loved me despite my darkness. He'd seen it and helped me overcome it. He'd been kind and good despite my hating him and lashing out.

Clang

All of the images from the last months flooded my brain as I realised in that moment that I wanted nothing more than to be with him.

Even like this.

Even, cold with murderous power, without his conscience, I loved him. He drew me in like a moth to a flame.

And I would burn if it meant I could save him.

Clang

He'd saved me once, from my own, personal demons. It only seemed right that I do the same for him. To love him, despite the dark, unholy, murderous absence of light in his eyes. I would follow him until the end, I realised. The end of all things, even if it destroyed the both of us.

Zale held out one large hand. A hand that had held my face, stroked my cheek with so much care I had not thought it possible.

I'm pulled by a force greater than me. A celestial force that had created us before we were human and would exist long

357

after we left this earth. We were a mated couple now. And that meant forever, with no boundary.

None.

Clang

So even though I heard Geravie let out a heartbroken wail from behind me. Even though I felt Malika's red rage on my back, and Rani's soft, broken eyes, I set my shoulders and crossed the space between us.

My darkness enveloped me completely as my wraith took over, pulling me down into that trap door of old heinous power, where I was nothing. Where I must *be* nothing, for Zale. For Ellythia. But I can control that trap door now.

Clang

A voice with a monster's rotting breath and the crunch of bones underfoot surged into my head without permission. And it laughed as if it were privy to some great, evil joke. *"Welcome, Altara Voltanius."*

I placed my hand inside Zale's cool one and went with him.

40
PIA

A little over half an hour ago, I knew something was deathly wrong when Cherimani appeared to me in my barracks at Xalya's sector. She was the trickster Goddess, and she danced into view, shimmying her hips as the air around me stilled and grew heavy from her power. Her impish, beautiful face was twisted into a wicked, mischievous smile. When I turned to follow her movements, she tilted her head back and giggled as if I'd told her some wonderful joke, before she leapt into the air with a flick of her foot and vanished with a spray of glitter. I'd rushed out of the barracks and headed straight for the palace when I found Rani charging out of Cholnayak's temple as a newly made acolyte. I couldn't even describe my shock until she showed me Kai's sketch. A black feeling told us something was very wrong.

Now I watched as six shadows stood on the horizon, under the malevolent green light cast by the Reaper's flames as the Lota death gong filled the night air.

Altara crossed toward them and placed her hand in Zale's. Ice gripped my very soul. She had chosen Zale. She had chosen the Reaper. Zale had called her and she'd went with only a moment's thought.

I could hardly blame her for wanting to follow her mate. So then why did it tear my heart in two to see my cousin choose to fight against us? To fight against our homeland with a creature who wanted destroy and damage our world?

But in the blink of an eye they were gone and everyone was released from the Reaper's power. The palace square became chaos around me, the death gong for my grandmother a deep resounding sound that struck me to the marrow. Malika screamed in anger or anguish, I wasn't sure, shooting a beam of pure red fire toward where they'd disappeared—the people that had once been our friends.

Rani clung onto Malika, crying something into her ear, but Malika was *raging*, shooting fire over and over again into the dark. Xalya's and Agnolthi's acolytes swarmed around us, shouting orders to close the city to prepare for attack, sending beams of defensive magic into the dome of light renewing above us.

My mother crashed down the steps, her sword held aloft. "I told you!" She turned to screech at me. "I told you!" She charged away from me, directing the palace guards.

The vision of Zale, Altara, Atax, Raen and Kai fighting together, without me, against me and this city, tipped me over the edge. We would lose against them. We wouldn't win.

"What do I do?" I screamed silently into the ether. *"Tell me what to do!"*

Xalya strode from behind me, her divine athletic grace was like a sharpened blade held to a soft throat. A battle axe was on one shoulder, a mace hanging from the other hand. Her face was the epitome of stoic, concentrated, warrior strength. Her muscles flexed under her black fighting clothes.

She turned to face me, fixing me to the spot with a black, raging glare.

"What do we do?" she hissed, her voice deep and rough. Her all-black eyes burning me right through. "We go to war."

—The End of The Archer Witch—

Get ready for our finale: The Archer Queen!

If you enjoyed this novel, pretty please leave a review at the retailer of purchase, it helps me make a living out of my work.

Signing up to my mailing list means that you get first peek at everything I produce, including book covers, new releases, exclusive excerpts and bonus material that I don't post anywhere else.

Check it out at www.ektaabali.com

ACKNOWLEDGMENTS

This book was incredibly cathartic and healing for me to write and I'm so grateful that, because of everyone's ongoing support, I get the opportunity to write these characters and their journeys.

A big thank you to everyone who has followed the world of the Ellythian Princesses up to this 5th book. I can't believe we have one last instalment left.

Thank you to Carly for this amazing cover. I feel like I keep saying this each time you come up with a new design but THIS one is my favourite to date!

C.K., I know this is the spiciest book you've ever edited, thank you for your kind words and patience along the way, I always appreciate your feedback on my manuscripts.

Sheree, you know you always have a place in my heart! Thank you for your proof reading eyes and encouragement, your notes on my stories ALWAYS make my day and god, I love you for it!

As always, thank you to my readers and the fans of this series. Without you guys I wouldn't be doing what I love every day.

ABOUT THE AUTHOR

Ektaa P. Bali was born in Fiji and spent most of her life in Melbourne, Australia.

After graduating Killester College in 2008, she studied nursing and midwifery at Deakin University, going on to spend eight years as a midwife in various hospitals.

She published her first novel in 2020, the beginning of a middle grade fantasy series, before going on to pursue her true passion: Young & New Adult Fantasy.

The Archer Witch is her tenth novel.

She currently lives in Brisbane, Australia.

facebook.com/ektaabaliauthor
instagram.com/ektaabaliauthor
youtube.com/ektaabali

ALSO BY E.P. BALI